John Ashton

Florizel's Folly

John Ashton

Florizel's Folly

ISBN/EAN: 9783337110703

Printed in Europe, USA, Canada, Australia, Japan

Cover: Foto ©Andreas Hilbeck / pixelio.de

More available books at **www.hansebooks.com**

BOOKS BY JOHN ASHTON.

Crown 8vo., cloth, 7s. 6d. each.

A HISTORY OF THE CHAP-BOOKS OF THE EIGHTEENTH CENTURY. With 334 Illustrations.

HUMOUR, WIT, AND SATIRE OF THE SEVENTEENTH CENTURY. With 82 Illustrations.

ENGLISH CARICATURE AND SATIRE ON NAPOLEON THE FIRST. With 115 Illustrations.

MODERN STREET BALLADS. With 57 Illustrations.

SOCIAL LIFE IN THE REIGN OF QUEEN ANNE. With 84 Illustrations. Crown 8vo., cloth. 3s. 6d.

BY

JOHN ASHTON

AUTHOR OF

'SOCIAL LIFE IN THE REIGN OF QUEEN ANNE,' 'MODERN STREET BALLADS,'
ETC., ETC.

WITH THIRTEEN ILLUSTRATIONS

LONDON
CHATTO & WINDUS
1899

CONTENTS

CHAPTER IV.

CHAPTER V.

CHAPTER VI.

CHAPTER VII.

CHAPTER VIII.

CHAPTER IX.

CHAPTER X.

CHAPTER XI.

CHAPTER XII.

CHAPTER XIII.

CHAPTER XIV.

CHAPTER XV.

CHAPTER XVI.

CHAPTER XVII.

CHAPTER XVIII.

CHAPTER XIX.

CHAPTER XX.

CHAPTER XXI.

CHAPTER XXII.

ILLUSTRATIONS

FLORIZEL'S FOLLY

CHAPTER I.

Early history of Brighthelmstone—Domesday Book—The Flemings—The French harry the South Coast—At Brighthelmstone—Defences of the town—Rumours of the Spanish
Armada—Armament of the town.

E who live in these latter days,
when Brighton, the 'London-on-
the-Sea,' has a standing population of 115,873,[1] and contains
19,543 houses, can hardly realize
its small beginnings. That it
was known to the Romans there
can be no doubt, for, about 1750,
an urn was dug up near the town, which contained a
thousand *denarii*, ranging from Antoninus Pius to

[1] Census, 1891.

1

Philip; and others have since been found. In the Anglo-Saxon time Brighthelmstone was a manor, and the great Earl Godwin succeeded in the lordship of it to his father, Ulnoth. On his banishment from the kingdom, this manor, with his other possessions, was seized by King Edward, but, afterwards, he recovered it, and held it until his death, on April 14, 1053, when it lapsed into the hands of his son Harold, who held it until his death at the Battle of Senlac, on October 14, 1066.

I should rather say that Harold held two of the three manors of Brighthelmstone, for his father, Godwin, had given the other to a man named Brictric, for his life only. This was the manor called 'Brighthelmstone-Lewes;' the other two were 'Michel-ham' and 'Atlyng-worth.' It is thus described in Domesday Book, A.D. 1086:

'Radulfus ten. de Will'o, Bristelmestane. Brictic tenuit de dono Godwini. T. R. E. et m°, se def'd p. 5 hid' et dimid'. Tra' e' 3 car. In d'nio e' dimid' car. et 18 vill'i et 9 bord' cu' 3 car. et uno servo. De Gablo 4 mill' aletium. T. R. E. val't 8 lib. et 12 sol. et post c. sol., modo 12 lib.

' In ead' villa, ten^t Widardus de Will'o 6 hid' et una v^a et p'tanto se defd'.

''Tres aloarii tenuer' de Rege E., et potuer' ire quolibet. Un° ex eis habuit aula': et vill'i tenuer' partes alior' duor. T'ra e' 5 car. et est in uno M. In d'nio un' car. et dim', et 13 vill'i, et 21 bord', cu' 3 car. et dimid': ibi 7 ac' p'ti et silva porc. In Lewes 4 hagæ. T. R. E. val't 10 lib., et post 8 lib., modo 12 lib.

'Ibide' ten' Wills. de Watevile Bristelmestune de

Willo. Ulovard tenuit de Rege E. T'c et modo se defd' p. 5 hid' et dim'. T'ra e' 4 car. In d'nio e' 1 car. et 13 vill'i, et 2 bord' cu' una car'. Ibi Æccl'a.

'T. R. E. val't 10 lib'. et post 8 lib', modo 12 lib'.'

Translation.

' Ralph holds of William (de Warren[1]) Bristelmestune. Brictic held it from the gift of Earl Godwin. In the time of King Edward, and now, it defends itself for 5 hides[2] and a half. The (arable) land is 3 carucates.[3] In demesne is half a carucate, and 18 villeins[4] and 9 bordars.[5] Of the Gabel (customary payment) 4 thousands of herrings. In the time of King Edward it was worth 8 pounds and 12 shillings, and, afterwards, 100 shillings. Now, 12 pounds.

' In the same vill,[6] Widard holds of William 6 hides and 1 virgate ;[7] and, for so much, it defends itself.

'Three aloarii (customary tenants) held it of King Edward, and could go where they pleased. One of them had a hall, and the villeins held the portions of the other two. The land is 5 carucates, and is in one manor. In demesne one carucate and a half, and 14 villeins and 21 bordars, with 3 carucates and a half;

---

[1] Earl of Surrey, son-in-law of William the Conqueror.

[2] A hide is an indeterminate quantity of land, varying from 20 to 4,000 acres. Eyton says it was a fiscal value, and not a superficial quantity.

[3] As much land as eight oxen could plough in a season—80 to 144 acres.

[4] Peasants, not serfs.

[5] Lord Coke says they were ' Boors holding a little house, with some land of husbandry, bigger than a cottage.'

[6] Manor.   [7] A perch of 16½ feet, or 5½ square yards.

there are 8 acres of meadow, and a wood for hogs. In Lewes 4 hagæ.[1] In the time of King Edward it was worth 10 pounds, and, afterwards, 8 pounds; now 12 pounds.

'In the same place William de Wateville holds Bristelmestune of William. Ulward held it of King Edward. Then, and now, it defends itself for 5 hides and a half. The land is 4 carucates. In demesne is 1 carucate, and 13 villeins, and 2 bordars with one plough.[2] There is a church.

' In the time of King Edward it was worth 10 pounds, and, afterwards, 8 pounds ; now, 12 pounds.'

We thus see how small was the population of the three manors in the time of William the Conqueror, and it is useful to note that there is no mention whatever of fisheries or fishermen except the Gabel of herrings. Concerning this matter Lee[3] propounds a very interesting theory. He says:

' From the surnames of some of the most ancient families in the town of *Brighthelmston*, the phrase and pronunciation of the old natives, and some peculiar customs there, it has, with great probability, been conjectured, that the town had, at some distant period, received a colony of *Flemings*. This might have happened soon after the Conquest, for we read of a great inundation of the sea, about that time, in *Flanders* ; and such of the inhabitants of the deluged

---

[1] Haga was a house in a city or borough—some think a shop.

[2] Eight oxen.

[3] 'Ancient and Modern History of Lewes and Brighthelmstone,' etc., printed for W. Lee, the editor and proprietor, Lewes, 1795, p. 458.

country as wanted new habitations could not have anywhere applied with a greater likelihood of success than
in *England*. *Matilda*, Queen of *William* the *Conqueror*,
was their countrywoman, being daughter to *Baldwin*,
Earl of *Flanders*. At her request, *William de Warren*,
her son-in-law, would have readily given a band of
those distrest emigrants a settlement on one of his
numerous manors; and, as they had been inhabitants
of the maritime part of *Flanders*, and lived chiefly by
fishing, *Brighthelmston* was the most desirable situation
for them within the territory of that nobleman.

'The *Flemings*, thus settled at *Brighthelmston*, were
led, by habit and situation, to direct their chief attention to the fishery of the Channel. Besides obtaining a
plentiful supply of fresh fish of the best kind and
quality for themselves and their inland neighbours,
they, every season, cured a great number of herrings,
and exported them to several parts of the Continent,
where the abstinence of Lent, vigils, and other meagre
days, insured them a constant market. The inhabitants of the town, now classed into *landsmen* and
seamen, or *mariners*, profited respectively by the advantages of their situation. The former, whose dwellings
covered the *Cliff*, and part of the gentle acclivity
behind it, drew health and competence from a fertile
soil. The latter, residing in two streets under the
Cliff, found as bountiful a source of subsistence and
profit in the bosom of the sea. In process of time the
mariners and their families had increased so far as to
compose more than two-thirds of the population of the
town, and had a proportionate share of the offices and
internal regulation of the parish.'

The people of Brighthelmstone were subject, in common with all the coast, to invasion and reprisals to the English raids on France, and their ships and boats were occasionally taken, and their fishery interrupted. In 1377 the French harried the South Coast, spoiled the Isle of Wight, and burnt Rye, Portsmouth, Dartmouth, Plymouth, and Hastings. There is no record of Brighthelmstone being attacked, but the French came parlously near, as Holinshed tells us: 'Winchelsie they could not win, being valiantlie defended by the abbat of Battell and others. After this, they landed, one day, not far from the abbeie of Lewes, at a place called Rottington (Rottingdean), where the prior of Lewes and two knights, the one named sir Thomas Cheinie, and the other, sir John Falleslie, having assembled a number of the countrie people, incountred the Frenchmen, but were overthrowen; so that there were slaine about an hundred Englishmen; and the prior, with the two knights, and an esquier called John Brokas, were taken prisoners, but yet the Frenchmen lost a great number of their owne men at this conflict, and so, with their prisoners, retired to their ships and gallies, and, after, returned into France.'

As far as I have read, Brighthelmstone had peace until 1514, when Holinshed tells us : 'About the same time, the warres yet continuing betweene England and France, Prior Jehan (of whom ye have heard before in the fourth yeere of this King's reigne), a great capteine of the French navie, with his gallies and foists[1] charged

---

[1] A foist was a light galley, a vessel propelled both by oars and sails.

with great basilisks[1] and other artillerie, came on the
borders of Sussex, in the night season, at a poore village
there, called Brighthelmston, and burnt it, taking such
goods as he found. But, when the people began to
gather, by firing the becons, Prior Jehan sounded his
trumpet, to call his men aboord, and by that time it
was daie. Then certeine archers that kept the watch,
folowed Prior Jehan to the sea, and shot so fast, that
they beat the gallie men from the shore; and wounded
manie in the foist; to the which Prior Jehan was con-
streined to wade, and was shot in the face with an
arrow, so that he lost one of his eies, and was like to
have died of the hurt; and, therefore, he offered his
image of wax before our ladie at Bullongne, with the
English arrow in the face for a miracle.'

These archers, who so stoutly resisted the French,
were, according to Lee, the land-owners and others of
the adjacent country, as well as the inhabitants of the
sea-coast, who were obliged to keep *watch* and *ward*
whenever there was the least appearance of danger.
The *Watch*, called *Vigiliæ minutæ*, in the King's mandate to the Sheriff, was nocturnal, and seldom exacted,
unless an immediate descent was apprehended. The
Ward consisted of men-at-arms, and *hobilers*, or *hoblers*.
The latter were persons who seem to have been bound
to perform that service by the nature of their tenure.
They were a sort of light cavalry, dressed in jackets
called *hobils*, and mounted on fleet horses. The bold
stand made against the French who landed at Rottingdean in 1377 was principally by the *Watch* and *Ward*

---

[1] Heavy ordnance, which, in the fifteenth century, could carry
stone balls of 200 lb. weight.

of this coast, which had been divided into districts, entrusted to the care of some baron or religious house by certain Commissioners called *Rectores Comitatus.* Thus it was that the Prior of Lewes and the Abbot of Battle were placed at several times at the head of an armed power, to oppose actual or threatened invasion. Certain hundreds and boroughs were also obliged, under pain of forfeiture, or other penalty, to keep the beacons in proper condition, and to fire them at the approach of an enemy, in order to alarm and assemble the inhabitants of the Weald.

Brighthelmstone had yet another hostile visit from the French, and to this we are indebted for the earliest recorded view of the town. It occurred in 1545, and Holinshed gives us the following short and pithy account of the affair.

'After this, the eighteenth of Julie, the admerall of France, monsieur Danebalte, hoised up sailes, and with his whole navie came forth into the seas, and turned on the coast of Sussex before Bright Hampsteed ; and set certein of his soldiers on land, to burne and spoile the countrie: but the beacons were fired, and the inhabitants thereabouts came downe so thicke, that the Frenchmen were driven to flie with losse of diverse of their numbers ; so that they did little hurt there.'

The French then tried the Isle of Wight, and got the worst of it, so returned to Sussex. 'The French Capteins having knowledge by certeine fishermen, whom they tooke, that the King was present, and so huge a power readie to resist them, they disanchored, and drew along the coast of Sussex ; and a small number of them landed againe in Sussex, of whome, few returned to

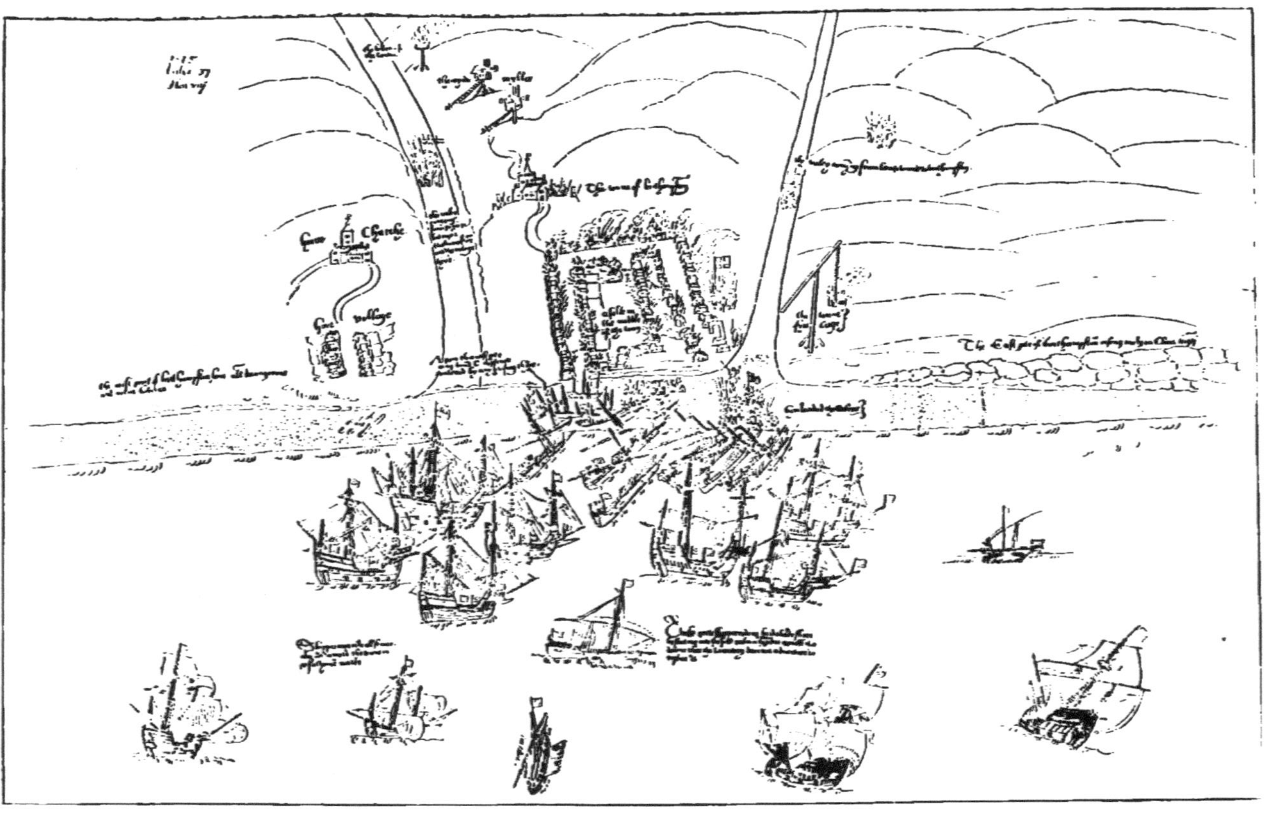

ATTACK MADE BY THE FRENCH FLEET UPON BRIGHTHELMSTONE, 1545.

their ships : for diverse gentlemen of the countrie, as sir Nicholas Pelham and others, with such power as was raised upon the sudden, tooke them up by the waie, and quickelie distressed them. When they had searched everie where by the coast, and saw men still readie to receive them with battell, they turned sterne, and so got them home againe without anie act acheived worthie to be mentioned. The number of the French-men was great, so that diverse of them that were taken prisoners in the Ile of Wight, and in Sussex, did report that they were three score thousand.'

This descent on Brighthelmstone is admirably shown in a water-colour drawing on parchment in the MS. Department of the British Museum (Cotton MSS., Aug. 1, vol. i. 18), which measures 3 feet by 2 feet; it is here reproduced. A tracing of it was engraved in 'Archæologia,' vol. xxiv., p. 298, as an illustration of a paper read by Sir Henry Ellis before the Society of Antiquaries, April 14, 1831.

Here we find the town, *apparently*, just where it is now, with a ' felde in the midle of the towne,' but with some houses on the beach opposite what is now Pool Valley, on the east side of which houses the French are landing. The following are the explanations inserted in the drawing :

' The Bekon of the Town.'

' The Wynde Mylles.'

' The towne of Brithampton.'

' Hoove Church.'

' Hove Village.'

' A felde in the midle of the Town.'

' The town Fyre Cage.'

' The Valley coming from Ponyng betwixt Brithampton and the village Hove.'

' Upon this west parte may lond $\frac{ML}{C}$ persons unletted
by any provisions there.'

' The east parte of Brithampston rising only on Cleves
(cliffs) high.'

' Here landed the Galeys.'

' Shippes may ride all somer within di. a myle the
towne in V fathome water.'

' These grete Shippes ryding hard abord shore by
shoting into the hille and valies over the towne, so sore
oppresse the towne that the Countrey dare not adventure
to reskue it.'

In consequence of this attack, Lee says that ' The
town of *Brighthelmston*, thus harassed by frequent
alarm, and the desultory attacks of an active enemy,
resolved to erect fortifications, which might afford them
some protection in future. Accordingly, at a Court
Baron held for the manor of Brighthelmstone-Lewes, on
the 27th of September, 1558, the Lords of the manor
granted to the inhabitants of the town, a parcel of land
on the cliff between Blacklyon street and Ship street,
and about two hundred and sixteen yards westward
from the lower end of East street, thirteen feet in
length and sixteen feet in breadth, to build thereon a
storehouse for armour and ammunition, afterwards called
the *Blockhouse*. This parcel, however, was only part of
the site of that building ; for, at a Court Baron held
for the Manor of *Atlyngworth*, on the 3rd day of January
1613, the homage presented that the north side of the
said building stood on the demesne lands of that manor.
The *Blockhouse*, the walls of which were about eight

feet in thickness, and eighteen feet in height, was circular, and measured 50 feet in diameter. Several arched apartments in its thick walls were repositories for the powder and other ammunition for the defence of the town. In front of it, towards the sea, was a little battery called the *Gun Garden*, on which were mounted four pieces of large iron ordnance. Adjoining the *Blockhouse*, on the east, stood the *Townhouse*, with a dungeon under it for the confinement of malefactors. From the summit of this building rose a turret, on which the town clock was fixed.

'At the same time, with the *Blockhouse*, were erected four Gates of freestone (three of which were arched) leading from the Cliff to that part of the town which lay under it; *viz.* the *East-gate* at the lower end of *East-street*; the *Portal*, vulgarly miscalled the *Porter's-gate*, which was less than any of the others, and stood next the *East-gate*; the *Middle-gate*, opposite the end of *Middle-street*, commonly called the *Gate of all nations*; and the *West-gate*, which stood at the end of *West-street*. From the *East-gate*, westward, there was, at the same time, a wall built about fifteen feet high, and four hundred feet long, where the *Cliff* was most easy of ascent: and, from the termination of that wall, a parapet, three feet high, was continued on the verge of the *Cliff* to the *West-gate*, with embrasures for cannon. The *Blockhouse* was built at the expense of the mariners of the town; but the gates and walls seem to have been erected partly, if not wholly, at the expense of Government.

'The upland part of the town, thus effectually secured on the south, might also, in case of any emergency, be rendered pretty secure on its three other sides, by cutting trenches at the ends of the streets which led into the town ; or barring the enemy's entrance with lumber carriages and household furniture, while the inhabitants annoyed them from every quarter.'

From 1545 to 1586 Brighthelmstone lived in peace; but when rumours of the Spanish Armada, which was in preparation, began to be bruited about, the town's folk had a scare, for a fleet of fifty vessels were descried off the town, apparently waiting for a favourable opportunity of landing. The terrified inhabitants lit the beacons, and sent off, post haste, to Lord Buckhurst, the Lord Lieutenant of the county, for assistance and protection. His lordship immediately attended with as many armed men as he could hurriedly muster, and posted them on the brow of the cliff between Brighthelmstone and Rottingdean, so that he might oppose the enemy should they try to land at either place. During the ensuing night, his force increased to the number of 1,600 men, and a considerable number of Kentish men were on their march to join him. However, when morning dawned, the ships were still there, but no one on board seemed to show any disposition to land ; so a few boats belonging to the town plucked up heart of grace, and ventured out a little way to reconnoitre this fleet, when they discovered, to their very great joy, that it only consisted of Dutch merchantmen, laden with Spanish wines, detained in the Channel by contrary winds !

But at the end of July, 1558, when the Armada was an accomplished fact, Brighthelmstone went to work in earnest to defend itself; and they then had in the town belonging to the Government, six pieces of great iron ordnance and ten ' qualivers.'[1] Luckily, they were not needed, and after the memorable storms of 1703 and 1705 the sea so encroached, that the *Blockhouse* and Gun Garden, together with the walls and gates, were sapped, and finally disappeared through stress of weather.

[1] Or caliver, a kind of harquebuse or musket—the lightest firearm, except the pistol, and it was used without a rest.

CHAPTER II.

Escape of Charles II. to France—The story of it—The 'Royal
Escape'—Brighton in 1730—In 1736—In 1761—Forty-five
different ways of spelling the name of the town.

HERE is nothing particularly noteworthy
with regard to Brighthelmstone until
we come to the embarkation of Charles II.
in July, 1651, from that place for France,
the culmination of his wanderings after
the disastrous Battle of Worcester. There are several
accounts of this event, including one dictated by the King
himself to Samuel Pepys; but the one that is considered
most reliable is Colonel Gounter's narrative, a manuscript
which was found in a secret drawer of an old bureau,
formerly in possession of the Gounter family, and purchased by a Mr. Bartlett of Havant, when their old
seat at Racton was dismantled about the year 1830.
It is now in the British Museum (Add. MSS., 9,008),
and is entitled, 'The last Act in the Miraculous Storie
of His M^{ties} Escape, being a true and perfect relation of
his Conveyance, through many obstacles and after many

dangers, to a safe harbour out of the reach of his tyrannical enemies. By Colonell Gounter, of Rackton, in Sussex, who had the happines to be instrumentall in the busines (as it was taken from his mouth by a person of worth, a little before his death).'

The following is the portion relating to Brighthelm-stone:

'When we were come to Beeding, a little village where I had provided a treatment for the King (one Mr. Bagshall's house), I was earnest that his majesty should stay there a while till I had viewed the coast; but my Lord Wilmot would by no means, for fear of those soldiers, but carried the King out of the road, I knew not whither; so we parted. They where they thought safest, I to Brightemston, being agreed they should send to me when fixed anywhere and ready.

'Being come to the said Brightemston, I found all clear there, and the inn (the George) free from all strangers at that time. Having taken the best room in the house, and bespoke my supper, as I was enter-taining myself with a glass of wine, the King, not finding accommodation to his mind,[1] was come to the inn: and up comes mine host (one Smith by name). "More guests," saith he to me. He brought them up into another room, I taking no notice. It was not long, but, drawing towards the King's room, I heard the

---

[1] This hardly agrees with Lee's account (p. 475), who says he 'was conducted at last to the house of a Mrs. Maunsell of Ovingdean, by Lord Wilmot and Colonel Gunter. . . . At Ovingdean the King lay concealed for a few days, as local tradition still relates, within a false wall or partition, while his friends were contriving the best means for his escape to France.'

King's voice, saying aloud to my lord Wilmot, " Here, Mr. Barlow, I drink to you." " I know that name," said I to mine host, now by me. " I pray inquire whether he was not a major in the King's army.' Which done, he was found to be the man whom I expected, and presently invited (as was likely) to the fellowship of a glass of wine.

' From that I proceeded, and made a motion to join company; and, because my chamber was largest, that they would make use of it, which was accepted, and, so, we became one company again.

' At supper, the King was cheerful, not shewing the least sign of fear or apprehension of any danger, neither then, nor at any time during the whole course of this business, which is no small wonder, considering that the very thought of his enemies, so great and so many, so diligent and so much interested in his ruin, was enough, as long as he was within their reach; and, as it were, in the very midst of them, to have daunted the stoutest courage in the world, as if God had opened his eyes, as he did Elisha's servant at his master's request, and he had seen an heavenly host round about him to guard him, which, to us, was invisible; who, therefore, though much encouraged by his undauntedness and the assurance of so good and glorious a cause, yet were not without secret terrors within ourselves, and thought every minute, a day, a month, till we should see his sacred person out of their reach.

' Supper ended, the King stood with his back against the fire, leaning over a chair. Up came mine host (upon some jealousy, I guess, not my certain knowledge); but up comes he, who called himself Gaius, runs to the King, catcheth his hand, and kissing it, said, "It shall not be said but I have kissed the best man's hand in England."

'He had waited at table at supper time, where the boatman also sat with us, and were there present. Whether he had seen, or heard anything that could give him any occasion of suspicion, I know not; in very deed, the King had a hard task so to carry himself in all things, that he might be in nothing like himself, majesty being so natural unto him, that, even when he said nothing, did nothing, his very looks (if a man observed) were enough to betray him.

'It was admirable to see how the King (as though he had not been concerned in these words, which might have sounded in the ears of another man as the sentence of death) turned about in silence, without any alteration of countenance, or taking notice of what had been said.

'About a quarter of an hour after, the King went to his chamber, where I followed him, craved his pardon with earnest protestation, that I was as innocent, so altogether ignorant of the cause how this had happened. "Peace, peace, colonel," said the King, " the fellow knows me, and I him ; he was one (whether so, or not, I know not, but so the King thought at the time) that belonged to the back stairs to my father. I hope he is an honest fellow."

'After this, I began to treat with the boatman (Tettersfield,[1] by name), asking him in what readiness he was. He answered he could not be off that night, because, for more security, he had brought his vessel into creek, and the tide had forsaken it, so that it was on ground.

[1] Tattersal.

' It is observable, that all the while the business had
been in agitation to this very time, the wind had been
contrary. The King, then opening the window, took
notice that the wind had turned, and told the master
of the ship; whereupon, because of the wind and a
clear night, I offered £10 more to the man to get off
that night; but that could not be: however, we agreed
he should take in his company that night.

' But it was a great business that we had in hand,
and God would have us to know so, both by the difficulties that offered themselves, and, by his help, he
afforded to remove them.

' When we thought we had agreed, the boatman starts
back, and saith, no, except I would insure the bark.
Argue it we did with him, how unreasonable it was, being
so well paid, etc., but to no purpose, so that I yielded
at last, and £200 was his valuation, which was agreed
upon.

' But then, as though he had been resolved to frustrate
all by unreasonable demands, he required my bond; at
which, moved with much indignation, I began to be as
resolute as he; saying, among other things, there were
more boats to be had besides his; and, if he would not
act, another should, and made as though I would go to
another.

' In this contest, the King happily interposed, " He
saith right," (saith his majesty), " A gentleman's word,
especially before witnesses, is as good as his bond." At
last, the man's stomach came down, and carry them he
would, whatsoever came of it: and, before he would be
taken, he would run his boat under the water: so it
was agreed that about two in the night they should

be aboard. The boatman, in the meantime, went to provide necessaries, and I persuaded the King to take some rest; he did, in his clothes, and my Lord Wilmot with him, till towards two of the night. Then I called them up, shewing them how the time went by my watch.

'Horses being led by the back way towards the beach, we came to the boat and found all ready, so I took my leave, craving his majesty's pardon if anything had happened through error, not want of will or loyalty; how willingly I would have waited further, but for my family (being many) which would want me, and I hoped his majesty would not, not doubting but in a very little time he should be where he would.

'My only request to his majesty was, that he would conceal his instruments; wherein their preservation was much concerned.

'His majesty promised nobody should know. I abided there, keeping the horses in readiness in case anything unexpected had happened.

'At eight of the clock, I saw them on sail, and it was the afternoon before they went out of sight.

'The wind (oh Providence) held very good till next morning, to ten of the clock brought them to a place in Normandy, called Fackham,[1] some three miles off Havre de Grace, Wednesday, Oct. 15.

'They were no sooner landed, but the wind turned, and a violent storm did arise, insomuch that the boatman was forced to cut his cable, and lost his anchor to save his boat, for which he required of me £8, and had it.'[2]

---

[1] Fécamp.

[2] The spelling of the MS. has been modernized.

On the King's restoration, Tattersal shared the fate of most of those who had helped the King in his need ; but he must have either had good interest or was very pertinacious in his claim, for his coal-brig, ornamented and enlarged, was taken into the Royal Navy as a fifth-rate, under the name of the *Royal Escape*, and on September 4, 1671, the Duke of York, as Lord High Admiral, appointed Tattersal to be her captain (a sinecure post), with pay as such, and an extra pension of £100 per annum. On August 29, 1672, the King granted the reversion of this appointment to his son Nicholas, to take effect after the death of Tattersal senior, which took place on May 20, 1674. He was buried near the south side of Brighton Church, under a marble slab, commemorative of his virtues. The *Royal Escape* was for some years moored off Whitehall ; afterwards she was relegated to Deptford, where she gradually decayed, and was broken up for firewood in 1791.

We get an account of Brighton in 1730 in ' Magna Britannia ' (pp. 510 and 511), which states that it is ' an indifferent large and populous town, chiefly inhabited by fishermen, and having a good Market weekly on Thursday, and a Fair yearly. The Situation is very pleasant, and generally accounted healthful ; for, tho' it is bounded on the North side by the *British Channel*, yet it is encompassed on the other Parts with large Cornfields and fruitful Hills, which feed great Flocks of Sheep, bearing Plenty of Wooll, which is thought by some concern'd in the Woollen Manufacture, to be of the finest Sort in *England*. . . . About 90 Years ago, this Town was a very considerable Place for Fishing, and in a flourishing Condition, being, then, one of the principal Towns of the County, containing nearly six hundred Families ; but since the Beginning of the Civil Wars, it hath decay'd much for want of a Free Fishery, and by very great Losses by Sea, their Shipping being very often taken from them by the Enemy : Nay, it is the Opinion of the most judicious Inhabitants that, had not Divine Providence in a great Measure protected them by their Town being built low, and standing on a flat Ground, the *French* would several Times have quite demolish'd it, as they had attempted to do ; but the low Situation of it prevented their doing it any considerable Damage, the Cannon Balls usually flying over the Town ; But the greatest Damage to the Buildings has been done by the breaking in of the Sea, which, within these 40 Years, hath laid Waste above 130 Tenements ; which Loss, by a modest Computation, amounts to near £40,000 ; and, if some speedy Care be not taken to stop the Encroachments of the Ocean, it is probable that the Town will, in a few Years, be utterly depopulated ; the Inhabitants being already diminished one third less than they were, and those that remain are many of them Widows, Orphans, decrepid Persons, and all very poor ; insomuch that the Rates for their Relief are at the Rack Rent of 8[d] in the Pound, for there are but few Charities given for their Support.'

Groynes, however, were introduced early in the eighteenth century, with such good effect as to do away with the above dismal apprehensions. Indeed, it was beginning to be a place for visitors to come to for the benefit of the bathing and sea-air, as we may see by the following letter from the Rev. William Clarke (grand-

father of the celebrated traveller, Edward Daniel Clarke
(1769-1822), to his friend Mr. Bowyer.[1]

'BRIGHTHELMSTONE,
'*July* 22, 1736.

'We are now sunning ourselves upon the beach at
Brighthelmstone, and observing what a tempting figure
this Island made formerly in the eyes of those gentlemen
who were pleased to civilize and subdue us. The place
is really pleasant; I have seen nothing in its way that
outdoes it. Such a tract of sea; such regions of corn;
and such an extent of fine carpet, that gives your eye
the command of it all. But then, the mischief is that
we have little conversation besides the *clamor nauticus*,
which is, here, a sort of treble to the plashing of the
waves against the cliffs. My morning business is
bathing in the sea, and then buying fish; the evening
is riding out for air, viewing the remains of old Saxon
camps, and counting the ships in the road, and the
boats that are trawling.

'Sometimes we give the imagination leave to expatiate
a little; fancy that you are coming down, and that we
intend to dine one day next week at Dieppe in
Normandy; the price is already fixed, and the wine
and lodging there tolerably good. But, though we
build these castles in the air, I assure you we live
here *almost under ground*. I fancy the architects here
usually take the altitude of the inhabitants, and lose
not an inch between the head and the ceiling, and then
dropping a step or two below the surface: the second

---

[1] 'The Brighton Ambulator,' by C. Wright, London, 1818,
p. 25.

story is finished something under 12 feet. I suppose
this was a necessary precaution against storms, that a
man should not be blown out of his bed into New
England, Barbary, or God knows where.

'But, as the lodgings are *low*, they are cheap; we
have *two parlours, two bed chambers, pantry, etc.*, for
5s. per week; and if you will really come down you
need not fear a bed of proper dimensions.

'And, then, the coast is safe; the cannons all covered
with rust and grass; the ships moored, and no enemy
apprehended.   Come and see.'

Lee tells us that about 1736 the delightful situation
of Brighthelmstone began to attract some visitors of
distinction as early in the summer as the deep miry
Sussex roads were in some way passable.   Hunting,
horse-racing, and water-parties were then the chief, or
sole, attractions; and a few indifferent inns their only
places of accommodation.

But Dr. Richard Russell, having removed from
Malling, near Lewes, to this town about the year
1750, called attention to the benefit of sea-bathing,
having written a treatise, which was translated into
English, and went through several editions—'De Tabe
Glandulari, sive de usu aquæ marinæ in morbis
glandularum dissertatio,' Oxford, 1750, 8vo.   This
brought visitors to Brighthelmstone; the erection of
lodging - houses became a profitable speculation, and
the town began to increase in population and celebrity.

Dr. Russell's successor, Dr. A. Relhan, wrote, in 1761,
'A Short History of Brighthelmston, with Remarks on
its Air, and an Analysis of its Waters, particularly of

an uncommon Mineral one, long discovered, though but lately used.' In this tract he thus describes the Brighthelmstone of his time:

' The town, at present, consists of six principal streets, many lanes, and some spaces surrounded with houses, called by the inhabitants Squares. The great plenty of flint stones on the shore, and in the cornfields near the town, enabled them to build the walls of their houses with that material when in their most impoverished state; and their present method of ornamenting the windows and doors with the admirable brick which they burn for their own use, has a very pleasing effect. The town improves daily, as the inhabitants, encouraged by the late great resort of Company, seem disposed to expend the whole of what they acquire in the erection of new buildings, or making the old ones convenient. And, should the increase of these, in the next seven years, be equal to what it has been in the last, it is probable there will be but few towns in England that will exceed this in commodious buildings.

' Here are two public rooms, the one convenient, the other not only so, but elegant; not excelled, perhaps, by any public room in England, that of York excepted: and the attention of the proprietor in preparing everything that may answer for the conveniency and amusement of the company is extremely meritorious.

' The men of this town are busied almost the whole year in a succeeding variety of fishing; and the women industriously dedicate part of their time, disengaged from domestic cares, to the providing of nets adapted to the various employments of their husbands.

'The spring season is spent in dredging for Oysters, which are mostly bedded in the Thames and Medway, and, afterwards, carried to the London market: the Mackerel fishery employs them during the months of May, June, and July; and the fruits of their labour are always sent to London; as Brighthelmston has the advantage of being its nearest fishing sea coast, and the consumption of the place, and its environs, is very inconsiderable. In the early part of this fishery, they frequently take the red Mullet; and, near the close of it, abundance of Lobsters and Prawns. August is engaged in the Trawl fishery, when all sorts of flat fish are taken in a net called by that name. In September they fish for Whiting with lines: and in November the Herring fishery takes place, which is the most considerable and growing fishery of the whole. Those employed in this pursuit show an activity and boldness almost incredible, often venturing out to Sea in their little boats in such weather as the largest ships can scarce live in. Part of their acquisition in this way is sent to London, but the greatest share of it is either pickled, or dried and made red. These are mostly sent to foreign markets, making this fishery a national concern. . . .

'From this account of the fishery of this town, the reader will be satisfied that it must supply a constant and good article in provision to the inhabitants. And although there are complaints made of the inconveniences experienced in the want of a regular and daily market; yet, as few who come here to take the waters can long want an appetite, and as fish of different sorts, excellent mutton, beef, and veal tolerably good, with all kinds of fowl, may be had in plenty twice or thrice a week, the rarities of a London market may be resigned un-regretted for a few months.'

It is probable that very few towns have so many variations on their names as Brighton, which modernized form began somewhere about 1775; at least, that is the earliest date I have met with. F. E. Sawyer, Esq., F.M.S., in an article on the 'Ecclesiastical History of Brighton' in the 'Sussex Archæological Collections,' vol. xxix., pp. 182, 183, gives forty-five different readings of the name, together with the authorities whence they are derived, and he repeated them in *Notes and Queries*, vi. S. ii. 376, with the dates of the authorities. They are as follow :

Brighthelm	ston	1252 and 18th cent.
	stone	1340.
	eston	1415.
	estone	1460.
	iston	1616.
	yston	1535 and 1411.
	sted	Camden.
Brighthelnisted		1616.
Brightehelmston		1621.
Brighte	lmeston	1440.
	lmiston	1616.
	lmyston	*ib.*
	elneston	?
	elniston	1616.
Brytthalmston		1340.
Brittelmston		?

Brist	elm	etune	1086.
		estune	*ib.*
		eston	?
		estona	Dugdale.
	alnerston		1292.
	halmestone		?
	helmstone		?
Bright	hem	pston	1509-14.
		son	1628.
		sted	1629.
		stone	1609.
	henstone		1509-14.
	Hampstead		Stow.
	healmertun		Saxon.
	on		Modern.
Brighelm	ston		1292.
	eston		1397.
Brihtelmston			1438.
Brithelm	ston		?
	eston		1404.
Brythelmston			1397.
Bryst	elmstone		1438.
	helmeston		?
Brishelmeston			?
Brichelmston			1292.
Brett	Hempston		1637.
	hempstone		*ib.*
Bredhemston			1724.
Brogholmestune			?

CHAPTER III.

Brighton becomes fashionable—Duke of Cumberland there— His character—The Royal Marriage Act—His influence over the Prince of Wales—The Duke and the King—Bad conduct of the Prince of Wales.

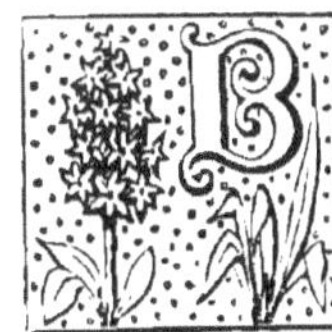RIGHTON rapidly became fashionable, and we find the announcement on June 1, 1761, of Lord Abergavenny, Lord Bruce, Mr. and Lady Jane Evelyn, Lady Sophia Egerton, etc.; and on June 25, 1775, arrived here the Duke and Duchess of Richmond, Duke and Duchess of Marlborough, Ladies Caroline and Eliza Spencer, etc. In 1782 it was patronized by Royalty, for the somewhat eccentric Princess Amelia Sophia Eleonora, the second daughter of George II., paid the town a visit, and Henry Frederick, brother to George III. and Duke of Cumberland, took up his residence there at Grove House. An extract from a letter from Brighthelmstone published in the *Morning Herald*, September 28, 1782, describes the state of society there at that time:

' *Sep.* 26.—This place is, at last, as full as an egg, but the company is a motley groupe, I assure you. The

Duke of C—— is at the head of the whole, and condescendingly associates with all, from the *Baron* down to the *Blackleg!—Play* runs high, particularly at Whist; his Royal Highness has touched a few hundreds by betting adverse to Major B——gs, who, apparently, is not like to make a very profitable campaign of it. We have every kind of amusement that fancy can desire for the train of folly and dissipation; and all are crowded beyond measure! *Barthelemon* has had two or three *boreish concerts* entirely of *his own* music, by which he has made much more than he merited. Lady *Worsley*, who is among us, is the life and soul of *equestrian parties*, riding *sixteen miles within the hour* every morning with all imaginable ease! Her Ladyship made a match the other day to ride over our revived course for fifty guineas, p. or p. against her aide du camp, Miss V——rs, and mounted her buckskins and half boots accordingly; but, to the mortification of a great number of spectators, who assembled to see this exhibition of *female jockeyship*, she declared off at the moment they were expected to start! Few people think of stirring from hence at present, so that it is probable we shall have a jolly season till the staghounds come down, about the middle of next month.'

This Duke of Cumberland (born 1744, died 1790) was the reverse of estimable in character. He was a confirmed gambler, and never missed a great horse-race when he was in England. In 1770 Lord Grosvenor brought an action against him, and obtained £10,000 damages from him on account of Lady G.; and in 1771 he married Lady Anne Luttrell, the widow of Mr. Christopher Horton, of Derbyshire, a lady much older than himself. This so enraged George III. that he forbade them the Court, and he sent a message to Parliament, recommending a legislative provision for preventing any of the Royal Family marrying without the consent of the King. Hence arose The Royal Marriage Act (12 George III., c. xi.), which was passed in 1772. By this Act none of the descendants of George II., unless of foreign birth, can marry under the age of twenty-five without the consent of the King. At and after that age, after twelve months' notice given to the Privy Council, they may contract such marriage, which shall be good unless both Houses of Parliament disapprove. Walpole gives us a ballad on the Marriage Act, a few verses of which I reproduce:

'THE MARRIAGE ACT NOT MADE BY THE LATE KING.

'A NEW BALLAD.

*   *   *   *   *

' The Duke was restored to his brother's high favour,
   And continued, as usual, his wanton behaviour;
   For adultery at Court was not thought an unfitness,
   As a twice married maiden of honour can witness.

' But Hymen, indignant to see his laws broke,
   Determined to bend the loose youth to his yoke;
   So a votary true, a bright widow, he chose,
   And the pert little Prince was soon caught in the noose.

' But, oh! all ye Gods, who inspire ballad-singers,
   Ye Muses, with nine-times-ten ivory fingers,
   I invoke ye to guide both my voice and my pen,
   While I sing of the fury that seized King and Queen.

' King and Queen, when they heard how th' undutiful whelp
   Had disgraced the great houses of Mecky and Guelp,
   Swore and cried, curs'd and fainted, and calling for Bute,
   Of your Luttrell connexion, cried George, see the fruit.

'This Irish alliance my projects all bilks,
　I'd as lief he had married the daughter of Wilkes ;
　While to humour my mother and you I conspire,
　I am out of the frying-pan into the fire.

　　　*　　　*　　　*　　　*　　　*

'From the Duke's breach of duty, my act shall receive
　The highest-flown doctrines of prerogative ;
　Plantagenets, Tudors, nay, Stuarts I'll quote,
　And what law cannot prove, shall be proved by a vote.

'To marry, unmarry, son, brother, or heir,
　Has been always his right, our good King shall declare ;
　Though as far from the truth as the north from the south,
　It is not the first lie we have put in his mouth.

'They may burn and be damn'd, but they never shall marry :
　George the Third as despotic, shall be, as Eighth Harry :
　He shall cut off the heads of his sons and his spouses,
　For we'll have no more war between red and white roses.'

　　　*　　　*　　　*　　　*　　　*

The Duke was ultimately reconciled to the King, but, during the time of his displeasure, the former was a very bad Mentor to the young Prince of Wales, with whom he was most intimate to the day of his death. We learn a great deal about them from Walpole. The following occurred in 1780, when the Prince was eighteen years old :[1] 'Two days afterwards the Duke told me the Prince of Wales had said to him : "I cannot come to see you now without the King's leave, but in three years I shall be of age, and then I may act for myself. I will declare I will visit you."'

Again[2] (1781): 'But an event soon happened that

---

[1] 'Journal of the Reign of King George the Third, from the Year 1771 to 1783,' by Horace Walpole, London, 1859, vol. ii., p. 416.

[2] *Ibid.*, p. 449.

changed that aspect, and made Cumberland House naturally the headquarters of at least part of the Opposition. The Duchess of Cumberland and the Luttrells openly countenanced the amour of the Prince of Wales, and Mrs. Armstead . . . joined that faction, and set themselves in open defiance of the King.

'The first project was to make a ball for the Prince at Cumberland House; but the King forbad his servants going thither. The Duke then made a great dinner for the Prince's servants, to which, as I have said, the King would not permit them to go. The Duke was so enraged, that he wrote a most insolent letter to the King, in which he told him he would go abroad, for this country was not fit for a gentleman to live in. The Duke, however, went to the Drawing-room again, and continued to go, the Duchess having certainly told him that if he absented himself he would lose his influence over the Prince of Wales.

'To the Queen's ball, as I have said, the Duke was not invited, yet went to Court the next day. At that ball the Prince got drunk, which threw him into a dangerous fever, but such a general irruption over his whole face and body of the humours in his blood came out, that it probably saved his life.

'At this moment the Duke and Duchess of Gloucester came to town from Weymouth. The King, as usual, vented his complaints to the Duke of Gloucester. The King told the Duke that though, on the reconciliation, he had told the Duke of Cumberland that all his doors would be opened to him, "yet," said the King, "he comes to the Queen's house fourteen times a week to my son, the Prince, and passes by my door, but never comes in to me ; and, if he meets me there, or when we are hunting, he only pulls off his hat, and walks, or rides away. I am ashamed," continued he, " to see my brother paying court to my son." The King resented it, and, though he invited the principal persons who hunted, to dinner, he never invited the Duke of Cumberland. The Prince of Wales seemed to be very weak and feeble. He drank hard, swore, and passed every night in ——— : such were the fruits of his being locked up in the palace of piety !

'The King further informed the Duke of Gloucester of his brother Cumberland's outrageous letter, and said, " He has forced himself every day into my son's company, even when he was at the worst." The Duke said he wondered his Majesty had suffered it. " I don't know," replied the King, " *I do not care to part relations.*" '

' *May* 4, 1781.[1]—The conduct of the Prince of Wales began already to make the greatest noise, and proved how very bad his education had been, or, rather, that he had had little or none; but had only been locked up, and suffered to keep company with the lowest domestics ; while the Duke of Montague, and Hurd, Bishop of Lichfield, had thought of nothing but paying court to the King and Queen, and her German women. The Prince drank more publicly in the Drawing room, and talked there irreligiously and indecently, in the openest manner (both which were the style of the Duchess of Cumberland). He passed the nights in the lowest debaucheries, at the same time bragging of intrigues with women of quality, whom he

---

[1] Walpole, vol. ii., p. 457.

named publicly. Both the Prince and the Duke talked
of the King in the grossest terms, even in his hearing,
as he told the Duke of Gloucester, who asked him why
he did not forbid his son seeing his brother. The King
replied that he feared the Prince would not obey him.

'The Duke of Cumberland dropped that he meant
by this outrageous behaviour to force the King to yield
to terms in favour of his Duchess, having gotten entire
command over the Prince. The latter, however, had
something of the duplicity of his grandfather, Prince
Frederick, and, after drawing in persons to abuse the
King, would betray them to the King. Nor in other
respects did his heart turn to good. In his letters to
Mrs. Robinson, his mistress, he called his sister, the
Princess Royal, a poor child, " *that bandy-legged b—h,
my sister ;*" and, while he was talking of Lord Chesterfield in the most opprobrious terms, he was sending
courier after courier to fetch him to town. That Lord's
return produced a scene that divulged all that till now
had been only whispered.

'One night, as soon as the King was gone to bed,
the Prince, with St. Leger and Charles Windham, his
chief favourites, and some of his younger servants, the
Duke of Cumberland, and George Pitt, son of Lord
Rivers, went to Blackheath to sup with Lord Chesterfield, who, being married, would not consent to send for
the company the Prince required. They all got immediately drunk, and the Prince was forced to lie down on a
bed for some time. On his return, one of the company
proposed as a toast, " *A short reign to the King.*" The
Prince, probably a little come to himself, was offended,
rose and drank a bumper to " *Long live the King.*" The

next exploit was to let loose a large fierce house-dog, and George Pitt, of remarkable strength, attempted to tear out its tongue. The dog broke from him, wounded Windham's arm, and tore a servant's leg. At six in the morning, when the Prince was to return, Lord Chesterfield took up a candle to light him, but was so drunk that he fell down the steps into the area, and, it was thought, had fractured his skull. That accident spread the whole history of the debauch, and the King was so shocked that he fell ill on it, and told the Duke of Gloucester that he had not slept for ten nights, and that whenever he fretted, the bile fell on his breast. As he was not ill on any of the disgraces of the war, he showed how little he had taken them to heart. Soon after this adventure, the King being to review a regiment on Blackheath, Lord Chesterfield offered him a breakfast, but the late affair had made such a noise that he did not think it decent to accept it.

'FOR THE "PUBLIC ADVERTISER," 1782.

MODERN WIT—(BLACKHEATH).

'Drink *like a* Lord, and *with* him, if you will.
Deep be the bumper : let no liquor spill ;
No *daylight* in the glass, though through the night
You soak your senses till the morning light ;
Then stupid rise, and with the rising sun
Drive the high car, a second *Phaeton*.
Let these exploits your fertile wit evince :
Drunk as a Lord, and happy as a Prince !'

' *Nov.* 28, 1781.[1]—The Duke of Gloucester had come to town, as usual, on the opening of Parliament, and

---

[1] Walpole, vol. ii., p. 480.

stayed five days, in which he was three times with the King, who, as if he had not used the Duke ill, opened his mind to him on his son, the Prince of Wales, and his own brother, the Duke of Cumberland, the latter of whom, he said, was governed by Charles Fox and Fitzpatrick, and governed the Prince of Wales, whom they wanted to drive into opposition. " When we hunt together," said the King, " neither my son nor my brother speak to me ; and, lately, when the chace ended at a little village where there was but a single post chaise to be hired, my son and brother got into it, and drove to London, leaving me to go home in a cart, if I could find one." He added, that when at Windsor, where he always dined at three, and in town at four, if he asked the Prince to dine with him, he always came at four at Windsor, and in town at five, and all the servants saw the father waiting an hour for the son. That since the Court was come to town, the Duke of Cumberland carried the Prince to the lowest places of debauchery, where they got dead drunk, and were often carried home in that condition.'

'*Feb.* 20, 1782.¹—The hostilities of the Prince of Wales were supposed to be suggested by his uncle, the Duke of Cumberland, who had now got entire influence over him. The Prince, though, at first, he did not go openly to her, frequently supped with the Duchess of Cumberland ; and, in a little time, they openly kept a faro bank for him—not to their credit ; and the Duke of Cumberland even carried bankers and very bad company to the Prince's apartments in the Queen's house. This behaviour was very grating to the

---

¹ Walpole, vol. ii., p. 502.

GEORGE IV. AS PRINCE OF WALES, 1 FEB. 1782.

King, and the offences increased. The Duke of Cumberland twice a day passed by the King's apartment to his nephew's, without making his bow to his Majesty; and the brothers, at last, ceased to speak. On hunting-days the Duke was not asked to dine with the King. He returned this by instilling neglect into his nephew. The King complained of this treatment to the Duke of Gloucester, who asked why he bore it. "What can I do?" said the King; 'if I resent it, they will make my son leave me, and break out, which is what they wish."

' But it was not long before the folly and vulgarity of the Duke of Cumberland disgusted the Prince. His style was so low that, alluding to the Principality of Wales, the Duke called his nephew *Taffy*. The Prince was offended at such indecent familiarity, and begged it might not be repeated—but in vain. Soon after, Mr. Legge, one of the Prince's gentlemen, and second son of the Earl of Dartmouth, growing a favourite, inflamed the Prince's disgusts; and the cool-ness increasing, the Duke of Cumberland endeavoured to counteract the prejudice by calling Legge to the Prince " Your *Governor* "—but as the Governor had sense, and the uncle none, Legge's arrows took place, the others did not. Yet, though the Prince had too much pride to be treated vulgarly, he had not enough to disuse the same style. Nothing was coarser than his conversation and phrases; and it made men smile to find that in the palace of piety and pride his Royal High-ness had learned nothing but the dialect of footmen and grooms. Still, if he tormented his father, the latter had the comfort of finding that, with so depraved and licentious a life, his son was not likely to acquire popularity.   Nor did he give symptoms of parts, or spirit, or steadiness.   A tender parent would have been afflicted—a jealous and hypocritic father might be vexed, but was consoled too.'

One more quotation from Walpole,[1] which shows us the Prince of Wales after he had attained his eighteenth year, when he had his own suite of apartments in the Queen's House (now Buckingham Palace):

'*Feb.*, 1781.—A new scene now began to open, which drew most of the attention of the public, at least of the town.   Since the family of the Prince of Wales had been established, and that he was now past eighteen, it was impossible to confine him entirely.   As soon as the King went to bed, the Prince and his brother Prince Frederick went to their mistresses, or to ——.   Prince Frederick, who promised to have the most parts, and had an ascendant over his brother, was sent abroad on that account, and thereby had an opportunity of seeing the world, which would only make him more fit to govern his brother (contrary to the views of both King and Queen) or the nation, if his brother should fail, and which was not improbable.

'The Prince of Wales was deeply affected with the scrofulous humour which the Princess of Wales had brought into the blood, and which the King kept down in himself by the most rigorous and systematical abstinence.   The Prince, on the contrary, locked up in the palace, and restrained from the society of women, had contracted a habit of private drinking, and this winter the humour showed itself in blotches all over his face.   His governor, the Duke of Montague, was utterly

---

[1] Vol. ii., p. 446.

incapable of giving him any kind of instruction, and his preceptor, Bishop Hurd, was only a servile pedant, ignorant of mankind. The Prince was good-natured, but so uninformed that he often said, " I wish anybody would tell me what to do ; nobody gives me any instructions for my conduct." He was prejudiced against all his new servants, as spies set on him by the King, and showed it by never speaking to them in public. His first favourite had been Lord Malden, son of the Earl of Essex, who had brought about his acquaintance with Mrs. Robinson.'

CHAPTER IV.

Mrs. Robinson—Her story of Florizel and Perdita—Her after-career—Coming of age of the Prince of Wales—His new establishment—His first visit to Brighton—His and Colonel Hanger's adventure.

HO was this Mrs. Robinson ?   She was of Irish extraction, and was born in Bristol in 1758.   In 1774 she married an attorney's clerk, named Robinson ; and, owing to pecuniary difficulties, she went on the stage, appearing at Drury Lane as Juliet on December 10, 1776, a part for which her fascinating beauty well fitted her.   On December 3, 1779, Garrick's adaptation of Shakespeare's *Winter's Tale* was produced by royal command, and Mrs. Robinson appeared in the part of Perdita.   It was then that she was seen and admired by the Prince of Wales.   Let her tell her own story as to that night, and what came of it.

'The play of the Winter's Tale was, this season, commanded by their Majesties.   I never had performed before the royal family; and the first character in which I was destined to appear was that of Perdita.   I had frequently played the part, both with the Hermione of Mrs. Hartley and of Miss Farren : but I felt a strange degree of alarm when I found my name announced to perform it before the royal family.

'In the green-room I was rallied on the occasion; and Mr. Smith, whose gentlemanly manners and enlightened conversation rendered him an ornament to the profession, who performed the part of Leontes, laughingly exclaimed, "By Jove, Mrs. Robinson, you will make a conquest of the Prince ; for to-night you look handsomer than ever." I smiled at the unmerited compliment, and little foresaw the vast variety of events that would arise from that night's exhibition !

'As I stood in the wing opposite the Prince's box, waiting to go on the stage, Mr. Ford, the manager's son, and now a respectable defender of the laws, presented a friend who accompanied him ; this friend was Lord Viscount Malden, now Earl of Essex.

'We entered into conversation during a few minutes, the Prince of Wales all the time observing us, and frequently speaking to Colonel (now General) Lake, and to the Honourable Mr. Legge, brother to Lord Lewisham, who was in waiting on his Royal Highness. I hurried through the first scene, not without much embarrassment, owing to the fixed attention with which the Prince of Wales honoured me. Indeed, some flattering remarks which were made by his Royal Highness met my ear as I stood near his box, and I was overwhelmed with confusion.

'The Prince's particular attention was observed by everyone, and I was again rallied at the end of the play. On the last curtsey, the royal family condescendingly returned a bow to the performers; but, just as the curtain was falling, my eyes met those of the Prince of Wales; and with a look that I *never shall forget*, he gently inclined his head a second time; I felt the compliment, and blushed my gratitude.

'During the entertainment Lord Malden never ceased conversing with me: he was young, pleasing, and perfectly accomplished. He remarked the particular applause which the Prince had bestowed on my performance; said a thousand civil things; and detained me in conversation till the evening's performance was concluded.

'I was now going to my chair, which waited, when I met the royal family crossing the stage. I was again honoured with a very marked and low bow from the Prince of Wales. On my return home, I had a party to supper; and the whole conversation centred in encomiums on the person, graces, and amiable manners of the illustrious Heir apparent.

'Within two or three days of this time, Lord Malden made me a morning visit. Mr. Robinson was not at home, and I received him rather awkwardly. But his Lordship's embarrassment far exceeded mine. He attempted to speak,—paused, hesitated, apologized; I knew not why. He hoped I would pardon him; that I would not mention something he had to communicate; that I would consider the peculiar delicacy of his situation, and then act as I thought proper. I could not comprehend his meaning, and therefore requested he would be explicit.

'After some moments of evident rumination, he tremblingly drew a small letter from his pocket. I

took it, and knew not what to say. It was addressed
to Perdita. I smiled, I believe, rather sarcastically,
and opened the billet. It contained only a few words,
but those expressive of more than common civility :
they were signed Florizel.

'" Well, my lord, and what does this mean ?" said I,
half angrily.

'" Can you not guess the writer ?" said Lord Malden.

'" Perhaps yourself, my lord," cried I, gravely.

'" Upon my honour, no," said the Viscount. "I
should not have dared so to address you on so short
an acquaintance."

'I pressed him to tell me from whom the letter came.
He again hesitated ; he seemed confused, and sorry that
he had undertaken to deliver it.

'" I hope I shall not forfeit your good opinion," said
he ; " but———"

'" But what, my lord ?"

'" I could not refuse—for the letter is from the
Prince of Wales."

'I was astonished ; I confess that I was agitated ; but
I was, also, somewhat sceptical as to the truth of Lord
Malden's assertion. I returned a formal and a doubtful
answer, and his lordship shortly after took his leave.'

It is not worth while pursuing the details of this
woman's fall ; she says her husband was neglectful of
her, and unfaithful ; and, besides, the Prince gave her a
bond for £20,000, payable when he came of age. He
soon tired of her, and terminated the connection in
1781. The lady seems to have been far from in-
consolable, for in 1782 she was under the protection
of Colonel Tarleton, and a caricature, said to be by

Gillray, called 'The Thunderer' (August 20, 1782), thus shows the then situation.

The engraving shows a dragoon officer (Colonel Tarleton) standing before the door of the 'Whirligig' Chop-house, with a drawn sword, boasting his wondrous feats of arms. Beside him stands a figure having a plume of three feathers instead of a head (the Prince of Wales). The sign, the 'Whirligig,' is Mrs. Robinson. The *Morning Post*, September 21, 1782, says: 'Yesterday, a messenger arrived in town, with the very interesting and pleasing intelligence of the Tarleton, armed ship, having, after a chace of some months, captured the Perdita frigate, and brought her safe into Egham port. The Perdita is a prodigious fine clean bottomed vessel, and had taken many prizes during her cruize, particularly the Florizel, a most valuable ship belonging to the Crown, but which was immediately released, after taking out the cargo. The Perdita was captured some time ago by the Fox, but was, afterwards, retaken by the Malden, and had a sumptuous suit of new rigging, when she fell in with the Tarleton. Her manœuvring to escape was admirable ; but the Tarleton, fully determined to take her, or perish, would not give up the chace ; and at length, coming alongside the Perdita, fully determined to board her, sword in hand, she instantly surrendered at discretion.'

The scandal about her being connected with Fox has, I think, no foundation in fact. He was infatuated with Mrs. Armstead, who afterwards became his wife ; and the foundation for the rumour was, probably, that Fox was the agent from the Prince to negotiate the return of the £20,000 bond from Perdita, which he succeeded in effecting, on condition that she was paid an annuity of £500 for life. Still, the caricaturist T. Colley gives us (December 17, 1782), ' Perdito and Perdita, or the Man and Woman of the People,' which shows Mrs. Robinson driving Fox in her chariot. This must have been a very smart affair, if we may trust a newspaper cutting of 1782.

' *Dec.* 4.—Mrs. Robinson now sports a carriage, which is the admiration of all the *charioteering* circles in the vicinity of St. James's; the body Carmelite and silver, ornamented with a French mantle, and the cypher in a wreath of flowers: the carriage scarlet and silver, the seat-cloth richly ornamented with silver fringe. Mrs. Robinson's livery is green, faced with yellow, and richly trimmed with broad silver lace; the harness ornamented with stars of silver, richly chased and elegantly finished. The inside of the carriage is lined with white silk, embellished with scarlet trimmings.'

The *Morning Herald*, June 16, 1783, says: ' The *Perdita's* new *vis-a-vis* is said to be the aggregate of a few stakes laid at Brooke's, which the competitors were not able to decide. Mr. *Fox* therefore proposed that as it could not be better applied than to the above purpose, that the *Perdita* should be presented with an elegant carriage. The ill-natured call it *Love's Last Stake*, or The Fools of Fashion.'

It is not worth while following her career until her death on December 26, 1800; and, indeed, unconnected as she was with the Prince and Brighton, the episode would not have been introduced were it not to tell the story of how the Prince got the name of Florizel, which stuck to him all his life.

The Prince came of age on August 12, 1783, but there were no great festivities over the event. The Court was quiet, because the Queen had just been confined, and the account we have of the doings at Windsor are very meagre. The *Morning Chronicle* of August 14 tells us that—

' *Windsor*, 13 *Aug*.—Yesterday, being the day on which his Royal Highness George, Prince of Wales, came of age, the same was observed, at this place, with every demonstration of joy, as far as could be consistent with the situation of Her Majesty. The Prince came down about eight in the morning, waited upon the King, with whom he breakfasted, and received the compliments from his brothers and sisters, the Duke of Cumberland, Duke of Montague, Lord Aylesbury, etc. After breakfast, his Highness retired to his own apartments, and, at noon, had a Levee ; Colonel Dalrymple, with all the officers belonging to the regiment, were introduced to the Prince, and gave him joy of the day. Several of the nobility and gentry around the country waited upon his Royal Highness, and were very politely received.

' The Prince had ordered a dinner for his own suite, from Clode's, at the White Hart, and had a turtle dressed in London, which was brought down by Weltje, of St. James's Street. His Royal Highness dined with his Majesty, three of his brothers, five of his sisters, the Duke of Montague, Lord Aylesbury, and Lady Charlotte Finch. After the cloth was removed, and a few glasses had gone round, the Prince went to his own apartments, and sat for some time with Lord Southampton, Lord Lewisham, Lord Boston, Lord Chewton and the rest of his suite. His Majesty went upon the Terrace at half past six; the Prince of Wales and his attendants soon followed. It is said, more genteel company scarce ever met on that spot.

'The Duchess of Ancaster, Lady Ferrers, the beautiful Miss Hudson, and a variety of women of rank, did honour to the day. It was quite dark before the company retired from the Terrace. The Duke of Queensbury joined his Royal Highness and his suite. The carriages were so numerous that they filled both Castle Yards.'

There were illuminations at Windsor and in London, where His Royal Highness's tradesmen and the Hon. Artillery Company (of which he was Captain-General) held good cheer; but it was felt that the coming of age had not been celebrated in a sufficiently national style, and a fête later on was talked of, which never came to pass. Perhaps the Prince's character had something to do with it, for the *Morning Herald* of August 15 says: 'The broad faced dissipation of a certain young gentleman, gives the most general disgust. Extravagance in the *extreme*, but ill suits the present state of the British empire.' They were outspoken in those days!

The Prince is now launched in life. He is Colonel of the 10th Light Dragoons, has £50,000 per annum allowed him by Parliament, and the revenues of the Duchy of Cornwall, about £13,000 more. He has Carlton House fitting up for him; he is his own master, being no longer under paternal control, and his soul yearns towards his *âme damnée*, the Duke of Cumberland. This Prince was at Brighthelmstone, and thither Florizel went. Every authority but one says that the Prince of Wales paid a visit to the Duke in 1782; but

I think that the one which has not slavishly copied from other sources is right, for two reasons: first, that in 1782 he was under strict paternal control, and could stir nowhere without his governor, and a visit to that uncle whom the King so disliked was the last thing to be thought of; and, secondly, we see (on p. 28) in the description of Brighton in 1782, 'The Duke of C. is at the head of the whole.' If the heir to the throne had been there, the Duke would have taken 'a back seat,' and the papers would have given due prominence to the visit; and therefore I incline to the opinion that, since the days of his childhood, his first visit to the watering-place he afterwards made so famous was in September, 1783, on which occasion the town was illuminated and there was a display of fireworks. During his stay of eleven days, he hunted, went to a ball, and to the theatre, besides the ordinary amusements of the place. In fact, his visit seems so to have impressed him, that from that date he made Brighthelmstone his abiding-place for, at least, a portion of the year. Huish,[1] however, gives another version for his liking for the place:

'The Prince had now begun to manifest that predilection for Brighton, which induced him at a future period to make that town his residence. The report, however, which was current at the time, and which is actually founded on truth, goes so far as to state, that it was neither the marine views, nor the benefit of change of air, nor the salubrity of the place, which possessed, in the eyes of his Royal Highness, at this time, any great attractions; but that he was drawn thither by the

---

[1] 'Memoirs of George IV.,' by Robert Huish, 8vo., vol. i., p. 80; London, 1831.

angelic figure of a sea nymph, whom he, one day, encountered reclining on one of the groins on the beach. In this amour, however, his Royal Highness was completely the dupe. As far as personal charms extended, Charlotte Fortescue was of " the first order of fine forms "; but, as far as mental qualifications were to be considered, she was one of the most illiterate and ignorant of human beings. In artifice and intrigue she was unparalleled; and, withal, she knew how to throw such an air of simplicity and innocence over her actions, as would have deceived even a greater adept than his Royal Highness, in the real nature of her character. She soon discovered the exalted station of the individual whom she believed she had captivated by her charms; and, on the principle that the thing is of little value which is cheaply or easily obtained, she, for a time, frustrated every attempt of his Royal Highness to obtain a private interview with her. She kept her residence a complete secret, and, for some days, she was neither seen nor heard of. On a sudden, she would make her appearance, and then, suffused in tears, would speak of her approaching marriage, and her consequent departure from the country; and could that idea be borne by her royal lover? Heaven and earth were to be moved to avert such a direful calamity; a regular elopement was proposed, and, in order to give the affair a highly romantic air, it was arranged that the dress of a footman was to be procured for the beautiful fugitive, and that the Prince was to have a postchaise in waiting a few miles on the London road, to bear away his valuable prize. There is, however, an old adage which says, that much falls between the cup and the lip, and, in this instance, the truth of it was fully confirmed. The hour was anxiously looked for which was to bring the lovers into the undisturbed society of each other; but, as the Prince was dressing for dinner, the arrival of George Hanger, who had just then begun his career of eccentricity and profligacy in the fashionable circles, was announced. The Prince invited him to dine; excusing himself, however, at the same time, for the early hour at which he would be obliged to leave him, as he had most important business to transact that night in the metropolis. Dinner being over, the Prince inquired the business which had brought his visitor to Brighton in so unexpected a manner.

'"A hunt, a hunt, your Royal Highness," said Hanger, "I am in chace of a d——d fine girl, whom I met with at Mrs. Simpson's in Duke's Place; and, although I have taken private apartments for her in St. Anne's East, yet the hussy takes it into her head every now and then to absent herself for a few days; and I have now been given to understand that she is carrying on some intrigue with a *fellow* in this place. Let me but catch him, and I will souse him over head and ears in the ocean."

'The Prince now inquired what kind of a lady he was in pursuit of; and, by the description given, he doubted not for a moment, that the lady with whom he was to elope that very evening, on account of her approaching marriage, was the identical lady who had eloped from the protection of his visitor, and he began to consider how he could extricate himself with the best possible grace from the dilemma in which he was involved. That he was a dupe to the artifices of a cunning, designing girl, was now apparent to him ; and, therefore, it would be his greatest pride and joy to outwit her. He, therefore, disclosed the whole of his intrigue with the runaway, and it was resolved that Hanger should put on one of the coats in which she was accustomed to see her royal lover, and take his seat in the chaise, instead of the Prince. The whole affair was well managed; the Prince remained at Brighton; Hanger bore off his lady to London, not a little chagrined at such an unexpected termination of her romantic elopement ; but not many months elapsed before the lady gained an opportunity of repaying the Prince tenfold for the trick which he had played her.'

CHAPTER V.

Memoir of, and anecdotes about, George Hanger.

HE HON. GEORGE HANGER (afterwards the fourth and last Lord Coleraine) was at one time an especial friend of the Prince. He was educated at Eton and Göttingen, and was for some little time an officer in the first regiment of foot guards, which regiment he soon left in disgust at someone being promoted over his head. He then received an appointment from the Landgrave of Hesse Cassel as Captain in the Hessian Jäger Corps, then serving in America, and he was with this corps throughout the war. He, afterwards (in 1782), was made a Major in Tarleton's Light Dragoons, which was disbanded the following year, and he retired on half-pay. It was then that he joined the Prince's set, and received the appointment of equerry at a salary of £300 per annum, and this, combined with raising recruits for the East India Company, enabled him for a time to vie with the jovial crew with which he

GEORGEY IN THE COAL-HOLE.

associated. But evil days fell upon him, and he dwelt in the King's Bench Prison from June 2, 1798, to April, 1799, and in 1800 set up for a time as a coal-merchant, and was nicknamed the Knight of the Black Diamond. He appears in many of Gillray's caricatures, but the most savage pictorial satire on him (by Cruick-shank) was issued with the *Scourge* for November 2, 1812, where he is represented as a tall, full-faced man, wearing a long drab-coloured coat with a cape, and a star upon his right breast. Each of his arms encircles a gin-drinking old woman, and at his feet, one of which is cloven like a satyr's, sprawls a young woman who applies a bottle to her lips. A dandy, standing near, inspects the scene through his quizzing glass, and observes : ' Hang her ! She's quite drunk.' A label issuing from the mouth of the principal person makes him observe : ' As for me, my name is sufficient ; I am known by the title of the Paragon of Debauchery, and I only claim to be the [Prince]s *Confidential Friend.*' The letterpress description of the caricature contains the following illustrative paragraph :

' A tall, strapping - looking person, shabbily, but buckishly attired, with a peculiar cast of countenance, now stepped forward, and cried out, " My *name* is sufficient. Whoever has heard of —— must know that I am without a rival in the annals of debauchery. I claim no higher honour than to be my *Prince's friend*." '

On the death of his brother, on December 11, 1814, he succeeded to the title of Lord Coleraine, but he never assumed the title, and disliked being addressed by it. On his death, unmarried, on March 31, 1824,

at the age of seventy-three, the barony of Coleraine
became extinct.

Huish tells several stories about Hanger.[1] 'It is
well known that the above-mentioned person was the
particular companion of his late Majesty, when Prince
of Wales, and many of the youthful improprieties which
he committed were ascribed, by the King, to the company which he kept; and, particularly, to the society
of Sheridan and Major Hanger. On a particular occasion, when the latter was raising recruits, the King,
hearing that the Prince was taken from place to place,
by him and others in high life, collecting mobs, and
throwing money to them in large quantities, for the
sake of creating the fun of seeing a scramble, and other
worse purposes, he, with much feeling, exclaimed, "D—n
Sherry, and I must hang—hang—Hanger, for they will
break my heart, and ruin the hopes of my country."'

The following will be read as a rich treat to the
lovers of fun and mischief: it shows the extraordinary
gaiety of the Prince of Wales's disposition, and the
familiar manner in which he lived with his companions:

It was at the celebration of her Majesty's birthday,
1782, that Major Hanger made his first appearance at
Court; and it may be said to have been a début which
proved a source of infinite amusement to all who were
present, and to no one more so than the Prince of
Wales, who was no stranger to the singularity of his
character, and the general eccentricity of his actions.
Being a Major in the Hessian service, he wore his
uniform at the ball, which was a short blue coat with
gold frogs, with a belt, unusually broad, across his

[1] Vol. i., p. 97, etc.

shoulders, from which his sword depended. This dress, being a little particular, when compared with the full-trimmed suits of velvet and satin about him, though, as professional, strictly conformable to the etiquette of the Court, attracted the notice of his Majesty and his attendants ; and the buzz, ' Who is he ?' ' Whence does he come ?' etc., etc., was heard in all parts of the room. Thus he became the focus of attraction, and especially when the contrast presented itself of his selecting the beautiful Miss Gunning as his partner. He led her out to dance a minuet, but when, on the first crossing of his lovely partner, he put on his hat, which was of the largest Kevenhüller kind, ornamented with two large black and white feathers, the figure which he cut was so truly ridiculous and preposterous, that even the gravity of his Majesty could not be restrained : the grave faces of the Ministers relaxed into a smile, and the Prince of Wales was actually thrown into a convulsive fit of laughter. There was such an irresistible provocation to risibility in the *tout ensemble* of his appearance and style of movement, that his fair partner was reluctantly obliged to lose sight of good manners, and could scarcely finish the minuet ; but Hanger himself joined in the laugh which was raised at his expense, and thereby extricated his partner from her embarrassment. This is, perhaps, the first time that the *pas grave* of a minuet has been considered as a mighty good jest, but there are moments when even the most serious circumstances serve only to produce a comic effect.

The Major now stood up to dance a country dance, but here his motions were so completely antic, and so

much resembling those of a mountebank, that he totally
discomfited his partner, put the whole set into confusion,
and excited a degree of laughter throughout the room
such as had never before been witnessed in a royal
drawing-room.

On the following day the subject of the Major's
ludicrous début at Court became the topic of conversation at the convivial board at Carlton House, when the
Prince proposed that a letter should be written to the
Major, thanking him in the name of the company which
had assembled in the drawing-room, for the pleasure
and gratification which he had afforded them. The joke
was considered a good one. Writing materials were
ordered, and the Prince himself indited the following
letter, which was copied by Sheridan, with whose handwriting the Major was unacquainted :

' ST. JAMES'S STREET,
 ' *Sunday morning.*

' The Company who attended the Ball on Friday
last, at St James's, present their compliments to Major
Hanger, and return their unfeigned thanks for the
variety with which he enlivened the insipidity of that
evening's entertainment. The *gentlemen* want words to
describe their admiration of the truly grotesque and
humourous figure which he exhibited : and the *ladies*
beg leave to express their acknowledgements for the
lively and animated emotions that his stately, erect,
and perpendicular form could not fail to excite in their
delicate and susceptible bosoms. His gesticulations and
martial deportment were truly admirable, and have
raised an impression that will not be soon effaced at
St James's.'

This letter produced a highly humorous scene, which often excited a laugh when the Prince related it to his guests, as one of the most humorous which had occurred to him during his life.

On the day subsequent to the receipt of this letter, the Prince purposely invited George Hanger to dine at Carlton House, and it formed part of the plot of his Royal Highness, that Sheridan should not be invited. After dinner the conversation turned, designedly, upon the leading circumstances of the late ball; and, on the Prince ironically complimenting the Major on the serious effect which his appearance must have had on the hearts of the ladies, he, in a very indignant manner, drew from his pocket the letter which he had received, declaring that it was a complete affront upon him, and that the sole motive of the writer was to insult him, and turn him into ridicule. The Prince requested permission to read the letter, and, having perused it, he fully coincided in the opinion of the Major, that no other motive could have actuated the writer than to offer him the greatest affront.

The Major's anger rose. 'Blitz und Hölle!' he exclaimed; 'if I could discover the writer he should give me immediate satisfaction.'

'I admire your spirit,' said the Prince; 'how insulting to talk of your grotesque figure.'

'And then to turn your stately, erect and perpendicular form into ridicule,' said Mr. Fox.

'And to talk of your gesticulations,' said Captain Morris.

'Sapperment!' exclaimed the Major, 'but the writer shall be discovered.'

'Have you not the slightest knowledge of the hand-writing?' asked the Prince; 'the characters are, I think, somewhat familiar to me. Allow me to peruse the letter again.' The letter was handed to the Prince. 'I am certain that I am not mistaken,' he said; 'this is the handwriting of that mischievous fellow, Sheridan.'

'Sheridan!' exclaimed the Major. 'Impossible—it cannot be!'

'Hand the letter to Fox,' said the Prince; 'he knows Sheridan's handwriting well.'

'This is undoubtedly the handwriting of Sheridan,' said Fox, looking at the letter.

'Then he shall give me immediate satisfaction,' said the Major, rising from the table; and, addressing himself to Captain Morris, requested him to be the bearer of his message to Mr. Sheridan. Having written the note, in which a full and public apology was demanded, or a place of meeting appointed, Captain Morris was despatched with it; and in the meantime he (the Major) would retire to his lodgings to await the answer from Mr. Sheridan. The Prince now pretended to interfere, expressing his readiness to be a mediator between the parties, but at the same time he contrived, every now and then, to increase the flame of the Major's resentment by some artful insinuations as to the grossness of the affront, and complimenting him on the spirited manner in which he had behaved on the occasion. The Major was determined not to be appeased, and he left the room, muttering, 'D—n the impudent fellow! grotesque figure! perpendicular form! gesticulations!'

The Major had no sooner retired than the whole party burst into a loud laugh. The Prince had brought

him to the very point he wished, and in about an hour
Captain Morris arrived with Sheridan, who entered immediately into the spirit of the adventure. It was
then agreed that Sheridan should accept the challenge,
appointing the following morning at daybreak in Batter-
sea Fields, and that Mr. Fox should be the bearer of
Mr. Sheridan's answer to the offended Major, Mr.
Sheridan undertaking, on his part, to provide the
necessary surgical assistance.

On the following morning the parties were punctually
on the spot; the Major, accompanied by Captain Morris,
Mr. Sheridan by Mr. Fox, the Prince of Wales, disguised
as a surgeon, being seated in the carriage which conveyed the latter gentlemen. The customary pre-
liminaries being arranged, the parties took their
stations. The signal to fire was given; no effect took
place. The seconds loaded the pistols a second time;
the parties fired again ; still no effect was produced.

'D—n the fellow!' said the Major to his second, ' I
can't hit him.'

''The third fire generally takes effect,' said Captain
Morris, who with the utmost difficulty could keep his
risible faculties in order, whilst the Prince, in the
carriage, was almost convulsed with laughter at the
grotesque motions of the Major.

The signal to fire was given the third time. The effect
was decisive ; Mr. Sheridan fell, as if dead, on his back.

' Killed, by G—d!' said Captain Morris. ' Let us
fly instantly;' and, without giving the Major time to
collect himself, he hurried him to the carriage, which
immediately drove away towards town. The Prince
descended from the carriage, almost faint with laughter,

and joined Sheridan and Fox, the former of whom, as soon as the Major's carriage was out of sight, had risen from his prostrate position, unscathed as when he entered the field, for, to complete the farce, it had been previously arranged that no balls should be put into the pistols, and that Sheridan was to fall on the third fire. The Prince, with his two associates, immediately drove off to town, and a message was sent to Major Hanger, desiring his immediate attendance at Carlton House. The Major obeyed the summons, and he entered the apartment of the Prince with a most dolorous countenance.

'Bad business this,' said the Prince—'a very bad business, Hanger; but I have the satisfaction to tell you that Sheridan is not materially hurt, and if you will dine with me this day, I will invite a gentleman who will give you an exact account of the state in which your late antagonist lies. Remain here till dinner-time, and all may yet be well.'

The Prince, from goodness of heart, and not wishing that the Major should have the painful impression on his mind that he had been the instrument of the death of a fellow-creature and one of the most convivial of their companions, had imparted to the Major the consolatory information that his antagonist was not seriously injured, and the Major looked forward to the hour of dinner with some anxiety, when he was to receive further information on the subject. The hour came. The party was assembled in the drawing-room.

'Now, Hanger,' said the Prince, 'I'll introduce a gentleman to you who shall give you all the information you can wish.'

The door opened, and Sheridan entered. The Major started back in wonder.

‘How—how—how is this?’ he stammered. ‘I thought I had killed you.’

‘Not quite, my good fellow,’ said Sheridan, offering the Major his hand. ‘I am not yet quite good enough to go to the world above; and, as to that below, I am not yet fully qualified for it, therefore I considered it better to defer my departure from this to a future period; and, now, I doubt not, that his Royal Highness will give you an explicit explanation of the whole business—but I died well, did I not, Hanger?’

The Prince now declared that the whole plot was concocted by himself, and hoped that when the Major next fought such a duel, he might be in a coach to view it. Conviviality reigned throughout the evening; the song and glass went round; the Prince singing the parody on ‘There’s a difference between a beggar and a queen,’ which was composed by Captain Morris, and which is to be found in the twenty-fourth edition of ‘Songs Political and Convivial,’ by that first of lyric poets.

One more anecdote of the Prince and George Hanger, from the same source,[1] and I have done with him.

‘That the immense losses which the Prince of Wales sustained at the gaming table were not, always, the consequence of a run of ill luck, may be easily conjectured. Scheme after scheme was devised by which a heavy drain was to be made upon his finances; and he became, eventually, the dupe of a set of titled sharpers, who fattened on his credulity, and who, by

---

[1] Huish, vol. i., 164.

acts of the most deliberate villainy, reduced him to a state of comparative pauperism. As a proof of the inventive spirit of these associates of the Prince, we have only to mention the celebrated wager between the turkeys and the geese, which emanated from the prolific head of George Hanger, and on the issue of which the Prince found himself minus several thousand pounds.

' During one of the convivial parties at Carlton House, George Hanger designedly introduced the subject of the travelling qualifications of the turkey and the goose, and he pronounced it as his opinion (although directly contrary to his real one), that the turkey would outstrip the goose. The Prince, who placed great reliance on the judgment of George Hanger on subjects of that nature, backed Hanger's opinion; and, as it may be supposed, there were some of the party who were willing to espouse the part of the goose: the dispute ended in the Prince making a match of twenty turkeys against twenty geese for a distance of ten miles, the competitors to start at four o'clock in the afternoon. The race was to be run for £500; and, as George Hanger and the turkey party hesitated not to lay two to one in favour of their bird, the Prince did the same to a considerable amount, not in the least suspecting that the whole was a deep laid plan to extract a sum of money from his pockets, for his chance of winning, from the natural propensity of the turkey, was wholly out of the question.

' The Prince took great interest in this extraordinary wager, and deputed George Hanger to select twenty of the most wholesome and high feathered birds which could be procured; and, on the day appointed, the Prince and his party of turkeys and Mr. Berkeley and his party of geese, set off to decide the match. For the first three hours everything seemed to indicate that the turkeys would be the winners, as they were, then, two miles in advance of the geese ; but, as night came on, the turkeys began to stretch out their necks towards the branches of the trees which lined the sides of the road. In vain the Prince attempted to urge them on with his pole, to which a bit of red cloth was attached : in vain George Hanger dislodged one from its roosting-place, before he saw three or four others comfortably perching among the branches—in vain was barley strewn upon the road ; no art, no stratagem, no compulsion, could prevent them taking to their roosting-place ! whilst, in the meantime, the geese came waddling on, and in a short time passed the turkey party, who were all busy in the trees, dislodging their obstinate birds ; but, as to further progress, it was found impossible, and the geese were declared the winners.

' Trifling as this circumstance may appear, it will have the tendency of exposing the characters of the intimates of the Prince of Wales, and the singular expedients to which they had recourse to restore their shattered fortunes at the expense of his character and fortune.'

On the death of Lord Coleraine, a contemporary[1] thus sums up his character : ' He was, formerly, admitted amongst the convivial companions of his present Majesty; but, as the Prince advanced in life, the eccentric manners of the Colonel became somewhat too free and coarse for the Royal taste, and the broad vivacity of the facetious Humourist gave way to associates of a more refined description. But, though the Colonel was free in his

---

[1] *Gentleman's Magazine*, 1824, part i., 457, 458.

manners, he never was inclined to give intentional offence, and the peculiarity of those manners precluded all idea of resentment, and laughter, rather than anger, was the result of his most extravagant sallies.

'He was capable of serious exertions of friendship, not by pecuniary sacrifices, for, of such, his situation hardly ever admitted, but by persevering zeal when he was likely to effect a beneficial purpose. He was well acquainted with military duty, and was never wanting in courage, or the spirit of enterprise. He is generally acknowledged to have been a very handsome man in early life, but his person was disguised by the singularity of his dress. Though disposed to participate in all the dissipations of higher life, he yet contrived to devote much of his time to reading, and was generally well provided with topics for the usual conversations of the table, even in the most convivial circles. He was so marked a character that he might be considered as one of the prominent features of his time, and he was courted as well for the peculiarity, as for the harmless tendency of his humour.'

CHAPTER VI.

The Prince goes to Brighton for his health—Description of
Brighton in 1784—Royal visitors—The Prince takes a
house — Weltje — Sam House — Fox and the Prince —
Brighton in 1785.

IN 1784 the Prince of Wales had a somewhat serious illness, and we read in the
Morning Herald of July 16 that ' His
Royal Highness, the Prince of Wales,
having been advised by his Physicians
to sea bathing, we are informed from good authority,
that his Royal Highness will set out on Monday next
for Brighthelmstone. Mr. Weltje, the Clerk of the
Kitchen, and Mr. Gill, the Purveyor of the Stables,
are now at Brighthelmstone, preparing everything for
his Royal Highness's reception.'

He left London on the evening of July 22, and the
following are some newspaper cuttings which describe his
visit and the general gaieties of that season at Brighton :

' *Brighthelmstone* will certainly prove the summer
residence of the *loves* and *graces*, on account of the
temporary residence there of the Heir apparent : not

5

a cock loft but what is taken by some *expectant fair*, who means to make an *innocent conquest*, or an *illicit sacrifice!*—The *Knights of the Dice box* are collecting there from all quarters, hoping for a plentiful harvest in so singular a season for universal *gul-* as well as *cullibility!* A pretty sprinkling of Princes of the *Gallic blood* is, likewise, hourly expected to complete the curious *dramatis personæ.*'[1]

' *Extract from a letter from Brighthelmstone, July 25.* The Prince of Wales is here quite as a private gentleman, attended by Colonel Leigh, etc. He walks frequently upon the Steine, and behaves with great affability and politeness.'[2]

' BRIGHTHELMSTONE INTELLIGENCE. *Brighthelmstone* is the center *luminary* of the *system* of pleasure : Lymington, Southampton and all other places within the *sphere* of its *attraction*, lose their gayest visitants, who fly to that resort :—the women, the pretty women, all hasten to see the *Paris* of the day!—On Monday last, the Dukes of *Chartres* and *Lauzun*, the Marquis *de Conflans*, the Comte *de Seguir*, and others, arrived to be present at the races. They came from France by the way of Dover, but had all their equipage sent over from *Dieppe*. The lively and engaging Comtesse *de Coniac* was to have met them by the latter route at Brighthelmstone ; but some dæmon, unfriendly to gallantry, and to this place, interposed, and procured an *arret* to be expedited from the Queen of France's bedchamber, just as the sprightly belle was casting a longing eye from *Dieppe* over to the British coast, and preparing to step into

---

[1] *Morning Herald*, July 27.

[2] *Parker's General Advertiser*, July 28.

the pacquet. This is a prodigious disappointment to the company, and particularly to the *Prince*. His Highness gave an elegant dinner at his house on the *Steine*. The *Duc de Chartres* and his friends were present: the meeting was festive and social. In the evening, this convivial party visited the Rooms: the company was genteel and numerous. The Prince danced with Lady *Elizabeth Conway*, and was acknowledged the best performer present.

'On Tuesday, the *Brighton Races* began, which afforded but very little sport. The Duke of Queensberry's was the favourite horse, but lost; and the *Duc de Chartres*, who betted him against the field, got rid of a good deal of money on the occasion. The sport was not better the next day, but rather worse, on account of the badness of the weather. All the Ladies attended both days, mostly in carriages. Lady *Charlotte Bertie* was the Constellation, or superior luminary of the course. *Micavit inter omnes, quantum inter ignes Luna minores.* Lady *Lincoln*, and her sister Lady *Betty Conway*, drove about in a phaeton, to the great annoyance of the beaux.

'The public entertainments at Brighthelmstone are, balls at the rooms twice a week, alternately at the *Ship*, and *Castle*, and plays, the other four nights, at the theatre. The balls are on Monday and Thursday; and no dress is required except in those that dance minuets. The rooms are, besides, open all the other nights for card parties, and on *Sunday* for a promenade. The Prince has not yet missed the Play house once, when there has been a performance at it, since his arrival. The pleasurable daughters of the place, have at their head, Mrs. *Smith*, Mrs. *Elliot*, and Mrs. *Walker*; between whom an equipoise of rivalship and jealousy prevails, and what one has in a *dimple*, is counteracted by the lip, or the eye of the others.'[1]

'LEWES RACES. The *Prince of Wales* is so regardless of weather, that a shower of rain is never known to interrupt his excursions. His Highness's indifference on this head, reminds us of a remark of *Henry the Great*, " that fate does not depend upon a sunbeam !"—The example of the British prince was followed by his *insular* friends and *Parisian* visitors. The road from Brighthelmstone to Lewes, was crowded by *gentlemen jockies* and *jockey sharpers*; carriages of various denominations, and a company of all descriptions. The *Steine* was depopulated of all save a few *living caricatures*, consisting of antique Females, and *balloonified* squires from the City, too awkward and unwieldy to wear boots, or venture on horseback : to this class of beings, the ball room was relinquished.

'The Course ground continued, during the races, frequented by fashionable guests. Besides the English and French princes, were present the Duc *de Lauzun*, Marquis *de Conflans*, Count *Seguir*, the Russian minister, and several others from the Continent. The Duke of Queensberry, Lord Cholmondeley, Lord Foley, and many more of the Jockey Club were on the ground.

'The Bets were high, though the sport was indifferent ; the Duke de Chartres, Duke of Queensberry and Sir Charles Bunbury, were principally engaged in the success of the day. The *Gallic Duke* was in such spirits, that it was said his Highness would have mounted an *Air balloon* had one been present.

[1] *Morning Herald*, August 9.

' A *Pedestrian Race* was, also, proposed between a *fat gentleman*, and a *lean one :* but the former complaining that the atmosphere was low, gave up the contest as he was fearful he should be *hard blowed !*[1]

The Prince being at Brighton made all the difference in the gaiety of the place, and his occasional absence in London is thus commented upon : ' Brighthelmstone, comparatively speaking, within these few days, has become almost a desert ; scarce a person of fashion remains ; the whole company now consists of *antiquated virgins, emaciated beaux,* and wealthy citizens, with their wives and daughters ; the latter of whom have some *weight* in continuing a few needy adventurers, who are as watchful as lynxes, for an opportunity of carrying off the golden prizes.'[2]

Note how this all changes when he returns. ' Extract from a Letter from Brighthelmstone, dated Sep. 5. We are all alive and merry here. Besides the honour of his Royal Highness the Prince of Wales's company, we are favoured with those of the Duchess of Ancaster, Lady Charlotte Bertie, Lady Mary Brudenell, the Bishop of Winchester, Lord and Lady Beauchamp, the Right Hon. Mr. Fox, with many others ; and, last night, the Right Hon. Mr. Pitt, accompanied by Mr. Steele, of the Treasury, arrived here.

' The Prince of Wales was, last night, at the Theatre, accompanied by the Hon. Mr. Erskine, and the Hon. Mr. Onslow, to see the Beggar's Opera, the principal parts of which were represented by gentlemen, and well represented they were. Captain Ash's *Macheath* much

---

[1] *Morning Herald*, August 10.

[2] *Ibid.*, August 21.

exceeded many of the professional men on either of
your London theatres. It was succeeded by a well-
timed address, written and spoken by Mr. Bonner,
craving the friendly attendance of the company to the
future benefits of the several performers.'[1]

We also learn by a newspaper paragraph[2] that 'the
house that the Prince of Wales has at Brighthelmstone,
is that which formerly belonged to Lord Egremont's
brother, Mr. Wyndham. The Duke of Cumberland
had it last year. The house is, or ought to be, the
best in the place.'

This is the house which we have seen was negotiated
for the Prince by Weltje, his clerk of the kitchen ; at
least, this was his nominal title, but in reality he was
the Prince's purveyor of his household, and was much
mixed up in his financial matters. Louis Weltje was
a German of obscure origin, and it is said, at one time,
sold cakes in the streets. However, he must have had
something in him, and must also have been thrifty, for in
the newspapers of 1782 and 1783 we find several
mentions of Weltje's Club, and he had a famous pastry-
cook's shop and restaurant in St. James Street, and
afterwards in Pall Mall. In the satirical prints in the
British Museum for 1783, drawn by Captain Hays, is
'Mr. Weltjee's Fruit Shop, Pall Mall.' Madame
Weltje, a large woman, is seated at a horseshoe counter,
on which is a variety of fruit. In the window are displayed pines, grapes, bottles, and jars. A manuscript
note says her shop was 'next door neighbour to
Mr. Neville.' He served the Prince for some years,

<hr>

[1] *Morning Herald*, September 9.
[2] *Ibid.*, August 27.

but was at last superseded. On his retirement he
bought a large house at Hammersmith, formerly in the
occupation of Lord Allington, the supporters of whose
arms, two talbots, decorated the gate-posts. In this
house, which he bequeathed to his brother Christopher,
he died, probably of apoplexy, in 1810, and was buried
in Hammersmith Churchyard. His name still exists
in the neighbourhood in Weltje Road, which runs from
the Upper Mall to King Street West, and consists of
sixty-eight houses.

We have seen that Fox was at Brighton in 1784.
Fox, who was the 'guide, philosopher, and friend' of
Prince Florizel, was at this time a man of about thirty-
five or thirty-six, having been born in 1749. By his
birth, education, and talents he should have been a
fitting companion for the Prince, but he was lax in his
morals, an inveterate gambler, and a hard drinker, and
a worse comrade for a young man could scarcely be
found. Indeed, at the end of the Westminster election
of 1784 Gillray caricatured him in a satirical print
entitled 'Preceptor and Pupil' as a loathsome toad
with a fox's brush, who is whispering into the ear of
the sleeping (or drunken) Prince : ' Abjure thy country
and thy parents, and I will give thee dominion over many
powers. Better to rule in Hell than serve in Heaven !'

Apropos of this election, which lasted forty days, and
brought Fox in second at the poll, it is perhaps as
famous as any in our electoral history. Much to the
disgust of his parents, the Prince threw himself heart and
soul into the fray, wearing a ' Fox cockade ' at Ranelagh,
and allowing members of his household to canvas for
his boon companion. During the election, Gillray

produced a satirical print (April 18, 1784) called 'Returning from Brooks's,' where the Prince, exceedingly drunk, and wearing the 'Fox cockade,' is being helped along by Fox and Sam House, a publican who kept a house, called The Intrepid Fox, at the corner of Peter Street and Wardour Street. 'Honest Sam House,' as he was called, was a violent politician and Whig, and during this election kept open house at his own expense. House figures in many caricatures of the time, and his fame was even enshrined in verse:

'See the brave Sammy House, he's as still as a mouse,
    And does canvas with prudence so clever;
See what shoals with him flocks, to poll for brave Fox:
Give thanks to Sam House, boys, for ever, for ever, for ever!
    Give thanks to Sam House, boys, for ever!

'Brave bald-headed Sam, all must own, is the man,
    Who does canvas for brave Fox so clever:
His aversion, I say, is to *small beer* and *Wray :*[1]
May his bald head be honour'd for ever, for ever, for ever!
    May his bald head be honour'd for ever!'

There is another satirical print, which is dated January, 1785, by an unknown artist, called 'Fox singing a Song to the P——e of W—l—s.' Fox and the Prince are playing cards and drinking. Fox sings:

1.

' Tho' matters at present go cross in the realm,
    You will one day be K—g, Sir, and I at the helm;
    So let us be jovial, drink, gamble and sing,
    Nor regard it a straw, tho' we're not yet the thing.
        Tol de rol, tol, tol, tol de rol.

---

[1] Sir Cecil Wray, one of the candidates.

RETURNING FROM BROOKS'S.

2.

' The proverb informs us, each dog has his day,
So those that oppose us, this fate must obey ;
But time's on our side, Sir, and now on the wing,
To make me a statesman, and you, Sir, the K—g.
Tol de rol, etc.

3.

' In vain are harangues, I as well may be dumb,
And let motions alone, till our day, Sir, is come ;
Then Thurlow and Pitt from their state we will fling,
They may go below stairs, Sir, so we are the thing.
Tol de rol, etc.

4.

' Thus seated in state, Sir, we'll fill all our soul,
At the fountain of Venus, at Bacchus's bowl ;
In all that we please, Sir, we'll take a full swing,
For who's to controul a Prime Statesman and K—g ?
Tol de rol, etc.'

The Prince remarks : ' Fox, are you not the shuffler ?'

'The Prince of Wales has again taken a house at Brighton for the season,' says the *Morning Post* of June 11, 1785, and he left London for his seaside residence on the 22nd of the same month. The same newspaper of June 28 reports that 'the visit of a certain gay, illustrious character at Brighton, has frightened away a number of old maids, who used constantly to frequent that place. The history of the gallantries of the last season, which is in constant circulation, has something in it so voluminous, and tremendous to boot, that the old tabbies shake in their shoes whenever his R——l H——ss is mentioned.'

' *Lewes, July* 2.—The Prince of Wales, on Monday last, at Brighthelmstone, amused himself for some time,

in attempting to shoot doves with single balls, but with
what success, we have not learnt ; though we hear that
his Royal Highness is esteemed a most excellent shot,
and seldom presents his piece without doing some
execution. The Prince, in the course of his diversion,
either by design, or accident, lowered the tops of several
of the chimnies of the Hon. Mr. Wyndham's house.'[1]

A few paragraphs from the *Morning Post* of this
year will give us a good insight into the Brighton of
the period.

July 6.—'The *Brighthelmstone intelligence* has no
novelty to recommend it ; merely a repetition of the
old story ; *morning rides, champaigne, dissipation, noise*
and *nonsense :* jumble these phrases together, and you
have a complete account of all that's passing at *Brighthelmstone !*

July 8.—' A correspondent says, Brighthelmstone is
much altered from what it was last season. Neither
money, nor any speculating jewellers who give good
tick, and discount upon a *gentle feeling*. The ——
has been tried and found wanting—all about him is
not sterling—but one good *endorser* in the whole set,
and he abroad. Times are bad.

'Mrs. Johnson and Windsor have undertaken to
provide for the necessities of Brighton this year. The
female adventurers of last season were totally ruined :
even *Bet Cox*, who made as good a hand of it as any,
swears she will not run the risk again, and that, *though
as how* she was with the Prince, one night when he was
drunk, yet that did not compensate her for the wear
and tear with his attendants. We have not yet heard

<hr>

[1] *Morning Post,* July 8, 1785.

Mrs. *Smith's* opinion on the subject; but, as she was nearer the fire, she could not well escape being scorched.'

August 4.—' Brighthelmstone is at present very thin of company, few females arriving there but the *corps d'amour.* Women of virtue and character shun these scenes of debauchery and drunkenness, ever attendant on the spot which is the temporary residence of a ——.'

August 18.—' His Royal Highness the Prince is so attached to his bathing residence, Brighthelmstone—he has so many sea nymphs there, rising from Old Ocean every morning to greet him; that, in the true spirit of an *English Prince*, his sole desire appears to *rule the waves:* and, when he comes to Town, he is actually like *a fish out of water.*'

August 25.—' Plague upon the *skippers* that they do not understand the navigation of their own coasts! for, surely, some of the Margate Hoys have blundered by both the North and South Foreland, and landed their cargoes on the Sussex Shore. Never were there such a set of curmudgeonly knaves and dowdies, before, in Brighton, say the conscientious keepers of the subscription books! The lodging-houses are full, the streets well frequented, and the Steyne crowded—but who bathes, who raffles, and who subscribes? They vow that they never had so little Gold in their Autumn crop, since they were obliged to content themselves with the profits of their fishing, to wash their smocks upon the beach, and to live on crabs and pickled herrings!

' In fact, the visitors of this place are either a wiser, or a poorer sort than formerly. *Snug* is the word with most of them; they give as little into amusements, dissipation and extra expences, as they can well avoid—

hence, the obvious policy of the inhabitants to render
the necessary ones as high and as productive as possible
—they treat Londoners in their town as we treat Dutch-
men and others, in our charge for lights and landmarks
—make them come down handsomely, as it is to be
done but seldom. The innkeepers here, are a kind of
beasts of prey, whose rapacity is in proportion to their
former abstinence: they are leeches, who think a
plethora of the purse is no less dangerous than that of
the body; and, though you come here only to have
your constitution put to rights, they will, also, gladly
take charge of your property.

' An Irish gentleman being asked, the other day, by
a friend, which Inn he thought the best, observed that
they were both bad enough ; at one you were *imposed
upon* ; at the other, *cheated.* The Rooms have been
pretty well frequented on a Sunday, when it is the
Vauxhall price of admission. The play house must,
long since, have shut up, were it not for the *extraordinary abilities* and *fertile resources* of Mr. *Fox*,[1] and
the patronage of the fair emigrants from Cleveland
Row, Jermyn Street, and King's Place—there have been
no gentlemen enactors, this year ; so much the worse.
With deference, be it said, to the judgement of certain
titled ladies, who, adding to their *purity* by every
successive plunge into the salt water, pronounced the
mixture of gentlemen with professed actors, a perfect
contamination. Better sense, however, and more extra
liberality prevail at present ; for ladies now ride to the
Downs to see Earls and great folks play at cricket, with
footmen and drivers, without having their delicacy

---

[1] The lessee and manager.

wounded, or their finer feelings deranged. That game
has become the favourite amusement with the young
men of fashion here. Mr. *St. John* is the best bowler;
Lord *Darnley* and *George Hanger* the best bats; *Bob*
the postillion, the best stopper behind the wicket. As
to his Royal Highness, he is but a young cricketer; the
ladies, however, commend his agility; and, since M^rs
J—n's squad arrived, he has been famous for catching
and running.

'On Saturday last, the *Marquis de Conflans* took his
departure for *Dieppe*. The Prince and his company
went to see the Marquis embark, when a very extraordinary and humorous scene was presented. It being
low water, the boat could not approach the shore—the
Marquis was anxious to get on board, and stood, for
some time, in suspence, when the Prince, to show him
that persons of their rank should not have the propensities of cats, or the frippery of *petits maîtres*, taking
one of his companions by the hand, rushed at once into
the water. The Marquis, *pour l'honneur de la France*,
could not do otherwise than follow him; the line
advanced with resolution, but could not long withstand
the force of the waves, which overset them; they then
rolled like porpoises in the water, till they got the
Marquis aboard the packet; when they despatched
him, in a proper state, to pay his respects to the
Dauphin. *Vive l'amour et l'allegresse, et bon voyage,
M. le Marquis!*'

September 10.—' The flux and reflux of company not
being so great here as at some other places, there has
been very little novelty since my last intelligence. The
lodging-houses are, still, in general, full, though there

are some occasionally to be disposed of at the following reasonable rates : for a house upon the Steine, eight guineas a week, or the same faced with blue and buff,[1] for the trifling addition of two guineas (for which you may have the credit of being a member of that party).[2] Two beds, with a dining-room or parlour (the former, perhaps, being supplied with a good *live stock*) for three guineas; and, for a guinea per week, a single gentleman may be accommodated with an apartment, where, if he finds himself streightened for want of room, he may be gratified, at least, with a prospect of better things, and have the view of a large piece of water, commonly called the English Channel. Hence, too, he may form some idea of our naval grandeur, by contemplating the fleet, as it lies at anchor before the town, consisting, at least, of an hundred sail—of fishing smacks; or, he may indulge in a peep of the ladies dipping into the water, or bobbing at a wave in rough weather; for the Master of the Ceremonies has judiciously assigned them the place nearest to the houses, and has sent the gentlemen, *for decency's sake*, two hundred yards further to the westward.

' If we may believe *the printed list*, half the fashionable persons, and about one-fourth of the w——s of London, have visited Brighton in the course of the summer; but, for those of the most consideration, who are to be seen in their shoes, as well as upon the List of the Company, take the following names : His Royal

[1] The builders have, since last year, erected a row of houses on the Steyne, with bricks of these colours, in compliment, I imagine, to the Prince's uniform.

[2] Whig.

Highness and suite, more respectable, though not as numerous as last year ; the Earl and Dowager Countess of Darnley, with her family ; Earl and Countess of Clermont ; Lord and Lady Beauchamp ; the Countess of Shaftesbury and family ; Baron and Baroness Nolcken ; Lord Belgrave ; Lord Lucan, with his family ; Lord and Lady Lisle ; Lord Gage ; Sir Sampson and Lady Gideon ; Sir Eardley Wilmot ; Earl and Countess of Sefton ; Lord Herbert ; Sir Godfrey Webster ; Mr. Wyndham ; Mr. T. Townsend ; Mr. St. John. Some city beaux sport their gigs upon the downs, and their persons upon the Steine : they would fain be thought men of fashion, but their very best airs in the ball-room partake of Coachmaker's Hall ; the City dancing-masters being ten years behindhand in the refinements of their profession. There is very little show of beauty in the Rooms. Among the young ladies of family, *Miss Bingham*, daughter of Lord Lucan, is almost the only one that deserves notice in that particular ; and, however singular, in this place, it is a fact that one of the ladies who has been most distinguished for elegance, is a Miss I——s, from *Cow Lane*, West Smithfield !

'The Rooms, as I hinted before, have been almost deserted, except on particular nights. At the last ball but one, at the *Ship*, only seven couple stood up, and the lady who took the lead, according to the etiquette established in pride and folly, was *pro summorum atque hominum fidem credite !*—no less a person than Mrs. Tr——d, daughter of the naval baronet, who, in his lifetime, gained many signal advantages over the tribes of Benjamin and Levi. The *Castle* has been somewhat more fortunate. But Fox, the manager, has been so successful, as to excite the envy of his rivals, who have it in contemplation to set up a theatre in opposition to his. It was for this purpose that *Signor Grimaldi's* journey was undertaken, which, by the newspaper accounts, proved so fatal to him ; and, as he, with Mr. *Spencer*, the harlequin, is to have the principal concern, we may expect that the prime parts of the entertainment at the new Theatre, will be pantomime, with *grinning* and *jumping* in abundance. If Mr. *Grimaldi* should bring down his young pupils from the Circus, it will, perhaps, be necessary for Mr. Fox to engage the General Jackoo, or the Dancing Dogs. At present, he confines his attempts to Comic Opera, Comedy, and Farce ; and, for these, it must be confessed, he has good materials. His company may be called a good one—for the country—though the greatest part are recruits, and want drilling. Yet, why for *the country*, when there are so many London performers without engagements in the summer.

'The most extraordinary event that has happened lately, was a violent gale on Tuesday, which caused many sad accidents. The wind blew with prodigious force from the southward, and brought an uncommonly high tide with it. This rendered it necessary to draw up all the small craft, and the machines upon the Steine, where most of the Company, particularly the Londoners, assembled to gaze at a sea storm. The Prince's curiosity got him a ducking, and an old man and his ass were drowned under the Cliff.'

CHAPTER VII.

The Prince's acquaintance with Mrs. Fitzherbert—His court-
ship and marriage—Satirical prints thereon.

HIS year was exceedingly fateful to Prince
Florizel, for, in it, he made the acquaint-
ance of a lady whose connection with him
influenced his whole life. This was Maria
Anne Fitzherbert, daughter of Walter
Smythe, Esq., of Brambridge, in the county of Hants,
second son of Sir John Smythe, Bart., of Eske, in the
county of Durham, and Acton Burnell, in Shropshire.
She was born in July, 1756, and married, in July, 1775,
Edward Weld, Esq., of Lulworth Castle, county Dorset,
who died in the course of the same year. She married,
secondly, Thomas Fitzherbert, Esq., of Swinnerton,
county Stafford, in the year 1778. This gentleman only
survived their union three years, losing his life in consequence of his exertions during the Lord George Gordon
Riots. Being much heated, he bathed, and brought on
the malady which, soon after, occasioned his death.

Behold her, then, in 1785 a fascinating young widow

6

with a competent fortune, moving in the highest society, and of so much importance as to be made the subject of newspaper paragraphs long before she met the Prince. *Morning Herald*, March 20, 1784.—'Mrs. *Fitzherbert* is arrived in London for the winter.' And again, *Morning Herald*, July 27, 'A new *constellation* has lately made an appearance in the *fashionable hemisphere*, that engages the attention of those whose hearts are susceptible to the power of beauty. The widow of the late **Mr. F—h—t** has in her train half our young Nobility : as the lady has not, as yet, discovered a partiality for any of her admirers, they are all animated with hopes of success.'

Cosway painted a charming picture of her, which, engraved by Condé, is reproduced as the frontispiece to this volume.

Huish[1] gives an erroneous account of the acquaintance of the Prince and Mrs. Fitzherbert, but I give it so that the reader may contrast it with that of Lord Stourton,[2] who was her intimate friend and near connection. 'The first time that the Prince of Wales saw Mrs. Fitzherbert, was in Lady Sefton's box at the Opera; and the novelty of her face, more than the brilliancy of her charms, had the usual effect of enamouring the Prince. But in this instance he had not to do with a raw inexperienced girl, but with an experienced dame, who had been twice a widow, and who, consequently, was not likely to surrender upon common terms. She looked forward to a more brilliant prospect which her ambition might artfully suggest, founded upon the feeble character of

---

[1] 'Memoirs of George IV.,' vol. i., p. 125.

[2] 'Memoirs of Mrs. Fitzherbert,' etc., by the Hon. Charles Langdale ; London, 1856, 8vo., p. 115.

an amorous young Prince; and, when his Royal Highness first declared himself her admirer, she gave him not the slightest hopes of success; but, in the true spirit of the finished coquette, she turned away from his protestations; and, in order to avoid his importunities, quitted the kingdom, and took up her residence at Plombiers, in Lorrain, in France. The lovely idol knew that an object which is easily gained, is seldom esteemed or prized: the Prince, indeed, from his peculiar situation as Heir apparent, could not follow her, although it is stated, in an anonymous letter preserved in the British Museum, that his Royal Highness did once travel to Paris incog. and that he had, there, an interview with Mrs. Fitzherbert, the consequence of which was, her immediate return to England. As there is no other authority for this act of his Royal Highness, and taking the improbability of the event into consideration, it must be left with all the doubt attached to it, acknowledging, at the same time, that the preponderancy leans to the side of its being a fiction.'

Now let us hear Lord Stourton's version, which bears the impress of truth upon it, judging by the almost universal testimony as to Mrs. Fitzherbert's character:

'In the midst of the afflictions, both of body and mind, which weighed down the latter years of Mrs. Fitzherbert, the thought which most soothed her pains, and assuaged her grief, was the consoling testimony which would be borne to her character, when she should be no more; when all the actors in this extraordinary drama being removed by the hand of death, the veil might be drawn aside which had prompted secrecy during her life; and her character might be shown to posterity in the light which it appeared to herself, unsullied by crime, and even untarnished by interestedness or ambition. With this view, she almost insisted, in our confidential communications, upon my requiring from her every information respecting her conduct, from her first connection with George the Fourth, down to his death—as evidence to satisfy my mind of the strictest propriety of every portion of her conduct, that I might deem doubtful, or objectionable.

'After disclosures so intimate, and, to my judgment, so satisfactory, I should not wish to descend into the tomb myself, leaving her reputation to the doubtful testimony of others, less informed, even if equally disposed to render her justice. Associated with some, in the custody of a few important papers relative to her history, I stand single in a nearer relationship to this distinguished person, in some important and intimate connections, and was, therefore, selected by her on that account, to be honoured with communications of so very delicate and confidential a nature. Having deliberately accepted the proffered confidence, I should not feel happy to leave to the chances of ill-advised or mercenary biographers the portraiture of one so difficult to pencil in her true and accurate lineaments.

'Mrs. Fitzherbert was first acquainted with the Prince when residing on Richmond Hill, and soon became the object of his most ardent attentions. During this period she was made the subject of a popular ballad, which designated her, under the title of the "Sweet Lass of Richmond Hill."

' " I'd crowns resign to call her mine,
Sweet lass of Richmond Hill."

She was, then, the widow of Mr. Fitzherbert, in possession of an independent fortune of nearly £2,000 a year, admired and caressed by all who were acquainted with her character and singular attractions.

'Surrounded by so many personal advantages, and the widow of an individual to whom she had been singularly attached, she was very reluctant to enter into engagements fraught with so many embarrassments; and, when viewed in their fairest light, exposing their object to great sacrifices and difficulties. It is not, therefore, surprising that she resisted, with the utmost anxiety and firmness, the flattering assiduities of the most accomplished Prince of his age. She was well aware of the gulf that yawned beneath those flattering demonstrations of royal adulation.

'For some time her resistance had been availing, but she was about to meet with a species of attack so unprecedented and alarming, as to shake her resolution, and to force her to take that first step, which, afterwards, led by slow (but on the part of the Prince, successful) advances, to that union which he so ardently desired, and to obtain which he was ready to risk such personal sacrifices. Keit (Keate), the surgeon, Lord Onslow, Lord Southampton, and Mr. Edward Bouverie, arrived at her house in the utmost consternation, informing her that the life of the Prince was in imminent danger—that he had stabbed himself, and that only *her* immediate presence would save him.[1] She resisted,

[1] At this time the great mooncalf would go to Fox's house at St. Ann's Hill, near Chertsey, and there blubber his love-woes into the sympathizing ears of Bridget Cane, alias Armistead, or Armstead, a woman of good manners and some education, who

in the most peremptory manner, all their importunities,
saying that nothing should induce her to enter Carlton
House. She was, afterwards, brought to share in the
alarm, but, still, fearful of some stratagem derogatory
to her reputation, insisted upon some lady of high
character accompanying her, as an indispensable condition : the Duchess of Devonshire was selected. They
four drove from Park Street to Devonshire House, and
took her along with them. She found the Prince
pale, and covered with blood. The sight so overpowered her faculties, that she was almost deprived of
all consciousness. The Prince told her that nothing would
induce him to live unless she promised to become his
wife, and permitted him to put a ring round her finger.
I believe a ring from the hand of the Duchess of
Devonshire was used upon the occasion, and not one
of his own. Mrs. Fitzherbert being asked by me,
whether she did not believe that some trick had been
practised, and that it was not really the blood of his
Royal Highness, answered in the negative ; and said
she had frequently seen the scar, and some brandy and
water was near his bedside when she was called to him
on the day he wounded himself.

' They returned to Devonshire House. A deposition
was drawn up of what had occurred, and signed and
sealed by each one of the party ; and, for all she knew
to the contrary, might still be there. On the next
day, she left the country, sending a letter to Lord

---

was said to have been waiting-woman to Mrs. Abington, the
actress, but who was then Fox's mistress, and afterwards his
wife.

Southampton, protesting against what had taken place, as not being then a free agent. She retired to Aix la Chapelle, and, afterwards, to Holland. The Prince went down into the country to Lord Southampton's, for change of air.

'In Holland, she met with the greatest civilities from the Stadtholder and his family, lived upon terms of intimacy with them, and was received into the friendship of the Princess of Orange, who, at that time, was the object of negotiation with the Royal Family of England, for the Heir apparent. Frequent inquiries were made about the Prince and the English Court, in confidential communications between her and the Princess, it being wholly unknown to the Princess that she was her most dangerous rival. She said she was often placed in circumstances of considerable embarrassment; but, her object being to break through her own engagements, she was not the hypocrite she might have appeared afterwards, as she would have been very happy to have furthered this alliance. She afterwards saw this Princess in England, and continued to enjoy her friendship, but there was always a great coolness on the part of the Stadtholder towards her.

'She left Holland in the Royal Barge, and spent above another year abroad, endeavouring to " fight off" (to use her own phrase) a union fraught with such dangerous consequences to her peace and happiness. Couriers after couriers passed through France, carrying the letters and propositions of the Prince to her in France and Switzerland. The Duke of Orleans was the medium of this correspondence. The speed of the couriers exciting the suspicion of the French Government, three of them were, at different times, put into prison. Wrought upon, and fearful, from the past, of the desperation of the Prince, she consented, formally and deliberately, to promise that she would never marry any other person ; and, lastly, she was induced to return to England, and agree to become his wife, on those conditions which satisfied her own conscience, though she could have no legal claim to be the wife of the Prince.

'I have seen a letter of thirty-seven pages, written, as she informed me, not long before this step was taken, entirely in the handwriting of the Prince ; in which it is stated by him that his Father would connive at the union. She was then hurried to England, anticipating too clearly and justly, that she was about to plunge into inextricable difficulties ; but, having insisted upon conditions, such as would satisfy her conscience, and justify her in the eyes of her own Church, she abandoned herself to her fate. Immediately after her return, she was married to the Prince, according to the rites of the Catholic Church in this country ; her uncle Harry Errington and her brother Jack Smythe being witnesses to the contract, along with the Protestant clergyman who officiated at the ceremony.[1] No Roman Catholic priest officiated. A certificate of this marriage is extant in the handwriting of the Prince, and with his signature and that of Maria Fitzherbert. The witnesses' names were added ; but, at the earnest request of the parties, in a time of danger, they were afterwards cut out by

---

[1] It is said that the Rev. Mr. Burt, of Twickenham, on his death-bed acknowledged marrying the Prince and Mrs. Fitzherbert, and that he received £500 for his fee.

Mrs. Fitzherbert herself, with her own scissors, to save them from the peril of the law.[1]

'This, she afterwards regretted; but a letter of the Prince, on her return to him, has been preserved, to supply any deficiency, in which he thanks God, that the witnesses to their union were still living; and, moreover, the letter of the officiating clergyman is still preserved, together with another document with the signature and seal, but not in the handwriting, of the Prince, in which he repeatedly terms her his wife.'

As a matter of fact, these papers are now deposited in Coutts's Bank, sealed up in a cover under the seals of the Duke of Wellington, Sir William Knighton, the Earl of Albemarle, and Lord Stourton. All other correspondence was destroyed, on the death of George IV., by Mrs. Fitzherbert herself in the presence of the Duke of Wellington and the Earl of Albemarle. The packet consists of:

1. The mortgage on the palace at Brighton.

2. The certificate of the marriage, dated December 21, 1785.

3. A letter from George IV. relating to the marriage (signed).

4. A will written by George IV.

5. Memorandum written by Mrs. Fitzherbert, attached to a letter written by the clergyman who performed the marriage ceremony.

With regard to this mortgage on the Pavilion, Lord Stourton says:[2] 'To the Duke of York and the Queen, Mrs. Fitzherbert was indebted for £6,000 a year in a

---

[1] She was married in her own drawing-room.

[2] Langdale's 'Memoirs of Mrs. Fitzherbert,' p. 141.

mortgage deed, which they procured for her on the
Palace at Brighton ; being aware, as she said, that till
that period, she had no legal title to a single shilling
should she survive the Prince. Indeed, at one period,
she had debts upon her own jointures, incurred principally
on account of the Prince ; and, when the Duke of Wellington, as executor to George IV., asked her if she had
anything to show, or claim upon the personalty of the
deceased Sovereign, she told him she had not even a
scrap of paper, for that she had never, in her life, been
an interested person.'

We have seen that the marriage took place on
December 21, 1785; but it was noised about before
then, as we may see by the two following cuttings from
the *Morning Post*, December 16, 1785 : ' It is whispered
in the circles of gallantry, that a certain illustrious
character has made a delicate and honourable engagement with a Lady of superior accomplishments ; that
she is to have the full direction of his household, with
a settlement of £8,000 a year, the ——'s liveries, with
an engagement to create her a Duchess, if ever he should
have the power.'

December 17, 1785.—' A very extraordinary treaty is
on the tapis, between a beautiful young Widow, who
resides about ten miles from London, in the county of
Surrey, and a Gentleman of *high rank*, in the neighbourhood of St. James's. Fame speaks highly of the Lady's
virtues, and her accomplishments ; and, as conscious of
her value, she has taken care to set a very high price
upon her person : the terms are that she should be the
mistress of the young Gentleman's town house, to pre-
side at his table, to have a settlement of Six thousand

pounds per annum : her equipages and liveries to be the same as her lover's ; and, when it shall be *in his power*, the Lady to be created a Duchess in her own right :—These conditions, it is said, are already agreed to ; and, in a very short time, the amorous treaty will be signed and sealed.'

The caricaturist did not linger long afterwards, and the earliest of the satirical prints bearing on this subject is one dated March 13, 1786, supposed to be drawn by ' Fitz,' called ' The Follies of a Day, or the Marriage of Figaro.' The Prince is just putting the ring on Mrs. Fitzherbert's hand. They are being married by a sham parson—Weltje, in fact, as is evidenced by the corkscrew which he wears in lieu of a crucifix, whilst out of his pocket appears a scroll endorsed ' Weltjie's Nat(uraliza-tio)" Bill.' The book from which he reads is ' Hoyle's Games,' and the page is headed ' Matrimony.' George Hanger is the sole witness.

Others follow, and they are all as wide of the real facts of the case as is this one.

March 20, 1786—' The Royal Toast—Fat, Fair, and Forty,' is a fancy portrait of Mrs. Fitzherbert, very stout, a fact as truthful as her age, which was but thirty.

March 21, 1786—' Wedding Night, or the Fashion-able Frolic.' The Prince and Mrs. Fitzherbert are dancing, and George Hanger is playing the ' Black Joke ' on a fiddle. A marriage certificate, torn up, lies on the floor.

March 21, 1786—' The Lovers' Leap.' The Prince and Mrs. Fitzherbert are preparing to jump over a broom (which is said to be the gipsies' marriage ceremony), which lies on the floor between them. George Hanger is pushing the Prince on, and a cat is jumping out of a bag.

Another version of this, by Gillray, was published on the same date, and is thus described in Wright and Grego's 'Gillray':

'21 *Mar.*, 1786.—'*Twas nobody saw the Lovers' Leap and let the Cat out of the Bag*. This title, which refers to the first disclosure of the scandal, is literally treated in the print. Fox appears as " nobody," and a cat is seen escaping from a bag. The Whig chief, with whom, as the occasional companion of the young Prince's excesses, the public were not slow to connect the transaction, is encouraging Florizel to " leap over the broomstick " with Mrs. Fitzherbert. The ex favourites, in a second apartment, surmounted by the Prince's crest, tranquilly regard the coming change. " All I desire of mortal man is to love whilst he can," says Perdita. " Well said, Robby," remarks a gentleman at table: " his father will broomstick him !" '

The best etching on the subject is dated March 27, 1786, and is called ' Wife and no Wife ; or, A Trip to the Continent.' The Prince is about to put the ring on Mrs. Fitzherbert's hand, and Fox is giving her away. Hanger and Sheridan are witnesses. Burke, as a Jesuit, is reading the marriage service, and Lord North, as a coachman, is fast asleep.

Then we have on May 1, 1786, ' The April Fool, or the Follies of a Night, as performed at the Theatre Royal, C——n House, for the Benefit of the Widow Wadman.' The Prince, Mrs. Fitzherbert, and George Hanger are dancing, while Fox is drumming with a pistol on a warming-pan, exclaiming, ' Damme, but 'tis

WIFE AND NO WIFE; OR, A TRIP TO THE CONTINENT.

sublime;' and Burke, who says, ' Burn the pan, is it not beautiful ?' plays on a gridiron with a pair of tongs. On the walls are two scenes from *Hamlet:* one where Polonius says to the King, ' I will be brief, your noble son is mad ;' the other where Hamlet says to Ophelia :

> ' He may not, as inferior persons do,
> Carve for himself, for on his choice depends
> The sanity and health of the whole state.'

On the ground lie two plays, ' A Bold Stroke for a Wife '[1] and ' The Clandestine Marriage.'[2]

May 1, 1786.—' An Extravaganza, or Young Solomon besieging Fitzhubbub, the Governess of the Fort and Garrison of Fitzhubbub, after a political resistance of time proper, surrenders to the besieger, as by the articles of capitulation.' The Prince is kneeling before Mrs. Fitzherbert, who, seated on a sofa, points to ' Articles of Capitulation, £8,000 per annum. A Duchess in my own right. The mockery of MARRIAGE by a Priest and a Parson.'

May 3, 1786.—' The Introduction of F—— to St. James's.' A view of the gateway of St. James's Palace. The Prince is carrying Mrs. Fitzherbert on his shoulders, preceded by George Hanger beating a drum, and by Fox and Captain Morris playing on trumpet and horn, whilst Burke brings up the rear playing on a flageolet.

The Prince, personally, took no heed of these pictorial satires; but others thought differently of them, as we learn by the *Morning Post*, April 24, 1786 : ' His Royal Highness the Prince of Wales has been frequently

---

[1] By Mrs. Centlivre.
[2] By George Colman and D. Garrick.

entreated to take legal cognizance of the numerous libellous prints, and other scandalous reports, which have lately been in circulation ; but, with a magnanimity of soul congenial with the spirit of British freedom, he constantly declined it, with expressions of jocularity: at the same time, thinking the authors unworthy of his notice. The laws of his country have, at last, interfered, and common decency requires that the most rigorous measures should now be pursued to punish the offenders. —Indictments have been preferred, and the Bills were found, on Friday last, at the Guildhall, Westminster, against — *Ford*, of Piccadilly, for having published and circulated some infamous prints, with an intent to satyrize and libel his Royal Highness, the Prince of Wales; which prints, we understand, were shown to a great law Lord, by an indifferent person ; and, in consequence, his Lordship pronounced them most infamous libels, and ordered the present prosecutions to be instituted against the publishers thereof.'

The newspapers notice the new opera-box of Mrs. Fitzherbert, and also her new house in St. James's Square, formerly in the occupation of Lord Uxbridge.

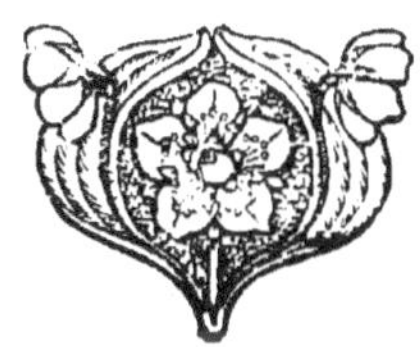

CHAPTER VIII.

The Prince's debts—Appeal to the King—His retrenchments
—'The Jovial Crew, or Merry Beggars'—Satirical prints
—Help from Parliament—Schedule of his debts.

ARLY in 1786 matters financial came to a crisis with Florizel. Notwithstanding his income of nearly £70,000, he had managed in less than three years to get some £300,000 in debt. Harassed by his creditors, he had no resource left but to apply to his father, but from him he got naught but good counsel. In this dilemma Pitt was applied to, and asked to furnish £250,000. This not being forthcoming, the King was written to, who replied, asking for a detailed statement of liabilities. This was furnished, and so astonished the King that he declined the proposal, and declared that he would never sanction an increase to his son's income. Then Florizel wrote another letter to his father, announcing his determination to retrench violently, and set aside £40,000 a year towards the payment of his debts. To which the King replied, that if he chose to take a rash step, he

must likewise take the consequences. Then the Prince once more took his pen in hand, and wrote a letter to his father, which closed the correspondence :

'SIR,

'I have had the honour of receiving your Majesty's written message, transmitted to me by Lord Southampton, and am greatly concerned that my poor sentiments cannot coincide with those of your Majesty, in thinking that the former message which I had the honour of receiving, in your Majesty's own hand, was not a refusal. After having repeatedly sent in various applications to your Majesty, for two years successively, representing that a partial reduction out of so incompetent an income as mine, was to no purpose towards the liquidation of a debt, where the principal and interest were so considerable, I, this year, humbly requested your Majesty that you would be graciously pleased (having previously laid my affairs before you, Sir, for your inspection, and painted them in the distressed colours which they so justly merited), whenever it suited your conveniency, to favour me with a decisive answer ; as the various delays which have occurred, through the course of this business, have, in reality, proved more pernicious to me in the situation in which I have been for some time past involved, than the original embarrassment of the debt. To not only these, but to any future delays, would I have, most willingly, submitted, had they really rested upon my own patience ; but the pressing importunities of many indigent and deserving creditors (some of them whose very existence depends upon a speedy discharge of their accounts),

made too forcible an appeal to the justice becoming my
own honour, and to the feelings of my heart, to be any
longer delayed. Another consideration is, that any
further procrastination might have exposed me to legal
insults, as humiliating to me, as, I am persuaded, they
would be to your Majesty. I, therefore, previously to
my having the honour of receiving that message, had
determined, that, should I not be so fortunate as to
meet with that relief from you, Sir, with which I had
flattered myself, and which I thought I had the greatest
reason to expect, I would exert every nerve to render
that just redress and assistance to my creditors, which I
cannot help thinking is denied to me. These are the
motives, Sir, that have actuated my conduct in the step
I have taken, of reducing every expence in my family, even
those to which my birth and rank entitle me (and which,
I trust, will ever continue to be the principle and guide
of my conduct), till I have totally liberated myself
from the present embarrassments which oppress me ; and
the more so, as I am persuaded that such a line, when
pursued with consistency, will meet with the approbation of every candid and dispassionate mind.

'I will not trespass any further on your Majesty's
time, but have the honour to subscribe myself,

       'Sir,

   'Your Majesty's most dutiful and obedient

       'Son and Subject,

         'GEORGE, P.'

'*July* 9, 1786.'

After the despatch of this letter he immediately acted
on it ; gave orders to curtail his household, to stop all

building and decoration of Carlton House, and to sell
his race and carriage horses, with a very few reserva-
tions, and go and ruralise at Brighton, which he reached
on July 11. The newspapers and caricaturists, of
course, immediately made capital out of it, *vide* the
Morning Post, July 13, 1786: ' A morning paper of
yesterday says that the *Prince of Wales* set off for
Brighton in a *hired chaise* and *hack horses;* but we are
informed by authority, which we trust will meet with
equal credit, that his Royal Highness was an *outside
passenger* by the *Brighton Dilly.*'

And the caricaturist followed quickly in the wake of
the newspaper men with a satirical print published on
July 15, called ' A Trip to Brighton, or the P——
and his reduced Household returning for the summer
season.' The Prince and Mrs. Fitzherbert are inside
the carriage, and the latter is studying the 'Principles
of Œconomy.' The carriage is laden with household
effects, vegetables, meat, etc., and with small beer and
raisin wine. One of the footmen is Fox, the other
George Hanger, who is reading, ' For Sale, at Tattersall's, the Prince's Stud.' Weltje, ' Purveyor, Coachman,
Cook and Butler,' is driving.

There is another, which, although not dated, is
evidently of the same period, called ' The Brighton
Stud,' in which is seen a groom leading three donkeys
—George Hanger, Fox, and Sheridan. The Prince
rides another donkey (Mrs. Fitzherbert), and Lord
Derby (as another) looks on. This evidently refers to
the sale of the Prince's stud, which realized somewhat
over £7,000. Mrs. Fitzherbert went to Brighton
immediately after the Prince.

There is a very amusing satirical print dated
August 23, 1786, the best part of which is the verse
attached. It is called 'The Jovial Crew, or Merry
Beggars. A Comic Opera, as performed at Brighton
by the Carleton Company.' The Prince and Mrs.
Fitzherbert occupy the centre of the picture. The
Prince has a hat full of money, '£7,586. By sale of
the Stud,' and Mrs. Fitzherbert carries a child on her
back. The other beggars, who are mostly on crutches,
are on either side.

'1ST BEGGAR, ⎱ I once was a poet at London,
  MR. S——. ⎰   I kept my heart still full of glee ;
  (*Sheridan.*)   There's no man can say that I'm undone,
                 For begging's no new trade to me.

'2ND BEGGAR, ⎱ In London I once shone with eclat,
  THE ——.   ⎰   A Stud and brave Household could boast ;
(*Prince of Wales.*) Give me a brisk wench in clean straw,
                 Aud I value not who rules the roast.

'3RD BEGGAR, ⎱ A widow I was, buxom and bold,
  MRS. F——. ⎰   So clos'd with a Royal attack ;
  (*Fitzherbert.*)   Tho' 'tis said the marriage won't hold,
                 But, ecod, I'll stick to his back.

'4TH BEGGAR, ⎱ Here comes a patriot polite, Sir,
  MR. F——.   ⎰   Who flatter'd the K—— to his face ;
      (*Fox.*)   Now, railing is all his delight, Sir,
                 Because he's turn'd out of his place.

'5TH BEGGAR, ⎱ I was a Jesuitical preacher,
  MR. B——.   ⎰   I turn'd up my eyes when I pray'd ;
    (*Burke.*)   But my hearers half starved their teacher,
                 For they believ'd not a word that I said.

7—2

'6TH BEGGAR,   } I still am a merry song maker,
  CAP. M——.   }   My heart never yet felt a qualm ;
    (*Morris.*)   Tho' poor, I can fiddle and caper,
                 And sing any tune but a psalm.

'7TH BEGGAR,   } Make room for a soldier in buff,
  COL. H——.   }   Who valiantly strutted about ;
    (*Hanger.*)   And, if the Peace should be breaking off,
                 Why, then he'll, most wisely, sell out.

'8TH BEGGAR,   } De Beggar vos I in Germany,
  MR. W——.   }   But alms vos here better agree ;
    (*Weltje.*)   For, by begging in coot company,
                 Begging vos de making of me.

'9TH BEGGAR,   } Since, Beggars, then, we are happy and free,
  L. N——.   }   Pray talk no more of state axes ;
    (*North.*)   For, by the War, you'll surely agree,
                 That, all, I have beggar'd with Taxes.'

There is a very clever satirical print which refers to
the breaking up of the Prince's establishment. It is
called ' The School for Scandal,' and parodies the scene
from Sheridan's play, in which Charles Surface helps to
knock down the portraits of his ancestors. George
Hanger is the auctioneer, and Lot 1 is a picture of the
King and Queen, ' Farmer George and his Wife.'
Hanger cries out, ' Going for no more than one Crown !'
and the Prince thus encourages the Colonel, ' Careless,
knock down the Farmer.' One of the audience bids
five shillings for the royal pair. Lot 2 is a portrait of
Mrs. Fitzherbert, and Lot 3 one of Perdita. Through
the open door is seen Tattersall's, where the Prince's
stud, etc., were sold. A carriage is numbered Lot 1,000

to show the extravagance of the Prince's stable arrangements.

A piece of gossip about the Prince at Brighton
appears in the *Morning Post* of September 25, 1786 :
' We hear that the Prince of Wales, a few days since,
was suddenly indisposed at Brighthelmstone ; and, at
the same time, several gentlemen who had dined with
the Prince at a friend's table, the preceding day, were
seized with symptoms similar to those of his Royal
Highness. They were all more or less affected, according to the quantity each eat of a particular dish
at table. Happily for his Royal Highness, he eat
but moderately ; and we have the pleasure to add, he
has now quite recovered. Mr. Keate, the Prince's
surgeon, has been sent for from London ; and the business terminated so favourably, no other assistance was
called in.'

During his stay this year he was very quiet, only
going to the races, and superintending the alterations
to his house, which were completed the ensuing spring.
He left Brighton for the season on October 17.

The Prince kept his promise of retrenchment for nine
long months, and was sorely put to it for money—a
fact of which the caricaturist took full advantage.
Thus, on January 18, 1787, we have ' The Prodigal
Son,' in which the Prince is depicted as seated on the
bare ground, feeding swine ; his coat is out at elbows
and breeches unfastened ; his Garter has gone, and his
three feathers lie on the ground.

Then, on February 26 there is ' Love's Last Shift,'
which represents the Prince and Mrs. Fitzherbert in
the last stage of poverty. The Prince sits before a

fire, turning a sheep's head, which hangs by a string,
and rocking a cradle in which a child lies sleeping, an
event which, happily, did not occur during his connection with Mrs. Fitzherbert.   He has no breeches on,
because Mrs Fitzherbert is mending them.   Weltje
has just brought in some potatoes, and George Hanger
has a small measure of beer.

The Prince's friends felt that this could not go on
longer.   It was resolved to appeal to Parliament for aid,
and Mr. Nathaniel Newnham, a merchant, Alderman,
and an M.P. for the City of London, was chosen to open
the matter, which he did on April 20, 1787, by asking
Mr. Pitt whether it was his intention to bring forward
any proposition to rescue the Prince of Wales from his
embarrassed and distressed situation.   Being answered
by the Minister that he had no commands to that
purpose from the King, the Alderman gave notice
that, on Friday, May 4, he would bring forward a
motion upon that subject for the consideration of the
House.

As a matter of fact, the motion was brought before
the House on April 27, and again on April 30, when
Fox supported the Prince, and in the course of his
speech, referring to the rumour of the Prince being
married to Mrs. Fitzherbert (a Roman Catholic), said:
'With respect to the allusion to something full of
"danger to the Church and State," made by the hon.
gentleman, one of the members of the County of Devon,
till that gentleman thought proper to explain himself,
it was impossible to say with any certainty to what
that allusion referred; but he supposed it must be
meant in reference to that miserable calumny, that low,

LOVE'S LAST SHIFT.

malicious falsehood, which had been propagated without doors, and made the wanton sport of the vulgar. In that House, where it was known how frequent and common the falsehoods of the times were, he hoped a tale, only fit to impose on the lowest order of persons in the streets, would not have gained the smallest portion of credit; but, when it appeared that an invention so monstrous, a report of a fact which had not the smallest degree of foundation, a report of a fact actually impossible to have happened, had been circulated with so much industry, as to have made an impression on the minds of the members of that House, it proved, at once, the uncommon pains taken by the enemies of his Royal Highness to propagate the grossest and most malignant falsehoods, with a view to depreciate his character, and injure him in the opinion of his country. . . . The whole of the debt the Prince was ready to submit to the investigation of the House; and he was equally ready to submit the other circumstance to which he had alluded, to their consideration, provided that the consideration of a House of Parliament could, consistently with propriety and decency, be applied to such a subject. Nay, his Royal Highness had authorised him to declare that, as a Peer of Parliament, he was ready in the other House to submit to any of the most pointed questions which could be put to him respecting it, or to afford his Majesty, or his Majesty's ministers, the fullest assurances of the utter falsehood of the fact in question, which never had, and which common sense must see, never could have happened.'

In a later part of the debate ' Mr. Fox answered, that he did not deny the calumny in question merely with regard to the effect of certain existing laws, alluded to by the hon. gentleman; but he denied it *in toto*, in point of fact, as well as of law. The fact not only never could have happened legally, but never did happen in any way whatsoever, and had, from the beginning, been a base and malicious falsehood.'

The debate was again resumed on May 4, when Mr. Alderman Newnham rose, and said: 'Sir, I am extremely happy that the motion which I was to have had the honour of making, this day, is no longer necessary; and it is with the most sincere and heart-felt satisfaction that I inform the House that I decline bringing it forward.'

The following is a note to p. 1074 of vol. xxvi. of Hansard: 'On Sunday the 29th, or Monday the 30th of April, an intimation was given at Cumberland House, that, if the Prince had no objection, Mr. Dundas would be glad to have an interview with his Royal Highness. On this being communicated to the Prince, he sent back word that he was ready to see him whenever he should call at Carlton House. Accordingly, on Wednesday, the 2nd of May, late in the evening, Mr. Dundas had a long general conversation with the Prince, which ended with Mr. Dundas requesting that the Prince would permit Mr. Pitt himself to wait upon him. To that, his Royal Highness assented; and Mr. Pitt, in conformity, was with the Prince at Carlton House, the next day, for more than two hours: in this long conversation, the Prince stated all his circumstances to Mr. Pitt, who then promised to lay the same before his Majesty, and to return an answer as speedily as possible.

' Mr. Pitt thence went immediately to the King, and the same evening a Cabinet Council was held at nine o'clock, which sat until midnight ; when an answer in writing, by his Majesty's command, was dispatched by Mr. Pitt to the Prince, informing him in general terms, that, in case his Royal Highness thought proper to withdraw the motion intended to be made, the next day, in the House of Commons, everything should be settled to his Royal Highness's satisfaction.   Agreeably to this, the motion was, the next day, withdrawn by Alderman Newnham, as being no longer necessary ; after which, to the infinite surprise of the House, the Minister rose up in his place, and said that he could not see, for his own part, that the motion was then either more or less necessary, than it ever had been ; and added, in answer to Mr. Rolle's question, that no terms of any kind were settled, but that matters remained *in statu quo.*

' This proceeding, being related to the Prince, his Royal Highness, the same night, wrote a letter, with his own hand, to Mr. Pitt, requiring an immediate explanation of the extraordinary speech delivered that day in the House of Commons.   Mr. Pitt, in answer, requested leave again to wait upon his Royal Highness. Accordingly the Minister went on Saturday, at noon, to Carlton House, and had another long conference with the Prince, in which his Royal Highness (in order to prevent any more mistakes) gave to Mr. Pitt, in writing, his proposals, which were in substance :—1. The Prince of Wales to have his debts paid off, in part, at least.   2. To have a sum granted sufficient to finish Carlton House.   3. To have such moderate increase made to his annual income, as may be sufficient to prevent his running in debt in future.

'With these propositions Mr. Pitt took his leave, and on Sunday, despatched them by a special messenger to Windsor, to the King; who, on Monday last, returned his answer, signed in form by his Majesty's own hand. This answer was on the same day delivered by Mr. Pitt to the Prince at Carlton House, and is nearly to the following effect:—1. That his Majesty was glad to find the Prince of Wales ready to submit his accounts to inspection. 2. That it would be necessary for the Prince, not only to ascertain the whole amount of his debts, but, also, the particulars thereof, with an exact account of how each debt was incurred. 3. That the Prince shall engage not to run in debt in future. That, upon the specifications above required, would depend his Majesty's determining upon whether he should agree to the payment of the whole, or any part of the Prince of Wales's debts. 5. That his Majesty cannot think any increase of income necessary, so long as the Prince of Wales shall remain unmarried. This answer cannot be supposed to have been, in any way, satisfactory to the Prince of Wales.

' However, nothing was said upon the business in the House, either on Monday, or Tuesday, and nothing on those days was done farther than that the Prince, on Tuesday, sent his commissioners, Colonels Lake and Hulse, with Mr. Lyte, his Treasurer, to Mr. Pitt, with all his accounts, etc., etc., for the inspection and information of his Majesty.'

The account of the Prince's debts which was furnished to the House is as follows:

Bonds and debts	...	...	...	... £13,000
Purchase of houses	...	...	...	... 4,000
Expenses of Carlton House	...	...	...	53,000
Tradesmen's bills	...	...	...	... 90,804
				£160,804

EXPENDITURE FROM JULY, 1783, TO JULY, 1786.

Household, etc.	...	...	...	£29,277
Privy purse	...	...	...	16,050
Payments made by Col. Hotham, particulars delivered to His Majesty	...	...	...	37,203
Other extraordinaries	...	...	11,406	
				£93,936
Salaries	...	...	...	£54,734
Stables	...	...	...	37,919
Mr. Robins, etc.	...	...	...	7,059
				£99,712
				£193,648

On May 21 the King sent a message to the Commons,
in which he says, ' His Majesty could not, however,
expect, or desire the assistance of the House, but on a
well grounded expectation that the Prince will avoid
contracting any new debts, in future. With a view to
this object, and from an anxious desire to remove every
possible doubt of the sufficiency of the Prince's income
to support amply the dignity of his situation, his
Majesty has directed a sum of £10,000 per annum
to be paid out of his civil list, in addition to the
allowance which his Majesty has hitherto given him ;
and his Majesty has the satisfaction to inform the
House that the Prince of Wales has given his Majesty
the fullest assurances of his firm determination to

confine his future expences within his income; and has, also, settled a plan for arranging those expences in the several departments, and for fixing an order of payment under such regulations as his Majesty trusts will effectually secure the due execution of the Prince's intentions.'

The King's message was considered on the 24th, and part of the Commons' reply runs thus: 'That his Majesty may depend on the zeal and affectionate attachment of his faithful Commons, to afford his Majesty the assistance he desires for the discharge of his Royal Highness's debts, and that, in full reliance on the assurances which his Majesty has received, this House humbly desires that his Majesty will be graciously pleased to direct the sum of £161,000 to be issued out of his Majesty's Civil List for that purpose, and the sum of £20,000 on account of the works of Carlton House, as soon as an estimate shall be formed, with sufficient accuracy, of the whole expence for completing the same in a proper manner, and to assure his Majesty that his faithful Commons will make good the same.'

Of course there was the inevitable satirical print, 'The Prince in Clover' (June 2, 1787). The Prince has his hands full of purses, with which he is, somewhat theatrically, paying his creditors. Three Ministers— Pitt, Dundas, and Thurlow—are abjectly grovelling behind him, to the intense delight of Fox, Sheridan, Burke and Lord North.

CHAPTER IX.

UT how about Fox's denial of the Prince's
marriage with Mrs. Fitzherbert? was
that to pass unnoticed? Certainly not,
and there was a slight disturbance in
Florizel's matrimonial establishment,
which may as well be told in Lord Stourton's suave
diction.

'The first signal interruption to this ill-fated engagement arose from the pecuniary difficulties of his Royal
Highness, when, on the question of the payment of his
debts, Mr. Fox thought himself justified by some verbal,
or written permission of the Prince, to declare to the
House of Commons that no religious ceremony had
united the parties. This public degradation of Mrs.
Fitzherbert so compromised her character and her
religion, and irritated her feelings, that she determined

to break off all connection with the Prince, and she was only induced to receive him again into her confidence, by repeated assurances that Mr. Fox had never been authorised to make the declaration ; and the friends of Mrs. Fitzherbert assured her, that, in this discrepancy as to the assertion of Mr. Fox and the Prince, she was bound to accept the word of her husband. She informed me that the public supported her, by their conduct, on this occasion ; for, at no period of her life, were their visits so numerous to her house, as on the day which followed Mr. Fox's memorable speech ; and, to use her own expression, the knocker of her door was never still during the whole day.

'I told her that I understood there was a scrap of paper from the Prince to Mr. Fox ; that Sir John Throckmorton, a friend of his, had assured me of the fact of the Prince wishing much to obtain possession of it ; but, though written on a dirty scrap of paper, it was much too valuable to be parted with. She said that she rather doubted the fact. I think that the difference between the assertions of the Prince and Mr. Fox may be accounted for under a supposition (which I have also heard) either that there was some ambiguity in the expressions used, or that Mr. Fox might have referred to what had passed, antecedently, at Devonshire House, without being privy to their subsequent more formal engagements.

'However this may be, an accommodation took place between Mrs. Fitzherbert and the Prince, though she, ever afterwards, resolutely refused to speak to Mr. Fox. She was, however, obliged to see him sometimes, and was much urged by the Prince to a reconciliation ; but, though of a forgiving disposition upon other occasions, and even benefiting some who most betrayed her confidence, she was inflexible on this point, as it was one of the only means left her to protect her reputation. She thought she had been ill-used, in a most unjustifiable manner, by this public declaration before the House of Commons; especially as she had been waited upon by Mr. Sheridan, who had informed her, that some explanation would, probably, be required by Parliament, on the subject of her connection with the Heir apparent. She then told him, that they knew she was like a dog with a log round its neck, and they must protect her. She went so far with respect to Mr. Fox, that when, afterwards, during his administration, he made overtures to her, in order to recover her good will, she refused, though the attainment of the rank of Duchess was to be the fruit of their reconciliation. On naming this circumstance to me, she observed that she did not wish to be another Duchess of Kendal.'[1]

Gillray published a satirical print on May 21, 1787, entitled 'Dido Forsaken. *Sic transit gloria Reginæ.*' Mrs. Fitzherbert, crucifix in hand, is seated on a heap of ruins, in utter despair, whilst a breeze, blown by Pitt and Dundas, carries away her crown, orb, sceptre, and coronet, as Princess of Wales. In a boat named *Honor*, bound for Windsor, sail away the Prince, Fox (who steers), Lord North, and Burke. The Prince says, 'I never saw her in my life.' Fox clinches this with, ' No, never in his life, Damme.' North and Burke asseverate ' No, never.' On the ground lie fetters, an axe, rods, and a harrow, 'for the conversion of heretics,' being a

---

[1] Mistress of George II.

delicate allusion to Mrs. Fitzherbert being a Roman Catholic.

However, the difference between the couple was made up, and they were in Brighton together early in July. The Prince evidently used some of his newly-got money on his seaside residence, for we read in the *Morning Herald* for July 3, 1787 : 'Last Tuesday morning (26 June) as the painters were beautifying the great dome of the Prince of Wales's house at Brighthelmstone, the scaffolding broke down, whereby several of the workmen were killed, and others terribly wounded. His Royal Highness has caused enquiry to be made into the condition of their families, in order to give them relief.'

We hear very little of his stay at Brighton during this year. The *Morning Herald* of July 24 tells us : 'The *Prince*, we are happy to say, has derived much benefit from the air of Brighthelmstone, and the exercise which he has taken in its environs. We have never seen his *Royal Highness* in better health, or more apparent spirits than in his evening walks on the Steyne. His companions in these promenades, exclusive of the gentlemen of his suite, are, in general, Mrs. F——, with the Countess of Talbot, and Lady Stawell.'

In the same newspaper of August 6, we find under the heading 'BRIGHTHELMSTONE, Aug. 3. This scene feels, at present, a temporary desertion from the general resort of the visitants to the races of Lewes. The Prince has also left it this morning, on hearing of the arrival of his brother, the Duke of York, from the Continent.

'The races above mentioned derived more celebrity from the brilliant attendance with which they were honoured, than from the sport which they afforded. The betting on the first day was so generally on the side of *Marplot* that eighty guineas to sixty, and immediately before starting sixty to forty were offered and refused. Mr. Fox took the odds that were offered against *Balloon*, to the amount of about five hundred pounds, and Mr. Tetherington is said to have cleared upwards of a thousand by the success of his horse *Marplot*.

'Amongst those present were the Prince, the Duke and Duchess of Cumberland, the Princesse de Lamballe, who was particularly distinguished through the day by the *enviable* attentions of the Duke of Queensberry. The Duchess of Rutland, the Countess of Talbot, Lord and Lady Abergavenny, Mrs. Fitzherbert, Lord Clermont, Lord Grosvenor, Sir John Lade, Sir Richard Heron, Mr. Fox, Mr. Wyndham, Mr. Pelham, Col. Fitzpatrick, etc., added to the fashion of the group.

' After the first race, the Prince, with a select party, retired to partake of an entertainment provided for them at the seat of Mr. Wyndham, near Lewes.'

In 1788 the Prince went to Brighton for the season on July 1, and very shortly, when driving with Mrs. Fitzherbert, they were both upset. Neither could have been much hurt, for the *Morning Post* of July 5 says that the Prince came to town the previous day, and that ' Mrs. Fitzherbert is totally recovered from the effects of her accident.' Still, this trivial event gave food to the caricaturist, ' The Prince's Disaster, or a fall in Fitz.' They have been for a drive in an open carriage, which has broken down. Mrs. F—— lies on the ground, and the Prince is being thrown out.

That their mutual relations were cordial is evidenced by a satirical print, April 3, 1788, where Mrs. Fitzherbert is seen leading the Prince in chains. She says, 'Who can behold without transport "the glass of fashion and the mould of form, the observ'd of all observers," smiling in chains?' He replies, 'Delightful slavery! A day, an hour, of such sweet bondage is worth an eternity of celestial happiness!'

We get a glimpse of what Brighton was, at this time, by the two following newspaper cuttings. *Morning Post*, July 14: 'Brighton, with the Prince, and such Company as follow the Prince, will do very well, though, of late years, it has not been so crowded as formerly. Many reasons have been assigned for this change—we, however, for *propriety's sake*, shall give none.' *Ibid.*, July 21 : ' Brighton, notwithstanding the return of the Prince, does not bear the appearance of pleasure and fashion.'

And it can hardly be wondered at, for the Prince had relapsed, since he had got his debts paid, and kept very bad company. He always was fond of seeing prize-fights, and he and the Duc d'Orleans saw the fight between Humphries and Martin at Newmarket, on May 3, 1786; but he had more than he bargained for at Brighton Races this year. The event is thus recorded in *Boxiana* (vol. i., p. 219, ed. 1818) : ' *Tyne* next entered the lists with *Earl*, upon a stage erected near the stand on the Brighton Race ground, on August 6, 1788. Never were more fashionables assembled at a boxing match than the above; the town of Brighthelmstone was literally drained of its company, and the race stand was crowded to excess with nobility and gentry; among whom was his Royal Highness the Prince of Wales. *Earl* was a tall, strong man, and, in point of appearance, the favourite, and was actually becoming so from his exertions, when *Tyne* put in a blow upon his temple, that made him reel against the rail of the stage, and he instantly dropped down dead : which unfortunate circumstance produced a most afflicting scene ; and the Prince declared he would never witness another battle. His Royal Highness, with great humanity and consideration, settled an annuity on Mrs. *Earl* and family. It appeared by the evidence before the Coroner's jury that *Earl* had been for some time previous to the battle engaged in an election contest at Covent Garden, and had been in one continued state of inebriety during the whole of it. It was the opinion of professional men, that the vessels being so overcharged with blood was the immediate cause of his death.'

The *Morning Post* of August 9 has the following from Brighton : 'The Prince of Wales gains many hearts by his great affability and good humour. His company is much better than it used to be, and he is certainly more sparing of his libations to Bacchus.

' Mrs. F——t looks more elegant than ever. One can, indeed, hardly help exclaiming with the army of Mahomet the Second, when he showed them his Irene— "Such a woman is worth a kingdom !"

' The Prince of Wales has won money on the races— more money than one would wish a Prince of Wales to win.'

The same newspaper of August 15 says: 'BRIGHT-HELMSTONE.—The celebration of the Prince's birthday was in a style of the utmost gaiety and conviviality, the more general and uniform, from the contracted circle in which it shone. The Prince gave a most sumptuous entertainment at the MARINE PAVILION,[1] of which all the Nobility and Gentry in the town and neighbourhood partook by invitation. In the evening the illuminations were general, and some of them conspicuous for taste, particularly the Castle, the front of which was covered with various coloured lamps. A Ball was given by the Jockey Club, in honour of the Prince, who honoured several ladies with his hand during the course of the evening.'

Ibid., September 6.—'The Prince of Wales does not slumber in dull indolence at his retreat at Brighton, but promotes and participates in many manly exercises. Cricket is, at present, the chief amusement patronized by his Royal Highness, who is dexterous and indefatigable. Most of the young noblemen in the neighbourhood join in this vigorous and wholesome exercise, in which the domestics of the Prince are permitted to partake.'

We get a good glimpse of our great grandfathers and grandmothers at Brighton in the *Morning Post* of September 18 : ' DRESS AT BRIGHTON.—The fashionable bathing dress at Brighton is chiefly a pair of buff trousers, and a slight jacket.

'This is adopted by all the young men of the place,

---

[1] This is the first instance I have met with in which it is so called.—J. A.

and such a number of idle, sauntering *land lubbers*
meet the eye, every morning, on the Steyne, that one
cannot help wishing for a sturdy press gang to give
them useful employment, or, at least, keep them out of
mischief.

' After breakfast, they are then accoutred for the
sports of the field.

' The sporting dress is a brown jacket, with a multi-
plicity of pockets on each side, that reach from the
bottom to the top, so that, from this appearance, it is
somewhat difficult to determine which the fashionable
tribe most resemble, a set of *grooms*, or a company of
smugglers.

' When the dinner hour arrives, after these sprightly
and heroic gentlemen have *slain their thousands and ten
thousands*, according to their own account, in the field,
with as little winking and blinking as *Major Sturgeon*
himself, they then attire themselves in order to enjoy
the pleasures of the table ; and, however deranged they
may, afterwards, be by convivial excess, they march,
or stagger away to the *Rooms*, as circumstances may
determine, and entertain the Ladies with *elegant* and
decent gallantry.

' The Ladies have no particular dress for the morning,
but huddle away to the bathing-place, in close caps and
gipsy bonnets, so that they look like a set of wandering
fortune tellers, who have just had the opportunity of
pillaging the contents of a *frippery warehouse*, with
which they have bedecked themselves in haste.

' It is to be remarked that the Ladies do not atone
for the negligence of the morning, by neatness and
elegance during the rest of the day, but *shuffle* on

something by dinner time, covering themselves with an enormous nondescript bonnet, which, to the confusion of all order, they, afterwards, think a proper garb for the assembly.

'If a spectator, not cognizant in the fanciful and capricious variations of *ton*, were to cast his eyes on the motley groupe contained in the Rooms, of an evening; far from supposing them persons of the first fashion attired for a Ball, he would consider them as a band of *Bedlamites*; or, at best, conclude that the whole presented the extravagant vagaries of a Masquerade.'

This year Mrs. Fitzherbert moved into a house in Pall Mall, which had a private entrance into the grounds of Carlton House. There was a question put in the *Morning Post* of October 10 which was never answered. 'A QUESTION, What is the reason that Mrs. FITZHERBERT, who is a lady of fortune and fashion, never appears at Court? She is visited by *some* ladies of high rank—has been in public with them—and, yet, never goes to the Drawing Rooms at St. James's. This question is sent for publication by a person who pays no regard to the idle reports of the day, and wishes to have the mystery cleared up.'

The house which Weltje had taken for His Royal Highness had the Castle Tavern on one side of its grounds, and Grove House on the other, and considerable alterations were made in it since it was leased to Weltje from Mr. Kempe for £150 per annum with the option of purchase (which was exercised) for £3,000, and the house and gardens were leased by Weltje to the Prince for a term of twenty-one years from Christmas, 1787.

When the King was taken ill with his first attack of mental aberration, in November, 1788, the Prince and Mrs. Fitzherbert came up to London, a fact which the pictorial satirist soon got hold of; and a print was published in that month, in which the King was depicted as being in bed, a Bishop reading prayers for his restoration to health. This solemn group is interrupted by the Prince of Wales bursting into the room, calling out, 'Damme, come along, I'll see if the old fellow's —— or not!' Following him are George Hanger, with a bottle, and Sheridan. To point this satire the more, a picture of the Prodigal Son hangs on the wall.

Miss Burney gives us an account of the King's seizure and of the arrival of the Prince, and although his conduct was not as heartless as shown in the etching, it was bad enough. 'Soon after, suddenly arrived the Prince of Wales. He came into the room. He had just quitted Brighthelmstone. Something passing within seemed to render this meeting awfully distant on both sides. She (the Queen) asked him if he should not return to Brighthelmstone. He answered, yes, the next day.'

But this he did not do, as there were already rumours of a Regency, yet his conduct towards his father seems to have been very bad. Grenville, writing to his brother, the Duke of Buckingham, November 23, 1788, says: 'Think of the Prince of Wales introducing Lord Lothian into the King's room when it was darkened, in order that he might hear his ravings at the time that they were at the worst. Do not let this fact come from you; it begins to be pretty well known here, and, no doubt, will find its way to Ireland; but it is important that

we should not seem to spread the knowledge of anything
which can injure his Royal Highness's character in public
opinion.'[1]

There was much intriguing as to a Regency, the
Ministry at first suggesting that the Government should
be carried on by a Commission ; but on December 30,
1788, Pitt wrote a letter to the Prince of Wales, stating
that His Majesty's Ministers had come to the conclusion
to offer him the Regency of the kingdom, under certain
restrictions.

The Prince replied at once, expressing his sorrow at
the occasion of his proposed elevation, but accepting
the trust. Of course, this suggestion of the Government could not be acted upon without mature delibera-
tion, and it was not until January 30, 1789, that the
following resolutions of the Lords and Commons were
presented to the Prince of Wales: 'That his Royal
Highness be empowered to exercise the Royal authority
under the title of Regent.'—'That the power given,
should not extend to the granting of any Peerage,
except to the Royal issue.'—'Nor to the grant of any
office in reversion, or any office, salary, or pension,
than during his Majesty's pleasure ; or to the granting
his Majesty's real, or personal estates.'—'That the
care of his Majesty be committed to the Queen, who
should nominate all persons to the offices in the household.'

Needless to say, the Prince made no objections, and
by February 12 the Regency Bill had gone through all

---

[1] 'Memoirs of the Court and Cabinets of George III.,' by
the Duke of Buckingham and Chandos; London, 1853, vol. ii.,
p. 11.

its stages in the House of Commons, and was ordered to be sent to the Lords. But the proverbial 'slip 'twixt cup and lip' occurred. On February 19 the Lord Chancellor informed the House of Lords that, according to the report of his physicians, the King's health was steadily mending, and they therefore abstained from further consideration of the Regency Bill.

The physicians' hopes were fully justified; the King got better rapidly, and on February 27 his perfect recovery was announced, the prayer for the same was discontinued, and a form of prayer of thanksgiving for his restoration to health was ordered to be read in all churches and chapels throughout England and Wales. Rejoicings and illuminations were the order of the day, and on April 23, the day of general thanksgiving, the King, Queen, and Royal Family went in state to St. Paul's Cathedral, to return thanks to God for His mercy in giving the King his health and reason once again.

Naturally, there were satirical prints going about, but not so many as might be thought. There was one in February, 1789, called 'The Rival Queens. *A Political Heat for Lege and Grege.*' Madame Schwellenburg, the Queen's Mistress of the Robes, armed with the Lord Chancellor's mace, is making a desperate onslaught on Mrs. Fitzherbert, who defends herself with a crucifix. Pitt officiates as second to the German lady, and Florizel performs the same office towards his wife.

On April 29 appeared 'The Funeral Procession of Miss Regency,' in which are numerous figures. On the coffin are a dice-box and two dice, the Prince of Wales's coronet, and an empty purse. The chief mourner is

Mrs. Fitzherbert, who is in deep grief at the loss of her
position. Of course Fox and Sheridan are among the
mourners, as are also the Prince's household, amongst
whom is the 'Clerk of the Dish Clouts,' Weltje, who
laments :

' Vor by Got, ve do pine, and in sadness ve tink
Dat it's long till de Prince vear de Crown.'

CHAPTER X.

The Prince as a musician—A *bon-mot* of his—Lady Lade—Her
husband, Sir John — The Prince's pecuniary difficulties
—His dealings with his jeweller—The latter's story—
Another financial mess.

HE King being ordered to Weymouth, the
Prince left, early in July, for Brighton.
We do not hear much of him there, and
more of what we read is pleasant. Fitzgerald[1] says : ' On one of the evenings
at the Pavilion (one of Sir P. Francis's daughters reports) his Royal Highness, after dinner, having proposed
music, and being actively engaged in performing, with
Mr. Francis and some other person, the pretty hunting
trio of " Azioli," of which the burden is *Ritorneremo a
Clori*. But the story is amusing, and bears such a
favourable testimony to the Prince's good humour, that
the lady must be allowed to tell it herself.

' " It is well known that, to an excessive love of
music, he added much real taste as an amateur, and

1 ' Life of George IV.,' by Percy Fitzgerald ; London, 1881,
8vo., vol. i., p. 238.

some power as a performer; but his execution was not
particularly good, and Mr. Francis, Sir Philip's son,
with whom he frequently sang, was, sometimes, comically
struck by the loudness of his voice, and his peculiar
manner. On one of the above-mentioned evenings at
the Pavilion, his Royal Highness, after dinner, having
proposed music, and being actually engaged in perform-
ming with Mr. Francis and some other person the
pretty hunting trio of ' Azioli,' of which the burden
is *Ritorneremo a Clori al tramontar del di*, Mr. Francis
suddenly found the full face of the Prince, somewhat
heated by the eagerness of his performance, in immediate contact with his own; and this circumstance,
combined with that of the loud bass tones in which
his Royal Highness was singing the words *Ritorneremo
a Clori*, striking him in some ludicrous point of view,
he became absolutely unable to resist the effect on his
nerves, and burst out laughing. The Prince evidently
perceived that his own singing had produced the un-
seasonable laughter; but, instead of showing a displeasure at a rudeness which, however involuntary,
would have been resented by many far less illustrious
persons, he only called the offender to order with the
words ' Come, come, Philip!' his countenance betray-
ing, at the same time, a strong inclination to join in
the laugh himself; and the trio proceeded to a conclusion. Sir Philip (adds his daughter) by his original
humour, and great powers of conversation, was, often,
the life of the Pavilion; though his temperate habits
made the excesses occasionally committed at the Prince's
table distasteful to him; and his royal host, perceiving
him ready to drop asleep when the revels were long

protracted, would say, 'We must carry grandpapa away to bed.' " '

The same ready good humour is shown in a pleasant scene which took place at the Pavilion. Cricket was often played on the lawn, and the dinner which followed was served in a marquee. On one of these occasions the Duke of York and Sheridan fell into dispute on some point of the game. Sheridan at length angrily told the Duke 'that he was not to be talked out of his opinion there, or anywhere else; and that, at play, all men were on a par.' The Duke was evidently about to make some peculiarly indignant reply, when the Prince stood up and addressed them both.

Dr. Croly, in his 'Life of George IV.,' tells the remainder of the story: ''The narrator of the circumstance, a person of rank, who was present, himself one of the most attractive public speakers of the day, has often declared that he never, on any occasion, saw any individual, under the circumstances, acquit himself with more ability. The speech was of some length—ten or fifteen minutes; it was alternately playful and grave, expressed with perfect self-possession, and touching on the occurrence of the game, the characters of both disputants, and the conversation at the table, with the happiest delicacy and dexterity. Among other points, the Prince made a laughing apology for Sheridan's use of the phrase "on a par," by bidding his brother remember that the impressions of school were not easily effaced; that Dr. Parr had inflicted learning upon Sheridan; and that, like the lover in *The Wonder*,[1]

[1] By Mrs. Centlivre, 1714. Revived by Garrick in 1757.

who mixes his mistress's name with everything, and calls to his valet, "Roast me these Violantes," the name of Parr was uppermost in Sheridan's sleep: he then ran into a succession of sportive quotations of the word *par*, in the style of *Ludere par impar, equitare in arundina longá*, until the speech was concluded in general gaiety, and the dispute was thought of no more.'

The rupture between the Prince and his father was complete, the Prince refusing to visit him while he was stopping at Weymouth, but sending the Duke of York instead ; he pursued his course of folly at Brighton, where Fox visited him, and they went to Lewes Races, where the Prince was received by the High Sheriff of the county, attended by a host of javelin men.   Three ladies were conspicuous at these races for their equipages, each drawn by four gray ponies—Mrs. Fitzherbert, the Duchess of Rutland, and Lady Lade.

This latter was no fit companion for any decent woman.   The first heard of her was in St. Giles's, where she was said to be the mistress of Jack Rann, commonly known as Sixteen String Jack, a highwayman, who was executed in 1774.   She married Sir John Lade, a boon companion of the Prince, and his tutor in the art of driving.   She was famous for her bad language and skill in riding and driving.   Of her the following lines were written :

> ' More than one steed Letitia's empire feels,
>   Who sits triumphant o'er the flying wheels ;
>   And, as she guides them through th' admiring throng,
>   With what an air she smacks the silken thong !

Graceful as John, she moderates the reins ;
And whistles sweet her diuretic strains ;
Sesostris like, such charioteers as these,
May drive six harness'd monarchs, if they please.'

Sir John Lade, of Haremere, was a mere country squire who, when he came of age, inherited a fair fortune, which he soon dissipated. Mrs. Thrale was his guardian, and it was when he attained his majority in 1780 that Dr. Johnson wrote the following prophetic verses :

' Long expected one and twenty,
    Ling'ring year, at length, is flown ;
Pride and pleasure, pomp and plenty,
    Great Sir John, are now your own.

' Loosen'd from the minor's tether,
    Free to mortgage, or to sell ;
Wild as wind, and light as feather,
    Bid the sons of thrift farewell.

' Call the Betsies, Kates and Jennies,
    All the names that banish care ;
Lavish of your grandsire's guineas,
    Show the spirit of an heir.

' All that prey on vice and folly,
    Joy to see their quarry fly ;
There the gamester, light and jolly,
    There the lender, grave and sly.

' Wealth, my lad, was made to wander,
    Let it wander as it will ;
Call the jockey, call the pander,
    Bid them come and take their fill.

' When the bonny blade carouses,
    Pockets full—and spirits high—
What are acres ?   What are houses ?
    Only dirt, or wet and dry.

> ' Should the guardian friend or mother
> Tell the woes of wilful waste ;
> Scorn their counsels, scorn their pother,
> You can hang, or drown, at last.'

He kept race-horses, and lost. He gambled and betted on anything. One of his bets is somewhat amusing. It is in the *Times* of October 2, 1795: ' A curious circumstance occurred here (Brighton) yesterday. Sir JOHN LADE, for a trifling wager, undertook to carry Lord CHOLMONDELY, on *his back*, from opposite the Pavilion, twice round the Steine. Several ladies attended to be the spectators of this extraordinary feat of the dwarf carrying a giant. When his Lordship declared himself ready, Sir JOHN desired him to STRIP. " Strip !" exclaimed the other : " why, surely you promised to carry me in my clothes !" " By no means," exclaimed the Baronet. " I engaged to carry *you*, but not an inch of clothes. So, therefore, my Lord, make ready, and let us not *disappoint* the ladies." After much laughable altercation, it was, at length, decided that Sir JOHN had won his wager, the Peer declining to exhibit *in puris naturalibus.*'

When he got poor, I presume the Prince cut him, for he ended his days as groom and coachman to the Earl of Anglesey.

The two following paragraphs from the *St. James's Chronicle* for 1789 tell us something about the Prince's doings at Brighton :

August 13-15.—' The Prince of Wales's birthday, on Thursday, was very splendidly celebrated at Brighthelmstone.—*St. George*, the famous fencing master, exhibited several trials of his skill, with two French masters, before the Prince and a large company, in a pavilion and marquees pitched about a mile from the town: an ox was roasted whole, and given to the populace. The Duke of Clarence gave prizes to several sailing boats, which afforded much diversion — the company dined in the pavilion, and the evening concluded with a supper and ball at the Castle Inn, given by the Dukes of York and Clarence.—The illuminations were universal and elegant.'

September 5-8.—' The foundation for the Prince's dog-kennel was laid, last week, in the *North fields* near Brighton.—Six or seven acres of these fields are to be inclosed as a paddock, with the building in the centre, which is to be finished in a month.'

Yes, the repentant prodigal had forgotten all his promises of never again running into debt. He was deeply dipped, and yet he kept altering his ' Marine Pavilion,' and now was building most expensive stables. He tried to borrow money on post-obits, and Weltje was the go-between with the money-lenders. A Mr. Cator lent £10,000 on condition of being repaid treble the amount, and about £30,000 was raised in £100 bonds, repayable in twelve years, which bonds were signed by the Prince, the Duke of York, and Prince William. They then tried to raise about £350,000 abroad on the security of the Duchy of Cornwall and the Bishopric of Osnaburg, and it is said they received over £100,000 in cash and jewels; but the story of this loan is a long one, and does not come within the scope of this book.

Here is a story of his dealings with his jeweller Jefferys, whom he eventually ruined by not paying him,

told by himself.[1] He was appointed jeweller to the
Prince in 1788 or 1789.

' About the period to which I allude, the Prince of
Wales (upon Mr. Gray[2] requiring a settlement of the
great demands he had upon his Royal Highness) was
so much displeased at that circumstance, as to cease
giving him farther employment. His Royal Highness
then sent for me to Carlton House, and conferred upon
me (most unfortunately) the favour which he had withdrawn from Mr. Gray. From this time, not a day
passed, for several years, in which, neglecting any
general business, I did not spend half my time at
Carlton House; and in which some entries were not
made in my books of large amounts for goods sold to
his Royal Highness.

*   *   *   *   *

' On the twenty eighth day of January, One Thousand
Seven Hundred and Ninety, the Prince of Wales sent
for me to Carlton House, at a much earlier hour in the
morning than he was accustomed to do ; and, taking
me into an inner apartment, with very visible marks
of agitation in his countenance and manner, said, he
had a great favour to ask of me, which, if I could
accomplish, would be doing him the greatest service,
and he should ever consider it accordingly. I replied,
that I feared what his Royal Highness might consider
a great favour done towards him, must be more than
my limited means could accomplish ; but, in all that

[1] ' A Review of the Conduct of the Prince of Wales in his
various transactions with Mr. Jefferys,' by N. Jefferys ; London, 1806, 8vo., eighth edition.
[2] The Prince's former jeweller.

I could do, I was entirely at his service, and requested his Royal Highness to name his commands.

'His Royal Highness then proceeded to state, that a creditor of Mrs. Fitzherbert had made a very peremptory demand for the payment of about sixteen hundred pounds : that Mr. Weltje had been sent by his Royal Highness to the creditor making such demand, to desire that it might be placed to the Prince's account : this, the creditor refused to do, on the ground that Mrs. Fitzherbert, *being a woman of no rank, or consideration, in the eye of the law, as to personal privilege, was amenable to an immediate process*, which was not the case with his Royal Highness. This, the Prince stated, to have caused in his mind the greatest uneasiness, for fear of the consequences that might ensue ; as it was not in the power of his Royal Highness to pay the money then, or to name an earlier period for so doing than three or four months. The request, therefore, that his Royal Highness had to make to me was, that I would interfere upon the occasion, and prevent, if possible, any personal inconvenience to Mrs. Fitzherbert, which would be attended with extreme mortification to the feelings of his Royal Highness.

'I assured his Royal Highness that I would do all I could in the business ; and I was appointed to attend, with the result of my endeavours, at Carlton House, the next morning. I did attend, as appointed, and presented the Prince of Wales with a receipt for the whole sum :—*fifteen hundred and eighty-five pounds, eleven shillings, and sevenpence, which I had, that morning, paid, being the only effectual means of pacifying the creditor, and removing from the mind of his Royal*

Highness, the anxiety he appeared so strongly to labor under.

' His Royal Highness was unbounded in his expressions of satisfaction at what I had so promptly accomplished, and in his assurances of future support, a support so strongly made, and so frequently repeated, as well as accompanied with such *apparent* marks of sincerity, as to have fixed my faith, (even had it been wavering) in the entire confidence I might place in all his promises and assurances.

' But what will the world think, or say, when I inform them, that in ten long years of the most bitter adversity, occasioned by a continuance of similar confidence, I have repeatedly applied, in vain, to his Royal Highness for relief, even in any degree to which he might have been induced, or enabled to have afforded it me, but he has ever been deaf to my entreaties.

' The moment misfortune overtook me, the Prince of Wales totally deserted me ; and my services, and his promises, were then alike forgotten.

*　　*　　*　　*　　*

' In the afternoon of the same day on which I had so highly gratified the Prince, and heard from his lips such kind expressions of regard ; the Prince of Wales came to my house, in Piccadilly, and brought with him, Mrs. Fitzherbert, for the express purpose, as His Royal Highness condescendingly said, that she might, herself, thank me for the great and essential service I had, that morning, rendered to her, by the relief my exertions had produced on the minds of his Royal Highness and Mrs. Fitzherbert. And his Royal Highness continued to repeat the same expressions of satisfaction, and assurances of support, which he had so abundantly made use of, in the former part of the day.'

Huish[1] is responsible for the following : 'The person of Mrs. Fitzherbert was, one morning, taken in execution for a debt of £1,825, *the Prince of Wales being in the house at the time.* The writ being returnable on the morrow, and no bail being available, the money must be paid, or the lady conveyed to prison. The Prince lost not a moment in making the application to his customary resources, but they appeared to be, most unaccountably, hermetically closed against him. In some instances, the most shallow excuses were returned ; in others, the impossibility of supplying so large a sum on so short a notice ; all of which the Prince knew to be false, and, therefore, he began, justly, to suspect that there was some secret machinery at work to prevent the necessary supplies from being advanced.

' In this emergency, Mr. C——l was despatched to an eminent pawnbroker in Fleet Street, who at that time was in the habit of lending large sums of money to the nobility, on their plate and jewels, and who was the actual holder of the celebrated jewels of the Duchess of Devonshire, the publicity of which hurried her prematurely to the grave. On the present occasion, Mr. Parker, the pawnbroker, lost no time in repairing to Park Lane, where the unfortunate lady was in the custody of the sheriff's officers ; and, here, a new difficulty presented itself in the way of her emancipation. The harpies of the law objected to any part of the plate or jewels being deposited in the hands of Mr. Parker, until their demand was satisfied. On the

<hr>

[1] 'Memoirs of George IV.,' vol. i., p. 266.

other hand, the wily pawnbroker refused to advance the money until the property was placed in his hands, as he did not know but what there might be other actions in reserve, for the liquidation of which the property in the house might prove inadequate.   Under these circumstances, C——l was secretly despatched to Carlton House, with instructions to bring away with him a particular casket, which contained the Prince's state jewels, which, although exceeding in value ten times the amount of the sum which he had to pay, was borne away by the pawnbroker to his depository in Fleet Street, but which, however, was redeemed on the following day by an advance which the Prince obtained from the wealthy Jew in St. Mary Axe.'

CHAPTER XI.

Rowlandson and Brighton—Poem on the Prince's birthday, 1790—Lord Barrymore—Anecdotes respecting him and his family.

ROM the pencil of Rowlandson the caricaturist, who with his friend Wigstead, a Bow Street magistrate, went a trip to Brighton in 1789, we have an excellent picture of the Pavilion, as it then was, and a view of the Steyne.

Their opinion of the building is that 'the *tout ensemble* is, in short, perfect Harmony. The whole was executed by Mr. Holland, under the immediate inspection and Direction of Mr. Weltjie, whose Attachment to his Royal Master was faithful and disinterested.' In the same book Rowlandson gives us a sketch of the beach at Brighton at the same period.

On July 23, 1790, the Prince went to Brighton for the season, being preceded by a day or two by the Duke of York, and his birthday was kept on August 17 in

a most festive fashion, immortalized in verse in the
Sussex Weekly Advertiser of August 23:

'HAIL BRIGHTON'S DOWN! Your velvet green,
Hill, ocean, dale, each varying scene,
The distant flock, the sloping mount,
And spring, of sparkling HEALTH, the fount ;
But chief, the dimpling Sea, where lave
A thousand *Naiads* in the wave.
Whilst, rising from th' abyss below,
The quicken'd vitals warmer glow,
And nerves, new strung, with vigour dance,
And every pleasing thought enhance,
And make men fonder of their lives,
And of their SWEETHEARTS, and their—WIVES—

These are the common joys and boast
Of BRIGHTON'S full frequented coast,
So honoured by the gay and fair,
By *Britain's* Princes, and her HEIR.

The Morning breaks—of jocund bells
The wat'ry sound melodious tells
The sports, that banishing delay,
Are treasured for the chosen day.

See, borne upon the smiling tide,
The Mariner triumphant ride,
And Cricketers, in Royal Match,
Pray Fortune for a tingling catch.

Two roasting steers, with novel sight
The neighbourhood to feast invite ;
Groan solid beams beneath the weight,
Hinds crowding round, with joy elate.
And now they're done—from knives and cleavers
Some fill their *pockets*—some their *beavers ;*
Loaves plentiful, in show'rs are thrown,
And pails of ale wash clean all down.
Better, like manna, loaves to rain,
Than flams prepare 'gainst haughty Spain ;

Cannons to ram, but their mouths muzzle,
And even *Solomon* to puzzle :
And like poor mice, when caught by cats,
Britons to turn to *Baltic* rats.

Meanwhile the FOUNDER circles round,
Six jetty steeds before him bound ;
And while the jolly huzzahs rise,
Of joy unfeign'd, and reach the skies,
Glad shiv'ring transports round him fly
And the tear trembles in his eye ;
And YORK's high Duke, with lively glee
Views, turned to spits, a mighty tree.

Now, music of two princely bands,
Sudden, attention mute commands ;
Alternate strains float sweet in air,
And thrill the breast of every Fair,
Bears to each manly heart their charms,
And all the trembling soul alarms.

When evening mild, at length invades
And spreads o'er earth and sea her shades,
Chequer well fancied lights her face,
Tell *Britain's charming Hope and Grace.*
Then hasten some to laugh their hour,
At the gay Stage's mirthful pow'r ;
Whilst gentry of the nobler sort
To a grand dance and treat resort.

Ah ! what avail the CASTLE's rays,
Of British beauty to the blaze,
Or the bright show of mimic fire,
To living flames of high desire ?
See, cull'd from Cytherea's dove,
Thick, nodding feathers scatter love ;
Beware the gem, the artful wreath
Where all Arabia's spices breathe,
The envious glove, the melting eye ;
Nor dare the heaving neck descry,
Nor quiv'ring ancle's sprightly bound
To Harmony's enraptured sound—

Or, vent'rous youths, too sure you'll find
Your *hearts* and *souls* are left behind.
    Did *Anstie's* Muse to me belong,
Brighton should rival *Bath* in song ;
Since, ocean sprung, great Beauty's Queen
Delights to trip along the *Steine.*'

It was in this year that one of the Prince's boon companions, Richard Barry, seventh Lord Barrymore, made himself somewhat notorious at Brighton. He had just come of age, and into a fortune of £20,000 a year, of which he tried to make ducks and drakes as quickly as possible, especially on the turf. A characteristic anecdote of him is related in the *Sussex Weekly Advertiser*, of June 21, 1790: 'Lord Barrymore had his watch taken from him at Ascot Heath races. He missed it immediately, and followed the fellow, who stopped, and entered into conversation with a well-known *boxer*. As soon as the conversation between these *gentlemen* ended, his Lordship went to the *champion of the fist*, and took his watch. The latter expostulating, Lord Barrymore informed him that his *friend* had just taken his watch, and that, if he would recover it, he should have his own. The *Knight of the Knuckle* soon regained his Lordship's watch from the pupil of *Barrington*, and retrieved his own.'

In compliment to his manners and language, his lordship was generally known as *Hell-gate ;* his next brother, the Hon. and Rev. Augustus Barry, was called *Newgate*, because he had been ' in prisons oft '; and their younger brother, the Hon. Henry Barry,[1] *Cripple-gate,*

[1] Gillray caricatured them on November 1, 1791, as ' Les Trois Magots '—The Three Scamps.

because of some physical deformity. To complete this delightful family, there was a sister, who from her habit of swearing was called *Billings-gate*.

We read in the *St. James's Chronicle*, July 29-31, 1790 : ' A pugilistick *rencontre* took place, a few days since, at Brighton, between Lord Barrymore and young Fox, son to the manager of the Theatre, in which the conduct of some of the parties is represented as very little to their credit.' The *Sussex Weekly Advertiser*, August 2, says : 'The Rencounter which took place on the Steine at Brighton, on Monday evening last, and the cause of it have been grossly misrepresented in the London papers ; they were set out with the wrong day : but, as Lord Barrymore has, through the goodness of the Prince, forgiven the insult he received, we shall not revive it by a relation of its attendant circumstances.'

The caricaturist soon caught hold of it, and we have ' Scrub and Boniface, or, Three Brave Lads, against one poor Roscius — London, pub. Aug. 9 by Steine Briton, Newgate Inv^t, Cripple-gate Direxit, Hell-gate Fecit.' Mr. Fox, son to the manager of the Brighton theatre is on the ground, calling out, ' Foul, foul.' The Earl of Barrymore is still raining blows upon him, and kicking him, encouraged by his two brothers, one of whom says, ' B——t me, I'll lay 3 to 1 we lick him.' The other calls out, ' Bloody Newgate to me, if I don't take his father's licence.' Sheridan deprecates with, ' Dam it, Newgate, fight like a man, no kicking.' The Duke of York, looking on, thus alludes to his duel with Colonel Lenox, ' Fie donc—If he had hit my head, instead of my curl, I would have fought fair.'

The World of August 2, 1790, says : ' A report was

circulated in town, that it was CHARLES Fox, and not the Manager's Son, who fought Lord Barrymore at Brighton. The report gained credit from the addition that the parties, immediately after the battle, *coalesced.*'

But fisticuffs were fashionable, *vide* the *Sussex Weekly Advertiser* of August 9, 1790 : ' Between the heats, on Saturday, a Boxing Match took place between a young man of this town, and one of the *black legged society ;* which, after a contest of about half an hour, terminated in favour of the latter. The number of spectators, we should think, were not less than 2,000.

' In making the ring, several scuffles ensued, that had like to have produced more battles. Captain Aston, who, lately, fought a duel, was with difficulty prevented in engaging in a conflict of the knuckle.

' One gentleman, who had struck a youth, as was supposed by some others that saw it, without provocation, was set upon, and had his shirt almost torn from his back.

' We could but both admire and applaud the singular good humour of the Duke of York, during the above battle. His Royal Highness, with a degree of freedom and politeness that might not have been expected even from a private gentleman, permitted *any one who chose it,* to take the benefit of his lofty Phaeton to see the fight, and actually accommodated, in, upon, and about it, near 30 persons, himself holding the reins, and observing the utmost care that the horses did not move forward, to endanger their lives and limbs, as on that, alone, depended the safety of many, who, either to gratify their Broughtonian curiosity, or ambitious desire to partake of so much of the Royal favour, had placed themselves on the wheels and every other part of the carriage, till it was completely covered.

'On the race-ground, on Saturday, Mr. Beeby, of Ringmer, near this town, feeling himself affronted at some words spoken by Lord Barrymore, told his Lordship, he should, in consequence, expect to see him the next morning. But an explanation, we hear, afterwards took place, and the matter was amicably adjusted ; the offensive words not being directed to Mr. Beeby.'

Here is another of his fights recorded in the same paper of September 19, 1791 : ' A circumstance occurred, last week, near the Steine at Brighton, that precipitated Lord Barrymore and Mr. Donadieu, a perfumer, in London, into a pugilistic encounter ; but his Lordship, after a few rounds, being likely to obtain no advantage in single combat, an interference ensued, that soon brought Mr. Donadieu into a situation so perilous, that he summoned the assistance of the spectators by the cry of *murder*, which so operated on the humanity of a young man, a linen draper, present, that he remonstrated on the violence offered to Mr. D., and, in consequence, got very roughly handled. The matter, we hear, has since been compromised with the perfumer to his satisfaction. But the linen draper, we understand, is seeking redress through the medium of the law.' There is another paragraph in the next week's paper, confirming the intention of the linen-draper to go to law.

The same newspaper of September 26 gives the following story, which has been universally credited to Lord Barrymore : ' A coffin has been borne about by men, through the streets of Brighton, for several evenings, in dismal annoyance to the peaceable inhabitant, and valetudinarian visitant. The *Merry Mourners* happened, unfortunately, to call at one, among many other houses, where pregnancy gave a natural increase of sensibility to the nerves of a poor woman, who opened the door at their wanton summons, and, soon after, by miscarriage, produced a premature candidate for a coffin, in melancholy earnest. An Italian, who, having heard, or, perhaps read, that Thespis, daubed with wine lees, squeaked his satire from a cart, got into this comic coffin, in order to *grin* a death's head moral to mortality. When his horizontal site got tiresome, Signor Cataletto resigned in favour of another, a dependent of the same household, who was conveyed in the coffin to the church-yard, whither, by consent between the parties, one of them, soon after, conducted a fair companion. On taking their stand near the coffin, Master *Dead-alive* rose, and sat up therein. The affrighted *Rep*, thinking it was some ghost which rose to avenge the profanation intended, scoured over the tombs with the pace of *Camilla*. Mr. O. a gentleman, having been honoured, one evening, with a visit by this drear procession, sallied out with a brace of pistols. They fled—but the bearers were, at last, obliged to drop their sable burden. The spirited pursuer soon brought the cased menial to own, that though so confined, he was yet alive, and belonged to the War-grave[1] family.'

One who knew him well thus describes him : 'His Lordship was alternately between the gentleman and the black guard, the refined wit and the most vulgar bully were equally well known in St. James's and St.

---

[1] An allusion to Lord Barrymore's country house at Wargrave, near Maidenhead.

Giles's. He could fence, dance, drive, or drink, box, or bet with any man in the kingdom. He could discourse slang as trippingly as French, relish porter after port, and compliment her ladyship, at a ball, with as much ease and brilliance, as he could bespatter in blood in a cider cellar.'

Henry Angelo,[1] the fencing master, tells many anecdotes of him; and, as he was very frequently in his company, owing to their mutual taste for amateur theatricals, they may be taken as authentic. I will only transcribe two of them : ' The year after I played Mother Cole, at Brighton, I received an invitation from Lord Barrymore to his house, then upon the Steyne. One night, when the champagne prevented the evening finishing tranquilly, Lord Barrymore proposed, as there was a guitar in the house, that I should play on it. I was to be the musician, and he, dressed in the cook-maid's clothes, was to sing " Ma chère amie." Accordingly, taking me to another part of the Steyne, under Mrs. Fitzherbert's window, (it was then three o'clock) he sang, whilst I played the accompaniment. The next day, he told me (quizzing, I should think,) that the Prince said, " Barrymore, you may make yourself a fool as much as you please; but, if I had known it was Angelo, I would have horsewhipped him into the sea." [2]

' Lord Barrymore's fondness for eccentricities ever engaged his mind. Whether in London, or at Wargrave, 'twas all the same, always in high spirits, thinking of what fun he should have during the day. I shall begin with London. Seated, after dinner, at eleven

[1] ' Reminiscences of Henry Angelo,' etc. ; London, 1830, 8vo.
[2] *Ibid.*, vol. ii., p. 94.

o'clock, on one of the hottest evenings in July, he proposed that the whole party should go to Vauxhall. The carriage being ordered, it was directly filled inside; and the others, outside, with more wine than wit, made no little noise through the streets. We had not been long at Vauxhall, when Lord Barrymore called out to a young clergyman, some little distance from us; who, when he approached, and was asked, " Have you had any supper?" to our surprise, he answered, " Vy, as how, my Lord, I have not, as yet, had none." A waiter passing by at the time, Lord Barrymore said, " You know me; let that gentleman have whatever he calls for:" when he told the parson to fall to, and call for as much arrack punch as he pleased. " Thank ye, my Lord," said he, " for I begins to be hungry, and I don't care how soon I pecks a bit."

' Lord Barrymore had, that morning, unknown to us, contrived to dress Tom Hooper, the tin man, (one of the first pugilists at that time), as a clergyman, to be in waiting at Vauxhall, in case we should get into any dispute. This fistic knight now filled the place of a lacquey, and was constantly behind the carriage, a sworn votary of black eyes and disfigured faces. His black clothes, formal hat, hair powdered and curled round, so far disguised him, that he was unknown to us all, at first, though Hooper's queer dialect must soon have discovered him to the waiters. This was a *ruse de guerre* of Lord Barrymore's. About three o'clock, whilst at supper, Lord Falkland, Henry Barry, Sir Francis Molineux, etc., were of our party; there was, at this time, a continual noise and rioting, and the arrack punch was beginning to operate.

'On a sudden, all were seen running towards the orchestra, the whole garden seemed to be in confusion, and our party, all impatience, sallied out, those at the farther end of the box, walking over the table, kicking down the dishes. It seems that the effects of the punch had not only got into Hooper's head, but had exerted an influence over his fists, for he was for fighting with everybody. A large ring was made; and, advancing in a boxing attitude, he threatened to fight anyone; but all retired before him.

'Felix M'Carthy, a tall, handsome Irishman, well known by everybody at that time, soon forced his way through the crowd, and collared him, at the same time saying, "You rascal, you are Hooper the boxer; if you don't leave the garden this instant, I'll kick you out." The affrighted crowd, who, before, retreated when he approached them, now came forward; when Hooper, finding himself surrounded, and hearing a general cry of "Kick him out," made his retreat as fast as possible, thus avoiding the fury of those who would not have spared him out of the gardens, if he had been caught. We found him, at five in the morning, behind Lord Barrymore's carriage, with the coachman's great coat on, congratulating himself upon having avoided the vengeance of those to whom, a short time previously, he had been an object of fear.'[1]

Lord Barrymore met with a sad fate on March 6, 1793, at the early age of twenty-four. He was an officer in the 2nd or Queen's Regiment, and, in pursuance of his duty, was escorting some French prisoners to Dover. He

[1] 'Reminiscences of Henry Angelo,' etc.; London, 1830, 8vo., vol. ii., p. 80.

had kindly halted by the wayside, and treated everybody at an inn, when, on resuming the march, being tired, he got into his curricle, driven by his servant, he himself smoking a pipe of tobacco. A loaded gun which was placed between them, slipping down to the bottom of the carriage, by some mischance went off, and lodged its contents in his head, the charge entering at his cheek and coming out at the upper part of his skull. He was buried at Wargrave, and the *Annual Register* says of him : ' He died in a few minutes, and so finished a short, foolish, and dissipated life, which had passed very discreditably to his rank as a peer, and still more so as a member of society.'

He was succeeded in his title by his brother Henry (Cripplegate), who had neither the brains nor the *bonhomie* of Hellgate. He is thus described by Captain Gronow :[1]

' This nobleman came of a very old family, and, when of age, succeeded to a fine estate. He acquired no small degree of notoriety from his love of pugilism and cockfighting ; but his *forte* lay in driving, and few coachmen on the northern road could " tool " a four-in-hand like him. His Lordship was one of the founders of the " Whip Club." The first time I ever saw Lord Barrymore was, one fine evening, while taking a stroll in Hyde Park. The weather was charming, and a great number of the *bon-ton* had assembled to witness the departure of the Four-in-hand Club. Conspicuous among all the " turn-outs " was that of his Lordship, who drove four splendid greys, unmatched in symmetry,

[1] Captain Gronow's ' Last Recollections ' ; London, 1866, 8vo., p. 97.

action and power. Lord Barrymore was, like Lord Byron and Sir Walter Scott, club-footed. I discovered this defect, the moment he got off his box to arrange something wrong in the harness. If there had been a competitive examination, the prize of which would be given to the most proficient in slang and vulgar phraseology, it would have been safe to back his Lordship as the winner, against the most foul-mouthed of costermongers; for the way he blackguarded his servants, for the misadjustment of a strap, was horrifying. On returning home, I dressed, and went to the Club to dine, where I alluded to the choice morsels of English vernacular that had fallen from the noble whip's mouth, in addressing his servants, and was assured that such was his usual language when out of temper.

'In addition to his " drag " in the Four-in-hand Club, Lord Barrymore sported a very pretty " Stanhope," in which he used to drive about town, accompanied by a little boy, whom the world denominated his " tiger." It was reported that Lord Barrymore had, in his younger days, been taken much notice of by the Prince Regent ; in fact, he had been the boon companion of his Royal Highness, and had assisted at the orgies that used to take place at Carlton House, where he was a constant visitor. Notwithstanding this, Lord Barrymore was considered by those intimately acquainted with him, to be a man of literary talents. He, certainly, was an accomplished musician, a patron of the drama, and a great friend of Cooke, Kean and the two Kembles ; yet I have heard a host of crimes attributed to his Lordship. This, if not a libel, showed that the connection existing between the Prince Regent and this nobleman could not have been productive of good results, and tends to confirm the impression that the profligate life led by his Royal Highness, and those admitted to his intimacy, was such, as to make it a matter of wonder that such scandalous scenes of debauchery could be permitted in a country like ours. Indeed, his acquaintance with the Prince ruined Lord Barrymore both in mind, body and estate. While participating in the Regent's excesses, he had bound himself to do his bidding, however palpably iniquitous it might be ; and, when he was discarded, in accordance with that Prince's habit of treating his favourites, he left Carlton House ruined in health and reputation.

' Lord Barrymore, during his last years, was a martyr to gout and other diseases : and, on his deathbed, he was haunted by the recollection of what he had been, and the thought of what he might have become : indeed, the last scene of his profligate life, when tortured by the inward reproaches of his accusing conscience, was harrowing in the extreme.'

CHAPTER XII.

NOTHER of the Prince's companions,
until they quarrelled, was Charles
Howard, eleventh Duke of Norfolk, who
possessed all the habits and attributes
of a hog.[1] Slovenly and dirty in his
attire, he was rarely washed, but when he was drunk,
and then by his servants ; and the story is told that one
day he was complaining to Dudley North that he
suffered terribly from rheumatism, for which he could
find no cure, and was answered by the question, 'Pray,
my lord, did you ever try a clean shirt ?'

Hear what the anonymous writer of ' The Clubs of

---

[1] Gillray caricatured him (May, 1792) in ' Le Cochon et ses
deux Petites,' where, holding a tumbler of wine in his hand, he
is toying with two very fleshly ladies.

London,' says of the old glutton, when writing of the Beefsteak Club. Speaking of a visit to that club in 1799, he says :

'I do not recollect all who were present on that day, but I particularly remarked John Kemble, Cobb of the India House, his Royal Highness the Duke of Clarence, Sir John Cox Hippisley, Charles Morris, Ferguson of Aberdeen, and his Grace of Norfolk. This nobleman took the chair when the cloth was removed. It is a place of dignity, elevated some steps above the table, and decorated with the various insignia of the Society; amongst which was suspended the identical small cocked-hat in which Garrick used to play the part of Ranger. As soon as the clock strikes fives, a curtain draws up, discovering the kitchen, in which the cooks are dimly seen plying their several offices, through a sort of grating, with this appropriate motto from Macbeth inscribed over it

 ' " IF IT WERE DONE, WHEN 'TIS DONE, THEN 'TWERE WELL
  IT WERE DONE QUICKLY."

' But the steaks themselves ;—they were of the highest order, and I can never forget the goodwill with which they were devoured. In this respect, no one surpassed the Duke of Norfolk. He was *totus in illis*. Eyes, hands, mouth, were all intensely exercised ; not a faculty played the deserter. His appetite, literally, grew by what it fed on. Two or three succeeding steaks, fragrant from the gridiron, rapidly vanished. In my simplicity, I thought that his labours were over. I was deceived, for I observed him rubbing a clean plate with a shallot, to prepare it for the reception of another.

'A pause of ten minutes ensued, and his Grace rested upon his knife and fork; but it was only a pause, and I found that there was a good reason for it. Like the epic, a rump of beef has a beginning, a middle, and an end. The palate of an experienced beef steaker can discern all its progressive varieties, from the first cut to the last; and he is a mere tyro in the business, who does not know, that towards the middle, there lurks a fifth essence, the perfect ideal of tenderness and flavour. Epicurism itself, in its fanciful combinations of culinary excellence, never dreamed of anything surpassing it. For this cut, the Duke had wisely tarried, and, for this, he re-collected his forces. At last he desisted, but more, I thought, from fatigue than satiety : *lassatus non satiatus*. I need not hint, that powerful irrigations of port encouraged and relieved, at intervals, the organs engaged in this severe duty.

'Nor could I help admiring that his Grace, pro-verbially an idolater of the table, should have dined with such perfect complacency upon beef steaks :—he, whose eyes and appetite roved every day amidst the rich variety of a ducal banquet, to which ocean, air and earth, paid their choicest contingents. His palate, I thought, would sigh, as in captivity, for the range in which it was to expatiate. A member, who sat next me, remarked that in beef steaks there was considerable variety, and he had seen the most finished gourmands about town quite delighted with the simple repast of the Society. But, with regard to the Duke of Norfolk, he hinted that it was his custom, on a beef steak day, to eat a preliminary dish of fish in his own especial box at the Piazza, and then adjourn time enough for the beef steaks.   He added also, and I heartily concurred in his remark, that a mere dish of fish could make no more difference to the iron digestion of his Grace, than a tenpenny nail, more or less, in that of an ostrich.

'After dinner, the Duke was ceremoniously ushered to the chair, and invested with an orange coloured ribbon, to which a silver medal, in the form of a grid-iron, was appended. . . .   I was astonished to see how little effect the sturdy port wine of the Society produced on his adamantine constitution ; for the same abhorrence of a vacuum, which had disposed him to do such ample justice to his dinner, showed itself no less in his unflinching devotion to the bottle.'[1]

Sir N. Wraxall, in his 'Historical Memoirs of My Own Time . . . 1772 to 1784,' writes thus of him : 'Drunkenness was in him an hereditary vice, transmitted down, probably, by his ancestors from the Plantagenet times, and inherent in his formation.   His father indulged equally in it, but he did not manifest the same capacities as his son, in resisting the effects of wine.   It is a fact that, after laying his father and all the guests under the table at the Thatched House Tavern in St. James's Street, he has repaired to another festive party in the vicinity, and there recommenced the unfinished convivial rites.'

The caricaturists openly made fun of his hoggish propensities, as did the public press, *vide* these two extracts from the *Times* (March 1, 1793) :

'ON THE LATE INUNDATION IN OLD PALACE YARD.

'On one side, Duke Norfolk pushed forward with strife,
FOR HE NEVER LIKED WATER throughout his whole life.'

---

[1] 'The Clubs of London,' etc. ; London, 1828, 8vo., vol. ii. p. 27.

February 17, 1794.—'The Duke of NORFOLK is attacked by the *Hydrophobia*, he can't bear the sight of *water*. His physicians have prescribed WINE. The Marquis of *Stafford*, Marquis of *Bath*, and Lord *Thurlow* who were present, sanctified this prescription with their most hearty consent.'

And yet it is over this wretched old sensualist that Thackeray, in his 'Four Georges,' gets maudlinly sentimental!

'And now I have one more story of the bacchanalian sort, in which Clarence and York, and the very highest personage of the realm, the great Prince Regent, all play parts. The feast took place at the Pavilion at Brighton, and was described to me by a gentleman who was present at the scene. In Gillray's caricatures, and amongst Fox's jolly associates, there figures a great nobleman, the Duke of Norfolk, called Jockey of Norfolk in his time, and celebrated for his table exploits. He had quarrelled with the Prince, like the rest of the Whigs; but a sort of reconciliation had taken place; and now, being a very old man, the Prince invited him to dine and sleep at the Pavilion, and the old Duke drove over from his Castle of Arundel with his famous equipage of grey horses, still remembered in Sussex.

'The Prince of Wales had concocted, with his royal brothers, a notable scheme for making the old man drunk. Every person at table was enjoined to take wine with the Duke—a challenge which the old toper did not refuse. He soon began to see that there was a conspiracy against him; he drank glass for glass; he overthrew many of the brave. At last, the First Gentleman of Europe proposed bumpers of brandy. One of

the royal brothers filled a great glass for the Duke.
He stood up and tossed off the drink. "Now," says he,
"I will have my carriage, and go home." The Prince
urged upon him his previous promise to sleep under the
roof where he had been so generously entertained. "No,"
he said, he had had enough of such hospitality. A trap
had been set for him; he would leave the place at once,
and never enter its doors more.

'The carriage was called, and came; but, in the half
hour's interval, the liquor had proved too potent for
the old man: his host's generous purpose was answered,
and the old man's grey head lay stupefied on the table.
Nevertheless, when his post chaise was announced, he
staggered to it as well as he could, and stumbling in,
bade the postilions drive to Arundel. They drove him
for half an hour round and round the Pavilion lawn;
the poor old man fancied he was going home. When
he awoke that morning he was in bed at the Prince's
hideous house at Brighton. You may see the place now
for sixpence: they have fiddlers there every day; and,
sometimes, buffoons and mountebanks hire the Riding
House, and do their tricks and tumbling there. The
trees are still there, and the gravel walks round which
the poor old sinner was trotted. I can fancy the flushed
faces of the royal princes as they support themselves at
the portico pillars, and look on at old Norfolk's disgrace;
but I can't fancy how the man who perpetrated it continued to be called a gentleman.'

Another of the Prince's intimates and visitor to the
Pavilion was that disreputable old roué William Douglas,
third Earl of March and fourth Duke of Queensberry,
commonly called 'Old Q,' well known on the turf as a

racehorse-owner and betting man, a thorough gambler and finished debauchee.

> 'And there, insatiate yet with folly's sport,
> That polished, sin-worn fragment of the Court,
> The shade of Queensb'ry should with Clermont meet,
> Ogling and hobbling down St. James's Street.'

Nearly forty years older than the Prince, he was his Mentor in every kind of vice, and rooked him of thousands of pounds at play and in betting.

Thackeray, in 'The Virginians,' portrays him under no pseudonym. He is called simply by his title of Lord March. In Chapter XXVI. Mr. Warrington is at the White Horse Tavern, where are Lords Chesterfield and March :

'"My Lord Chesterfield's deuce is deuce ace," says my Lord March. "His Lordship can't keep away from the cards, or dice."

'"My Lord March has not one, but several devils. He loves gambling, he loves horse-racing, he loves betting, he loves drinking, he loves eating, he loves money, he loves women, and you have fallen into bad company, Mr. Warrington, when you lighted upon his Lordship. He will play you for every acre you have in Virginia."

'"With the greatest pleasure in life, Mr. Warrington !" interposes my Lord.

'"And for all your tobacco, and for all your spices, and for all your slaves, and for all your oxen and asses."

*　　　*　　　*　　　*　　　*

'"Unfortunately, my Lord, the tobacco, and the slaves, and the asses, and the oxen, are not mine, as yet.

I am just of age, and my mother—scarce twenty years older—has quite as good chance of long life as I have."

' "I will bet that you survive her. I will pay you a sum now, against four times the sum to be paid at her death. I will set a fair sum over this table against the reversion of your estate in Virginia at the old lady's departure." '

Certainly, it is pleasant to turn from such companions of Florizel's to another, whose only fault was his conviviality. I mean Captain Charles Morris, punch-maker and bard to the Beefsteak Society, where he met with the Prince, at his admission into the society, in 1785; and the author of the 'Clubs of London' thus describes him :

' But Charles Morris—can anyone think of the Beefsteaks without including thy revered image in the picture? The faculties of man are not equal to an abstraction so metaphysical. For many, many years, during which several of man's autumnal generations have fallen, he has been faithful to his post. He is the bard of the Society, who, in the person of this, her favourite disciple, may still boast *non caret vate sacro*, fortune has not yet struck this old deer of the forest. You should have seen him, as was his wont at the period I am speaking of, making the Society's punch, his ancient and rightful office. It was pleasing to see him at his laboratory at the side board, stocked with the varied products that enter into the composition of that nectareous mixture ; then, smacking an elementary glass, or two, and giving a significant nod, the fiat of its excellence ; and what could exceed the extasy with which he filled the glasses that thronged round the

CAPTAIN MORRIS.

bowl ; joying over its mantling beauties with an artist's
pride, and distributing the fascinating draught

> ' " That flames and dances in its crystal bound." '

Morris's songs, which after his death were published
in two volumes, under the title of ' Lyra Urbanica,'
rendered him a welcome guest at Carlton House and the
Pavilion ; and, strange to say, he enjoyed the favour
and countenance of Florizel, both as Prince and King,
until the death of his royal patron.

We have a very good portrait of Captain Morris,
dated July 1, 1789, with the lines :

> ' When the fancy stirring Bowl
>   Wakes its World of pleasure,
>   Glowing Visions gild my Soul,
>   And Life's an endless treasure.'

These were some of the more notorious of the Prince's
intimates at that time ; some of the minor ones may be
mentioned later on.

We hear very little of the Prince at Brighton in
1791. He went there, for the season, on June 13, and
he soon had his old set round him. I can only find one
record of their doings, and that is in the *Sussex Weekly
Advertiser* of September 26 : ' Between six and seven
o'clock, on Monday morning last, the Prince, accompanied by Sir John Lade, in his curricle, drove through
this town, on a shooting excursion, to Haremere, an
estate belonging to Sir John ; but no day ever proved
more unfavourable to the sport, for the gamekeeper
who attended on the occasion, with all his diligence,
was unable to spring more than one solitary bird.

About seven in the evening his Royal Highness returned here, and, after taking fresh horses, which were in readiness at the White Hart, proceeded on to Brighton.

'Lady Lade and the Barrys had the honour to be of the party. Her Ladyship, in rallying the Prince and Sir John, on their bad success, observed she thought even an object as large as a goose, might, with great safety, come in their way; but was, soon after, convinced of her error, by being presented with a goose, which the Prince and Sir John had shot in a neighbouring pond. The joke was accompanied with great pleasantry; and the farmer, who owned the goose, had the benefit of it, by receiving a handsome present from the Royal purse.'

In 1792 the Prince went down to Brighton earlier than usual—in April—and his regiment was quartered there for the defence of the coast; things on the Continent were very disturbed, and war with France broke out the next year. We read in the *Sussex Weekly Advertiser* of May 21: 'On Friday the 10th Regiment of Light Dragoons had a grand field day, in honour of the Prince; after which, his Royal Highness honoured the officers with his company to dinner, at the Old Ship tavern; and, the next morning, set out for town. The Prince is expected at Brighton this day, previous to the grand review of his regiment to-morrow, by Gen. Lascelles, on the Downs, near that place. On Friday next, the above regiment is to have another field day, in review order, at which the Duke and Duchess of York are expected to be present.'

The French Revolution was seething, and prudent

people were leaving France. We read in the same newspaper : ' There has been, lately, a great importation of *French Emigrants* to Brighthelmstone. Last Wednesday, twelve of them, seemingly persons of distinction, passed through this town, in four post chaises, on their route to Dover, in order to embark there for Brussels. Another cargo of the same quality, has also been smuggled in an open boat to Bulverhithe,[1] on our coast, likewise on their way to the ex-Princes.'

En passant, let me just give one anecdote of the manners and customs of Brighton at this time *re* smuggling (*Sussex Weekly Advertiser*, August 27, 1792): ' On Wednesday last, a smuggling cutter, having been closely chased at sea, in order to lighten her lading, threw 300 tubs of spirits overboard, and, by means thereof, escaped her pursuers. The Brighton fishermen seeing many of the tubs float on a very rough sea before that town, swam out at the hazard of their lives and saved some of them. Two Revenue officers, who looked on while these hardy sons of Neptune buffeted the angry waves for the sake of their favourite grog, endeavoured to seize the fruits of their labour. But, one of them, in pursuing a woman, who had received a tub from her husband, or brother, fell down the bank and broke one of his legs, in a manner that the bone appeared through his stocking. The other, having gone down on the beach, in order more effectually to intercept his prey, was hustled by the crowd off one of the groins, and broke three of his ribs in the fall.

---

[1] One mile from St. Leonards Station, and two miles west of Hastings. It is supposed to be the landing-place of Julius Cæsar.

Honest Jack, seeing his foes thus disabled, secured every tub that fell in his way, and in his dripping jacket, drank confusion to Excise.'

On August 27 Florizel gave a fête to celebrate his birthday, and this is a contemporary account of it (*Sussex Weekly Advertiser*, September 3): 'At the Prince's fête on Brighton Level, last Monday, no fewer than four thousand persons were supposed to have attended ; the majority to feast their eyes, while the others feasted more substantially on a fine ox, with a proportionate quantity of bread and strong beer prepared for the occasion. The ox was taken from the fire about 3 o'clock, and very skilfully dissected by Mr. Russel, at the bottom of a large pit, while the spectators and expectants stood, in theatric gradation, on its sloping sides. The day proved very favourable to this rustic festivity. His Royal Highness's guests were very accommodating and good humoured to each other, until the strong beer began to operate. The Prince and Mrs. Fitzherbert looked on for a considerable time with great good humour, and had the satisfaction of hearing that no accident nor injury occurred in so large a concourse, except a few blackeyes and bloody noses, at the close of the evening.'

The French Revolution grew apace. On August 10 the Royal Swiss Guards were cut to pieces and 5,000 persons massacred. On August 26 there was a decree of the National Assembly against the priests, and 40,000 of them were exiled. From September 2 to 5 there was a fearful massacre in Paris ; the prisons were broken open, and 1,200 persons, including 100 priests, were slain.

Of these priests Charlotte Smith speaks in her poem called 'The Emigrants':

'SCENE—*On the Cliffs to the Eastward of the Town of Brighthelmstone, in Sussex.*

'TIME—*A morning in November,* 1792.

*   *   *   *   *

'Behold, in witness of this mournful truth,
A group approach me, whose dejected looks,
Sad Heralds of distress ! proclaim them Men,
Banish'd for ever, and for Conscience' sake,
From their distracted Country, whence the name
Of Freedom misapplied, and much abus'd
By lawless Anarchy, has driven them far
To wander ; with the prejudice they learn'd
From Bigotry (the Tut'ress of the blind),
Thro' the wide World unshelter'd ; their sole hope,
That German spoilers, thro' that pleasant land
May carry wide the desolating scourge
Of War and Vengeance ; yet unhappy Men,
Whate'er your errors, I lament your fate :
And, as disconsolate and sad ye hang
Upon the barrier of the rock, and seem
To murmur your despondence, waiting long
Some fortunate reverse that never comes ;
Methinks, in each expressive face, I see
Discriminated anguish ; there droops one,
Who in a moping cloister long consum'd
This life inactive, to obtain a better,
And thought that meagre abstinence, to wake
From his hard pallet with the midnight bell,
To live on eleemosynary bread,
And to renounce God's works, would please that God.
And now the poor pale wretch receives, amaz'd,
The pity, strangers give to his distress ;
Because these strangers are, by his dark creed,
Condemn'd as Heretics—and, with sick heart,
Regrets his pious prison, and his beads,' etc.[1]

---

[1] 'The Emigrants : a Poem,' by Charlotte Smith ; London, 1793, 4to., p. 7.

CHAPTER XIII.

The *émigrés*—Duchesse de Noailles—The nuns—Camp at Brighton—The Prince as a soldier—His debts—Interview with the King—Breaks with Mrs. Fitzherbert—Her account—Satirical prints—Newspaper paragraphs.

BOUT this time the *émigrés* poured into Brighton, and happy were those who could thus save their lives. Here is a contemporary account, given in the *Sussex Weekly Advertiser*, September 3, 1792:

' Brighton once favoured the escape of a sovereign from his enraged subjects. The former town is now become the refuge of the persecuted *noblesse* of a neighbouring state. The former returned to his country and kingdom, untaught by affliction, and ungrateful to loyalty that had bled in his service. And it is to be feared, that if the bayonets of combined despotism restore the latter to their late rank and power, petty tyranny will revive, and human nature, exhausted in the unequal struggle for freedom, again lick the feet of her oppressors, in debility and despair.

'On Wednesday last (*Aug*. 29) Madame (*Duchesse de*) Noailles arrived at Brighton from France, and was received with the most polite and cordial hospitality, by his Royal Highness the Prince of Wales, and Mrs. Fitzherbert. Her husband being a counter revolutionist, she found it very unsafe to remain any longer in Paris, or any other part of France, and sent her child and nurse before her, who took their passages from Dieppe to Brighton, where they arrived about a week ago. The lady, herself, had more difficulty in leaving her native land; but we are far from vouching for the reality of all the sufferings which are said to have attended her emigration. Travelling in breeches[1] was no very great distress; but the coil of cable which is said to have enclosed her for *fourteen hours*, smells not less of the *marvellous*, than the *tar*. This, in the hands of a novelist, might be spun out to something *monstrous pathetic*.

'It is also said that the Marchioness de Bouillé (? Beaulé), whose safety in France might have been no less precarious than that of the other fair fugitive, hired an open boat at Dieppe, in which she committed herself to the mercy of the winds and waves; and, after a very tempestuous passage, arrived safe, on Wednesday last, at Brighton.

'Some Frenchmen, seemingly of distinction, landed last Wednesday morning, after a very rough passage, in an open boat, at Newhaven; and, on Friday, went post from this town for the Capital.'

September 10.—'On Wednesday and Thursday last, no less than *one hundred and seventy* French emigrants,

---

[1] She was disguised in male attire.

mostly priests, were landed from the packets, and an open boat at Brighton. More are daily arriving; and, many of them being observed to labour under very distressed circumstances, we hear a subscription has been opened for their relief, at Mr. Crawford's library.

'On Friday and Saturday last, near three hundred unfortunate Frenchmen of the above description were put on shore at Eastbourne, many of whom were hospitably received by Lord George Cavendish, Lord Bayham, A. Piggott, Esqre, and many other of the Nobility and Gentry of that place. They, afterwards, took different routes for the Metropolis. Many, from the above place and Brighton, came to this town, and such as could not get places on the stage coach, hired carts for their conveyance. Five of them, seemingly of a superior order, who brought a letter of recommendation to a gentleman of this town, have fixed their abode there.

*	*	*	*	*

' Mrs. Fitzherbert, the Duchess de Noailles, and many other ladies of distinction, were present at the Cricket match, and dined in a marquee pitched on the ground, for that purpose. The Prince's band of music attended, and played during the whole time the ladies were at dinner. In the evening, Mrs. Fitzherbert, the Duchess, Lady Clermont, and Miss Piggott, walked round the ground, seemingly the better to gratify the spectators with a sight of the French lady.

'The Duchess de Noailles appears to be 21, or 22 years of age, is very handsome, and her figure and deportment are remarkably interesting.'

September 17, 1792.—'Upwards of five hundred unfortunate emigrants were, last week, landed on our coast, who have had the fury of the elements to contend with, after escaping that of their barbarous countrymen. The Brighton packets, heavily laden with them, were driven by the winds far eastward of their usual track ; and, with difficulty, made Hastings, Pevensey, and Eastbourne. At the former place, on Wednesday morning, *seventy six*, all ecclesiastics, came on shore; among whom were the *Bishop of Avranches*, the *Dean of Rouen*, and several other dignitaries. The Bishop, with great difficulty, escaped from *Avranches* with the assistance of one of his Grand Vicars, who, with one of his domestics, accompanied him to *Rouen*, where they were, for some days, concealed. The populace, however, having discovered them, they were, again, obliged to fly. They travelled thence, on foot, in disguise, to *Dieppe*, at which place they arrived in the night, and took refuge, for a few hours, at a hotel. Thence, at the time appointed for the departure of the packet, they ran to the sea side, and, as it was, providentially for them, high water, they were enabled to put off, and instantly get out of the reach of the rabble, who, in less than one minute afterwards, pursued them to the shore, and, with savage fury, declared that it was their intention to have murdered them on the spot.

' The Bishop and his Grand Vicar were hospitably received at Hastings by the Rev. Mr. Whitear, who entertained them till Saturday, when they left that place for London. It is the duty of every Magistrate and Gentleman to prevent the lower classes in this country from imposing upon these poor fugitives. We are sorry to learn that, at Hastings, the *exactions* of the boatmen, on Wednesday last, were shameful in the extreme. They refused to bring any of the Frenchmen on shore for less than four *shillings* a man ; and some even raised their fare to *five shillings.*—Among *English* mariners, we thought that such *unjust* and *unfeeling* wretches were not to be found.'

A notice of the nuns who took refuge here must close this episode :

October 29, 1792.—' The Nuns, whose arrival at Brighthelmstone was mentioned in our last paper, were driven from a convent at *Lisle*. At the time of their debarkation they had only about thirty pounds in specie remaining, all the valuables of their convent having been seized on by the *regenerate* French. The Prince and Mrs. Fitzherbert paid them a very long visit at the New Ship Inn ; after which, his Royal Highness set on foot a subscription for their relief, which, in a short time, amounted to upwards of one hundred pounds.

' The above ladies, on the evening of their arrival, celebrated High Mass, with great solemnity, in an apartment at their inn.

' 'Twas remarkable that no two of the above nuns could be prevailed on to sleep in one bed.'

October 1, 1792.—' The Prince, we hear, has it in contemplation, to take down, and entirely rebuild, on a much larger scale, his Marine Pavilion at Brighthelmstone ;' but he did not do it just then, as he was woefully hard up.

Of course, during the year the Prince did not escape the pencil of the satirist, and there was a print published

A VOLUPTUARY UNDER THE HORRORS OF DIGESTION.

on May 23, to understand which it must be premised that formerly, at the opening of Courts of Assize and Quarter Sessions in England, a proclamation against vice and immorality was always read. This print is called 'VICES OVERLOOKED IN THE NEW PROCLAMATION,' in which are depicted the King and Queen as AVARICE, the Prince as DRUNKENNESS, the Duke of York as GAMBLING, and the Duke of Clarence and Mrs. Jordan as DEBAUCHERY.

Another, published July 2, is 'A Voluptuary under the Horrors of Digestion.'

This is an excellent likeness of the Prince, who, with unbuttoned waistcoat, lolls in an armchair, picking his teeth with a fork. On the ground are dice, a New-market List, Debts of Honour unpaid, and Faro partner-ship Account, Self, Archer,[1] Hobart and Co.

In February, 1793, war was declared between France and England, and volunteers were enrolled for the defence of their country. Camps were formed at different parts of the coast, and there was one at Brighton in August of that year. Needless to say that the Prince's regiment was quartered there, and he him-self showed in great force. A contemporary[2] gives us an account of this camp, written by a volunteer:

'*Brighton Camp, August* 22.—On the Monday, whatever mistakes (if commanders can make any) had prolonged the order of march from Waterdown, they were removed, and the line reached Chailey in good time. With equal glee and regularity, they set off, the

---

[1] Lady Archer and Mrs. Hobart, both notorious keepers of high-class faro-tables.

[2] *Gentleman's Magazine*, vol. lxiii., part ii., p. 785.

next morning, for Brighton : about four miles before
they arrived on their ground, their regiments were
formed in battalions, in which order they moved, keeping good wheeling distance. The irregularity of the
Downs frequently gave an opportunity of seeing every
regiment with a *coup d'œil.* Numbers of people came
out to meet us. The town, with the sea and the music,
and the universal animation around, somewhat dissipated the fatigue of a long march. Conspicuous
among the spectators, was the Prince of Wales, in the
honourable garb of his regiment, looking both the
Soldier and the Prince. We marched by his Royal
Highness by divisions, officers saluting, and then
wheeled round the town to our new ground, which
appeared a little Paradise, in comparison.

'The water at our former stations had too much
chalybeate in it to be pleasant. On Chailey common it
was good ; and, on our arrival here, we had the luxury
of finding it could not be better. This necessary part
of the comforts of life, with the delightful ground we
are encamped upon, a full advantage of the sea breeze,
and the lively scene continually passing and repassing
in our front, make us hope we shall have more oppor-
tunities of frequenting the Steine Parade than we had
of visiting Tunbridge Wells. Besides, the Commander
in Chief wonderfully gave us an overslaugh from Wednesday until Monday ; on which day we were out six
hours and a half ; five of the hours dragged on with the
usual having nothing to do. We then began to form
columns and lines. This intention was by way of drilling
in the new system. General Dundas, the modeller of it,
gave his personal assistance ; and I could not help

remarking how gracefully and expeditiously he moved his sun burnt hand, explanatory of his formation of the divisions into battalion. I dare say, when we have brought his theory to practical perfection, we shall never be a hair's breadth out. Old officers, who have been accustomed to fight after the old school, find great fault with many parts of this celebrated system.'

This camp consisted of about 10,000 men, regulars, militia, and volunteers, and was situated at Hove, where it continued till October 28. Two new batteries were built, one on the west cliff, which mounted eight twenty-four pounders, and the other on the east cliff, where were four guns of the same weight.

The *Annual Register*, August 21, gives the following : ' Last Sunday, the Rev. Dr. Knox (a gentleman well known in the literary world as the author of several essays) preached at Brighton church. He took his text from St. Luke ; " Glory to God in the highest, and on earth peace and good will towards men !" In enlarging on this subject, he spoke in very strong terms of the calamities of war, and said that the tinsel of military parade was but a poor compensation for the innumerable miseries that were the too sure attendants upon a state of warfare ; that the voice of religion was but little heard amidst the roar of cannon, the shouts of conquerors, and the splendour of victory. In another part of his discourse, he said that religion and philosophy seemed to have but little weight in the councils of the rulers of the world.

' Several military officers in the church, officiously took upon themselves to think that the sermon was an attack upon the constitution of the country, and that it contained improper reflections upon the profession to which they belonged.

'Last night, Dr. Knox and his family being in one of the boxes at the theatre, there were, also, several officers in the house. At the end of the play, a note was handed by the boxkeeper, to Dr. Knox, stating that it was the desire of several gentlemen then present, that he should withdraw. The note being without a signature, Dr. Knox took no notice of it. Several officers then stood up, and insisted on his leaving the house immediately.

'A scene of much confusion, nearly bordering on personal violence, ensued. Dr. Knox attempted to speak, but was, absolutely, forcibly hindered from proceeding; and himself, Mrs. Knox, and two or three of their little children, were compelled to leave the house, to avoid *military* coercion.'

Florizel, commanding his regiment, and playing at soldiers, was in his element, as the following extracts from the *St. James's Chronicle* show:

August 13-15.—'Monday, being the anniversary of the Prince of Wales' birth, the same was celebrated at Brighton; the morning was ushered in by the ringing of bells; and, at one o'clock, the guns of the salute battery were fired. Several of the nobility, who went down to pay their compliments to the Prince, visited his Royal Highness in the Pavilion, who gave a very superb entertainment to the officers of his regiment, etc., in his Marquee. In the evening there was a grand ball in the Castle, which was numerously attended.'

September 5-7.—'In the high winds of Wednesday night, the Prince of Wales's Marquee, in the Camp at

Brighton, was blown down; his Royal Highness, however, suffered nothing; for, except on the nights when he is Colonel of the Camp, his residence is in the Pavilion. Many of the officers and men had their tents blown down on the same night.'

This marquee was a very splendid and spacious affair, with a kitchen and all sorts of conveniences attached. Indeed, Florizel was ever attentive to his own comfort, *vide* the following account of his new travelling-carriage:

August 22-24.—'The Prince of Wales has just built a long carriage for travelling—it is so constructed, that, in a few moments, it forms a neat chamber, with a handsome bed, and every other convenience for passing the night in it, on the road, or in a camp.'

It is all very nice to have travelling-carriages and marquees, and whatever one's soul desires, but if the income is a fixed one, albeit over £70,000 a year, there must be a limit to expenditure. Poor Florizel was deeply in debt, and one of his best friends, the Earl of Malmesbury, tells us about it:[1]

'Landed at Dover on Saturday, June 2nd, 1792. . . . Saw Prince of Wales early the 4th—he was very well pleased with what I had done at Berlin, thanked me for it, etc.—Stated his affairs to me as more distressed than ever—Several executions had been in his house—Lord Rawdon had saved him from one—that his debts amounted to £370,000. He said he was trying, through the Chancellor, to prevail on the King to apply to Parliament to increase his income.

---

[1] 'Diaries and Correspondence of James Harris, first Earl of Malmesbury;' London, 1844, vol. ii., p. 450, etc.

'On the Wednesday following, I was with him by appointment. He repeated the same again ; said that if the King would raise his revenue to £100,000 a year, he would appropriate £35,000 of it to pay the interest of his debts, and establish a Sinking fund. That, if this could not be done, he must break up his establishment, reduce his income to £10,000 a year, and *go abroad*. He *made a merit* of having given up the turf, and blamed the Duke of York for remaining on it. He said (which I well knew before), that his racing stable cost him upwards of £30,000 yearly. He was very anxious, and, as is usual on these occasions, nervous and agitated. He said (on my asking him the question), that he did not stand so well with the King, as he did some months ago, but that he was better than ever with the Queen—that *she* had advised him to press the King, through the Chancellor, to propose to Mr. Pitt to bring an increase of the Prince's income before Parliament, and that, if this was done, she would use her influence to promote it.

'I strongly recommended his pressing the Queen. He suggested the idea of going to Mr. Pitt *directly* through the Chancellor, etc. I doubted both the consent of the Chancellor to such a step, at the moment he was going out, and his influence and weight if he did consent to it. I took the liberty of disapproving his going abroad, on any terms, and, particularly, under the circumstances he mentioned ; said, that if he should, unfortunately, be reduced to the necessity of lowering his income to the degree he had mentioned, it would be much better to live in England, than *out* of it. That the showing, in England, that he *could* reduce his expences, and live economically, would do him credit, prove him in earnest, and if he kept up to such a plan, would, in the event, be much more likely to induce the public to take his situation into consideration, than any attempts through Ministry, Opposition, or even the Queen herself.

'I saw the Prince again on the 7th June, at Carlton House, as before. He repeated the same things, and added, that, if he could not obtain some assurance from the King that he would apply to Parliament in the next Session of Parliament, before this ended, that he should be ruined, and *must go abroad*—I, again, combated this idea; but he appeared to have a wish and some whim about going abroad, I could not discover.— He talked coldly and unaffectionately about the Duke and Duchess of York, and very slightingly of the Duke of Clarence.

'Colonel St. Leger called on me on the 8th June. He said the Prince was more attached to Mrs. Fitzherbert than ever; that he had been living with Mrs. Crouch[1]; that she (Mrs. Fitzherbert) piqued him by treating this with ridicule, and coquetted on her side. This hurt his vanity, and brought him back; and he is, now, more under her influence than ever.'

And yet he could sacrifice her, in order to get his debts paid, and himself have a larger income to squander. There was but one way out of his mess: that he must commit bigamy, and deliberately repudiate his wife.

---

[1] Anna Maria Crouch, actress and famous singer; born 1763, died 1805. Separated from her husband in 1791.

On August 24, 1794, the King wrote thus to Pitt from Weymouth :

' Agreeable to what I mentioned to Mr. Pitt before I came here, I have this morning seen the Prince of Wales, who has acquainted me with his having broken off all connection with Mrs. Fitzherbert, and his desire of entering into a more creditable line of life, by marrying ; expressing, at the same time, that his wish is that my niece, the Princess of Brunswick, may be the person. Undoubtedly she is the person who, naturally, must be most agreeable to me. I expressed my approbation of the idea, provided his plan was to lead a life that would make him appear respectable, and, consequently, render the Princess happy. He assured me that he perfectly coincided with me in opinion. I then said that till Parliament assembled, no arrangement could be taken, except my sounding my sister, that no idea of any other marriage may be encouraged.

' G. R.'

At this time Lady Jersey, a lady of mature age, had great influence over the Prince, and this probably made his rupture with Mrs. Fitzherbert the easier. The caricaturist (this time J. Cruikshank), who always seems to have been as well posted up in any Court scandal as one of our Society papers, has a picture, August 26, 1794, ' My Grandmother, alias the Jersey Jig, alias the Rival Widows.' Old Lady Jersey, who is taking snuff, sits on the knee of the Prince, who says:

' I've kissed & I've prattled with fifty Grand Dames,
    And changed them as oft, do you see ;
  But of all the Grand Mammys that dance on the Steine,
    The Widow of Jersey give me.'

Mrs. Fitzherbert, one hand clasping her forehead, and in the other holding a bond for £6,000 per annum, cries distractedly : ' Was it for this Paltry Consideration I sacrificed my—my—my—? for this only I submitted to—to—? Oh ! shame for ever on my ruin'd Greatness ! ! !'

It came very suddenly. Both Mrs. Fitzherbert and the Prince were to dine with the Duke of Clarence; the lady was there, but Florizel was not; instead, a letter from him was handed to his wife repudiating her. Lord Stourton had the story from her own lips. Let him tell it :

' Her first separation from the Prince was preceded by no quarrel, or even coolness, and came upon her quite unexpectedly. She received, when sitting down to dinner at the table of William the Fourth, then Duke of Clarence, the first intimation of the loss of her ascendancy over the affections of the Prince ; having, only the preceding day, received a note from his Royal Highness, written in his usual strain of friendship, and speaking of their appointed engagement to dine at the house of the Duke of Clarence. The Prince's letter was written from Brighton, where he had met Lady Jersey. From that time she never saw the Prince, and this interruption of their intimacy was followed by his marriage with Queen Caroline ; brought about, as Mrs. Fitzherbert conceived, under the twofold influence of the pressure of his debts on the mind of the Prince, and a wish on the part of Lady Jersey to enlarge the Royal Establishment, in which she was to have an important situation.

' Upon her speaking to me of this union (confiding

in her own desire that I should disguise from her
nothing that I might conceive to be of doubtful
character as affecting her conduct to the Prince), I
told her I had been informed that some proposals had
been made to her immediately preceding the marriage
of the Prince, of which her uncle, Mr. Errington, had
been the channel, offering some terms upon which his
Royal Highness was disposed to give up the match.
She told me there was no truth whatever in the report;
that a day or two preceding the marriage, he had been
seen passing rapidly on horseback before her house at
Marble Hill, but that his motive for doing so, was
unknown to her; and that, afterwards, when they were
reconciled, she cautiously abstained from alluding to
such topics; as the greatest interruptions to their
happiness, at that period, were his bitter and pas-
sionate regrets and self accusations for his conduct,
which she always met by saying—" We must look to
the present and the future, and not think of the past."

'I ventured, also, to mention another report, that
George the Third, the day before the marriage, had
offered to take upon himself the responsibility of
breaking off the match with the Princess of Brunswick,
should the Prince desire it. Of this, too, she told me,
she knew nothing; but added, that it was not improbable, for the King was a good and religious man. She
owned, that she was deeply distressed and depressed in
spirits at this formal abandonment, with all its consequences, as it affected her reputation in the eyes of the
world.

'One of her great friends and advisers, Lady Clare-
mont, supported her on this trying occasion, and coun-

THE RAGE.

selled her to rise above her own feelings, and to open her house to the town of London. She adopted the advice, much as it cost her to do so; and all the fashionable world, including all the Royal Dukes, attended her parties. Upon this, as upon all other occasions, she was principally supported by the Duke of York, with whom, through life, she was always united in the most friendly and confidential relations. Indeed, she frequently assured me, that there was not one of the Royal family who had not acted with kindness to her. She particularly instanced the Queen; and, as for George the Third, from the time she set foot in England, till he ceased to reign, had he been her own father, he could not have acted towards her with greater tenderness and affection. She had made it her constant rule to have no secrets of which the Royal Family were not informed by frequent messages, of which, the Duke of York was, generally, the organ of communication, and, to that rule, she attributed, at all periods, much of her own contentment and ease in extricating herself from embarrassments which would, otherwise, have been insurmountable.'

Compare this paragraph with the ideas of the pictorial satirist on her abandonment. Take, for instance, 'The Rage,' published November 21, 1794. Here we see Mrs. Fitzherbert, having thrown off her Princess of Wales's coronet, with clenched fists and dishevelled hair, sparring at the new Princess of Wales.

Another, which is of the same date, and is called 'Penance for past Folly,' shows Mrs. Fitzherbert weeping, and on her knees, before a Roman Catholic priest, who holds a birch rod in his hand.

The newspapers had an early inkling of the state of affairs between Mrs. Fitzherbert and the Prince, and the following cuttings from the *Times* of 1794 do not redound much to the paper's credit, or knowledge:

July 21.—'A CERTAIN LADY has not been so improvident as the beauteous harlot in the days of EDWARD. She has, wisely, laid up ample provision for a rainy day; and, therefore, her approach, unlike to that of SHORE, is still as likely as ever to make " a little holiday!" '

July 23.—' We have, hitherto, forborne to mention the report in circulation for many days past, of the FINAL SEPARATION between a GENTLEMAN of the most DISTINGUISHED RANK, and a LADY who resides in *Pall Mall*, until we had an opportunity to ascertain the FACT beyond all doubt.

' We are now enabled to state from the most undoubted authority, that a final separation between the parties in question has ACTUALLY TAKEN PLACE; that the agreements formerly entered into, have been given up by mutual consent; that a new contract has been signed, by which the lady is *secured* in the possession of £4,000 per annum, for her life, besides retaining her house in Pall Mall, plate, jewels, etc.

' MRS. FITZHERBERT has no intention of retiring into Switzerland, as has been reported. She is looking out for a house at, or near, Margate, where she means to reside for six months, in the society of the Duchess of CUMBERLAND, Lady E. LUTTRELL, Mrs. CONCANNON,[1] and others of her old acquaintance.'

---

[1] All notorious gamblers and keepers of faro-tables.

August 5.—'Mrs. FITZHERBERT, we learn, wished to have a title and £4,000 annuity settled on her, but this was peremptorily refused.'

August 7.—'Much has been said respecting the jointure settled on Mrs. FITZHERBERT, in consequence of a late separation ; but the precise fact has never been hitherto stated.—The truth is this:—When the incumbrances of a certain GREAT PERSONAGE were put in a state of settlement, two, or three years since, £3,000 a year was allotted out of his revenues, for Mrs. FITZHERBERT, which has been punctually paid by Mr. COUTTS, the banker. This sum has been lately settled on the lady for life ; which, with her own private fortune of £1,800 annually, will make her present income £4,800 a year. Unincumbered as she now is, the lady will, probably, be a happier woman than she has ever been.'

CHAPTER XIV.

Another camp at Brighton—The Prince's second marriage—
His debts—Parliamentary debate thereon—Prince and
Princess at Brighton—'Moral Epistle from the Pavilion at
Brighton to Carlton House'—Manners at Brighton, 1796—
Description of the town.

ARLY in the summer of 1794 another
encampment took place at Brighton,
about a mile and a half to the west of
the town, as it then was. It consisted
of about 7,000 men, and did not break
up until the second week in November. The Prince
was at the Pavilion in May, but not much afterwards.
Mrs. Fitzherbert did not go there this year.

The King, in his speech in opening the session of
Parliament, on December 30, 1794, said : ' I have the
greatest satisfaction in announcing to you the happy
event of the conclusion of a treaty for the marriage
of my son, the Prince of Wales, with the Princess
Caroline, daughter of the Duke of Brunswick ; the
constant proofs of your affection for my person and

family persuade me that you will participate in the
sentiments I feel on an occasion so interesting to my
domestic happiness, and that you will enable me to make
provision for such an establishment, as you may think
suitable to the rank and dignity of the Heir apparent to
the crown of these kingdoms.'

As soon as possible afterwards the pictorial satirist
has (January 24, 1795) THE LOVER'S DREAM.

> ' A thousand virtues seem to lackey her,
>   Driving far off each thing of sin and guilt.'
>
> MILTON.

The Prince is represented as asleep in bed, and
dreaming of his coming bride, who is descending from
heaven, accompanied by Cupids, and driving away
Bacchus, Fox, the Jews, Mrs. Fitzherbert and fiends,
racehorses, etc.; and by the bedside are the King and
Queen, the former holding a bag labelled £15,000 per
annum.

Much Florizel cared for reforming his character; he
only wanted to get clear of debts, and have an increased
income; and, not caring how he obtained this relief, he
committed bigamy on April 8, 1795, in order to obtain
the longed-for relief.   His debts were, according to a
schedule presented to Parliament, up to April 5, as
follows:

Debts on various securities, and bearing interest...	£500,571	19	1
Amount of tradesmen's bills unpaid	86,745	0	0
Tradesmen's bills and arrears of establishment (from October 10, 1794, to April 5, 1795)	52,573	5	3
	£639,890	4	4

On April 27 the King sent a message to his faithful
Commons respecting an establishment for the Prince
and Princess of Wales, and in the last paragraph he
says : 'Anxious as his Majesty must necessarily be,
particularly under the present circumstances, to relieve
the Prince of Wales from these difficulties, his Majesty
entertains no idea of proposing to his Parliament to
make any provision for this object, otherwise than by
the application of a part of the income which may be
settled on the Prince; but he earnestly recommends it
to the House, to consider of the propriety of thus
providing for the gradual discharge of these incumbrances, by appropriating and securing, for a given
term, the revenues arising from the Duchy of Cornwall,
together with a proportion of the Prince's other annual
income; and his Majesty will be ready and desirous to
concur in any provisions which the wisdom of Parliament may suggest for the purpose of establishing a
regular and punctual order of payment in the Prince's
future expenditure, and of guarding against the possi-
bility of the Prince being again involved in so painful
and embarrassing a situation.'

On May 14 the House went into Committee on the
subject. Pitt pointed out that fifty years previously
the Prince's grandfather, as Prince of Wales, had an
annual income of £100,000. ' He, therefore, now proposed, that the income of his Royal Highness should be
£125,000, exclusive of the Duchy of Cornwall, which
was only £25,000 a year more than was enjoyed 50
years ago. This being the only vote he had to propose, he should merely state, in the nature of a notice,
those regulations which were intended to be made here-

after. The preparations for the marriage would be stated at £27,000 for jewels and plate ; and £25,000 for finishing Carlton House. The jointure of the Princess of Wales, he proposed to be £50,000 a year, being no more than had been granted on a similar occasion.'

The addition to the Prince's income was carried by 241 to 100.

In the course of the debate Pitt proposed that the revenues of the Duchy of Cornwall and part of the income of £125,000 should be applied to the payment of the interest of the debts, and to the gradual discharge of the principal ; that the sum so taken should be vested in the hands of Commissioners. From the income of £125,000 a year he should propose that £25,000 should be deducted annually for the payment of the debts at 4 per cent., and that the revenues of the Duchy of Cornwall should be appropriated as a sinking fund, at compound interest, to discharge the principal of the debts, which they would do in twenty-seven years.

Finally, by an Act which received the royal assent on June 27, 1795 (35 Geo. III., c. 129), £60,000 per annum was to be set apart and vested with Commissioners from the Prince's income, as well as £13,000 per annum from the Duchy of Cornwall, to pay the Prince's debts, a proceeding which found small favour in Florizel's sight.

Of the wretched marriage nothing need be said. Public appearances were kept up until the birth of the Princess Charlotte, and the Prince and his consort visited Brighton together, as we see from the following extracts from the *Sussex Weekly Advertiser* :

June 22, 1795.—'Their Royal Highnesses the Prince and Princess of Wales arrived at Brighton between one and two o'clock on Thursday morning last. They alighted at the house of Mr. Hamilton, on the Steine, which is to be made the Royal residence, till the alterations that are going forward at the Pavilion, can be completed.

'In the evening the whole town was illuminated, in honour of their Royal Highnesses' arrival; but the effect of the illumination was greatly lessened by the wetness of the night, as it prevented the lamps with which the Castle, the Libraries, and other houses were decorated, from burning.

'The Prince, we are informed, perambulated the town, in his great coat, to view the different devices.

'Though the untowardness of the weather has, hitherto, obscured the beauties of Brighton from the Princess of Wales, it has had no effect whatever on her Royal Highness's spirits; on the contrary, her cheerfulness and pleasantry strongly bespeak her approbation of the place.

'The Prince, about noon yesterday, set off for town, but we understand his Royal Highness signified his intention of returning to Brighton some time in the course of this day.

'On Wednesday morning, should the weather prove favourable, the Prince and Princess of Wales intend visiting the Camp, when the whole line will be drawn up, and fire a Royal salute, on the occasion. After which, there will be a grand field day.'

June 29.—'The Prince and Princess of Wales did not visit the Camp, last Wednesday, as was expected, owing to the absence of his Royal Highness, who, on that day, went to town, in order to attend the Privy Council. The whole line was, nevertheless, out, and had a field day.

'On Saturday morning, however, their Royal Highnesses honoured the Camp with their promised visit, when the whole line was drawn up in readiness to receive them; after which, the troops marched to Goldstone Bottom, where they had a very grand field day, and fired a Royal salute, on the occasion.

'We are glad to hear, from the best authority, that the air of Brighton proves extremely agreeable to the above illustrious Princess. Since her arrival at that place, her Royal Highness has enjoyed an excellent flow of spirits, and has frequently been heard to declare she had never before experienced so good an appetite. Her Royal Highness has signified her intention of continuing at Brighton, the whole of the summer.'

July 6.—' The Prince and Princess of Wales removed from Mr. Hamilton's house, on the Steine, to the Royal Pavilion, on Thursday last.'

They stopped at Brighton till November, and Queen Caroline never again revisited it, as, after the birth of the Princess Charlotte (January 7, 1796), the royal couple separated for good.

The Prince went to Brighton for the season on July 28, 1796, and the Pavilion, as it then was, is thus described in a contemporary pamphlet :[1]

' The Pavilion is built principally of wood; it is a nondescript monster in building, and appears like a mad house, or a house run mad, as it has neither beginning,

[1] 'The New Brighton Guide ;' London, 1796, 8vo., p. 16.

middle, nor end ; yet, to acquire this design, a miserable bricklayer was despatched to Italy, to gather something equal to the required magnificence, and actually charged two thousand guineas for his expenses.—There are four pillars in *scagliola*, in a sort of oven, where the Prince dines ; and, when the fire is lighted, the room is so hot, that the parties are nearly baked and incrusted : the ground on which it is erected was given to the Prince by the town, for which he allows them fifty pounds yearly, to purchase grog and tobacco ; and has so far mended their ways, as to make a common sewer to hold the current filth of the parish.'

The same pamphlet contains ' A Moral Epistle from the Pavilion at Brighton to Carlton House, London,' which gives an account of the style of company kept there :

' When he first nestled here, he was handsome and thin,
No razor had then mown his stubbleless chin :
He was sportive and careless, bland, upright and young,
And I smiled on his feats when he said, or he sung :
Then youth bore its own pardon, while stumbling o'er ill,
As the passions o'erthrew what was meant by the will.
    *   *   *   *   *
I have seen him inwove with a pestilent crew,
Who, nine tenths came undone, and the rest to undo !
When those caitiffs came thund'ring in impudent state,
And drew up their *tandems* and *gigs* at my gate,
Full of wrath at their daring, I rav'd and I swore,
Then I let in an Eddy that slamm'd to the door :
But, alas ! it avail'd not—'twas open'd again,
And the P—— rose, and welcom'd the toad eating train !
He, urbane, smil'd on all, where 'twas sin to look sad,
As God's light aids, in common, the good and the bad.
I tore off Folly's cloak, to exhibit the wrong ;
How I toil'd to advise, but was stunn'd with a song :

I made signs on my plaster to rally them all,
But no *Daniel* was there to decipher the wall.—
Ah ! I know his large heart, and beneficent plan ;
Though he's run from the course, yet HE FEELS LIKE A MAN :
Though he dissipates seeds of an undeserv'd sorrow,
And, gaily, puts off half his ills till the morrow,
His radical nobleness knows no decay ;
He will act, but not cant ;—he'll relieve ere he'll pray :
As Charity's retinue own, while embrac'd,
IN HIS GIFT HE GIVES TWICE, 'TIS A DEED SO WELL GRAC'D.

    When their mirth grew to madness, and jests met the ear,
Which Philosophy scorns, and no maiden should hear,
Convuls'd with disdain, I soon alter'd their note,
For I shut up the principal valve of my throat ;
Till the smoke, in vast volumes, pour'd into the room,
And enwrapp'd the loud mob in a horrible gloom,
More fœtid than Vulcan inhal'd with his breath ;
More thick than e'er pass'd o'er the threshold of Death ;
More choking than Cyclops drank in at their forge ;
More rank than the reptile of Thebes could disgorge :
As they gasp'd, it rush'd down their intestines, and clogg'd 'em,
And from *pharynx* to *rectum* begrim'd and befogg'd 'em :
While, hoarsely, they growl'd at the house, and the smother,
Though, by knowing the cause, they had curs'd one another.
'Mid their baneful carousals, I've fum'd and I've fretted,
Till from kitchen to garret, I've croak'd, and I've sweated ;
By pressure, I made my joints crack—I can't bawl—
And drops, drawn from my heart, ran from every wall :
But, his H——s, not knowing my woes, or displeasure,
Renew'd the broad catch, and refill'd every measure ;
While the rascals around him. revil'd the damp mansion,
And my marrow, scorch'd up by the fire's expansion :
Which so heated my fibres and bones—I mean wood—
That a putrescent fever polluted my blood ;
Which settled behind the bed's head of the P——e,
And I've not had my health, or my ease, ever since ;
Yet I'm sure he would grieve, his politeness is such,
Had he known that a lady had suffered so much.

Thus they swill'd and re-swill'd, and repeated their boozings,
Till their shirts became dy'd with purpureal oozings.
When the *taster* sought wine of a primary sort,
I have cough'd 'neath the bin, and shook all the old port,
Till 'twas muddy as WILL B——CK'S brains—yet each varlet
Said 'twas as bright as a ruby, and toasting some harlot,
Would then smack his lips, in despite of my labour !
Oh, ye Gods ! how I wish'd for a fist and a sabre,
To cut down the hiccupping roist'rers with glee,
That is, if their heads could be injur'd by me.
When WELTJE has cook'd for the half famish'd group,
How oft have I belch'd pecks of soot in his soup :
Yet e'en that could not drive them from board, or from bed,
Though 'twas render'd as black as an Ethiop's head :
When I've made it as foul as a Scot's ragged tartan,
The rogues gulp'd it down, and all swore it was Spartan.
When they've sat near the fire, in knee squeezing rows,
I have spit out a coal, and demolished their hose :
All my grates have breath'd sulphur to stifle their powers ;
I'd a watch at my side to beat minutes and hours :
When I've seen a Blight glide 'twixt the earth and the skies,
I've coax'd in the demon, and ruin'd their eyes :
I've edg'd down a poker on legs swell'd with gout,
Till the miscreant has roar'd like swine stuck in the snout ;
When Lord —— from my windows was making a beck,
I have hurl'd down my sashes, and wounded his neck ;
Though my rage could but bruise him black, yellow and blue,
'Twas a hint that might show what the nation should do :
But each knave all the arts of my anger withstood,
For the leeches will suck while the body has blood.
I'd have prophecied much, had I Cerberus' three tongues ;
I would fulminate oaths, but, alas ! I've no lungs.
When they thought 'twas an earthquake that palsied my walls,
It was I who was shudd'ring to witness their brawls.
There's no office so dirty but they would fulfil ;
There's no sense of debasement could alter their will :
When the munching of immature codlings might gripe him,
They would tear out the leaves of the Psalter to wipe him.

Yet these summer fed vermin will fly him, if e'er
His wintery fortunes should leave his trunk bare ;
Then he'll know that but virtue can keep the soul great,
As they'd make their past meanness the *cause* of their hate !
I have dropp'd lumps of lime in their glasses while drinking ;
I've made thieves in the candle to move him to thinking ;
I have clatter'd my casements and chairs to confound 'em ;
I have let in the dews and the blast all around 'em ;
I have elbow'd my timbers 'gainst many a head ;
I have stirr'd up the sewers to stink 'em to bed :
Yet this mass of antipathy marr'd my own liver,
And my tears fill'd the gutter like Egypt's deep river.
—My eyes, my dear Coz, are exhausted with crying ;
So I'll give o'er at present—I'm yours till I'm dying.

' Pavilion.'

We learn what the society at Brighton was like at this time by the following excerpt from the *Times* of July 13, 1796 :

' Brighton.—The Prince and Princess of Wales's arrival has been talked of much in London ; but, as yet, we have no signs of it here. The Duke and Duchess of Marlborough pass their time in a very retired manner indeed. His Grace walked for some time yesterday evening upon the *Steyne ;* the company consisted chiefly of opulent Jews, needy fortune hunters, broken down Cyprians, fishermen's daughters, and several fat city dowdies, from the environs of Norton Folgate. Her Grace commands the play on Friday evening, which will be her *first appearance* in public, here, for this season. The Officers of the Blues are the *great dashers* of the place ; they associate with no one but their own Corps. The most of them keep their blood horses, their curricles, and their girls. At one o'clock they appear on the parade, to hear the word of command given to the Subaltern Guard : afterwards, they toss off their *goes* of brandy, dine about five, and come about eight to the Theatre. *Vivent L'Amour et Bacchus.*'

The latter part of this quotation seems to be borne out by the first of ' TWELVE GOLDEN RULES *for young Gentlemen of Distinction, to be observed at Brighton for the year* 1796 ':

' Young and inexperienced officers must confederate with several of their mess, as young as themselves, and reel into the theatre, during the performance, in a state of assumed intoxication, and be sure to disturb the audience in the most important part of the drama, by taking liberties with any of those Cyprian nymphs who harbour in the green boxes, and are, unhappily, devoted to insult : by this manœuvre, if dexterously managed, they will gain three enormous points ;—the first is, the credit of having consumed more wine than their income will allow; the second is, a disposition for unlimited intrigue ; and the third is, an opportunity of displaying their contempt for good manners, without any hazard of personal danger.—This behaviour will be totally out of character if any of the parties have seen service, or arrived at the years of discretion.

' N.B.—All descendants, or members of the tribes of Israel, must neither mention lottery tickets, *omnium,* *bonus,* scrip, navy, nor exchequer bills ; they must pay their tradesmen on Saturdays, laugh at the paschal, eat swine, and shave every day.'

Let us look at Brighton as shown us by a contemporary publication[1] :

<hr>

[1] ' New Brighton Guide,' 1796.

'There are two taverns, namely, the Castle, and the Old Ship, where the richer visitors resort; and, at each of these houses, a weekly assembly is held, where a master of the ceremonies attends, to arrange the parties, not according to the scale of morality, but that of aristocracy. There is a ball every Monday at the Castle, and, on Thursdays, at the Old Ship; every subscriber pays three shillings and sixpence, and every non-subscriber, five shillings; for which they are entitled to a beverage which they call *tea* and *coffee*.—The masters of the respective inns receive the profits, except on those nights appointed for the benefit of the Master of the Ceremonies; to whom, all who wish to be arranged as people of distinction, subscribe one guinea—and who would not purchase distinction at so cheap a rate!— Independently of this vain *douceur*, they must pay most liberally for their tickets! The card assemblies are on Wednesdays and Fridays.—There is a hotel, which was intended for a country Hummums, or grand dormitory; but, in my weak opinion, the establishment is somewhat inefficient, unless it can be supposed that the tumultuous equipment of stage coaches, at the dawn of day, is contributory to the purposes of rest.—There is a theatre, commodious, and, generally, well directed; the nights of performance are Tuesdays and Wednesdays, Fridays and Saturdays.—At the lower end of North Street is a sort of Birmingham Vauxhall, called the *Promenade Grove;* it is a small inclosure of a paddock, tormented from its native simplicity, befringed with a few gawky poplars, and decorated with flowers, bowers, zigzag alleys, a ditch, and a wooden box for the minstrels.—The coast is like the greater part of its visitors, bold, saucy, intrusive, and dangerous.—The bathing machines, even for the ladies, have no awning, or covering, as at Weymouth, Margate, and Scarborough; consequently, they are all severely inspected by the aid of telescopes, not only as they confusedly ascend from the sea, but as they kick and sprawl and flounder about its muddy margin, like so many mad Naiads in flannel smocks;—the shore is so disastrously imperfect, that those beginners who paddle in, are injured by the shocking repulsion of the juices to the brain; and, of those who are enabled to plunge in, and swim beyond the surge, it is somewhat less than an even bet, that many never return—in truth, the loss of lives here, every season, would make any society miserable, who were not congregating in the mart of noisy folly.—There is a Subscription House, or Temple of Fortune, on the Steyne, where the minor part of our blessed nobility are accustomed to reduce their characters and their estates in the same period;—the signal for admission is *habeo*,—for rejection, *debeo*.—There are lodgings of all descriptions and fitness, from twenty pounds per week, on the Cliffs, to half a crown per night in a stable—the keepers of the lodging houses, like the keepers of madhouses, having but one common point in view—to *bleed* the parties sufficiently.—There are carriages and caravans of all shapes and dimensions, from a waggon to a fish cart; in which you may move like a king, a criminal, or a crab, that is, forwards, backwards, or laterally.—There are two libraries on the Steyne, replete with every flimsy species of novels, involving the prodigious intrigues of an imaginary society; this kind of recreation is termed *light reading*:

perhaps, from the certain effect it has upon the brains
of my young country women, of making them *light
headed !*—'There is a parish church, where the *canaille*
go to pray; but, as this is on a hill, and the gentry
found their Sabbath visit to the Almighty very trouble-
some, the amiable and accommodating *master* priest has
consigned the care of his common *parish mutton* to his
journeyman, the curate, and has kindly raised a Chapel
Royal for the *lambs of fashion*, where a certain sum is
paid for every seat; and this, it must be admitted, is
as it should be; as a well bred Deity will, assuredly,
be more attentive to a reclining Duchess, parrying the
assaults of the devil, behind her fan, than the vulgar
piety of a plebeian on his knees.—'There were books
open in the circulating libraries, where you were
requested to contribute your mite of charity to the
support of the rector, as his income is somewhat less
than seven hundred pounds a year; the last incumbent
died worth thirty thousand pounds.'

CHAPTER XV.

Reconciliation of the Prince and Mrs. Fitzherbert—Her scruples,
etc.—The Prince at Brighton—Satirical prints—The Prince
and the Pavilion—Increase of income—The Prince and his
regiment—A race—Guests at the Pavilion—The Prince and
his daughter.

T was in this year that the separation of
the Prince and the titular Princess of
Wales was complete, and Florizel's heart
(if he had such a thing) went back to
his wife.   Let us hear Lord Stourton's
account of their reconciliation :

'When she thought her connection with the Prince
was broken off for ever, by his second union, she was
placed by him in difficulties from the same earnest and
almost desperate pursuit, as she had been exposed to
during the first interval of his attachment.   Numbers
of the Royal Family, both male and female, urged a
reconciliation, even upon a principle of duty.

'However, as she was, by his marriage with Queen
Caroline, placed in a situation of much difficulty,

involving her own conscience, and making it doubtful whether public scandal might not interfere with her own engagements, she determined to resort to the highest authorities of her own Church upon a case of such extraordinary intricacy. The Rev. Mr. Nassau, one of the chaplains of Warwick Street Chapel, was, therefore, selected to go to Rome and lay the case before that tribunal, upon the express understanding that, if the answer should be favourable, she would again join the Prince; if otherwise, she was determined to abandon the country. In the meantime, whilst the negotiation was pending, she obtained a promise from his Royal Highness that he would not follow her into her retreat in Wales, where she went to a small bathing place. The reply from Rome, in a Brief, which, in a moment of panic, she destroyed, fearful of the consequences during Mr. Percival's administration, was favourable to the wishes of the Prince; and, faithful to her own determination to act, as much as possible, in the face of the public, she resisted all importunities to meet him clandestinely. The day on which she joined him again at her own house, was the same on which she gave a public breakfast to the whole town of London, and to which he was invited.

'She told me, she hardly knew how she could summon resolution to pass that severe ordeal, but she thanked God she had the courage to do so. The next eight years were, she said, the happiest of her connection with the Prince. She used to say that they were extremely poor, but as merry as crickets; and, as a proof of their poverty, she told me that once, on their returning to Brighton from London, they mustered their common means, and could not raise £5 between them. Upon this, or some such occasion, she related to me, that an old and faithful servant endeavoured to force them to accept £60, which he said he had accumulated in the service of the best of Masters and Mistresses. She added, however, that even this period, the happiest of their lives, was much embittered by the numerous political difficulties which frequently surrounded the Prince.'

We can scarcely, nowadays, when the judicial separation of man and wife is an everyday occurrence, and divorce is rendered as easy as possible, properly conceive Mrs. Fitzherbert's feelings in this matter of reconciliation. We must, however, remember that she was a strict Catholic, that her Church teaches that marriage is indissoluble, except by death, and that she invoked and followed the highest ecclesiastical authorities for guidance. Let us hear a modern opinion of her conduct. It occurs in the *Dublin Review* of October, 1854, p. 21, in a criticism of 'Lord Holland's Memoirs ':

' The doctrine of the Catholic Church regarding marriage is plain and simple. She teaches that the marriage contract itself, which is perfected by the words, "I take thee for my wife," on the part of the man, and " I take thee for my husband," on the part of the woman, or by any other words, or signs, by which the contracting parties manifest their intention of taking each other for man and wife, is a sacrament. Protestants are apt to fall into the mistake that it is the priest who administers the sacrament to the wedded pair. He does no such thing. As far as the validity of the contract and of the sacrament is concerned, even when the contracting parties are both Catholics, the priest need not utter a word. His presence is only necessary as a *witness* to the contract between the parties. Up to the time of the Council of Trent, the presence of a priest was not necessary for the validity of either the contract, or the sacrament. Nor was it by any means to confer the sacrament that the Council enacted a law requiring his presence. The law was made in consequence of the abuses which arose from clandestine marriages, because an immoral person who had married without witnesses, could, afterwards, deny the existence of the contract, and wed another publicly, and in the face of the Church. To prevent this abuse, the Council of Trent enacted that the parish priest of one of the contracting parties, or some other priest deputed by him, and two other witnesses should, *for the future* (*in posterum*), be present (*præsente parocho*) at the marriage contract. The presence of the two other witnesses is required exactly in the same way as that of the parish priest. The law is simply that marriage should be contracted in the presence of three witnesses, one of whom should, necessarily, be the parish priest.

'Nor was this law made, at once, obligatory, even on Catholics. By an ordinance of the Council, it was not to have effect *in any parish* until thirty days after it had been published there. This allowed a large discretion to each bishop with regard to the time of its publication in his diocese, and, in fact, it is not long since it has been introduced into England.

'But it does not, and never did apply to any marriage in these countries, where one of the parties is not a

Catholic. Neither in such marriages, which are called mixed, nor in those contracted between parties, neither of whom belong to the Catholic Church, is the presence of any priest required for the validity of either the contract, or sacrament. It is not even necessary that the contracting parties should *know* that marriage is a sacrament. The sacrament exists wherever Christians marry as Christ intended ; and, if they be properly disposed, they will receive grace to live happily together, and to bring up their children in the fear and love of God.

' Mrs. Fitzherbert's marriage was, therefore, perfectly valid, both as a contract and as a sacrament, in the eyes of the whole Catholic Church, and to imagine that she alone, of all those who professed the same faith, should look upon it as invalid, is monstrously absurd. Neither the Pope, nor the whole Church could have annulled it, nor allowed her to marry another.

' But it was illegal ! Why, so was the whole Catholic religion, at the same period. It was, not very long ago, unlawful to celebrate Mass, but the sacrifice was not, therefore, invalidly offered. To say that Mrs. Fitzherbert considered the marriage ceremony to be nonsense, because it was illegal, at the time when the penal code against Catholics—and especially that part of it which regarded matrimony—was in full operation, is about as reasonable, as to prove that she did not believe in transubstantiation, because the law declared it to be damnable and idolatrous.'

For the next two or three years we hear little about the Prince, the newspapers leaving his doings unrecorded. We learn (May 15, 1797) that ' On last Thursday evening, the Prince of Wales, accompanied by a single gentle-

man, arrived at his Pavilion at Brighton. His Royal
Highness, the next day, reviewed the Monmouth and
Brecon Militia, on the Downs, near the above place.
To-day, we hear, the Prince leaves Brighton, having
come there only for a few days, by the advice of
Dr. Warren, for the benefit of the sea air. His Royal
Highness has lost much of his corpulence since he was
last at Brighton.'

He went again, on July 24, to be present at the races,
and it is recorded that, on October 23, 'The Prince of
Wales amused himself with a day's shooting at Petworth,
on an invitation from the Earl of Egremont. The next
day, his Royal Highness being on his way to London,
with post horses, very narrowly escaped being overturned,
about a mile and a half on the other side of Cuckfield,
where the horses, by some means, took the carriage off
the main road to the side of a bank, and with an inclination that threatened its overturn, for the space of
many yards, but fortunately, and owing to the lowness
of the carriage, it was kept upon its wheels.'

He was present at the races on August 1, 2, and 3,
1798, and a newspaper remarks that 'The change of
society and manners which has taken place at the
Pavilion, gives the most heartfelt satisfaction to every
lover of his country; it is, now, every way worthy of
the Heir apparent of the British Empire.'

In 1799 we hear of him being at Brighton, both in
July and October. In 1800 he was at the races in
August, when his horse Knowsley won a race. In the
'Brighton New Guide,' fourth edition, there is a good
view of the Pavilion as it was in 1800, with the follow-
ing text :

' Adjoining to Marlborough House stands the MARINE PAVILION, built by his Royal Highness the Prince of Wales, in the year 1784.

' This handsome structure extends upwards of 200 feet in front, towards the Steyne; the centre is a circular building, with a lofty dome, supported by pillars; on each side are two elegant rooms on the ground floor, with bed chambers over them: in addition to these, in the spring of 1802, two wings were added, which gives a light, airy appearance to the building; gravel walks, grass plats, and plantations towards the Steyne, add a great degree of elegance to the whole.

' The front, towards the street, forms a square, with a handsome colonnade in the middle, supported by columns; in the wings are commodious apartments for his Royal Highness's suite; in the court is the figure of a negro supporting a dial, executed in a superior style of beautiful sculpture.'

The Prince was at Brighton in 1801. *Vide* the following extract from a newspaper:

' *Rejoicings for Peace. Oct.* 14.—On Monday, the joyful tidings of Peace were celebrated here; the bells rang from six in the morning till twelve at night; never was the satisfaction of the people more fully displayed. Young and old wore ribbons emblematic of the occasion —*Peace* and *Plenty!* The sea fencibles fired a *feu de joie*, marched from thence to the Prince's house, and gave him three loud huzzas: with that liberality which has ever marked our Royal guest, he ordered them two hogsheads of beer. Brilliant illuminations took place in the evening; the whole town appeared in a blaze. The most distinguished were those of his Royal Highness the Prince of Wales, flambeaux burning round his house, and every window lighted. This happy day closed with a ball and supper at the Castle, attended by near five hundred visitors; at one o'clock the room was opened with the most sumptuous entertainment; every delicacy that could be procured.'

The Prince was in Brighton in 1802, and in the latter part of the year hunted almost daily with his harriers, and had concerts at the Pavilion two or three times a week. He left it for the season on December 27.

A newspaper cutting tells us that 'The charitable donations and willing assistance which Mrs. Fitzherbert has bestowed, and continues to bestow on the unfortunate individuals of this place, have justly endeared her to the inhabitants of every description.'

But the miserable caricaturist, who knew nothing of her noble nature, depicts her in a scurrilous drawing (October 21, 1802), entitled 'A BRIGHTON BREAKFAST, OR MORNING COMFORTS.' Mrs. Fitzherbert and Lady Lade are at breakfast; Mrs. Fitzherbert is pouring Hollands into a huge tumbler labelled 'Comfort,' and says, 'Won't you take another Comforter? We must make haste, I expect Noodle here presently.' Lady Lade, who takes Brandy, says, 'I think your Comforters are bigger than my John's.'

The next day brought out another satirical print, indicative of the Prince's intimacy with the Lades. It is called 'Birds of a Feather Flock Together; Diversions of Brighton.' Sir John Lade and the Prince are on the box of an open carriage, in which are seated Mrs. Fitzherbert and a lady (Miss Snow). Sir John is lashing one of the four horses, and says to the Prince, 'There,

B——t it, don't you see ? that's the Cut.' Miss Snow observes to Mrs. Fitzherbert, ' Did Noodle bring your physic this morning ?' To which she replies, ' Oh, yes, he calls regularly every morning.'

We read in the *Sussex Weekly Advertiser* (February 28, 1803) that ' The Prince's Pavilion at Brighton is undergoing other considerable alterations and improvement, under the direction of Mr. Holland, the architect ; and is ordered to be got ready for the residence of his Royal Highness, at an early part of the ensuing season.'

On October 14, 1800, just before Weltje died, the Prince took from him a lease of the Pavilion for ninety-nine years at a rent, annually, of £1,150, and on April 18, 1803, he went to Brighton to see how the alterations were getting on. ' His Royal Highness slept at the house, late Weltje's, adjoining the Pavilion, the repairs and alterations of which are not yet completed. The Prince, after minutely inspecting the works going on, returned to town on Thursday.'

In this extravagance he was somewhat justified, for on February 16 the Chancellor of the Exchequer brought before the House of Commons the following message from the King :

' GEORGE R.

' His Majesty having taken into consideration the period which has elapsed since the adoption of those arrangements which were deemed, by the wisdom of Parliament, to be necessary for the discharge of the incumbrances of the Prince of Wales ; and, having adverted to the progress which has been made in carrying them into effect, recommends the present situation of the Prince to the attention of this House.

'Notwithstanding the reluctance and regret which his Majesty must feel in suggesting any addition to the burthens of his people, he is induced to resort, in this instance, to the experienced liberality and attachment of his faithful Commons, in the persuasion that they will be disposed to take such measures, as may be calculated to promote the comfort, and support the dignity of so distinguished a branch of his Royal Family.'

On February 23 the House went into Committee to consider the King's message ; and the Chancellor of the Exchequer (Addington) pointed out that on the 5th of the previous January £563,895 had been paid off the Prince's debt of £650,000, and that the whole would be discharged in July, 1806. He moved 'That his Majesty be enabled to grant a yearly sum, or sums of money, out of the Consolidated Fund of Great Britain, not exceeding, in the whole, the sum of Sixty thousand pounds ; to take place, and be computed from the 5th day of January, 1803, and to continue until the 5th day of July, 1806, towards providing for the better support of the station and dignity of his Royal Highness, the Prince of Wales.' This resolution was agreed to.

In September, 1803, the royal stables, now the Dome, were commenced, and that the Prince was there in October we have evidence in the following newspaper cutting :

'*Oct. 2.*—The Prince of Wales, at the conclusion of the Concert at the Pavilion, some time after midnight, on Thursday last, addressing himself to Colonel

Leigh, expressed an anxious desire to know in how short a time his regiment of dragoons could be under arms, and ready to face the enemy, should necessity require their exertions in the night. The Colonel immediately proposed, as the best method of satisfying his Royal Highness, instantly to ride to, and order an alarm to be sounded at, the barracks ; and, afterwards, to return, and give his Royal Highness a correct account of the conduct of his troops. This measure being approved by the Prince, the Colonel's horse was soon brought to the door, and he set off, with all possible speed to see it carried into effect.

'On reaching the advanced guard at the entrance of the barracks, the Colonel commanded a black trumpeter on duty, to sound to arms. The man, in obedience to the mandate, raised the trumpet to his lips ; but the surprise of the moment so greatly overpowered him, that he wanted breath to put it in execution. An English trumpeter, who overheard the order, as he lay in bed, in an instant arose, dashed open the window of his room, and without waiting for further advice, put the bugle to his mouth, gave the proper signal, and the troops, in every part, were, in an instant, in motion. The greater part of the soldiers had been in bed many hours ; the whole of them were properly accoutred, and on their horses, together with the flying artillery, in readiness to depart, in time sufficient to have reached Brighton within 15 minutes after the bugle gave the alarm. The barracks are situated something better than a mile and a half to the north of the town.'

The following excerpt from the *Annual Register* shows the diversions of Brighton :

' *Aug.* 20, 1803. — A whimsical exhibition took place on the race ground at Brighton. Captain Otto, of the Sussex Militia, booted, and mounted by a grenadier of 18 stone weight, was matched to run 50 yards, against a poney, carrying a feather, to run 150; but Capt. Otto's rider tumbled over his neck, which he was very near cracking ; and, consequently, he lost the bet. The next match was, the same gentleman, mounted by the same grenadier, to run 50 yards, against a noble lord, carrying a feather, who was to run 100. He was considerably distanced by the latter.'

The following is taken from the *Times* of September 7, 1804 :

' BRIGHTON ANECDOTE.—Some ill timed pleasantry was played off, a few days ago, at Brighton, on a respectable *Law Officer* and his wife, who have made a summer excursion there. An invitation, couched in due form, and bearing all the marks of authenticity, was sent to them, desiring their company at the Pavilion in the evening. The Gentleman and Lady, justly proud of the distinguished honour thus conferred on them, they knew not how, attended at the hour appointed, and were ushered into the Saloon, in which were many persons of distinction, to whom they were wholly unknown. Some embarrassment necessarily ensued, but it was increased to a ten fold degree, when they were announced to the *illustrious* Master of the house, who had no recollection either of his guests, or the invitation in his name ; an explanation ensued, and his Royal Highness, with all that urbanity that distinguishes him as the most finished Gentleman in Europe, was pleased to declare " that he felt himself much indebted to the ingenious person, who (by forging his invitation, in order, perhaps, to sport with their feelings) had afforded him the pleasure of their society and acquaintance, however unexpected ; and that he was perfectly happy in the opportunity of receiving them." His Royal Highness conducted himself towards them during the whole of the evening with the most liberal and marked attention, and thus converted a *rencontre*, which was produced by the most malignant motives, into a source of honour and perfect satisfaction.'

Of the Prince's connection with Brighton in 1804 we have very little trace. He was averse to having his doings chronicled, probably because they were immediately pictorially satirized ; but we have a very fine one by Gillray, called THE RECONCILIATION, published on November 20, 1804.

The Prince and the King had been at daggers drawn, principally as to the guardianship of the little Princess Charlotte. A peace was temporarily patched up between them, and the King wrote on November 7 to the Chancellor that he was ready to receive the Prince. The letter being forwarded to the latter, he at once replied :

'BRIGHTON,
'*Nov.* 8, 1804.

' The Prince of Wales, without delay, acknowledges the receipt of the Chancellor's letter ; and will, in consequence of the gracious intention signified from his Majesty, be in London to-morrow evening, with Lord Moira, who has just arrived at Brighthelmstone. The Earl of Moira is authorised by the Prince to wait upon the Chancellor at any hour on Saturday morning, that his lordship may please to appoint.'

The meeting between father and son took place on November 12, and next day the King wrote to the Princess of Wales :

'WINDSOR CASTLE,
'*Nov.* 13, 1804.

'MY DEAREST DAUGHTER IN LAW, AND NIECE,

'Yesterday, I and the rest of the family had an interview with the Prince of Wales, at Kew. Care was taken on all sides to avoid all subjects of altercation, or explanation, consequently, the conversation was neither instructive, nor entertaining ; but it leaves the Prince of Wales in a situation to show whether his desire to return to the family, is only verbal, or real, which time, alone, can prove. I am not idle in my endeavours to make inquiries that may enable me to communicate some plan for the advantage of the dear child. You and I, with so much reason, must interest ourselves ; and its effecting my having the happiness of living more with you, is no small incentive to my forming some ideas on the subject, but you may depend on their not being decided upon, without your thorough and cordial concurrence ; for your authority as a mother, it is my object to support.

'Believe me, at all times,
'My dearest daughter and niece,
'Your most affectionate Father in Law and Uncle,
'GEORGE R.'

Nothing really came of this so-called 'Reconciliation,' and soon father and son were as much estranged as ever. Gillray gives us a picture of the Prodigal Son's return. '*And he arose and came to his Father ;*

and his Father saw him, and had compassion and ran, and fell on his neck, and kissed him.' The Prince of Wales is in tatters, with his empty pockets turned inside out, his stockings slipping down, and his shoes down at heel. Lord Moira and Pitt stand by, looking on, and Queen Charlotte, with her arms outspread, and two of the Princesses, are beaming with delight.

CHAPTER XVI.

The case of Miss Seymour — Satirical prints thereon — The
Prince at Brighton, 1806—His birthday—The Green Man
—Visit of the Princess Charlotte.

IN 1805 the Prince was much at Brighton,
but we hear but little of him except
in connection with Mrs. Fitzherbert's
guardianship of Miss Mary Seymour,
a child of whom the Prince of Wales
was very fond, and Lord Stourton tells the story in a
pleasant way:

'A circumstance now took place, which ended by
blasting all her happy prospects, and, finally, terminated
in a rupture with the Prince, which lasted till the end
of his life. One of the dearest friends of Mrs. Fitzherbert, Lady Horatia Seymour, in the last stage of
decline, was advised to go abroad, to seek, in change of
climate, her only chance of recovery. She had, at that
time, an infant, and, not being able to take it with her,
she entrusted her treasure to the care of her attached
friend, Mrs. Fitzherbert, who, having no child of her

14

own, soon became devotedly attached to the precious
child, and her affection for the child increased with the
loss of the parent. Some time afterwards, one of the
near relatives of the family, desirous of having the
education of the child placed in other hands, and being
jealous of the religion of its protectress, applied to the
Chancellor to obtain possession of Miss Seymour, as
guardian. Mrs. Fitzherbert, now more than ever
devoted to the child, and sharing, in this affection,
with the Prince himself, exerted every means to retain
the custody of it; and, after all others had failed, had,
at last, recourse to Lady Hertford, with whom she was,
formerly, intimately acquainted. She requested her to
intercede with Lord Hertford, as head of his house,
to come to her aid; and, demanding for himself the
guardianship of the child, to give it up to her,[1] upon
certain conditions as to its education.'

The satirical prints, of course, were to the fore on
this subject, although it was a purely private matter.
First of all comes (January 9, 1805) 'To Be, or Not
to Be, a Protestant.' Miss Seymour is sitting on a
sofa, holding in her hand a book, '*Mother's advice to
her Daughter, respecting the true principles of the Protestant religion*'; Mrs. Fitzherbert, wearing a rosary
and crucifix, and having in her hand a book, '*Directions
from the clergy, respecting the Duty of a true Catholic,
in converting all, etc.*,' says: 'I say I have the undoubted right to have the care of her, and to bring her
up as I like. Do I not Rule the Roast?' At an open
door appears a monk, who says: 'Well done, my Child,

---

[1] An arrangement which was satisfactorily effected.

THE GUARDIAN ANGEL.

you are now serving our holy religion; you shall next use your influence to procure us Emancipation.'

'THE CONVENTION, OR A HINT AT EMANCIPATION,' is another on the same subject (February 18, 1805). Mrs. Fitzherbert, who has been reading 'The Reign of Queen Mary,' is seated at a table with a monk, who is making a hearty meal of roast beef and port wine. She says: 'Oh, Father, they want to rob me of my charge, I will not part with her; entrusted to my care, I have the will and the power to make her as mine own, and save one Heretic, at least. I know my power, and will exert it for our cause.' Says the monk: 'Dear Child! the labours of the faithful claim their due regard. That thou hast laboured to promote our cause, full well I know, and have my brethren well informed. Emancipation is at hand, and all *depends on thee*.'

But the best print is 'THE GUARDIAN ANGEL. The print taken from the Rev. Mr. Peter's sublime Idea of an Angel conducting the Soul of a Child to Heaven.' Mrs. Fitzherbert, with an apron full of 'play things,' such as rosaries, monstrances, thuribles, service-books, etc., is the angel, who, ascending from the Pavilion at Brighton, with Miss Seymour in her arms, points to an altar surrounded by lighted candles, flowers, etc., and surmounted by a Virgin and Child. All round are cherubs—Fox, Sheridan, Earl of Derby, etc., all friends of the Prince.

We learn the following from a newspaper cutting in 1805:

'On Friday and Saturday, the Prince, attended by Col. Leigh and Col. Hanger, rode for several hours.

Soon after six o'clock, on the former evening, his Royal Highness, in his carriage, left the Pavilion to dine with the Marchioness of Downshire, at Westfield Lodge. Among the *elegantes* present, on this occasion, were, Lord and Lady Harrington, the beautiful and accomplished Lady Ann Maria Stanhope, Mrs. Fitzherbert, Baron Eben, Col. Hanger, Col. Leigh, etc., forming, on the whole, a select and sociable party of fourteen. About nine o'clock, the Prince, the Marchioness, and the whole of her guests from Westfield Lodge, removed to the Pavilion, where a most splendid entertainment, consisting of a ball and supper, etc., was given by the Prince, and of which the greater part of the most distinguished persons, here at present, partook, in number somewhat exceeding one hundred and sixty. . . . On the night following (Saturday) it being the natal day of the interesting little *protégée* of Mrs. Fitzherbert, Miss Seymour, this young lady gave a ball and supper to a party of juvenile nobility, at the Pavilion.'

The Prince's birthday in 1806 was celebrated at Brighton with great festivity.

'*Aug.* 12.—At the Pavilion dinner yesterday, the Prince entertained five of his Royal brothers, the Dukes of York, Clarence, Kent, Sussex, and Cumberland. Of the splendid party were also the Duke of Orleans, M. Beaujolais, the Marquis of Winchester, Count Stahremberg, Mr. Sheridan, Colonels Turner and Lee, etc. This being the natal day of the Heir apparent, the morning was ushered in by the ringing of bells, and the flag was hoisted on the tower of the church. Two oxen, *pro bono publico*, are roasting whole, on the Level. Such an agreeable bustle as this town at present exhibits, was never witnessed here before. Business is totally given up, and pleasure is the standing order of the day. At ten o'clock a.m., the *Otter* sloop of war, decorated with the colours of all nations, hoisted the Royal Standard at the main, and announced the event by a discharge of her guns. The *Gallant* and *Calypso*, armed brigs, and Earl Craven's yacht, were, also, dressed out with colours. About this time, the Carabineers from Shoreham, and the Fourth Dragoons, passed to the north and south of the town for the Downs. The Artillery, the King's Dragoons, and the Nottingham and South Gloucestershire Militias were under arms as early as four o'clock in the morning. At half past twelve, the Prince of Wales, habited as a Field Marshal, a star at his breast, accompanied by his Royal brothers, and a numerous suite of noblemen, etc., and mounted on a grey charger, splendidly caparisoned, left the Pavilion for the Downs. The Royal brothers were all in regimentals, with stars at their breasts. The Duke of Sussex wore his Highland uniform. The Earl of Moira, General White, Count Beaujolais, Lord E. Somerset, the Earl of Barrymore, etc., were in the Prince's suite. Lady Haggerstone, and Miss Seymour, the Lord Chanceller, Lord Headfort, Mr. Sheridan, and Mrs. Smith were in the Prince's landau. Mrs. Fitzherbert was detained at home by indisposition.

'As soon as the Royal cavalcade was distinguished by the military on the Downs, signal guns were discharged, and every necessary adjustment was, in an instant, made for its reception. The Royal party now advanced, and passed down the centre of the line, each regiment saluting,

and the bands alternately playing " God save the King."
Having reached the extremity of the line, the cavalcade
turned back, and the Commander in Chief and staff,
took their stations in the centre of the line, the Prince
and the other Royal Dukes facing them. The whole
line now saluted the Prince. This ended, the line passed
the Prince, in review order, to slow time ; the bands of
each regiment wheeling off, and playing until the regiment to which they were attached, had gone by. The
regiments again passed in quick time, the Duke of York,
etc., having stationed themselves by the Prince of Wales.
The line was again formed, when a *feu de joie* was fired
in a very capital style. Huzzas and "God save the King"
concluded the proceedings, this day, on the hill, when
a signal was hoisted at the Telegraph, for the shipping
to salute, which was instantly obeyed ; and every house
in the town was shaken by the explosion. The Princes
returned to the Pavilion about half past three o'clock.
At six, all the splendour and fashion of Brighton were
assembled to dine at the Pavilion.

' *Tuesday Evening*.—The crowd on the Level in
number are many thousands ; and his Royal Highness's
butcher, Russell, habited in a white jacket, the sleeves
ornamented with buff and blue ribbons, and a blue sash
containing the words " Long live the Royal Brothers,"
with a white apron, and steel, and a fanciful cap to
correspond, has just given the signal for the grand carver
to do his duty. The acclamations of the multitude are
deafening, and all, now, is confusion, expectation and joy.
The Nottingham Militia, whose encampment adjoins
the public kitchens, are busy actors in this scene. They
distinguish themselves manfully, and many a heavy joint,

after severe struggles for victory, is borne by them, triumphantly, to their tents. Amongst the splendid party at the Pavilion are, the six Royal Brothers, the Lord Chancellor, Earl Moira, Count Beaujolais, Mr. Sheridan, Mr. Tierney, with a numerous assemblage of persons, the most distinguished for their rank and talents. Two bands of music, the Prince's own, and the South Gloucester, play alternately on the Lawn. The Steyne is crowded with pedestrians. The town is generally illuminated ; Pollard's and Donaldson's libraries have, both, a very brilliant appearance. The Theatre, Fisher's lounge, Mr. Russell's, the Old Ship, the New Inn, the Coach Offices, Blaker's, Alexander's, and the greater part of the houses at the bottom of North Street, are, also, lit up in a very radiant style.

'At ten o'clock, the Princes and the whole of the Royal dinner party left the Pavilion, for the ball at the Castle. The rooms had a good show of company as early as half past eight, but, towards nine, they began to arrive in crowds. Carriages with four and six horses rattled through the town from Worthing, Rottingdean, Lewes and Eastbourne. Before ten o'clock, not less than four hundred persons were present ; and, before eleven, the assemblage had received an addition of two hundred, at least. The crowd occasioned heat, and many ladies nearly fainted, though every possible precaution was taken to prevent it.

'When the Royal Brothers entered the ball room, the band (the Prince's) struck up, "God save the King," all the company standing until they had passed down the room. All the rank, elegance, fashion and beauty in Sussex were present. A few minutes subsequent to the arrival of the Princes, dancing commenced with the *Honey Moon*. About fifty couple stood up; who led off, it was impossible correctly to ascertain. This dance was succeeded by *Lord Macdonald's reel;* at the end of which, about half an hour after midnight, the Prince and his Royal brothers removed to the supper rooms: tables were laid in three separate rooms, but the company was so numerous, that many could not be accommodated with seats; and, consequently, *sans* refreshment, they were compelled to remain in the ball room. The tables were decorated with every delicacy of the season. The ladies were dressed in an unusual style of elegance ; such a rich display of diamonds we never saw at a public entertainment before, and such a fascinating display of beautiful women, in one house, was not to be found, perhaps, in any other part of the world. The Princes were all in regimentals, and all appeared in high health and spirits. The attention paid by those illustrious personages to the company was highly flattering. They entered into conversation with all they knew ; and the ladies were highly gratified with the marked attention which was so peculiarly bestowed upon them ; and all ultimately retired, highly gratified with the entertainment they had received.'

My readers must pardon my introducing an episode unconnected with this book, except as regards Brighton ; but it is so curious that I cannot refrain. It is chronicled in the *Annual Register* for 1806 :

' *Oct.* 25.—Among the personages who lately attracted public notice at Brighton, was an original, or *would be* original, generally known by the appellation of THE GREEN MAN. He dressed in green pantaloons, green waistcoat, green frock, green cravat : and, though his ears, whiskers, eyebrows, and chin were powdered, his countenance, no doubt, from the reflection of his clothes, was also green. He ate nothing but greens, fruits and vegetables ; had his rooms painted green, and furnished with green sofa, green chairs, green tables, green bed, and green curtains. His gig, his livery, his portmanteau, his gloves and his whip were all green. With a green silk handkerchief in his hand, and a large watch chain with green seals, fastened to the green buttons of his green waistcoat, he paraded every day on the Steine.

'This morning, at six o'clock, this gentleman leaped from the window of his lodging, on the south parade, into the street, ran thence to the verge of the cliff nearly opposite, and threw himself over the precipice, to the beach below. The height of the cliff whence he precipitated himself, is about 20 feet perpendicular. From the general demeanour of the above gentleman, it is supposed he is deranged. His name, we understand, is Henry Cope, and that he is related to some highly distinguished families.'

There were some contemporary verses on Mr. Cope :

' A spruce little man in a doublet of *green*,
  Perambulates, daily, the streets and the Steyne.
  Green striped is his waistcoat, his small clothes are *green*,
  And, oft, round his neck a green 'kerchief is seen.
  Green watch string, green seals, and, for certain, I've heard,
  (Tho' they're powdered) *green* whiskers, and eke a *green* beard ;
  Green garters, *green* hose, and, deny it who can,
  The Brains, too, are *green*, of this little green man.'

Another account of him says :
' Mr. Cope, at four o'clock, walked on the Steyne ;

he wore a huge cocked hat, with gold tassels. He was surrounded with company, who expressed their surprise at the size of his hat: when he answered that he was then performing a different character from that of the preceding day. He is the gaze of Brighton.'

In 1807 the Princess Charlotte was staying at Worthing, and paid a surprise visit to the good folks of Brighton.

'*July* 27.—About eight o'clock yesterday evening, an open barouche, with four horses, halted for a few minutes nearly opposite to the Pavilion, and, shortly afterwards, it was ascertained that the carriage contained the Princess Charlotte of Wales. The carriage at length moved for the Buff and Blue houses, and, afterwards, down the North and South Parades, followed by an immense confluence of people, anxious to obtain a view of the interesting blossom of royalty. As if to gratify the populace, the carriage moved but slowly, and, on the North Parade, it again halted for a few moments. Her Royal Highness was habited in a very plain and simple style, white frock and slouch straw hat. She appeared in charming health, and much pleased with the respectful notice she obtained. Her extreme likeness to her Royal parent was loudly spoken of, and, on that subject, there could be but one opinion. Her Royal Highness, prior to her arrival here, yesterday, had paid a visit to Lewes. She returned from hence to Worthing.'

The Prince liked to spend his birthdays at Brighton, and 1807 was no exception. Here is a contemporary account of the festivities :

'*Aug.* 12.—His Royal Highness the Prince of Wales's birthday was announced, this morning, by the ringing of bells, and every demonstration of joy: colours were hoisted on the church. The gun brig, the Strenuous, and Earl Craven's boat, were dressed in national colours, and placed in a situation to be seen from the Pavilion. By eight o'clock, the whole town was in motion, the Marine Parade was lined with company, the balconies were full of beauty and fashion, and all the telescopes were in use. At ten o'clock, the gun brig fired a royal salute, which was answered by Earl Craven's boat. His Royal Highness the Prince of Wales's band, in full uniform, played on the lawn in front of the Pavilion; and, on the outside of the railing, the carriages formed a complete line, the ladies sitting on the boxes, surrounded by a vast number of gentlemen on horseback, viewing the lawn in front of the Pavilion, where all the Royal Dukes were walking.

'At eleven o'clock, her Royal Highness the Princess Charlotte of Wales arrived at the Pavilion from Worthing, in one of her Royal father's carriages, drawn by four beautiful bays. Her Royal Highness was dressed in white muslin, trimmed with point lace, Vandyked at the edges, and wore a Leghorn gipsy hat, with wreaths of small roses round the edge of the leaf, and a second row round the crown. Her Royal Highness looked most charmingly, and was received at the grand entrance by her Royal father and uncles, who conducted her to the Chinese apartment, with which she appeared greatly delighted. The Pavilion was surrounded on all sides by a most numerous concourse of spectators, who waited anxiously to see the Royal party proceed to the ground, where the grand review was to take place.

' At twelve o'clock, a Royal salute was fired from the batteries; and, immediately after, two of the Royal carriages came out, the first, drawn by four bays, with two postilions dressed in blue striped jackets, and brown beaver hats; in this carriage were Viscount and Viscountess Melbourne, Lord Erskine, and Mr. Dalmy; in the second, her Royal Highness, the Princess Charlotte of Wales, attended by the Dowager Lady De Clifford, and another lady; the carriage was drawn by six fine bay horses; after which, followed his Royal Highness the Prince of Wales, mounted on a beautiful iron grey charger. His Royal Highness was most superbly dressed in the hussar uniform, and wore a diamond belt, with a diamond crown on his breast: the feather in his cap was most superb, encircled with diamonds round the bottom, and fixed in a diamond loop: never did we witness his Royal Highness in better health and spirits. The accoutrements of his charger were most superb. They proceeded slowly to the ground, where the troops were formed in a line, which was on the beautiful hills at the four mile course, which command a grand view of the sea.

' At within half a mile from the ground, his Royal Highness the Duke of York galloped up to the line, extended upwards of a mile, and passed them without any form. At half past twelve the whole of the Royal party arrived on the ground, and took their station in the centre of the line; her Royal Highness the Princess Charlotte of Wales's carriage stood just behind her Royal father. As soon as the party had taken their

station, a royal salute of twenty one guns was fired from
the horse artillery ; the ranks formed into open order,
when the Royal party went down the front of the line,
returned by the rear, and retook their station in the
centre, when the whole of the line passed in ordinary
and quick time, the different bands playing " God save
the King." Some ships passing at the time, received
signals from the telegraph ; they immediately fired a
Royal salute, and hoisted a Royal Standard.

' There was, also, a sham fight on the sea with small
boats, which had a very pretty effect. The day was
uncommonly fine, and not one accident occurred to damp
the joy manifested on this happy occasion. A good
deal of mirth was occasioned by the firing, several of
the horses that had been taken from the carriages,
having broken loose, and run in all directions, leaving
many of the company fixed in their carriages until the
horses were caught.

' At half past three the Royal party returned to the
Pavilion, where the Prince of Wales's band was playing
to receive them. Her Royal Highness, the Princess
Charlotte of Wales, after partaking of some refresh-
ments, walked on the lawn with her Royal uncles, who
seemed to vie with each other in attention to her. The
Duke of Cambridge danced with her on the lawn, and at
six o'clock she returned to Worthing. At eight o'clock
the Royal party, the Duke of St. Albans, the Marquis
of Headford, Earls Berkeley, Craven, Dursley, Bathurst
and Barrymore, Viscount Melbourne, Lords Petersham,
Erskine, and Charles, Edward and Arthur Somerset,
and several military officers, sat down to dinner. The
Pavilion was most brilliantly lighted, and the South

Gloucester band played on the Steyne. The illuminations were splendid. The Prince attended the ball at
the Castle in the evening, which was crowded with
fashion and beauty, but none of the Royal party joined
in the dance. The supper was of the first description,
but would have been better enjoyed had the company
been less numerous. The Prince retired at an early
hour.'

CHAPTER XVII.

Final rupture between the Prince and Mrs. Fitzherbert—That
lady and William IV.—Her kindly relations with the Royal
Family—Her death—The King's illness—The Regency—
Visitors at the Pavilion — Queen Charlotte there — The
'Royal Rantipoles.'

HE episode of Miss Seymour indirectly
led to the final separation of the Prince
and Mrs. Fitzherbert, which was mainly
brought about by her false friend, Lady
Hertford.   Lord Stourton, speaking of
the Mary Seymour incident, says :

'This long negotiation, in which the Prince was the
principal instrument, led him, at last, to those confidential relations which, ultimately, gave to Lady Hertford, an ascendancy over him, superior to that possessed
by Mrs. Fitzherbert herself; and, from a friend, converted her into a successful rival.   Lady Hertford,
anxious for the preservation of her own reputation,
which she was not willing to compromise with the
public, even when she ruled the Prince with the most

absolute sway, exposed Mrs. Fitzherbert, at this time,
to very severe trials, which, at last, almost, as she said,
ruined her health and destroyed her nerves. Attentions
were required from her towards Lady Hertford herself,
even when most aware of her superior influence over
the Prince, and these attentions were extorted by the
menace of taking away her child. To diminish her
apparent influence in public, as well as in private, was
now the object. When at Brighton, the Prince, who
had passed part of his mornings with Mrs. Fitzherbert
on friendly terms at her own house, did not even
notice her in the slightest manner at the Pavilion on
the same evenings, and she, afterwards, understood
that such attentions would have been reported to her
rival.

' She was frequently on the point of that separation
which afterwards took place, but was prevented by the
influence of the Royal Family from carrying her resolution into effect. A dinner, however, given to
Louis XVIII.[1] brought matters, at last, to a conclusion ; and, satisfied of a systematic intention to degrade
her before the public, she then, at last, attained the
reluctant assent of some of the members of the Royal
Family, to her determination of finally closing her connection with the Prince, to whom, in furtherance of this
decision, she never, afterwards, opened the doors of her
house. Upon all former occasions, to avoid etiquette
in circumstances of such delicacy as regarded her own
situation with reference to the Prince, it had been
customary to sit at table, without regard to rank.

---

[1] On June 19, 1811.

Upon the present occasion, this plan was to be altered, and Mrs. Fitzherbert was informed, through her friends at Court, that, at the Royal table, the individuals invited were to sit according to their rank.

'When assured of this novel arrangement, she asked the Prince, who had invited her with the rest of his company, where she was to sit. He said, " You know, Madam, you have no place." " None, Sir," she replied, " but such as you choose to give me." Upon this, she informed the Royal Family that she would not go. The Duke of York, and others, endeavoured to alter the preconcerted arrangement, but the Prince was inflexible ; and, aware of the peculiar circumstances of her case, and the distressing nature of her general situation, they no longer hesitated to agree with her, that no advantage was to be obtained by further postponement of her own anxious desire to close her connection with the Prince, and to retire once more into private life. She told me, she often looked back with wonder that she had not sunk under the trials of those two years.

'Having come to this resolution, she was obliged, on the very evening, or on that which followed the Royal dinner, to attend an assembly at Devonshire House, which was the last evening she saw the Prince previously to their final separation. The Duchess of Devonshire, taking her by the arm, said to her, " You must come and see the Duke in his own room, as he is suffering from a fit of the gout, but he will be glad to see an old friend." In passing through the rooms, she saw the Prince and Lady Hertford in a *tête-à-tête* conversation, and nearly fainted under all the impressions which then rushed upon her mind; but, taking a glass of water, she recovered, and passed on.[1]

'Thus terminated this fatal, ill-starred connection, so unfortunate, probably, for both the parties concerned. Satisfied as I was with the very full explanation of all the circumstances, and of the propriety, and almost necessity of the course which Mrs. Fitzherbert was compelled to pursue, I yet felt, that her intimate relations with the Prince might have imposed upon her some duties during his last illness, the non-fulfilment of which would have left my mind not fully satisfied. I, therefore, again availed myself of the confidence which had been so repeatedly urged upon me, to inquire of her, whether any communication had taken place previous to his demise. She told me " Yes," and that she would show me the copy of a letter which she had written to the King, a very short time before his death, which, she said, had been safely delivered by a friendly hand; the person assuring her, that the King had seized it with eagerness, and placed it immediately under his pillow; but, that she had not received any answer. She was, however, informed that, on the few last days of his life, he was very anxious to be removed to Windsor Cottage.

[1] On June 1, 1812, *Town Talk* published a satirical print, Worse and Worse, or the Sports of the 19th Century.' Mrs. Fitzherbert and Lady Hertford are playing at shuttlecock with the Prince of Wales's feathers. Mrs. F. says, ' This shuttlecock is too light for me. I'll have no more to do with it.' Lady H. calls out, ' You have play'd with it till you are tired, but it suits me to a nicety ; the game's mine. Y—h, take care of the shuttlecock.' Lord Yarmouth, who is behind Mrs. F., says, ' O yes, Ma'am, I'll take care of the shuttlecock, I warrant you.'

' " Nothing," she said, " had so cut her up," to use her own expression, as not having received one word in reply to that last letter. It is true, she observed, that she had been informed by the Duke of Wellington, that he, more than once, expressed his anxiety that a particular picture should be hung round his neck, and deposited with him in the grave ; and it seemed to be the opinion of his Grace, that this portrait was one which had been taken of her in early life, and was set round with brilliants. It appeared the more likely, as this portrait was afterwards missing when the others were returned to her. The copy of the letter, which, in answer to my question, she went into her bedroom to fetch, she put into my hands to read. It was an expression of her fears that the King was very ill, and an affecting tender of any services she could render him, in a strain which I could not read without sympathising deeply in her distress.

'Soon after his death, she left town for Brighton. There, she, a second time, received the kindest messages from William the Fourth ; but, upon his inquiry, why she did not come to see him, she stated the peculiar difficulties of her situation, and a wish, if it was not asking too much from his condescension, that he would graciously honour her with a personal communication at her own house, previously to her visit to the Pavilion.

'The King complied with her request, without delay, and she told him that she could not, in her present circumstances, avail herself of the honour of waiting upon his Majesty, without asking his permission to place her papers before him, and requesting his advice upon them.   Upon her placing in his hands the Documents which have been preserved, in justification of her character, and, especially, the certificate of her marriage, and another, and most interesting paper, this amiable Sovereign was moved to tears by their perusal, and expressed his surprise at so much forbearance with such Documents in her possession, and under pressure of such long and severe trials.   He asked her what amends he could make her, and offered to make her a Duchess.   She replied, that she did not wish for any rank; that she had borne through life the name of Mrs. Fitzherbert ; that she had never disgraced it, and did not wish to change it; that, therefore, she hoped his Majesty would accept her unfeigned gratitude for his gracious proposal, but that he would permit her to retain her present name.

' " Well, then," said he, " I shall insist upon your wearing my livery," and ended by authorising her to put on weeds for his Royal brother.   He added, " I must, however, soon see you at the Pavilion "; and, I believe, he proposed the following Sunday, a day on which his family were more retired, for seeing her at dinner, and spending the evening at the Pavilion.   " I shall introduce you myself to my family," said he, " but you must send me word of your arrival."

' At the appointed hour, upon her reaching the Pavilion, the condescending monarch came himself and handed her out of her carriage, and introduced her to his family, one after the other, as one of themselves. He, ever after, treated her in the same gracious manner, and, on one occasion, upon her return from Paris, made her a present of some jewels, which he said he had had some time, but would not send them to her abroad, as he wished to give them to her himself, on her return to England. He afterwards entered into conversation on matters relating to her dearest interests, and to sanction the custody of such papers as were thought most available in support of her honour and fair reputation with posterity.

'Mrs. Fitzherbert told me that, the first day, when, in compliance with the commands of the King, she went to the Pavilion, and was presented by him to the Queen and Royal Family, she was, herself, much surprised at the great composure with which she was able to sustain a trial of fortitude which appeared so alarming at a distance; but she believed the excitement had sustained her. It was not so the next dinner at which she was present in the same family circle; and the many reflections which then oppressed her mind, very nearly overpowered her. Afterwards, she frequently attended the King's small Sunday parties at Brighton, and then, as upon all other occasions, she was received with uniform kindness and consideration.

'Many letters of hers, even when writing from abroad to fight off her marriage, had been preserved by the King. Some were in the possession of Sir William Knighton,[1] who had obtained possession of the King's correspondence, either as being his executor, or from having Colonel MacMahon's letters in his custody. She had, also, various letters of her own, from the Prince. It was, therefore, agreed, by the friends of both parties, that, with a few exceptions, the whole correspondence should be destroyed.

[1] Physician-in-ordinary to George IV.

'In this arrangement, William the Fourth kindly concurred, and it was carried into effect; only such papers being preserved as Mrs. Fitzherbert thought fit to select to bear witness to her character.

*   *   *   *   *

'Upon one memorable exception, only, she was called upon by the Prince; and, indeed, expressly sent for to Brighton, to give her opinion on a step of great political importance which he was about to take, but her influence, then, had been, some time, on the wane. He told her that he had sent for her to ask her opinion, and that he demanded it of her, with regard to the party to which he was about, as Regent, to confide the administration of the country. At his commands, she urged in the most forcible manner that she was able, his adherence to his former political friends. Knowing all his engagements to that party, she used every argument and every entreaty to induce him not to sever himself from them. "Only retain them, Sir, six weeks in power. If you please, you may find some pretext to dismiss them at the end of that time; but do not break with them without some pretext or other." Such was her request to him. He answered, "It was impossible, as he had promised"; but, at the same time, she observed that he seemed much overpowered by the effort it cost him. Finding that resistance to a determination so fixed was unavailing, she asked to be allowed to return to Brighton, which she did; but, previously to leaving him, she said that, as he had done her the honour of imposing upon her his commands of freely declaring her sentiments upon this occasion, she hoped he would permit her, before she left him, to offer one suggestion, which she trusted he would not take amiss.

'She then urged upon him, as strongly as she was able, the disadvantages which must accrue to his future happiness from treating his daughter, the Princess Charlotte, with so little kindness. "You, now, Sir," she said, "may mould her at your pleasure, but, soon, it will not be so; and she may become, from mismanagement, a thorn in your side, for life." "That is your opinion, Madam," was his only reply.

'I must, here, also add that, not only with the Royal Family, but, also, with the Princess Caroline, Mrs. Fitzherbert was always on the best terms. As to the Princess Charlotte, Mrs. Fitzherbert said, the Prince was much attached to her for some years; indeed, he was generally fond of children and young people, and it was only when the Princess Charlotte became the subject of constant altercation betwixt him and those who took part with Queen Caroline, that he, at last, began to see her with more coolness. Upon one occasion, Mrs. Fitzherbert told me, she was much affected by the Princess Charlotte throwing her arms round her neck, and beseeching her to speak to her father, that he would receive her with greater marks of his affection; and she told me that she could not help weeping with this interesting child.'

She spent the latter part of her life almost entirely at Brighton, beloved by the townsfolk for her goodness and charity, and whilst she lived her servants invariably wore the Royal livery. She died in 1837, and was buried in the Old Catholic Church[1] at Brighton, where a hand-

---

[1] St. John the Baptist in Upper St. James's Street.

some monument was erected to her memory by the Hon.
Mrs. Lionel Dawson Damer, whom we have known as
Miss Mary Seymour.   It bears the following inscription :

'In a vault near this spot, are deposited the remains of
Maria Fitzherbert.   She was born on the 26th July,
1756, and expired at Brighton, on the 29th March, 1837.
One, to whom she was more than a parent, has placed
this monument to her revered and beloved memory, as a
humble tribute of her gratitude and affection.'

On her wedding-finger are three rings, in allusion to
her three marriages.

The Prince was more or less at Brighton in 1808,
1809, and 1810, when came the death of the Princess
Amelia, and the mental aberration of the poor old King.
On February 11, 1811, the Prince of Wales was sworn in
as Regent, and for the next two or three years Brighton
saw little of him ; only the Pavilion was always growing
bigger.   Marlborough House was purchased, in 1812,
for £9,000, and in 1813 a series of improvements and
additions were made, which lasted till 1818.   In 1814
the King of Prussia and the Emperor of Russia came
to England on a visit—the former, in passing through
Brighton, spending ten minutes at the Pavilion for
refreshment, and the latter going all over it, besides
walking on the Steine.

Queen Charlotte paid a visit to the Prince Regent at
the Pavilion on October 24, 1814, accompanied by the
Princesses Elizabeth and Mary, and they stopped until
the 29th, visiting, during their stay, various parts of
the town, and expressing themselves much satisfied
with the situation and appearance of the place, and the
general respectability and conduct of the inhabitants.

Before her Majesty left the town, she ordered £50 to be distributed among the poor, and became the patroness of the Dollar Society for their relief, towards which both she and the Princesses liberally subscribed.

They paid another visit to Brighton the next year, as the *Gentleman's Magazine* for 1815 records :

'*Brighton.   Dec.* 14.—Her Majesty and the two Princesses arrived on a visit to the Prince Regent, at the Pavilion. The principal inhabitants, having received permission, went to Patcham, dressed in buff and mounted, to escort her Majesty ; a dutiful address was presented on the occasion, to which her Majesty returned a gracious verbal answer. Her Majesty, on entering Brighton, seemed to be highly pleased with the attention paid her, and repeatedly bowed to the gentlemen who escorted her. The Prince Regent remained from three o'clock until the arrival of his august mother, outside the gate of the Pavilion, with the Duke of Clarence and several of the nobility, to receive the Queen and Princesses.—On the 16th, her Majesty, accompanied by the Duke of Clarence, with the two Princesses, in a carriage, passed through the principal streets of the town, notwithstanding the dampness of the atmosphere, and was every where received with the most marked respect and homage.'

It was of this visit that the following satire[1] (believed to have been written by C. F. Lawler) was penned. I can only give a portion, as it is too long ; but I give it, as it exhibits the popular belief of the doings at the Pavilion :

[1] 'Royal Rantipoles ; or the Humours of Brighton.' A poem, by Peter Pindar, Esq. ; London, 1816, 8vo.

'Royal Rantipoles.

' " I'll stick to state affairs no more,
　　But banish toil and sorrow ;
So order, Mac,[1] my coach and four
　　And we'll away to-morrow.

' " Of Rhenish take an ample store ;
　　Be careful how you pack it ;
My whiskers, too, my hearty cock ;
　　And eke my shooting jacket.

' " I mean to pass a month or so,
　　'Midst rural scenes so pleasant ;
In waging war with buck and doe,
　　With partridge, hare and pheasant.

' " The pockets of the coach well cram
　　With brandy, gin and carraway
That we may take a social dram,
　　When snugly riding far away."

' Thus spake the Prince, a demi-god,
　　The pink of earthly Regents,
Who shakes three nations with his nod,
　　And bows them to obedience.

*　　　　*　　　　*　　　　*　　　　*

' Thro' Brighton streets the carriage rolls,
　　Loud greeted by the million,
Who, crowding thick as herring shoals,
　　Block'd up the gay Pavilion.

' Now from his carriage Cæsar hopp'd,
　　(No second Master Ellar[2])
Just like a butt of porter dropp'd
　　Into an alehouse cellar.

---

[1] Colonel MacMahon, the Regent's Privy Purse.
[2] A famous equestrian at Astley's Amphitheatre.

' Then happy Cæsar cry'd " Huzza !
  As sure as thou'rt a sinner,
Since here we are, Mac, here we'll stay,
  And eat our Christmas dinner.

' " And we will sport and feast away,
  In one unbroken revel ;
Venus all night, and wine all day,
  We'll play the very devil."

*   *   *   *   *

' The next day came a group of lords,
  And eke of ladies plenty ;
Deck'd out in jewels, wigs and swords,
  Of each not less than twenty.

' High at the head of this gay throng
  Shone mighty Cæsar's mother ;
And, like a pine, the shrubs among,
  Stood Y—k, his favourite brother.

' And brother K—t, too, shew'd his face ;
  And Austria's budding roses,[1]
To swell th' attractions of the place,
  Thrust in their royal noses.

' And Cæsar's glorious sisters came,
  Each like a butter firkin,
A round, unwieldy, greasy dame,
  With visage gay and smirking.

' And H——d,[2] too, the prince of peers,
  The monarch of the stables.
Who, like a glutton leech, for years
  Had suck'd the royal tables.

' And H——d's frisky Mar——ss,[2]
  The very pink of beauty,
Came, Cæsar's banquet to caress,
  And pay her humble duty.

---

[1] The Archdukes John and Lewis, who spent a few days at
Brighton with the Prince.

[2] Marquess and Marchioness of Hertford.

' And then came quibbling Cast——gh,[1]
  And C——h's proud spousy ;[1]
And placemen green, and placemen grey,
  And many a Lady Blowsy.

' But sure some dire mishap befel
  Red-headed Whiskerandos,[2]
Or frolick'd he with wanton belle,
  In that fam'd street call'd *Chandos?*

' Or had he some contusion gain'd
  While at the Fives court sparring ?
Or, murky thought ! a scratch obtain'd
  In some domestic jarring ?

' No, truth to tell, for truth will out,
  Cæsar and this hot stager,
Had quarrell'd, as the thing fell out,
  About some trifling wager.

' Says Redhead, " One to five, this pea
  (And in the fire he cast it) ;
Will bounce against your Grace's knee,
  As soon as fire shall blast it."

' " Done !" Cæsar cry'd.—The hot pea bounc'd,
  Outrageously disloyal,
And with most trait'rous aim it pounc'd
  Against the forehead royal.

' " Knave !" Cæsar roar'd, and Cæsar look'd
  With most prodigious fury ;
And said—" Such pranks shall not be brook'd,
  No, Redhead, I assure ye !"

' Then Redhead swore his Highness jok'd,
  And seem'd but to be fluster'd ;
At which his Grace grew more provok'd,
  And still more loudly bluster'd.

---

[1] Lord and Lady Castlereagh.

[2] Lord Yarmouth, who had red hair and was a notable
bruiser.

' And then he d——d the pea so vile,
  And d——d poor Redhead's folly ;
Whilst he stood staring all the while,
  Quite dumb with melancholy.

' And from that hour, as courtiers say,
  High ran the mutual malice;
Nor was hot Redhead, from that day,
  Seen in the Royal Palace.

    *   *   *   *   *

' Then Cæsar quoth—"My friends, give ear :
  This Christmas, to my thinking,
Is the fit season for good cheer,
  For frolic, fun, and drinking :

' " And, since my Mother will not stay
  A week for recreation,
Our Christmas sports will have, to-day,
  A sweet anticipation :

' " So, pray you, name, some lord or gent,
  How we may all make merry,
How best the moments may be spent,
  How we dull care may bury."

' Then quoth the Q—n, and with her snuff,
  Rais'd thick terrestrial vapours—
" Suppose we play at blindman's buff,
  Or cut some country capers."

' " Faith " (Cæsar cry'd) " catch who catch can,
  I'll do my best endeavour ;
So blind my eyes ; 'ware maid and man,
  And blindman's buff for ever !"

' Queen Dollalolla[1] straightway bound
  Round Cæsar's eyes the linen,
And three times thrice she turn'd him round,
  While all the group sat grinning.

---

[1] According to the novelist Fielding, in his play of 'Tom Thumb,' 1730, Dollalolla was the consort of King Arthur, very fond of stiff punch, but scorning 'vulgar sips of brandy, gin and rum.'

' " Now !" cry'd the Q—n ; and, at the word,
   Off hood-wink'd Cæsar started ;
While lady, from his grope, and lord,
   With cunning archness darted.

' Now, Cæsar's hand profanely press'd
   The bosom of his mother ;
Now, grasp'd this fair one's naked breast,
   Now wandered to another.

' Now, on some lady's carmine cheek,
   His erring fingers lighted,
But not one timid shrug, nor shriek,
   Told that the fair was frighted.

' At length, with am'rous fire, he seized
   Round her white neck, his sister ;
And clasp'd her to his heart, well pleas'd,
   And, still mistaking, kiss'd her.

' And Heaven alone knows when and where
   Had paus'd the panting Cæsar,
But the dame whisper'd in his ear—
   " 'Tis Mary ; pray don't teaze her."

' Then Cæsar quick relax'd his hold,
   And grip'd to find another ;
And, soon, with hand most lewd and bold,
   He clasp'd his wither'd mother.

' But she, too old for am'rous guile,
   For Cupid's conflagration,
Felt his embrace, and stood the while
   Secure from perturbation.

' Yes, like a stock or stone, she stood,
   While naughty Cæsar linger'd,
Her gay attire and attitude,
   Her varying graces finger'd.

'But gay, good temper'd Y—k, just by,
    Felt for his brother's blunder,
And, whisp'ring in his ear, so sly,
    Soon tore the pair asunder.

'"Take care, the belles!" then Cæsar cry'd,—
    "I'll hug 'em if I reach 'em!"
Then Cæsar made a desp'rate stride,
    And caught young Lady B——mp.[1]

'Young Lady B ——mp, strange to tell,
    Was much attached to virtue ;
And scream'd, and Cæsar said, "Sweet belle,
    I'll tickle, but not hurt you."

'And, then, his wicked fingers stray'd
    About the fair one's graces ;
The neck and bosom of the maid,
    And such forbidden places.

'Then, in the maiden's eyes, a tear
    Glisten'd, and seem'd to linger ;
And then, she loudly cry'd "O, dear !"
    And pinch'd the Royal finger.

'But, still, the Royal finger stay'd
    And show'd no signs of flinching ;
But, further in the lab'rinth stray'd,
    In spite of sighs and pinching.

'So high then grew the maiden's fears,
    Lest scandal should traduce her ;
That hard she box'd great Cæsar's ears,
    And called him " *Vile Seducer !*"

'Then, dumb with anger and surprise,
    And not without much reason,
Cæsar unveil'd his royal eyes,
    To see who did the treason.

---

[1] Beauchamp, pronounced 'Beacham.'

'Then Lady B——mp's mother rush'd,
    Nor lords, nor ladies heeding,
And vow'd to Cæsar that she blush'd
    To see the girl's ill breeding.

'But, if his Highness would, for once,
    Benignantly forget her,
She would take home the silly dunce,
    And teach the rustic better.

'Queen Dollalolla interpos'd,
    To wipe off the transgression,
And Cæsar's wounds, at length, were clos'd
    By this most vile concession.'

Then they played at 'hunt the slipper,' and would
have tried forfeits, only none of the gentlemen could be
found with wit enough to invent the penalties, and—

'Now wearied Cæsar call'd for wine,
    And Y— his brother Gracchus,
With Momus cut, and left his shrine,
    To pay his vows to Bacchus.

'The peers, of sport and frolic cur'd,
    Soon put their chairs in motion,
And join'd, by high example lur'd,
    The jolly god's devotion.

'Then rose the dame of mighty mind,
    The graceful Dollalolla,
And walk'd across the room, and sign'd
    The peeresses to follow.

'But whether, as the Frenchman notes,
    They went to closet handy,
To wet their pretty little throats,
    And glut themselves with brandy :

' Or, whether, as the aforesaid saith,
   Adjourning to their houses,
They went to plan their plans of death
   Against their thoughtless spouses :

' Of this, the bard relateth not,
   Nor with the ladies went he, ·
But chose to stay (far happier lot !)
   Where claret flow'd in plenty.

' Now Cæsar at the head took place,
   With Y— and K— beside him ;
And those who said he shew'd no grace,
   Most wofully belied him.

' Quoth he, when in his brain, a rout
   The wine began to kick up,
Tho' lamely hopp'd the language out,
   Delay'd by many a hiccup.

' Quoth he—" Upon my soul, Lord L.,[1]
   You are a funny fellow,
And it would please me vastly well
   If you a song would bellow ;

' " Or, if Lord C.[2] and you will try
   To sing my favourite duet,
I'll dub you dukes before you die,
   So mind and keep me to it."

' Then did Lord C—— most gravely swear,
   For songs he could not hum 'em ;
For sharps and naturals made him stare,
   He could not overcome 'em.

' " And," said Lord L——, " I gravely vow
   By him the blessed Saviour,
I, never, from my youth, could know
   A crotchet from a quaver."

---

[1] Liverpool.   [2] Castlereagh.

16

' Then Cæsar cry'd—" Well, sing in flats,
    I want no grace nor science ;
  And, if you mew like two Tom Cats,
    I'll have a prompt compliance."

' When these two nobles saw 'twas vain,
    To oppose his R——l Highness,
  They pick'd them out a simple strain,
    Suited to birds of shyness.

' The key once pitch'd, they puff'd their cheeks,
    And gave the ears a griper,
  Like the discordant sound that breaks
    From an old Scotch bagpiper.

' But L——l soon got before,
    And C——h jogg'd after,
  While all their friends were in a roar,
    And Cæsar shook with laughter.

' Cry'd Cæsar—" Of your notes be spare,
    A little economic ;
  For though a vastly tragic air,
    Your genius makes it comic.

' " When next, with long, Munchausen hop,
    The Post[1] your praise is ringing,
  Your politics the knave should drop,
    And blazon out your singing."

' Then Cæsar volunteer'd a song,
    And volunteer'd it gaily ;
  And bellow'd out, in cadence strong,
    " Unfortunate Miss Bailey !"

' But, as his voice approach'd the close,
    Its tones began to woddle ;
  The claret fumes so quickly rose,
    While reaching to the noddle.

---

[1] The *Morning Post.*

' Dimly the lights began to burn,
    And care appear'd a bubble,
And ev'ry noble, in his turn,
    Saw wine and glasses double.

' Now Cæsar from his cushion popp'd,
    And none to help were able ;
For, one by one, the whole group dropp'd,
    Like logs, beneath the table.

' And now, God bless all men who breathe,
    And shield the Royal *crania*,
That they may never break beneath
    The Bacchanalian mania.'

CHAPTER XVIII.

The Regent and Admiral Nagle—A quiet time at the Pavilion
—The Regent's extravagance—His yacht—Sham fight and
caricature thereon—A cruise to the French coast—Royal
visitors—The Regent's statues—'High life below stairs,'
etc.—Satirical prints—Closing days—Last appearance at
the Pavilion.

THE Regent was always being satirized by
the publication of some of his own
puerilities, or those of his suite, who, of
course, took their tone from him. The
Brighton Herald is responsible for the
following anecdote :

'A gallant Admiral (Nagle) residing at the Pavilion,
was, a few days since, presented by a certain Great
Personage, with a beautiful milk white mare, which, it
was stated, had just arrived from Hanover. Nothing
was talked of but this fine creature ; and every one
seemed anxious to have her merits put to the test. The
Admiral mounted, tried her in all her paces, and, though
he could but approve, yet he pronounced her to be

greatly inferior to a favourite black mare of his own. The present, however, coming from so high a quarter, was, of course, received with every expression of duty and thankfulness. The long switching tail of the animal not exactly suiting the Admiral's taste, he sent her to a farrier to have it cropped—when, lo! he speedily received intelligence that it was a *false* tail, and that, beneath it appeared a short black one. This curious fact led to a minute inspection, when it was discovered that this *beautiful white Hanoverian horse* was no other than the good humoured Admiral's own *black mare*, which had been painted in a manner to elude his detection.'

This anecdote is probably true, as Captain Gronow ('Reminiscences,' second series, p. 212) tells a similar story, only he changes the venue from Brighton to Carlton House:

'Admiral Nagle was a great favourite of George the Fourth, and passed much of his time with his Majesty. He was a bold, weather beaten tar, but, nevertheless, a perfect gentleman, with exceedingly pleasing manners, and possessed of much good nature and agreeability.

'The late Duke of Cambridge, on one occasion, sent his brother a cream coloured horse from the Royal stud at Hanover, and the King gave the animal to Colonel Peters, the riding master. Admiral Nagle ventured to express a hope that, if his Majesty received a similar present from Hanover, he would graciously make him a present of it; upon which the King replied, " Certainly, Nagle, you shall have one."

'The Admiral was, shortly afterwards, sent to Portsmouth, to superintend the building of the Royal Yacht, during which time Strohling, the fashionable painter of the day, was summoned, and ordered to paint the Admiral's favourite hack, to make it appear like one of the Hanoverian breed. The horse was, accordingly, placed in the riding school, and, in an incredibly short period, the metamorphosis was successfully completed. In due time the Admiral returned from Portsmouth, and, as usual, went to the Royal Stables, and was charmed to see that his Majesty had fulfilled his promise. He lost no time in going to Carlton House to return thanks, when the King said, " Well, Nagle, how do you like the horse I sent you ?" " Very much," was the reply, " but I should like to try his paces before I can give your Majesty a decided opinion about him." " Well, then, let him be saddled, though it does rain, and gallop him round the park and return here, and let me know what you think of him." It rained cats and dogs ; the paint was gradually washed off the horse, to the Admiral's great astonishment, and he returned to Carlton House, where the King and his friends had watched his departure and arrival with the greatest delight. The Admiral was welcomed with roars of laughter, which he took with very great good humour ; and, about a month afterwards, the King presented him with a real Hanoverian horse of great value.'

These Christmas festivities probably produced a fit of gout, which brought the Queen and Princesses, together with the Princess Charlotte, to the Pavilion, on a visit, from January 6, 1816, to January 20—a visit which covered the birthdays of the Princess Charlotte and Her Majesty, both of which were nobly celebrated.

This seems to have been a quiet time at the Pavilion, if we may credit a letter from the Dowager Countess of Ilchester to Lady Harriet Frampton, dated from Cranborne Lodge, February 2, 1816 :[1]

'. . . I must tell you that the fortnight at Brighton has had a very happy effect on Princess Charlotte's health and spirits. . . . You have no idea how her manners are daily softened by witnessing the address of the Queen and Princesses, with whom she went regularly round the circle, paying individual attention to the company, and she looked, really, very handsome, being always elegantly dressed, and every one seemed delighted to have her under her father's roof.

' It certainly was a great satisfaction to the Prince to find it gave so much pleasure to the Princess, for he had been led to suspect she did not like to come—a complete mistake, of which he is now convinced. . . . The Chinese room is gay beyond description, and I am sure you would admire it, as well as the rest of the Pavilion, though the extreme warmth does not suit every one.

' In the morning, all the guests were free from Court restraint, and met only at six o'clock, punctually, for dinner, to the number of between thirty and forty daily ; in the evening, about as many more were invited. A delightful band played till half past eleven, when the Royal family retired, and the rest of the company dispersed, after partaking of sandwiches : the evenings were not in the least formal. As soon as the Queen sat down to cards, every one moved

[1] ' The Journal of Mary Frampton from 1779 to 1846,' 8vo., pp. 264, 265 ; London, 1885.

about as they pleased, and made their own back gammon, chess, or card party, but lounging up and down the gallery was most favoured. All the rooms open into the beautiful gallery, which is terminated at both extremities by the lightest and prettiest Chinese staircases you can imagine, and illuminated by the gayest lanterns. There are mandarins and pagodas in abundance, and plenty of Japanese and Chinese sofas. In the centre of the gallery is a skylight. Each staircase opens into a large room, one of these communicating with the Queen's suite of rooms, and the other with that of the Princess and mine. The effect of the central room is very good. There was a bright fire, and it is supplied with books and newspapers, and from one set of rooms to the other is a private communication.'

Prince Leopold also stopped at the Pavilion for some time previous to his marriage with the Princess Charlotte, which took place May 2, 1816.

In spite of the enormous taxation, the dearness of bread, etc., the extravagances of Florizel knew no bounds. What cared he, so long as every whim and wish of his was gratified, who found the money for it? In three years he had spent £160,000 on furniture for Carlton House; the previous year china cost £12,000, ormolu nearly £3,000, and during three years he owed his silversmith £130,000. He had £100,000 allotted him for an outfit when he came to the Regency; that had to go to pay some of his debts, and Lord Castlereagh was obliged to admit that the Prince's debts amounted to £339,000!

Yet, forsooth, the great baby must have another toy

at the expense of the nation—a yacht, all over gilding. William Hone published a single-sheet broadside (August 26, 1816) with a picture and description of this rococo vessel. Here is his 'DESCRIPTION OF THE REGENT'S NEW GILT YACHT:

'This superb yacht, the *Royal Sovereign*, was launched from Deptford Yard on Thursday, the 8th of August, 1816, having been newly copper bottomed, and entirely new *gilt*, and fitted up throughout.—She is between three and four hundred tons burthen, has three masts, is ship rigged, and is the most splendid vessel, beyond all comparison, ever launched in England. —The bust of his Majesty forms the head, *richly gilt;* surmounted by a canopy, painted crimson, with fringe and tassels in *gold.*—The head rails have carved figures of Peace and *Plenty* (!) which *support* the bust, with a frieze of devices to the bows, carved and *gilt.*—Above the channels is a frieze—boys supporting the Cardinal Virtues, united by festoons of laurel, *all gilt.* The quarter badge, representing the Star and Garter, supported by the Lion and Unicorn, is a complete blaze of *gilding.* The stern is most superbly *gilt*—in the centre of the taffrel is a King's Coat of Arms, supported by Prudence and Fame, carved and *gilt.* Fortitude and Truth are carved at the sides of the stern, richly *gilt.* The lower counter is an emblematical painting, *gilt.* On the right of the rudder is Neptune, drawn by four Sea Horses, a painting, *gilt.* On the left of the rudder is Britannia, pointing to the Arts, a painting, *gilt.* Above the rudder is a Star, presumed to be the Star of Brunswick, as if presiding,—*gilt.* The upper counter is Cupids with laurel, painted and *gilt.* Over the poop

are three magnificent lanterns, in blue and *gold*, with
stars on the top, *gilt*. The quarter deck is separated
from the main deck by a rich carved breast rail, *gilt*.
The sides of the quarter deck are devices painted in
compartments, *gilt*.

'The gallery is fitted up for a kitchen, with steam
boilers and other cooking apparatus. Adjoining it is
the Lord's room, in white, with panel mouldings *gilt*—
the roof supported by fluted pilasters, with Ionic caps,
all *gilt*. The passages are white and *gold*. The roof
of the King's room is panelled mahogany and *gold*; the
sides crimson damask panels, the framings *gold*; twenty
carved emblematical figures, the four Elements, etc., are
on pedestals with Ionic caps of mahogany and *gold*.
Round the rudder case are three beautiful plates of
looking glass, entirely concealing the wood, in frames
to correspond, *gilt*. The Queen's room is fitted up, in
every respect, with the same grandeur as to materials
and *gilding*. The descent to the State rooms is by
a superb mahogany winding staircase, the balustrades
richly carved and *gilt*; the sides panelled with
mahogany and *gold*. The ceilings and doors to the
State rooms are of the finest mahogany, in panels, with
carved borders, richly *gilt*. The doors in the centre
cabin are covered with mirrors. The chairs and sofas
are of crimson damask, in mahogany frames, *gilt*. The
windows are of plate glass, and draw up and down, like
those of a coach, the sides painted a deep vermilion,
the edges *gilt*. To suspend the tables, that they may
swing with the vessel, chains descend from the ceilings,
as if for lamps, elegantly *gilt*. The side windows, one
on each side the stern, are two immense concaves of

plate glass, like mirrors; from each of which, on the outside the vessel, rays diverge, to form a splendid star, superbly *gilt*. The predominant feature of the decorations is *costly gilding*; even the blocks carrying the ladders and the rigging, are fully *gilt*. The vessel has been put in its present state, for the Prince Regent, at an estimated expence of SIXTY THOUSAND POUNDS; the *gilding*, alone, is supposed to have cost nearly *Thirteen Thousand, Five Hundred Pounds!* She now lies off the Dockyard at Deptford, with the workmen on board; and, when completed, will, with the Divine permission, sail to Brighton, for his Royal Highness's use. Her apparatus for roasting, baking, boiling, frying, stewing, broiling, etc., is complete. And it is remarkable that the Cardinal Virtues are amongst the most prominent decorations *outside*.'

This new plaything was at Brighton in the summer of 1817, and we read in a newspaper cutting that:

'On the 10th September, for the Regent's especial delectation, a sham fight took place at sea, immediately off the town, the vessels taking part in it being the *Inconstant* and *Tigris* frigates, the *Grecian* armed schooner, and the *Rosario* brig. The Channel was thickly dotted with packets and pleasure boats, and every species of floating craft, each and all crowded with spectators, anxious to witness the coming conflict; the cliffs from one end of the town to the other were also thronged. The Prince Regent embarked at 10 a.m., and, as soon as the Royal barge was afloat, simultaneous salutes were fired from the ships of war, and were repeated as soon as his Royal Highness was on board his yacht was announced, by the Royal standard being hoisted at the main.

'The order of battle was, that the *Inconstant* and the *Grecian* were to defend the yacht against the designs of the supposed enemy, in the *Tigris* and the *Rosario*. The vessels, respectively, were most skilfully manœuvred, and broadside after broadside sent their rattling reports to land. At length, the escape of the yacht was effected ; but the enemy still stood to their guns. In fact, the conflict between the frigates became still more severe, during which, within pistol shot of each other, many discharges of musketry marked the apparently determined progress of the action. The spectacle was grand, and wrought the feelings of the spectators to the highest pitch. The battle over, which ended in the retreat of the enemy, the *Royal George* stood in, and the whole returned to the roadstead about 2 p.m. In the evening a boat was sent ashore, to announce the Regent's intention of remaining on board all night.'

Apropos of this naval engagement, a humorous print was published in October, 1817, entitled, 'Fun at Sea—the sham fight off Brighton, and the capture of the Knight of the Larder, Privateer, or, the Alderman in Chains.' Alderman Sir William Curtis is brought on board the Regent's yacht a prisoner, bound in chains of sausages,[1] accompanied by sailors bearing turtles, fowls, soup, etc., whilst an officer exhibits a scroll of 'Ammunition Stores taken in the Larder Sloop. Ammunition—500 Forced meat *balls*, 5 Barrels Curry *Powder*, 2 casks

---

[1] A turkey hung round with festoons of sausages is called 'an Alderman in Chains.'

whole Pepper, 200 Bottles Sauce piquant.—Stores—
1 whole Calf, 25 Sheep, 12 dozen Capons, 50 Haunches
of Venison,—Westphalia Hams, 2 cwt. of Sausages,
100 Rounds of Beef, 100 Sir Loins, 150 doz. of
Pigeons, 50 Sucking pigs.' Sir William Curtis is
kneeling, and, offering the Regent a carving knife
and ladle, he says:

> 'Great conqueror, see your captive kneel;
> Your clemency now let him feel!
> Here's all my arms, upon my life,
> My Ladle and my Carving Knife.
> My Vessel Fame "the Larder" calls,
> My Ammunition Forced meat balls,
> My Powder, Curry, whole Pepper, Shot,
> All, by my Capture, going to Pot:
> Then, let me hope you'll grant this Boon,
> *Release me speedily, and soon!*
> I'm bit of a poet, you see, this is rare fun.'

The Regent, looking at him, says, 'What! we have
caught you, have we? and in arms against your
Sovereign! We'll just drench you with grog, and keel-
haul you—and then release you, my old buck. You
love fun!'

Sir William was fond of the sea, and the Whig and
Radical wits were never tired of laughing at the sumptuous fittings of his yacht, in which the Regent often
accompanied him in his cruises. He was very badly
educated, and is said to have been the author of the
famous 'Three R's: Reading, Riting and Rithmetic.'

According to the *Gentleman's Magazine* for 1817,
the Regent had quite a cruise in his new toy:

'*Monday, Sept.* 15.—The Prince Regent arrived last
night at Carlton House from Brighton, having, during

the week, been four days, and three nights at sea! The Prince commenced his aquatic excursions on Monday, when His R.H. remained at sea ten hours; and, on Wednesday, accompanied by Admirals Sir George Campbell, and Sir Edmund Nagle, Lord William Gordon, Sir William Keppel, the Hon. Capt. Paget, and Capt. Horace Seymour, His R.H. embarked in the *Royal George* yacht on a second voyage, under salutes from the *Tigris, Inconstant, Rosario, Grecian, Viper* and *Hound:* and, at half past one, the ships of war went through all the manœuvres of an engagement. At night, the vessels proceeded to sea; and, the next day, they stood over to the coast of France, and were off Dieppe, close in with the land, early on Friday morning; where, communication being had, the yacht and squadron cruised across the Channel again, and reached Brighton at one clock on Saturday, when the Prince landed, regretting that his presence being required in town, he was obliged to disembark.

'His Royal Highness was gratified beyond description, and enjoyed the highest state of health and spirits during the excursion. On disembarking, the Prince presented the Hon. Capt. Paget with a most elegant snuff box, in testimony of his high gratification and esteem; and so ardent and perfect was the pleasure that His R.H. felt, that, among other gracious intimations of his attachment to the Naval service, he said that, if he should land at any other place besides Brighton, it was his intention to wear the full dress uniform of an Admiral, and which he should continue to wear, at his *levées*, alternately with the dress of the army.'

On January 15, 1817, the Grand-Duke Nicholas (afterwards Emperor) of Russia visited the Prince at the Pavilion, and stayed four days.

Directly after the funeral of the Princess Charlotte, who died on November 5, the Prince went to Brighton, and stayed there eleven weeks.

In September, 1818, the Grand-Duke Michael of Russia paid a visit to the Pavilion, which in that month was lit by gas. '*The Brighton Ambulator*,' by C. Wright (*London and Brighton*, 1818) gives a very good description of the Pavilion, and mentions that 'a statue of the Prince of Wales, by Rossi, 7 feet high, on a pedestal 11 feet high, was, in the year 1802, placed in front of the Royal Crescent. The Prince is represented as dressed in his regimental uniform, with his arm extended towards the sea. This statue cost upwards of £300. The likeness is not considered very striking, and, since it has been injured by the loss of one of the arms, it is not even deemed a pleasing ornament.'

In 1821 it was proposed to erect, on some conspicuous spot in the town, a large bronze statue of George IV., and £3,000 was very quickly subscribed for it. For this sum Chantrey agreed to produce it, and pay for the casting; but he made a bad bargain, as it cost nearly double the sum. It was unveiled on October 11, 1828.

The alterations to the Pavilion were not altogether finished; yet the Prince made shift somehow, as he was most certainly there in March, 1819, for we read in the *Times* of March 15:

'ROYAL CONDESCENSION.—We are assured that, a few

nights ago, the PRINCE REGENT, in a merry mood, determined to sup in the kitchen of the Pavilion. A scarlet cloth was thrown over the pavement, a splendid repast was provided, and the good humoured PRINCE sat down, with a select party of his friends, and spent a joyous hour. The whole of the servants, particularly the female part, were, of course, delighted with this mark of condescension (*Brighton Herald*).'

Then the pictorial satirists swooped down upon him, and curious were their different conceptions of the event. I give the one I consider best, as it is the least offensive, and the Regent is so 'royally drunk.' It is by J. R. Cruikshank, and was published on March 25. It is called ' HIGH LIFE BELOW STAIRS ! a new Farce, as lately perform'd at the Theatre Royal, Brighton, for the edification and amusement of the Cooks, Scullions, Dishwashers, Lick trenchers, Shoe blacks, Cinder sifters, Candle snuffers, etc., etc., of that Theatre, but which was unfortunately Damn'd the first night by Common Sense !'

Others are (all in the same month), ' ROYAL KITCHEN STUFF ! or a Great Man *come down* to visit his most Obed[t] humble Servants ! ! ! (vide the amusements of Brighton).' The Prince has a fat cook round the neck, kissing her, and saying, ' Don't be alarmed, my dear ! I only want to see how my private affairs get on below here, so show me your Kitchen Stuff.' The cook, who beats him with a ladle, says, ' La, Sir ! what will the people say when they hear of your meddling so often with things beneath you ? Depend upon it, you'll be call'd over the Coals, and finely roasted for this.' A maid-servant has hold of his coat-tails, and calls out,

HIGH LIFE BELOW STAIRS.

' Baste him well! Give him Goose without Gravy!'
On the floor lie two papers—one, ' Theatre Royal,
Brighton, By Command of the Prince Regent, High
life below Stairs, with Animal Magnetism '; the other is,

> ' When *Bottle the eighth*, I get through,
>   I make love in a style so bewitching,
>   That most female hearts I subdue,
>   From the Drawing-room down to the Kitchen.'

Another is, ' He stoops to Conquer, or the Royal
George *Sunk*. This is not the Royal George that was
sunk at Spithead, this was sunk at Brighton.' A third
is entitled ' Beauties of Grease, or Luxuries of the
Kremlin '; and a fourth is, ' Royal George in the Kitchen,
or High life below Stairs.' The Prince, with a bumper
in his hand, nurses a cook on his knee, to whom he
remarks :

> ' You may baste meat at leisure,
>   It's my will and pleasure
>   Distinctions between you and me,
>   Henceforward shall cease,
>   In love, and in peace,
>   The P—e and his Cook shall agree.'

It would seem, also, that he gave a servants' ball at
Christmas, 1820, at the Pavilion, for there is a satirical
print, published January 24, 1821, called ' Low LIFE
ABOVE STAIRS, *or the Humours of the* Great Baby *at*
B . . . ht . n.' The King is dancing with a fat kitchen-
maid, whilst Lady Conyngham looks on in rage and
wonder.

> ' Releas'd from all the toils of State,
>   From care and sorrow free,
>   The humorous Wag of pond'rous weight,
>   Gives way to mirth and glee.

' " To all the Servants of my house,"
   Said G—e, " I'll give a ball ;
  Haste, mirth and revelry let loose,
   Come forward, one and all.

' " I've supped within my Kitchen range,
   But I'll descend no more ;
  The scene, this night, I'll wholly change,
   Upstairs invite uproar.

' " No virtuous women visit me—
   They dread to lose their name—
  I'll condescend—with those make free
   Who never blush'd with shame.

' " 'Twas wrong when C——c[1] eat, perchance,
   With Vassali and Bergami,
  I'll eat with Cooks, with Scullions dance—
   I can't do wrong, G—d d—n me."

' The Orchestra made noble sport,
   Old Bags,[2] the bag-pipes squeez'd,
  A ricketty Cabinet pianoforte
   Old Sid[3] and L——l[4] teaz'd.

' The R–y–l Host, in livery clad,
   (An honour long design'd her),
  Waltz'd with his scullion, nearly mad,
   To *Terry O, the grinder*.

' Ben Bloomy[5] and the fat old Cook,
   Herself a perfect larder,
  A simple jig together took,
   The tune was *Shave the Barber*.

---

[1] Queen Caroline.   [2] Lord Eldon.
[3] Viscount Sidmouth.   [4] Earl of Liverpool.
[5] Sir Benjamin (afterwards Lord) Bloomfield.

> ' And Cunning-one[1] mov'd not a limb,
>   But stood amazed with wonder !
> To see the K—'s disgraceful whim,
>   And vow'd she'd pull'm asunder.
>
> ' The fiddlers play'd, the dancers scream'd,
>   And all was in commotion ;
> Like waves they roll'd—the noise it seem'd
>   Just like a troubled ocean.
>
> ' Great G—e at supper next attends,
>   Amidst his new compeers ;
> When drunk " Low life above Stairs " ends
>   With thrice three times three cheers.'

In the beginning of January, 1820, the inhabitants of Brighton were allowed, for a fortnight, to visit the Pavilion and view its wonders, as far as it was then completed ; on the 29th of the same month the old King died, and Florizel, then in his fifty-ninth year, succeeded him, as George IV. He came to the Pavilion at the end of February, and stayed at Brighton nearly the whole of March.

A satirical print represents him as being at the Pavilion in November of this year. It is called ' MOMENTS OF PAIN.' The scene is an apartment in the Pavilion, and the surroundings are all Chinese. The King is dressed in full Chinese costume, the great ' Fum ' bird being embroidered on his bosom ; he is very ill, and a physician is feeling his pulse. On the floor lies a huge roll of a ' List of Addresses presented to Caroline, Queen of England,' and an attendant is trying to prevent the entrance of a messenger, who

[1] Lady Conyngham.

brings the news of 'The Bill turned out.' This was the Bill of pains and penalties brought into Parliament against her by Lord Liverpool on July 5, 1820; the trial began on August 19, and the Bill was abandoned on November 18.

The King spent his Christmas at Brighton, and as he was a full-fledged monarch, his ideas expanded as to his country residence, and the assembly-room of the Castle Tavern was absorbed into the building, and converted into a chapel. Then also was arranged the alterations which have made the Pavilion the extraordinary conglomeration of buildings it now is. The chapel was consecrated on January 1, 1822.

He left Brighton in April, went to Scotland in August, and returned to Brighton in October. In January, 1823, he had a terrible attack of gout, and he did not leave the Pavilion till April. Naturally, now that he was King, he had to spend much of his time in London; but he spent the Christmas of 1824 at Brighton, and stayed there till the following February. He never made but one more visit to Brighton—from January 23, 1827, to March 7—and Florizel's stupendous Folly knew him no more.

CHAPTER XIX.

The books by Nash and Brayley on the Pavilion—Description
and history of the building—Its exterior—Entrance hall—
Red Drawing-room.

E left behind him a more abiding monu-
ment of his 'folly' than the building
itself in a magnificent folio volume of
etchings, plain and coloured, a task
which he entrusted to Nash, the archi-
tect, who employed the artistic assistance of Wilks,
Moore, and the elder Pugin, especially the latter, and
it took five years (1820 to 1825) to complete.

I have reserved the description of this building until
the end of my book, because it ended only with the
King's life. The Lord alone knows what it might have
become had he lived longer! And I transcribe the best
description, that of E. W. Brayley,[1] who in the spring

---

[1] 'Illustrations of Her Majesty's Palace at Brighton, formerly
the Pavilion ; executed by command of King George the Fourth,
under the superintendence of John Nash, Esq., architect. To

of 1836 made a careful survey of the Pavilion, which had but very slightly been altered since the death of George IV.

'THE ROYAL PALACE AT BRIGHTON,

'FORMERLY THE PAVILION.

'This Edifice, which, in respect to architectural form, has no parallel in Europe, nor perhaps on the globe, is indebted for its origin to his late Majesty GEORGE THE FOURTH, who, when Prince of Wales, first went to Brighton in the autumn of the year 1782 (?), on a visit to his uncle the late Duke of Cumberland, then residing at his house, near the south end of the Steyne, and not far from the cliff. The consequences of that visit have been extraordinary.

*   *   *   *   *

'The greatly increased and still augmenting prosperity of this town, however, is almost wholly due to the patronage which it received from the late Prince of Wales, who, whilst the guest of his uncle, as above noticed, became so pleased with the situation and air, and the bold, open, and diversified character of the downs and neighbouring country, that he, again, visited Brighton in the following summer, and in the next year (1784) the Prince commenced the erection of the *Marine Pavilion*, now the Royal Palace, for the purpose of forming a distinct and appropriate habitation for himself and suite.

---

which is prefixed a History of the Palace by Edward Wedlake Brayley, Esq., F.S.A.' London, 1838, fol.

'The *éclat* attending the residence of such an illustrious person as the Heir apparent to the Crown, attracted a great resort of company to Brighton, and numerous respectable mansions and rows of houses were quickly built for the accommodation and entertainment of those continually flocking thither. The impulse thus given cannot be said to have yet ceased; and, though the town has been so greatly extended, that it already covers full six times as much ground as when it first engaged the notice of the Prince of Wales, scarcely a year passes without a considerable augmentation, both in the number of its inhabitants, and of its buildings. A still further increase is also contemplated, to which the projected *Railway* from the metropolis (that occasioned so much controversial enquiry during the sitting of Parliament in 1837) is expected essentially to contribute, by the superior accommodation it will afford for speedy intercourse. Having, thus, briefly adverted to the vast change in the state of Brighton, which has resulted from princely patronage and abode, we shall proceed to the immediate object of this work, *viz.*, the description of the Palace itself.

'The *Marine Pavilion*, as it was originally called, was commenced in 1784, under the superintendence of the late Henry Holland Esq^ro, architect, whose professional talents were, afterwards, so eminently displayed by the magnificent Drury Lane Theatre, which was destroyed by fire in February, 1809. In its first state, the Pavilion, as completed by Mr. Holland in 1787, consisted of a circular edifice, attached by semicircular projections to two adjoining buildings, forming wings. The central part (which was crowned by a dome, or cupola, and fronted by an Ionic colonnade and entablature, supporting statues), and the north wing, were new erections, but the south wing was merely altered from the villa which had been first hired for the occasional residence of the Prince of Wales, and was, subsequently, purchased by his Royal Highness. In succeeding years, and, particularly, in 1801 and 1802, additional buildings were raised by the same architect, or, rather, by his pupil, Mr. F. P. Robinson, F.S.A., who was stationed at the Pavilion, and, during Mr. Holland's absence on some mining affairs in Cornwall, had the special direction of the works in progress.

' Whilst the improvements were going on, in the year 1802, several pieces of very beautiful Chinese paper were presented to the Prince, who, for a time, was undecided in what way to make use of them. As the Eating room and the Library, which were between the Saloon and the new Northern wing, were no longer required for their original purposes, Mr. Robinson, on being consulted, advised the Prince to have the partition removed, and the interior formed into a Chinese gallery. This was immediately agreed to ; the walls were hung with the paper described, and the other parts of the Gallery were painted and decorated in a corresponding style. About the same time, the passage room between what was, then, called the Small Drawing Room, and the New Conservatory, or Music room, at the south end of the Pavilion, was constructed in a singular manner. A space was enclosed within it, measuring twelve feet by eight, the sides and upper part of which were entirely formed of stained glass, of an oriental character, and exhibiting the peculiar insects, fruits, flowers, etc., of China. It was illuminated from without; and through it, as through an immense Chinese lantern, the communication was carried on; its effect is stated to have been extremely beautiful. Such, then, were the circumstances under which the Eastern style of decoration was first adopted at the Pavilion; and, soon afterwards, between the years 1803 and 1805, the same principle was extended to its architecture; the new Stables, which were then erected by Mr. William Porden, being considered as designed in the Hindû style.

' Although the Pavilion itself had been much enlarged, and had, recently, undergone extensive alterations, the Prince had still further changes in contemplation; and, in 1805, he issued his commands to Mr. H. Repton (who was much celebrated for his judicious practice in landscape gardening, and had already been employed in improving the grounds at Brighton), to deliver his opinion " concerning what style of architecture would be most suitable for the Pavilion." The result was made known to the Prince early in the ensuing year; and, in the spring of 1808, was communicated to the public in a folio work of much interest, which includes a series of coloured plates of proposed improvements, both in the House and Grounds. Though Mr. Repton's designs in respect to the Pavilion were never carried into effect, the arguments which he employed for giving it an Eastern character, had, doubtless, considerable influence over its present form; a short extract from his work will, therefore, be admissible.

' Mr. Repton ingenuously owns that his knowledge of the various forms of Hindû architecture was derived from communications first made to him by the proprietor of Sesincot, in Gloucestershire (Sir Charles Cockerell, who had been long resident in the interior of India); and, afterwards, corroborated by the accurate sketches and drawings made on the spot by his ingenious friend, Mr. Thomas Daniell. He then says, "Immediately after I had reconciled my mind to the adoption of this new style at Sesincot, I received the Prince's commands to visit Brighton, and there saw, in some degree, realised, the new forms which I had admired in the drawings. I found, in the Gardens of the Pavilion, a stupendous and magnificent building, which, by its lightness, its elegance, its boldness of construction, and the symmetry of its proportions, does credit both to the genius of the Artist, and the good taste of his Royal employer. Although the outline of the Dome resembles rather a Turkish Mosque than the buildings of Hindûstan, yet, its general character is distinct from either Grecian or Gothic, and must both please and surprise every one not bigoted to the forms of either.

' " When, therefore, I was commanded to deliver my opinion concerning the style of architecture best adapted to the additions and Garden front for the Pavilion, I could not hesitate in agreeing that neither the Grecian, nor the Gothic style could be made to assimilate with what had so much the character of an Eastern building. I considered all the different styles of different countries, from a conviction of the danger of attempting to invent anything entirely new. The Turkish was objectionable, as being a corruption of the Grecian ; the Moorish, as a bad model of the Gothic ; the Egyptian, as too cumbrous for the character of a Villa ; the Chinese, too light and trifling for the outside; however it may be applied to the interior; and specimens from Ava were still more trifling and extravagant. Thus, if any known style were to be adopted, no alternative remained, but to combine from the architecture of Hindûstan such forms as might be rendered applicable to the purpose."

'Acting on this principle, Mr. Repton produced the series of drawings which have been referred to; and it is but just to add, that his designs for the Pavilion evince a clearness of conception, and a boldness and accuracy of outline, and combination of forms in the Hindû style, which far surpass the anomalous conceptions that determined the external character of the present edifice.

'The Plan of Brighton, published in 1809, shews that the Pavilion was still in a state of progressive enlargement. Several neighbouring houses had been previously bought, and annexed to the premises, and the whole assumed, in a great measure, the form and arrangement represented by the Ground Plan in Plate I., in which state it remained until the late John Nash, Esqre, architect, commenced his alterations in the year 1817. Those alterations were carried on during a considerable time, under the direct *surveillance* of the Prince himself, whose own facility of invention, and correctness of taste, tended greatly to increase the elegance of the interior. Numerous additions were also made to the buildings, until, at length, about the year 1824, the edifice was completed in the manner in which it now appears. Instead of the plain and humble character of a *Marine* abode, it assumes, in its external architecture, the varied characteristics of an Oriental style, and domes, and

cones, and minarets spring from its roofs to a considerable altitude.

'In the general design of this *unique* edifice, much
fancy is exhibited, and great ingenuity and professional
skill are displayed in the construction of its domes and
conical cupolas; yet there is little in the composition,
exteriorly, that would elicit praise from an admirer of
classic elegance. There is, however, ornament in pro-
fusion, and this, in combination with the singular aspect
of the entire fabric, makes a considerable impression on
the eye, and especially so, if the spectator be unacquainted with the details of classic architecture; this
effect would, doubtless, be stronger, if the Pavilion
stood upon elevated ground. With the exception of
the minarets, pinnacles, and minor ornaments, which
are of Bath stone, nearly the whole building is of brick,
stuccoed.

'The expense of completing and furnishing this
building was very great; and, independently of many
lavish sums issued for those purposes from the Civil
List, upwards of £100,000 was paid from the Privy
purse of its magnificent founder in aid of the charges
for furniture and decorations. On the accession of the
Prince Regent to the Crown, after the decease of his
father, in January, 1820, the Pavilion became a Royal
Palace; and, on his own decease, in 1830, it descended,
together with the succession, to his brother, the Duke
of Clarence, the late King William the Fourth. It,
afterwards, became a favourite residence of this sovereign
(and his now dowager, Queen Adelaide), who passed
some portion of every year there until his death in
June, 1837. During a few weeks in the past autumn,

the Palace was inhabited by his successor, VICTORIA, her present Majesty; WHOM GOD PRESERVE!

'EXTERIOR OF THE PALACE.

'The Ground-plot forms a long parallelogram; the extent of the building from north to south being 480 feet, and from east to west, about 125 feet: of this space, upwards of two thirds is occupied by the Royal apartments and their appendages; and the remainder by the great kitchen, chapel, servants' rooms, and domestic offices.

'Since the Pavilion was first built, it has been greatly and progressively enlarged, as above detailed, and, together with the adjoining grounds and stabling, it now occupies an extensive plot of ground, nearly in the centre of the town, and immediately contiguous to the far famed Steyne and Parade. The whole of the demesne comprises ten acres, the principal part of which was obtained by purchase, and the rest by grant from the manorial owners and town's people.

'The principal, or eastern front of the Palace, opens on to a lawn, which is merely separated from the Steyne Parade by a low wall and dwarf enclosure, at the distance, from the building, of 170 feet. On the north side are shrubberies; and, on the west, which includes the main entrance, are the pleasure grounds and carriage drive. The southern extremity, comprehending the Chapel Royal and offices, projects into Castle Square.

'From this Plate, it would seem that this front might be described as consisting of seven parts; namely, a centre, of a curvilinear form, connected by adjoining divisions to two wings, and those again flanked by square buildings, forming returns to the north and south : yet this is not strictly the case, the southern return never having been completed. In all other respects the Elevation is correct.

'The Centre division which includes the *Rotunda*, or *Saloon*, and has a semicircular arcade in front, is crowned by a vast dome, presenting the appearance of an inverted balloon, tapering upwards into a lofty pinnacle, the point of which is more than one hundred feet from the ground. The dome is surrounded by a horizontal band of twenty eight conjoined ovals (crossing a similar number of vertical ribs), most of which are pierced as windows to the several small apartments contained in its concavity. It is also flanked by two octagonal minarets, and appears to rise from a basement cone, faced with scale work. Smaller domes, of a more compressed form, surmount the semicircular recesses which adjoin the Saloon; these have ornamental bands and vertical ribs, but no windows. The arcade spandrils are filled up with curvilinear trellis work, inclosing quatrefoils ; and, over the middle part, is the Prince of Wales's crest, and this inscription :

'" H.R.H. G eorge. P.W.

A.D. MDCCCXI."

'Similar domes to those last described, surmount the *Green* and *Yellow Drawing Rooms* (as they are now called), which connect the Saloon with the wings, and are each curved at the ends. The upper chambers recede, and before each range is a balcony and pierced parapet. The wings, which are of a square form, are

WEST FRONT OF THE PAVILION, 1825.

surmounted by lofty cones, rising to the height of about ninety feet ; at the angles are minarets. In front of both wings is an open arcade, composed of seven arches, separated from each other by octagonal columns, and ornamented by similar trellis work to that of the Saloon arcade. The Southern extremity terminates in a square tower crowned by a dome, and minarets corresponding with those already described. A sort of running battlement, with very narrow embrasures, surmounts the upper line of the whole building.

'The *West Front* of this edifice is shewn in all its variety of detail. In its general character it corresponds with the Steyne front, but there are many differences in the minor ornaments. The Perspective View (drawn from a North West point) exhibits this front in nearly its entire length ; the octagon tower in the distance is that which encloses the water reservoir.

'The principal entrance to the palace is constituted by a Porch and Vestibule, which open from the drive on the western side of the building. The Porch, which forms a square of about twenty two feet, is supported at each angle by three oriental columns, and crowned by a small dome in the general style of those already described. Over the cornice is the following inscription, recording the date when the alterations at the Pavilion were commenced by Mr. Holland :

'" H.R.H. GEORGE. P.W.

A.D. MDCCLXXXIV."

'The Porch leads directly to the Vestibule, which is of an octagonal form, and about twenty feet in diameter.

It is surmounted by a tented roof, neatly decorated, and a Chinese lantern is suspended from the centre.

'The Entrance Hall forms a square of twenty six feet, exclusive of an angular recess which slopes to the Vestibule. The recess has a tented roof, supported by two columns in the oriental style, and pierced by a horizontal sky light, illumined, in parts by tinted glass; there are also two side windows in the recess, independently of its glazed doors. The square of the Hall is surmounted by an ornamental cornice, supporting the ceiling, which resembles an azure sky, diversified by fleecy clouds. On the entrance side, below the cornice, is neatly painted a long range of dragonish forms and other devices; and four globular lamps, similarly embellished, are suspended from the angles of the ceiling. The walls are of a delicate pale green, relieved by circular and vertical compartments, in which dragons and serpents are depicted in subdued colouring. The chimney piece is of white marble, neatly executed.

'The Red Drawing Room, which is chiefly used as a Breakfast Room, adjoins the Entrance Hall on the south side; its length is about thirty feet, and its breadth twenty two feet, independently of a considerable recess towards the north. The timbers which cross the ceiling are sustained by reeded columns in imitation of bamboo. A number of small Chinese pictures, mostly of a bluish tone, exhibiting domestic or family scenes, ornament the walls, which are painted in resemblance of the crimson japan.'

CHAPTER XX.

The Chinese Gallery—The Music Room—The Yellow Drawing-room—The Saloon—The Green Drawing-room.

HE CHINESE GALLERY which ranges immediately behind the Saloon and its communicating apartments, is 162 feet in length, and 17 feet wide. This space is partially separated into five divisions, of unequal extent and elevation, by trellis work in imitation of bamboo.

'The central division is surrounded by a Chinese Canopy of similar trellis work, hung with bells, and surmounted by a coved ornamental ceiling, which projects through the upper floor, and is illumined by a horizontal light of stained glass, measuring twenty two feet in length, and eleven feet in width. On this light is represented *Lin-Shin*, the god of thunder, surrounded by his drums, and flying, as described in the mythology of China. His right hand wields a mace, or sceptre, " wherewith to strike the drums, and arouse the thunder "; and, with his left, he apparently upholds

18

an elegant glass lamp, ornamentally tinted and enriched by clusters of brilliant drops. Other sections of the light exhibit the Imperial five clawed dragon, amidst fancy borderings of different hues. Vertical transparencies, in a similar style, in imitative frames of bamboo, enrich the ends immediately below the ceiling, and corresponding embellishments are painted on each side.

'On the west side, beneath the canopy, and directly facing the middle entrance, is a curiously designed chimney piece worked in brass and iron to imitate bamboo ; and, over it, is a looking glass of considerable magnitude. At a little distance, right and left, are two large niches, lined with yellow marble, containing cabinets ; and, on them, in erect positions, are plaster casts, painted, of a male and female Chinese figure, in their proper costume. There are, also, four similar niches in the other divisions of the gallery, occupied by Indian cabinets, etc. ; as well as two recesses, each containing a pagoda of six stories, wrought in porcelain. At various angles of the ceiling, in place of the Chinese standards, to which they were formerly attached, tasteful lanterns of stained glass are suspended, exhibiting, on their respective sides, mythological devices, with flowers, birds, insects and other ornaments, tinted in a very effective and striking manner.

' The walls are battened, and the canvas is painted throughout with a delicate peach blossom, as a ground colour, on which rocks, trees, shrubs, birds and other embellishments in the Chinese style are very neatly pencilled in a subdued tone of pale blue. There are three fire places, over which stand beautiful jars and vases of china and porcelain, intermingled with open tulips and lotus flowers of stained glass, inclosing branches for lights. Many large jars and other vessels and figures of China ware, are, also, distributed throughout the gallery, the furniture of which is entirely of an oriental description. All the couches and chairs, which are numerous, are of ivory, curiously figured; and, in some instances, variegated with black.

' The extreme compartments to the north and south, are occupied by double Staircases, rendered light and airy in appearance by the steps being fronted with perforated brass and iron work; the railings are of cast iron, wrought and painted to resemble bamboo. These compartments are illumined by horizontal lights of stained glass, of similar elevation and accordant adornments to that of the central division of the Gallery; the southern one exhibiting the Imperial five clawed dragon, surrounded by flying bats, and the northern one the Chinese bird of Royalty called the *Fum*, with other ornaments. Above the landing place, at the north end, are also three windows, each being embellished with a full sized representation, in stained glass, of a Chinese god; and corresponding imitative windows are depicted over the southern landing place. The staircases lead into an upper gallery, or corridor, which communicates with the superior bed rooms and other apartments. When the doors at the ends of the Gallery, which are fronted with looking glass, are closed, an almost magical illusion is produced, the perspective appearing interminable. The carpeting is of English manufacture, and accords, in decoration, with the other furniture. From the respective extremities of this Gallery, access is obtained to the Music Room and the Banqueting Room.

'THE MUSIC ROOM.

' No verbal description, however elaborate, can convey to the mind, or imagination of the reader, an appropriate idea of the magnificence of this apartment; and even the creative delineations of the pencil, combined with all the illusions of colour, would scarcely be adequate to such an undertaking. Yet, luxuriously resplendent and costly as the adornments are, they are so intimately blended with the refinements of an elegant taste, that every thing appears in keeping, and in harmony.

' The ground plan of this apartment forms a square of forty two feet, enlarged to the north and south by rectangular recesses, ten feet in depth; thus extending the entire length to sixty two feet. The square part, at the height of twenty three feet, is surrounded by a splendid canopy, or cornice, ornamented with carved shield work, flower drops, stars, etc.; and supported, at the angles, by slender, reticulated, tree like columns, richly gilt. Immediately above this is an octagon gallery, ten feet high, formed by a series of eight elliptical arches, pierced by windows of a similar shape, and connected by intervening spandrils. The windows, which are so contrived as to be illumined from the exterior, are enriched with stained glass displaying numerous Chinese devices, and similar decorations, in green gold, surround them. A convex cove, four feet in elevation, forms the next architectural feature, and, upon that, is based a very elegant dome, or cupola (thirty feet in diameter), which is faced, throughout, with scale work, in green gold, resembling escallop shells; these ornaments, by decreasing in size as they ascend, add much to the apparent height of the room, which, at this point, is forty one feet.

'At the apex, expanding in bold relief and vivid colouring, is a vast foliated ornament, bearing a general resemblance to a sunflower, with many smaller flowers issuing from it, in all the luxuriancy of seeming cultivation. From this, apparently projected from the calyx, depends a very beautiful lustre of cut glass, designed in the pagoda style, and sustaining, by its chain work, an immense lamp in the form of the *Nelumbrium*, or Water-lily. The upper leaves are of white ground glass, edged with gold, and enriched with transparent devices derived from the mythology of the Chinese; the lower leaves are of a pale crimson hue. At the bottom are golden dragons, in attitudes of flight. Eight smaller lamps, but of corresponding forms and decoration, are suspended from the projecting angles of the canopy; adding greatly to the general effect when illumined for evening parties.

'On the eastern side of this room, light is admitted by five windows, the draperies of which, composed of blue and crimson satins, and yellow silks, richly fringed, are upheld by golden dragons, and supported, at the sides, by large serpents of a silvery hue. In front of the intervening piers (on elevated pedestals, manufactured by Spode) stand four pagoda towers of oriental porcelain, each of which consists of eight stories, and is fifteen feet in height; the pedestals are embellished with varied landscapes and flowers. Many other rare and valuable specimens of oriental china and jasper, in large jars, vases, etc., are included among the ornamental furniture of this room.

'On the west side is a magnificent chimney piece, of statuary marble, designed by Westmacott, and very beautifully wrought. The sweep of cornice in the centre is supported on the expanded wings of a finely sculptured dragon; and each of the jambs, which are, in fact, short, circular columns, having bases and capitals of conjoined lotus leaves, is surrounded by eight small columns of *or molu*, and otherwise enriched. The stove, fender, fire irons, etc., which were manufactured by Cutler, in a superior style of workmanship to most others, are of polished steel and *or molu*. Over the chimney piece is an effulgent looking glass, measuring nearly twelve feet by eight, surmounted by a tasteful and glittering canopy, supported by tree like columns of radiant gold. In front, stands a superb time piece, of curious and elaborate design; the base exhibits a rock and a palm-tree; around the latter a dragon entwines, and appears to be darting its sting at a figure behind, who wields an uplifted spear. At the top are Venus and Cupid, with the peacock of Love; and, below them, is the god Mars, who is climbing upwards, as though to view the beauties of the Paphian queen. Large and elegant China vases, with golden branches for lights, are placed on each side the time piece, together with other vessels of rich jasper.

'The walls, where not otherwise adorned, are covered with paintings, in imitation of the crimson japan. The subjects introduced are twelve in number, and consist of views in China principally taken in the neighbourhood of that " far famed, but little known, metropolis " Pekin; they are of a bright yellow colour, heightened with gold; and, in delicacy of execution, and beauty of pencilling, are scarcely to be exceeded by the best miniature paintings. Much fancy is displayed in the framework; the inner borderings being composed of a running pattern of rich foliage, and the outer ones of blue and yellow fret work, heightened with gold: at the upper corners are flying dragons.

'The recesses at the north and south ends are each canopied by a convex curve representing rows of bamboos, confined by ribands, and terminating in the square of the room; these are partly sustained by large columns of crimson and flowered gold, which are entwined by enormous serpents, depicted in all their glowing diversity of colour, and vivid expression of animal power. Similar columns, but of greater height, are ranged on the western side of this apartment. Within the northern recess, and a separate room extending behind it to the depth of twenty feet, stands a large organ, which was built by Lincoln in the year 1818, and is celebrated both for great powers, and peculiar delicacy of tone. It has three rows of keys, twenty eight stops, and twenty pedals; and its compass extends from C.C.C. with a double diapason throughout.

'There are two entrances to this apartment, one from the Chinese Gallery, and the other from the Yellow Drawing-room, each under a superb canopy of crimson and gold, ornamented with dragons and musical bells, and supported by golden columns entwined by dragons. There is no outlet on the opposite side, but the general uniformity is preserved by apparent entrances, corresponding in embellishments with those described.

'The carpet, which was manufactured in Axminster,

to fit the room, is one of the largest in the kingdom, its dimensions being sixty one feet by forty, and its weight about 1,700 lbs. It is wrought with Chinese subjects in gold colour, on a light blue ground, including suns, stars, serpents, dragons, birds, insects, and other forms. The sofas and chairs, which are of yellow satin and gold, accord with the surrounding objects; the arm chairs are partially dove coloured.

'The Yellow Drawing Room, has been so much altered since it was fitted up by the Prince of Wales, that it now bears little resemblance to Pugin's drawing of it. As there delineated, the walls displayed a series of pictures in the Chinese style, intermingled with other characteristic embellishments, and numerous Chinese lanterns were suspended from flying dragons issuing from the cornice.

'This is the intervening apartment between the Saloon and the Music Room, and is the one that usually becomes the sitting room of the Royal party when residing at the Palace. Its length is fifty six feet, and its extreme breadth, to the windows, about thirty three feet. The ceiling is partly supported by two oriental columns, of white and gold, enwreathed by serpents, and branching into umbrella capitals hung with bells. The Cornice, or Canopy, which surrounds the room, is also diversified by pendent bells. The draperies, etc., are of striped satin; and the walls are panelled in white, with richly gilt borderings. The principal chairs and sofas are covered to match the drapery; and, on the back of every chair, is a small Chinese figure, seated, with a bell in each hand. There are five windows on the east side (besides two others in

the semicircular returns), and, in front of each inter-
mediate pier, is a sexagon stand of porcelain, sustaining
branch lights. The chimney piece, which is of brown
coloured marble, is elegantly designed ; at the angles
are small columns, and within a niche in each jamb is a
Chinese figure. On the mantel shelf is a handsome
dial, by Vulliamy, with ornamental accessories, including Chinese figures of white china, in draperies
enriched with gold. Among the furniture are Buhl
tables, with grotesque borderings, beautifully inlaid.
On the side and end tables are many jars and vases of
Asiatic and Sèvres porcelain ; several of which are of a
pale sea green colour, elegantly wrought with flowers,
butterflies, and other forms. The doors are panelled
with plate glass.

‘ The Saloon, which forms the centre of the suite in
the eastern front, is magnificently decorated, almost
every part being effulgent with gold. Its general plan
is a circle, thirty five feet in diameter, surmounted by a
cupola, and enlarged to the north and south by coved
semicircular recesses (of a ten feet radius), which include
the entrances from the apartments communicating with
the Music and Banqueting rooms. The Cupola springs
from a boldly projecting cornice, composed of various
mouldings, apparently, of massive gold, crowned by a
running ornament of flowers, and pendent bells. The
ceiling represents a lightly clouded sky (the sun being
dimly seen) ; in the centre of which is a gorgeous bird,
in full relief, with wings of flowered gold and silver, enwreathed with serpents, resplendently coloured crimson
and green. This sustains one of the most elaborate
and finely devised lustres, of cut glass, that was ever

executed. Its height is about eighteen feet, and its varying and brilliant tiers of glittering drops are surrounded, towards the bottom, by radiant burners, the light of which is softened and diffused around by globes of ground glass. Four smaller lustres, but of corresponding fancy and workmanship, are pendent from the ceilings of the recesses.

'On the eastern side are three large windows, splendidly adorned with festooned curtains of flowered satin, crimson and gold: and the panels, and other divisions, are enriched with corresponding drapery. Between the windows are two very large pier glasses, reaching nearly from the ground to the cornice; and other large glasses surmount the entrance doorways; all the framework is of an elegantly conceived pattern, designed from the lotus leaf; and every frame has a rich canopy, springing from dragons' heads. On the west side is a sumptuous chimney piece of statuary marble, with enrichments of *or molu*; and, in each jamb, within a niche, stands a Chinese figure; these figures, which are of metal, are highly painted and varnished, and the dresses are finely pencilled. Over the chimney piece is a vast looking glass, thirteen feet high, and eight feet wide, in front of which stands an elegant dial by Vulliamy; this is supported by couchant dragons of blue porcelain, and enclosed in a China case surrounded by golden wreaths of the lotus and sunflower plants. Surmounting the dial, is a Chinese male figure seated, with a boy on his shoulder, a girl at his side, and a dog on his lap.

' At the sides of the recesses are enriched pilasters; each shaft of which exhibits a kind of caduceus, enwreathed by double headed serpents, in gold. The doors, which are folding, and also double, are beautifully ornamented in Japan work, in panels, curiously embossed with flowering shrubs, birds of different kinds (including peacocks, parrots, and cockatoos), rabbits, a porcupine frightened by snakes, insects, etc., in variously coloured gold. On the side piers, between the doors, are represented pagodas in rockery scenery, together with a lake teeming with water flowers of many species, and, in the sky, flying dragons. Great invention and very skilful execution are displayed by all these designs.

'Large vases of china, and other vessels in rich settings, beautifully wrought with sundry kinds of insects, in low relief, constitute a part of the ornamental furniture of the Saloon; which, also, includes some fine cabinets, and splendid ottomans of ruby coloured silk, fringed with gold, with couches and chairs of corresponding elegance. The carpet, which is of Axminster manufacture, is wrought on a circular plan, to fit the room, accords with the other decorations. In the centre is a dragon and two serpents, surrounded by lotus flowers and leaves; roses, stars, serpents, and other forms, in alternating succession, diversify the borderings.

'The Green Drawing Room, or Banqueting Room Gallery, which connects the Banqueting Room with the Saloon, was originally called the *Blue Drawing Room*, from the general tone of its decorations. Chinese lanterns were suspended from the cornice and ceiling, and paintings of Chinese scenery and trellis work covered the walls; but it was, subsequently, altered, and scarcely a vestige of its former state remains except the stoves and chimney pieces.   It is now called the *Green Drawing Room*, from the prevalent hue of its draperies, which are of richly woven silks, of a pale green colour, tastefully wrought with groups of fruit and flowers.

' This apartment is fifty two feet in length, and about thirty three feet in extreme breadth.   The ceiling, which is surrounded by an enriched cornice, is partly sustained by two oriental columns, crowned with spreading foliage.   The walls are panelled white, with broad fret like borders, in gold ; and, on the west side, under a festooned canopy, is a recess for a couch, with fluted drapery at the back, radiating from a central flower. On the same side, surmounted by large looking glasses, are two handsome chimney pieces of white marble, having ornamental accessories in *ormolu* and bronze. A clock by Vulliamy, and two beautiful jars of porcelain, upholding branch lights, stand on each shelf ; and many other rich vessels of china and porcelain are ranged on Indian cabinets and side tables, in different parts of the room.   But the most *récherché* of all, are two vases, and two ewers of Chinese manufacture, which occupy high pedestals in front of the window piers ; they approach to the Egyptian form, and are of a sea green colour, variegated with gold ; each of these vessels is about three feet in height.   Several of the tables are of rosewood inlaid with *ormolu ;* and one table is of rich tortoise shell, similarly embellished.   The door panels are of looking glass.'

CHAPTER XXI.

The Banqueting Room—The Library—Royal Bedroom—North
and South Galleries—Queen Adelaide's apartments—Great
Kitchen—Chapel—Stables—Riding House.

'THE BANQUETING ROOM.

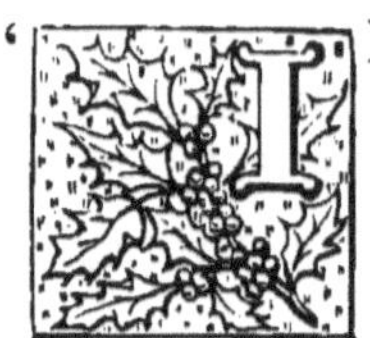N its general plan, dimensions, and
principal architectural features, this
apartment nearly corresponds with the
Music Room ; but the decorations and
ornamental work are entirely different,
although equally impressive in effect, from the good
taste displayed in their well harmonized combinations,
and in the professional ability which pervades the
whole.

'Like the Music Room, the square of this apartment,
at the height of twenty three feet, is bounded by a most
elegant cornice, apparently inlaid with pearl and gold :
the upper members exhibit the lotus leaf, and the lower
ones are adorned with pendent trefoils, alternating with
silver bells. This is supported, at the angles, by golden
columns, each surrounded, in two divisions, by fasces of

lances and darts entwined by serpents. Over each side
of the cornice extends an elliptical arch, about seven feet
high in the clear, having, in the central part, a narrow,
oblong window of stained glass (so contrived as to be
illumined from without), and, in smaller arched compartments, at the extremities, golden dragons of various
forms. The windows, which are glazed lozenge wise,
include in their embellishments radiant suns within
circles, on a blue ground, involving dragons and serpents
in their blaze, in accordance with oriental imagery.
Cove-like spandrils, faced with ornamental fret work,
connect the elliptical arches with a cupola of an unique,
yet graceful form; the base being a regular cone,
about six feet in height, and the surmounting part
composed of curves struck from different centres, and
partly convex. The cove is bordered with gold mouldings, and faced with scale work of a whitish-green
colour, studded with golden flowerets. An Eastern sky,
partially obscured by the broad and branching foliage
of a luxuriant and fruited plantain tree, is depicted in
the upper part; and, from this, appears to issue a vast
dragon, finely carved, and most brilliantly coloured, the
wings and scales being redolent of metallic green and
silver.

'From a ring, environed by the claws of the dragon,
was, formerly, suspended a magnificent lustre, of unparalleled size and beauty; but this was taken down,
about three years ago, under the express command of
his late Majesty, King William, who was fearful lest,
from its immense weight, the supports should give way,
and some fatal accident occur. It is still, however,
carefully preserved, and may be replaced, whenever

desirable.   Its height is thirty feet, its extreme diameter about twelve feet, and its weight about one ton.   This elaborate specimen of ingenious art consists of two divisions, connected with each other by chains richly gilt.   The upper division is, apparently, formed of conjoined links of pearls and rubies diverging to a horizontal star; below which is a radiant circle of open flowers and bands of pearls, etc., combined with festoons of sparkling jewellery.   The lower division consists of a vast bulb, gradually expanding, composed of seeming pearls, and connected with four large and glittering dragons, from whose upturned mouths proceed as many lotus flowers (of ground glass slightly tinted), "the expressive Eastern emblems of perfection and brightness."   Festoons of pearls, with rosettes, stars, etc., and tassels of brilliant drops, complete the form of this unique ornament.

'Four other lustres, designed in a style of corresponding elegance, but much smaller, and more simple in construction, are suspended from an equal number of beautifully carved figures of the Chinese *Fum*, which appears to issue, in the act of flight, from the spandrils beneath the cupola, and are richly and variously coloured to resemble nature.   Each minor lustre displays only a single lotus flower, which crowns the lower division, and appears studded, at the joining of the leaves, with superb jewels; twenty four burners are contained within the cup of each flower.

'Of the enchanting effect produced by the diffusive rays of these lustres, when fully illumined, it is scarcely possible to conceive an adequate idea.   "Creating," (if the figure may be allowed), "in mid air, a diamond blaze, yet so chastened by the semi-transparent medium through which it streams, that the eye gazes on the beauteous scene, undazzled ; the effulgence assumes the character of an artificial day.

' The recesses to the north and south of this apartment are united to the main cornice by convex curves (rising from a subordinate cornice enriched with gold and pendent bells), each of which is divided into five semi-elliptic compartments, curiously embellished with a variety of shadowy mythological forms, in pale gold, on a slate coloured ground. The intervening spaces above the cornice, are crimson and gold, with silver studs.

' On the east side are five spacious windows, the draperies of which are of the richest crimson silks, adorned with gold, and sustained by flying dragons. The dividing piers are covered by fluted silks of celestial blue ; and, in front of each pier, is a beautiful candelabrum, about ten feet in height. Each of the latter consists of a circular pedestal (including descending dragons, in relief, among its ornaments), supporting a cylindrical vase of blue porcelain, resembling lapis lazuli, surmounted by a lotus flower, of seven leaves, slightly tinged with red, and having its stem entwined by golden dragons. Similar candelabra, but with varied pedestals, stand before the main piers on the opposite side. The windows are glazed with plate glass in large panes, set in frames of dark wood, with gold beadings, and borders of amber coloured glass ; the jambs are black and red, edged with gold ornamental work.

' There are four entrances to this apartment (*viz.*, two at each end), all of which are uniform in character

and decoration. They have folding doors embellished
in imitation of Japan work ; each leaf presenting an
elegant pagoda, embossed with gold of different hues,
and hung with silver bells. Small columns ornament
the sides of the doorways, and each impost exhibits two
finely carved dragons, apparently of solid gold. Above
these, in an arched compartment, is a group of dragons,
issuing from an expanded flower cup, expressive of the
chimæra of oriental mythology : these, also, are richly
gilt, and beautifully sculptured.

'The walls above the dado (independently of a general
decoration of silver chequer work, heightened with
flowered crosses, on a deep blue ground) are divided
into compartments of large size, containing a series of
beautiful paintings in illustration of the domestic
manners and costume of the Chinese people. The
grouped subjects are eleven in number, and there are
four others of single figures, holding screens of peacock's
feathers. The ground of these masterly productions
is an imitation of inlaid pearl, richly and ingeniously
wrought with all the varied forms of the mythology of
China ; yet so delicately executed as scarcely to intrude
upon the eye. The central picture on the west side
represents the conveyance home of a Chinese bride. She
is seated in a palanquin, under a parasol canopy, with a
peacock by her side, and carried by six bearers in rich
habits. An attendant with cymbals, and two boys,
respectively carrying a banner and a trumpet, lead the
procession. In the adjoining are a lady looking at a
vase containing gold fish, which an attendant is feeding,
and a Chinese grandee giving audience to a suitor. On
the same side, but within the recesses, family parties

are represented, in one of which is a female on a settee, with two children, and, at her knee, a boy playfully holding a macaw. Among the other subjects represented are, a lady playing on a guitar, with a much pleased child, kneeling at her side, and listening; a lady, with a peacock fan, receiving fruit from a boy; a lady and child tending flowers; and a child amusing itself with a tame snake, in the presence of its parents. These paintings are executed with a precision and delicacy equal to miniature, and the colouring is extremely brilliant: the figures are nearly the size of life; and the dresses are richly embroidered. They are all inclosed within painted framings of trellis work, edged by narrow gold mouldings. On the west side are, also, painted two Chinese standards, hung with pennons, and guarded, at the base, by dragons.

'At each end of this room (facing each other) is a chimney piece of the finest statuary marble, ornamented with *ormolu*, and having canopied niches in the jambs, occupied by Chinese figures, richly gilt. Above each is a looking glass, extending to the cornice, and measuring ten feet in height, by five feet nine inches in width. Before the northern glass stands a time piece, of most excellent design and workmanship. The dial forms the centre of an opening sunflower, on each side of which, as though reposing in the shade of its exuberant and varied foliage (chased in gold), is a Chinese figure, male and female, the one with a bow, the other with a fan. These figures are of brass, highly coloured in beautiful Japan work; and the garments are enriched with golden ornaments, finely pencilled. On the opposite chimney piece is a thermometer, of similar design and execution as the time piece : each dial is surmounted by a peacock, or *Fum*.

'There are five sideboards of rose wood in this apartment, ornamented with *ormolu* and Chinese emblems. The dining table, which is of the best mahogany, is forty two feet in length, and seven feet six inches in width. The seats and backs of the chairs are covered with red morocco.

'Among the other furniture appropriate to a dining room, are five Chinese Cisterns, mounted in *ormolu*, of superior workmanship; and numerous jars and vessels of blue porcelain, of great brilliancy and excellence; the latter are of Staffordshire manufacture, and were provided by Spode and Copeland. The carpeting, which is of Axminster manufacture, and made expressly for the room, consists of a large square, and two end pieces to correspond. A dragon, with three serpents coiled round, and involving it, forms the central ornament: this is surrounded by circles, diversely wrought, and increasing in diameter towards the border.

'The illustration represents the Banqueting Room as it appeared during one of the splendid entertainments given there, by the Prince Regent; whose portrait may be distinctly recognised among the company.

'On the same side, at the end of the dining table, is his Royal brother, the late King, when Duke of Clarence. The table is set out with rich plate, splendid candelabra, and elegant and costly statuary.

'THE LIBRARY.

'Behind the Music Room, and, partly, forming the north west of this edifice, are the private apartments

which were occupied by his late Majesty, George the
Fourth. They consist of a Library, Bed room, Bath,
Sitting and Dressing rooms, and several offices.

'The Library comprehends two rooms, the largest of
which is thirty five feet in length, by twenty feet in
breadth, and the other, about half those dimensions.
Divided into three compartments, *viz.* a square and two
oblongs, the ceiling of the large room is painted to
represent an azure sky, diversified by light clouds; and,
in the oblong compartments, are delineations of Chinese
standards. The square part is surrounded by a gilt
cornice, supported, at the angles, by fluted pillars,
crowned with capitals of fan-like tracery. Dragons of
grotesque and varied forms, combined with flowers and
other devices, on a green ground, are curiously painted
on the walls. The hangings are composed of rich yellow
coloured drapery. Over the chimney piece, which is of
statuary marble, and very elegant, is a splendid looking
glass; and another is fixed over the chimney piece in
the smaller room. Though still called the Library,
these apartments present but few indications of that
appropriation, all the books having been removed during
the residence, here, of William the Fourth. A great
variety of China jars, and other vessels, form a part of
the ornamental furniture, and, in the smaller room, is a
very pretty Indian Cabinet, containing numerous articles
of *bijouterie* and *vertû.*

'HIS MAJESTY'S (GEORGE THE FOURTH) BEDROOM.

'This apartment adjoins to the Library, on the north
side: it forms a square of about forty feet, with a recess
for a bed on the eastern side. A kind of dado of trellis

work surrounds the lower part, and the upper parts are decorated with dragons, stars, flowers, etc., pencilled in white, on a light green ground : the doors, also, are painted to correspond. The adjoining *Bath Room* is lined white marble : the principal bath, which is sixteen feet long, ten feet wide, and six feet deep, is supplied with salt water from the sea, by a succession of pipes, and other machinery. In the Ante room (or Page's room) are eighteen small paintings, very neatly executed, of Chinese Landscapes, and other subjects connected with China.

'THE NORTH AND SOUTH GALLERIES, or LOBBIES, as they are now called, serve as avenues of communication with the adjoining apartments. From the trellis work and general style of fitting up, they have a light and airy appearance, and the furniture is correspondent. Each doorway is flanked by two half columns, ornamented by lozenge-shaped reticulations, and crowned by dragons' heads in relief. Several models of Chinese ships and Pagodas, finely carved in ivory, are preserved here, and exhibit extraordinary examples of patient labour and dexterity in that branch of art.

' QUEEN ADELAIDE'S APARTMENTS, are very neatly fitted up, though with little splendour; being far more adapted for domestic comfort than for state display; for which, indeed, they were never designed. Both the Drawing and Bed-rooms are battened with a very handsome paper, teeming with flowers upon a yellow ground, and including many beautiful parrots and other birds and insects among its other ornaments. Several Indian cabinets, and an elegant Buhl table, form part of the Drawing room furniture; and, in the adjoining Lady's

Room, is a fine head, by Lawrence, of his late Majesty, William the Fourth. These apartments open to the balcony in the West Wing, over the Library.

'GREAT KITCHEN.

'Nearly the whole of the south end of the Palace is occupied by the various offices belonging to the establishment,—of which, both in appearance, and interest, the *Great Kitchen* must be regarded as the principal. Its form is rectangular ; the extent from east to west is about forty-five feet, and, from north to south, thirty-six feet. It has a lantern roof, which is supported by four iron columns, in the shape of palm trees, and is carried up to a considerable elevation. The interior of this necessary adjunct to social comfort is to be seen in a contemporary illustration, wherein its busy inmates are seen in active preparation for a Royal entertainment. The dishes, when placed on the central table, are kept hot by a steam apparatus, until everything is ready for the banquet. Several smaller kitchens, and two larders, are attached to the principal one ; and, on the western side of the servants' corridor, are two pastry rooms and a confectionary. Some alterations were made here about two years ago, during a repair. It is scarcely necessary to add, that all the arrangements, fittings up and furniture of these offices, as well as the great variety of articles of culinary use, are of the best and most convenient description. In an open court, there is, also, an octagon tower, containing a water reservoir ; the water is raised and supplied for domestic purposes, by ingenious and powerful machinery.

'THE CHAPEL.

'Near the south east angle of the palace is a large building of red brick, forming part of Castle Square. This was, originally, the Castle Inn ; but, it having been purchased by the Prince Regent, the Ball room was converted into a CHAPEL for the Royal household, soon after his accession to the Crown. It was consecrated with great solemnity, on the 1st of January, 1822, by the late Dr. John Buckner, Bishop of Chichester, in the presence of the King and his suite, and a numerous congregation. The interior forms a rectangle of eighty feet by forty ; the height is about thirty feet. The Royal gallery, which is at the north end, is supported by fluted columns and pilasters, and hung with crimson drapery : it includes three divisions, the central one being for the sovereign, and those to the right and left, for the attendant ladies and gentlemen. At the south end is a large organ gallery, with seats for the household servants. The area is appropriated to a general congregation, but no person is admitted without a ticket : the number of tickets issued is about 400. The chapel is neatly wainscoted ; and has two fire places on each side : it communicates with the Palace by a covered passage leading to an apartment adjoining the Banqueting room. The original Chapel Royal was in Prince's Place, North Street, at a short distance westward from the Pavilion ; and it is still occupied as a Chapel of ease to Brighton. It was erected in 1793, under the patronage of the Prince of Wales, who deposited the first stone ; and contains accommodation for about 1,000 persons.

'THE ROYAL STABLES.

'It has already been stated that the Pavilion Stables were erected from the designs of the late William Porden, Esqre, between the years 1803 and 1805. They stand on the northern side of the pleasure grounds, at the distance of about ninety or one hundred yards from the Palace itself, and occupy a part of the site of the Elm, or Promenade Grove, which had, for some years, been used as a place of public recreation, and was purchased by the Prince of Wales, in 1800. Shortly afterwards, the adjoining shrubberies and grounds of Grove House, belonging to the Duke of Marlborough, were also purchased; and, in consequence of those acquisitions, the *New Road*, connecting North Street with Church Street, was made. The thoroughfare connecting East Street with the North Steyne (which had, previously, run immediately behind the Pavilion) was then closed up, and the intervening space annexed to the demesne.

'The arrangement and construction of this extensive pile are highly honourable to the professional skill of its talented architect, who was the first person in this country that adopted the Oriental style in modern composition; at least, on an enlarged scale. In the boldness of the design, particularly of the dome crowned Rotunda, and in the judicious allocation of the parts, "which" (as was justly remarked by a contemporary writer), "while they produce all the conveniences in the contemplation of his Royal Highness, contribute, equally, to advance the general effect," the architect has been eminently successful; yet, as correct specimens of Oriental composition, neither the Pavilion, nor Stables, will be ever regarded as examples for imitation. The expense of erecting this building was upwards of £70,000.

'The principal entrance to the Royal Stables is from Church Street, and leads through a wide and lofty arch, of the pointed form, into a spacious quadrangular court, containing the coach houses, coach house stabling, and various servants' rooms and offices. Opposite to this, is another archway, conducting to the area of the Rotunda, which is a circle of 249 feet in circumference, surrounded by the stables for the saddle horses, and an open gallery; and the whole of which receives its light through the glazed compartments of the vast cupola by which it is surmounted. From the extent and height of this interior, and the lofty elevation of the four arches which open from it towards the cardinal points, an impressive effect, associated with surprise and admiration, is produced on the mind of every spectator.

'The Dome, or Cupola, which surmounts the Rotunda, combines strength and lightness in an extraordinary degree. Although upwards of eighty feet diameter in the clear, its thickness is only twelve inches at the bottom, and nine inches at the top. It is constructed on the same principle as was the celebrated Cupola of the *Halle au Blé* at Paris, and it was the first example of that mode of construction, in this country, upon a large scale. The main ribs, which are twenty-four in number, are twelve inches by nine inches at the bottom, diminishing to nine inches square at the top; they are each constructed of three thicknesses of fir planks, in lengths of nine feet, breaking joint, and firmly bolted together, every three feet ; the whole planed smooth, and the heading joints fitted together with the greatest accuracy. Of the space between the ribs, by far the largest proportion is divided into sixteen glazed compartments, spreading fan wise, which diffuse an abundant light throughout the Rotunda. The remaining eight compartments are embellished with panels in stucco work, instead of glass, which adds variety, without destroying the symmetry, and relieves the eye from the repulsive glare that a skylight of that magnitude must, otherwise, produce. In the middle of the Cupola is a circular opening, surmounted by a lantern, which forms a ventilator for the Rotunda and Stabling, and is wrought, exteriorly, in the form of a coronet. Where not interrupted by the skylights, the ribs are connected by horizontal purlins, and further strengthened by iron chains surrounding the whole contour. The curvilinear plate, or curb, at the springing of the dome, measures twelve inches by nine inches, and that at the top, nine inches by nine ; both are constructed in thicknesses in the same manner as the ribs above described.

'The great arches on the east and west of the Rotunda lead to the Riding House, and to a new wing of stablings, erected in 1832, for Queen Adelaide, on the site of what had been intended for a Tennis Court. They, also, contain the staircases connected with the gallery, around which are the Harness and Saddle rooms, and numerous apartments for the grooms and other servants. The southern arch opens to the pleasure grounds, and the view through the arches, from the entrance gateway, across the Rotunda, is singularly striking. The stables, surrounding the area, forty-four in number, are so arranged that, when the doors are open, a spectator, standing under the central part of the Cupola, may see into every stall, without changing his situation. The fronts of the stables, and the arcades of the surmounting gallery, are finished in a corresponding manner to the dome, and this gives an harmonious character to the whole interior.

' It has been frequently stated that the ventilation of the Royal stables, though aided by extensive archways connected with the Rotunda, was inadequate to disperse the heat attracted, and retained, by the glass and lead work covering the dome; and, that the health of all horses kept there for any length of time was much injured in consequence. These assertions, however, are contrary to facts; the writer having been recently assured by the chief groom, who has held his situation many years, that no stabling in the kingdom can be more healthful, nor better adapted for its purpose than this.

' The RIDING HOUSE, which is to the west of the Rotunda, is a very capacious building; its length being 176 feet, its width 58 feet 6 inches, and its height 34 feet, in the clear. It is covered with a roof of a peculiar construction, differing, probably, from every other example. For the purpose of gaining as much height as possible, this roof was constructed without the beams, the main timbers, of twelve inches by nine inches scantling, being built in the form of an arch, of forty-seven feet six inches radius, in three thicknesses of fir plank ; precisely in the same manner as the ribs of the dome, above described. These curvilinear beams rest on plates of fir, and are further strengthened by curvilinear oak struts, of ten feet three inches radius, forming the ceiling into an elliptical arch 58 ft. 6 in. in the span (as before stated), and of 15 feet rise ; with groins 15 ft. 4 in. wide over each of the five windows on the west front, and corresponding groins on the east side. Over the arched beams are principal rafters, framed at the top with a king post, in the usual manner; and, at the bottom, forming tangents with the beams, and connected with them by keys and iron straps. The main trusses of the roof are 18 ft. 5 in. apart over the windows, and 6 ft. 9 in. over the piers, measuring from centre to centre ; and the number of main beams is eighteen, or three over each pier.'

CHAPTER XXII.

EORGE the Magnificent was buried on July 16, 1830, and at the earliest opportunity his brother and successor William the Fourth visited the Pavilion (August 16), and at once began to plan alterations. The following is the account, from the *Brighton Herald* of August 21, of his reception :

'On Monday last, it being generally known that his Majesty would arrive at the Palace on that day, the town, at an early hour, was in full bustle and active preparation for receiving the Sovereign ; and, by two o'clock, the various public bodies and institutions were assembled, and proceeded to take up their stations on the line of road by which the King would pass, as allotted to them by a Committee appointed at a public meeting, on Saturday, to conduct the various matters. By three o'clock, Brighton had poured forth its thousands of every grade, and dense masses of people flanked the road, from the Palace gates to Preston, and even beyond ; while vehicles of every description, from the gay barouche of the Peer, to the humble hackney fly, formed a continuous line for nearly a mile. · The manner in which the various authorities were stationed to receive his Majesty, was as follows :

' At the Palace gates,—the local Magistrates, the High Constable, and the Clergy, in their Canonicals ; at St. George's Place, the body of the Commissioners and their officers ; opposite St. Peter's Church, the Over-seers, Directors, and Guardians ; at the Elephant and Castle, the Revenue Officers ; at the Hare and Hounds, the Friendly and Benefit Societies of the town ; and, from the Dairy to Preston, the children of the various Charity Schools.

' Precisely at half past four o'clock, a gun, fired from the battery, announced to the expectant multitude that their Royal Prince was approaching ; and, soon after, one of the Royal carriages, containing his Majesty's pages, arrived. Twenty minutes elapsed, when the acclamations of the distant throng made known that the King, himself, had appeared.

' At Preston, the King, in his travelling chariot, (the glasses of which were down) accompanied by Sir Frederick Watson, entered, amidst huzzas, the line which had been formed, when his Majesty, to meet the wishes of his delighted people, directed the postilions to proceed at a walking pace.

' The King, who looked extremely well, and was in

the highest spirits, acknowledged the loyal gratulations and respectful obeisances, with which he was, on both sides, saluted, frequently bending to the elegant and beautiful females who filled the balconies and windows, waving their handkerchiefs as he passed.

' The line of road was pretty well kept, until his Majesty had nearly cleared Marlborough Place, when the anxiety of the crowd, who stood in the back ground, in Church Street, to see the King, was not to be withstood ; and, despite the endeavour of the Headborough and Committee, the populace rushed in, and the Royal carriage was literally beset : and it was with extreme difficulty that the postilions wended their way through the dense crowds, who rent the air with deafening acclamations, which were continued for a considerable time after the King had entered the Palace Gates.

' *Never was a monarch more heartily and joyfully welcomed, than was William the Fourth, on Monday last, by the inhabitants of this town.*'[1]

Poor Florizel ! only absent a little more than three years from the town which he had made ; superseded in a moment by another rising sun, and all but clean forgotten ; and even his own brother, as soon as he possibly could, began alterations on poor Florizel's Folly !

' His Majesty, as early as nine o'clock the next morning after his arrival, attended by Sir Frederick Watson, and Mr. Nash, walked from the Palace Grounds to the gravelled space outside the south gate of the Palace, fronting East Street, where he continued for some time, familiarly conversing, and marking the ground with his stick, evidently suggesting certain alterations; after

---

[1] The *italics* are mine.—J. A.

which, his Majesty and attendants retired into the Palace. It is conjectured that the unsightly boards, which hide from public view the western front of the Palace, and the beautiful grounds, will be removed, and a light iron fence and gates, extending from Messrs. Brewster and Seabrook's to the Royal Kitchen, will be substituted in lieu thereof.'

A few days afterwards (on August 30), the King, with Queen Adelaide, visited Brighton, and stayed at the Pavilion until October 25. Anent this visit, I cannot refrain from quoting an anecdote of the present Duke of Cambridge, who was then not twelve years old.

Brighton Herald, October 2, 1830.—'The following has been related to us as a fact : A few days since, Prince George of Cambridge went into a saddler's shop, in the King's Road, and requested to be shewn some whips. An assortment being produced, his Royal Highness selected one of costly manufacture, and enquired the price. The cautious shopkeeper, ignorant of the rank of his visitor, stated the charge, and added : " Perhaps, Sir, you had better consult your friends before you purchase so expensive an article." The Prince, with infinite good humour, acquiesced, and left the shop ; and a servant was, soon after, sent for the whip, and announced to the astonished saddler the name of his customer.'

The Pavilion was altered and added to according to the King's instructions ; in 1831 the southern gateway and the dormitories were completed, as were the northern gateway and Queen Adelaide's stables in the next year. The Queen was very fond of Brighton, and the royal visits were frequent. None, however, deserve a notice, except, perhaps, that which commenced on October 19, 1836, the only noteworthy episode in which was that on Saturday, December 24, the whole royal establishment were unable to stir forth owing to the very heavy fall of snow. Several people were frozen to death ; the theatre was closed, and no carriages, except in cases of absolute necessity, left the town. One short paragraph out of a long account in the *Brighton Patriot* of December 27, 1836, will suffice to show the severity of the storm :

' The King's messenger left the Palace, with despatches, for London, on Sunday evening ; but, when he had arrived at Patcham, he was compelled to leave the carriage; he then took horse, and proceeded towards London. A gentleman left in a postchaise and pair, about the same time, in spite of the most pressing remonstrances. On the other side of Clayton Hill, the carriage and horses were buried in the snow. The gentleman and driver, it is understood, with great difficulty reached the Friar's Oak, leaving the horses in the snow ; and it is said, they have both perished. The London Mail left on the same evening, at the usual time ; but, having got to Patcham, it returned, the road being impassable ; but the mail bags were taken on by a man on horseback.'

The old King was then ill with the gout, and he died on June 20, 1837, and it was not long after her accession that Queen Victoria visited the Pavilion. She came to Brighton on October 4, and left November 4. It is needless to say that she received an ovation, which

may be tersely expressed in the following acrostic taken
from the *Brighton Gazette* of October 5, 1837 :

'View now the crowds who throng the joyous scene,
In anxious hope to greet our youthful Queen ;
Can loyal hearts their joy now fail to show ?
To Heaven the shouts ascend of all below.
O ! may thy reign with every bliss be crowned,
Round the vast world may thy renown abound,
In Brighton, may'st thou health and peace acquire,
And Heaven grant thee all thy heart's desire.'

Her Majesty's next visit to the Pavilion was in the
following year, arriving on December 18, and keeping
Christmas there. The Queen married in 1840, but did
not visit Brighton until February 10, 1842, when she
and Prince Albert, together with the Prince of Wales
and the Princess Royal, paid a visit to the Pavilion.
A notice of this visit, in the *Brighton Herald* of
February 12, says :

'In the third carriage came the infant Prince of
Wales and the Princess Royal, for whose failing health,
it is said, this journey has been made : and never has it
been our lot to witness a more interesting scene. The
Prince, a fine chubby little fellow, was held up by his
nurse to the right window, so as to be visible to every
one, and he appeared to return the gaze of the thousands
who were looking on him and hailing him, with almost
as much joy as they felt. On the opposite side, the
Princess Royal was displayed in a similar manner, and
received with equal enthusiasm. Indeed, her Majesty
must feel that she enjoys a double existence in these
Royal infants, who call forth from her subjects so large
a share of loyalty and love.'

This visit terminated on March 8.

In September, 1843, the Queen and Prince Albert paid visits to the Kings of France and Belgium, and the royal children were sent to Brighton ; but the Queen and Prince Albert paid them a visit at the Pavilion on September 7, stopping till the 12th. This was the Queen's fourth and last visit to Brighton.

The royal children—the Prince of Wales, the Princess Alice, and Prince Alfred—were sent to the Pavilion next year, on September 10, and stopped till October 2. This was the last time the building was used as a royal residence.

A marine palace with greater privacy was considered necessary, and, as Osborne fulfilled the requirements, the Pavilion was doomed. In August, 1846, it was rumoured it was to be sold, and we see, from the following cutting from *Punch* of August 22, what was thought of it :

'RUBBISH FOR SALE.—As there is a doubt about a purchaser coming forward to bid for the Pavilion at Brighton, we suggest that it be bought up for the Chinese Collection, unless No. One St. Paul's* should purchase it for their tea establishment. We know of no other purpose it could be turned to ; and, with a few paper lanterns, and a real native at the door, we feel confident a deal of business in selling tea, or exhibiting curiosities, might be done. If it is pulled down, it will be a fine specimen of broken china.'

From 1846 to 1848 the Pavilion was quietly dismantled, and in the latter year the organ was presented to the town. In June, 1849, leave was given to bring

* Then Alderman Dakin's tea warehouse.

a Bill into the House of Commons for its sale, and the town was given the option of purchasing it for £53,000, although Messrs. Cubitt were prepared to give £100,000 for the site for building purposes.　On June 13, 1850, the town paid £53,000 to the Commissioners of Woods and Forests, and possession was given them on June 19. Thackeray, speaking of it in 1861, says :

'You may see the place now for sixpence : they have fiddlers there every day ; and, sometimes, buffoons and mountebanks hire the Riding House and do their tricks and tumbling there.'

THE END.

BILLING AND SONS, PRINTERS, GUILDFORD.

AN ALPHABETICAL CATALOGUE
OF BOOKS IN FICTION AND
GENERAL LITERATURE
PUBLISHED BY
CHATTO & WINDUS
111 ST. MARTIN'S LANE
CHARING CROSS
LONDON, W.C.
[SEPT. 1899.]

About (Edmond).—The Fellah: An Egyptian Novel. Translated by Sir RANDAL ROBERTS. Post 8vo, illustrated boards, 2s.

Adams (W. Davenport), Works by.
A Dictionary of the Drama: being a comprehensive Guide to the Plays, Playwrights, Players, and Playhouses of the United Kingdom and America, from the Earliest Times to the Present Day. Crown 8vo, half-bound, 12s. 6d. [Preparing.
Quips and Quiddities. Selected by W. DAVENPORT ADAMS. Post 8vo, cloth limp, 2s. 6d.

Agony Column (The) of 'The Times,' from 1800 to 1870. Edited with an Introduction, by ALICE CLAY. Post 8vo, cloth limp, 2s. 6d.

Aidé (Hamilton), Novels by. Post 8vo, illustrated boards, 2s. each.
Carr of Carrlyon. | Confidences.

Alden (W. L.).—A Lost Soul: Being the Confession and Defence of Charles Lindsay. Fcap. 8vo, cloth boards, 1s. 6d.

Alexander (Mrs.), Novels by. Post 8vo, illustrated boards, 2s. each.
Maid, Wife, or Widow? | Blind Fate.

Crown 8vo, cloth, 3s. 6d. each; post 8vo, picture boards, 2s. each.
Valerie's Fate. | A Life Interest. | Mona's Choice. | By Woman's Wit.

Allen (F. M.).—Green as Grass. Crown 8vo, cloth, 3s. 6d.

Allen (Grant), Works by. Crown 8vo, cloth, 6s. each.
The Evolutionist at Large. | Moorland Idylls.
Post-Prandial Philosophy. Crown 8vo, art linen, 3s. 6d.

Crown 8vo, cloth extra, 3s. 6d. each; post 8vo, illustrated boards, 2s. each.

Babylon. 12 Illustrations.	The Devil's Die.	The Duchess of Powysland.
Strange Stories. Frontis.	This Mortal Coil.	Blood Royal.
The Beckoning Hand.	The Tents of Shem. Frontis.	Ivan Greet's Masterpiece.
For Maimie's Sake.	The Great Taboo.	The Scallywag. 24 Illusts.
Philistia.	Dumaresq's Daughter.	At Market Value.
In all Shades.	Under Sealed Orders.	

Dr. Palliser's Patient. Fcap. 8vo, cloth boards, 1s. 6d.

Anderson (Mary).—Othello's Occupation. Crown 8vo, cloth, 3s. 6d.

Antipodean (The): An Australasian Annual. Edited by A. B. PATERSON and G. ESSEX EVANS. Medium 8vo, with Illustrations, 1s.

Arnold (Edwin Lester), Stories by.
The Wonderful Adventures of Phra the Phœnician. Crown 8vo, cloth extra, with 12 Illustrations by H. M. PAGET, 3s. 6d.; post 8vo, illustrated boards, 2s.
The Constable of St. Nicholas. With Frontispiece by S. L. WOOD. Crown 8vo, cloth, 3s. 6d.

Artemus Ward's Works. With Portrait and Facsimile. Crown 8vo, cloth extra, 3s. 6d.—Also a POPULAR EDITION post 8vo, picture boards, 2s.

Ashton (John), Works by. Crown 8vo, cloth extra, 7s. 6d. each.
History of the Chap-Books of the 18th Century. With 334 Illustrations.
Humour, Wit, and Satire of the Seventeenth Century. With 82 Illustrations.
English Caricature and Satire on Napoleon the First. With 115 Illustrations.
Modern Street Ballads. With 57 Illustrations.
Social Life in the Reign of Queen Anne. With 85 Illustrations. Crown 8vo, cloth, 3s. 6d.
Crown 8vo, cloth, gilt top, 6s. each.
Social Life under the Regency. With 90 Illustrations.
Florizel's Folly: The Story of GEORGE IV. With Photogravure Frontispiece and 12 Illustrations.

Bacteria, Yeast Fungi, and Allied Species, A Synopsis of. By
W. B. GROVE, B.A. With 87 Illustrations. Crown 8vo, cloth extra, 3s. 6d.

Bardsley (Rev. C. Wareing, M.A.), Works by.
English Surnames: Their Sources and Significations. Crown 8vo, cloth, 7s. 6d.
Curiosities of Puritan Nomenclature. Crown 8vo, cloth, 3s. 6d.

Baring Gould (Sabine, Author of 'John Herring,' &c.), Novels by.
Crown 8vo, cloth extra, 3s. 6d. each ; post 8vo, illustrated boards, 2s. each.
Red Spider. | Eve.

Barr (Robert: Luke Sharp), Stories by. Cr. 8vo, cl., 3s. 6d. each.
In a Steamer Chair. With Frontispiece and Vignette by DEMAIN HAMMOND.
From Whose Bourne, &c. With 47 Illustrations by HAL HURST and others.
Revenge! With 12 Illustrations by LANCELOT SPEED and others.
A Woman Intervenes. With 8 Illustrations by HAL HURST.
The East While You Wait : Being some Notes on a Visit to the Farther Edge of the Mediter-
ranean. Crown 8vo, cloth, 6s. [Shortly.

Barrett (Frank), Novels by.
Post 8vo, illustrated boards, 2s. each ; cloth, 2s. 6d. each.

Fettered for Life.	A Prodigal's Progress.
The Sin of Olga Zassoulich.	John Ford: and His Helpmate.
Between Life and Death.	A Recoiling Vengeance.
Folly Morrison.	Honest Davie.	Lieut. Barnabas.	Found Guilty.
Little Lady Linton.	For Love and Honour.

Crown 8vo, cloth, 3s. 6d. each ; post 8vo, picture boards, 2s. each ; cloth limp, 2s. 6d. each.
The Woman of the Iron Bracelets. | The Harding Scandal.
A Missing Witness. With 8 Illustrations by W. H. MARGETSON.
Crown 8vo, cloth, 3s. 6d. each.
Was She Justified?
Under a Strange Mask. With 19 Illustrations by E. F. BREWTNALL.

Barrett (Joan).—Monte Carlo Stories. Fcap. 8vo, cloth, 1s. 6d.

Beaconsfield, Lord. By T. P. O'CONNOR, M.P. Cr. 8vo, cloth, 5s.

Beauchamp (Shelsley).—Grantley Grange. Post 8vo, boards, 2s.

Besant (Sir Walter) and James Rice, Novels by.
Crown 8vo, cloth extra, 3s. 6d. each ; post 8vo, illustrated boards, 2s. each ; cloth limp, 2s. 6d. each.

Ready-Money Mortiboy.	By Celia's Arbour.
My Little Girl.	The Chaplain of the Fleet.
With Harp and Crown.	The Seamy Side.
This Son of Vulcan.	The Case of Mr. Lucraft. &c.
The Golden Butterfly.	'Twas in Trafalgar's Bay. &c.
The Monks of Thelema.	The Ten Years' Tenant. &c.

₊ There is also a LIBRARY EDITION of the above Twelve Volumes, handsomely set in new type on a
large crown 8vo page, and bound in cloth extra, 6s. each ; and POPULAR EDITIONS of The Golden
Butterfly and of All Sorts and Conditions of Men, medium 8vo, 6d. each ; cloth, 1s. each.

Besant (Sir Walter), Novels by.
Crown 8vo, cloth extra, 3s. 6d. each ; post 8vo, illustrated boards, 2s. each ; cloth limp, 2s. 6d. each.
All Sorts and Conditions of Men. With 12 Illustrations by FRED. BARNARD.
The Captains' Room, &c. With Frontispiece by E. J. WHEELER.
All in a Garden Fair. With 6 Illustrations by HARRY FURNISS.
Dorothy Forster. With Frontispiece by CHARLES GREEN.
Uncle Jack, and other Stories. | Children of Gibeon.
The World Went Very Well Then. With 12 Illustrations by A. FORESTIER.
Herr Paulus: His Rise, his Greatness, and his Fall. | The Bell of St. Paul's.
For Faith and Freedom. With Illustrations by A. FORESTIER and F. WADDY.
To Call Her Mine, &c. With 9 Illustrations by A. FORESTIER.
The Holy Rose, &c. With Frontispiece by F. BARNARD.
Armorel of Lyonesse : A Romance of To-day. With 12 Illustrations by F. BARNARD.
St. Katherine's by the Tower. With 12 Illustrations by C. GREEN.
Verbena Camellia Stephanotis, &c. With a Frontispiece by GORDON BROWNE.
The Ivory Gate. | The Rebel Queen.
Beyond the Dreams of Avarice. With 12 Illustrations by W. H. HYDE.
In Deacon's Orders, &c. With Frontispiece by A. FORESTIER. | The Revolt of Man.
The Master Craftsman. | The City of Refuge.
Crown 8vo, cloth, 3s. 6d. each.
A Fountain Sealed. With a Frontispiece. | The Changeling.
The Orange Girl. With 8 Illustrations by F. PEGRAM. Crown 8vo, cloth, gilt top, 6s.
The Charm, and other Drawing-room Plays. By Sir WALTER BESANT and WALTER H. POLLOCK
With 50 Illustrations by CHRIS HAMMOND and JULE GOODMAN Crown 8vo, cloth, gilt edges, 6s. ;
or blue cloth, to range with the Uniform Edition of Sir WALTER BESANT'S Novels, 3s. 6d.
Fifty Years Ago. With 144 Illustrations. Crown 8vo, cloth, 3s. 6d.
The Eulogy of Richard Jefferies. With Portrait. Crown 8vo, cloth, 6s.
London. With 125 Illustrations. Demy 8vo, cloth, 7s. 6d.
Westminster. With Etched Frontispiece by F. S. WALKER, R.E., and 130 Illustrations by
WILLIAM PATTEN and others. Demy 8vo, cloth, 7s. 6d.
South London. With Etched Frontispiece by F. S. WALKER, R.E., and 118 Illustrations.
Demy 8vo, cloth, gilt top, 18s.
Jerusalem : The City of Herod and Saladin. By WALTER BESANT and E. H. PALMER. Fourth
Edition. With a new Chapter, a Map, and 11 Illustrations. Small demy 8vo, cloth, 7s. 6d.
Sir Richard Whittington. With Frontispiece. Crown 8vo, art linen, 3s. 6d.
Gaspard de Coligny. With a Portrait. Crown 8vo, art linen, 3s. 6d.

Bechstein (Ludwig).—As Pretty as Seven, and other German Stories. With Additional Tales by the Brothers GRIMM, and 98 Illustrations by RICHTER. Square 8vo, cloth extra, 6s. 6d.; gilt edges, 7s. 6d.

Bellew (Frank).—The Art of Amusing: A Collection of Graceful Arts, Games, Tricks, Puzzles, and Charades. With 300 Illustrations. Crown 8vo, cloth extra, 4s. 6d.

Bennett (W. C., LL.D.).—Songs for Sailors. Post 8vo, cl. limp, 2s.

Bewick (Thomas) and his Pupils. By AUSTIN DOBSON. With 95 Illustrations. Square 8vo, cloth extra, 3s. 6d.

Bierce (Ambrose).—In the Midst of Life: Tales of Soldiers and Civilians. Crown 8vo, cloth extra, 3s. 6d.; post 8vo, illustrated boards, 2s.

Bill Nye's Comic History of the United States. With 146 Illustrations by F. OPPER. Crown 8vo, cloth extra, 3s. 6d.

Biré (Edmond). — Diary of a Citizen of Paris during 'The Terror.' Translated and Edited by JOHN DE VILLIERS. With 2 Photogravure Portraits. Two Vols., demy 8vo, cloth, 21s.

Blackburn's (Henry) Art Handbooks.

Academy Notes, 1899.

Academy Notes, 1875-79. Complete in One Vol., with 600 Illustrations. Cloth, 6s.

Academy Notes, 1880-84. Complete in One Vol., with 700 Illustrations. Cloth, 6s.

Academy Notes, 1890-94. Complete in One Vol., with 800 Illustrations. Cloth, 7s. 6d.

Academy Notes, 1895-99. Complete in One Vol., with 800 Illustrations. Cloth, 7s. 6d.

Grosvenor Notes, Vol. I., 1877-82. With 300 Illustrations. Demy 8vo, cloth 6s.

Grosvenor Notes, Vol. II., 1883-87. With 300 Illustrations. Demy 8vo, cloth, 6s.

Grosvenor Notes, Vol. III., 1888-90. With 230 Illustrations. Demy 8vo, cloth, 3s. 6d.

The New Gallery, 1888-1892. With 250 Illustrations. Demy 8vo, cloth, 6s.

English Pictures at the National Gallery. With 114 Illustrations. 1s.

Old Masters at the National Gallery. With 128 Illustrations. 1s. 6d.

Illustrated Catalogue to the National Gallery. With 242 Illusts. Demy 8vo, cloth, 3s.

Demy 8vo, 3s. each.

The Illustrated Catalogue of the Paris Salon, 1899. With 300 Illustrations.

Illustrated Catalogue of the Exhibition of the Société Nationale des Beaux Arts, 1899. With 300 Sketches.

Blind (Mathilde), Poems by.

The Ascent of Man. Crown 8vo, cloth, 5s.

Dramas in Miniature. With a Frontispiece by F. MADOX BROWN. Crown 8vo, cloth, 5s.

Songs and Sonnets. Fcap. 8vo, vellum and gold, 5s.

Birds of Passage: Songs of the Orient and Occident. Second Edition. Crown 8vo, linen, 6s. net.

Bourget (Paul).—A Living Lie. Translated by JOHN DE VILLIERS. With special Preface for the English Edition. Crown 8vo, cloth, 3s. 6d.

Bourne (H. R. Fox), Books by.

English Merchants: Memoirs in Illustration of the Progress of British Commerce. With 32 Illustrations. Crown 8vo, cloth, 3s. 6d.

English Newspapers: Chapters in the History of Journalism. Two Vols., demy 8vo, cloth, 25s.

The Other Side of the Emin Pasha Relief Expedition. Crown 8vo, cloth, 6s.

Boyle (Frederick), Works by. Post 8vo, illustrated bds., 2s. each.

Chronicles of No-Man's Land. | Camp Notes. | Savage Life.

Brand (John).—Observations on Popular Antiquities; chiefly illustrating the Origin of our Vulgar Customs, Ceremonies, and Superstitions. With the Additions of Sir HENRY ELLIS, and numerous Illustrations. Crown 8vo, cloth extra, 7s. 6d.

Brayshaw (J. Dodsworth).—Slum Silhouettes: Stories of London Life. Crown 8vo, cloth, 3s. 6d.

Brewer (Rev. Dr.), Works by.

The Reader's Handbook of Famous Names in Fiction, Allusions, References, Proverbs, Plots, Stories, and Poems. Together with an ENGLISH AND AMERICAN BIBLIOGRAPHY, and a LIST OF THE AUTHORS AND DATES OF DRAMAS AND OPERAS. A New Edition, Revised and Enlarged. Crown 8vo, cloth. 7s. 6d.

A Dictionary of Miracles: Imitative, Realistic, and Dogmatic. Crown 8vo, cloth, 3s. 6d.

Brewster (Sir David), Works by. Post 8vo, cloth, 4s. 6d. each.

More Worlds than One: Creed of the Philosopher and Hope of the Christian. With Plates.

The Martyrs of Science: GALILEO, TYCHO BRAHE, and KEPLER. With Portraits.

Letters on Natural Magic. With numerous Illustrations.

Brillat-Savarin.— Gastronomy as a Fine Art. Translated by R. E. ANDERSON, M.A. Post 8vo, half-bound, 2s.

Bryden (H. A.).—An Exiled Scot: A Romance. With a Frontispiece, by J. S. CROMPTON, R.I. Crown 8vo, cloth, 6s.

Brydges (Harold).—Uncle Sam at Home. With 91 Illustrations. Post 8vo, illustrated boards, 2s.; cloth limp, 2s. 6d.

Buchanan (Robert), Novels, &c., by.

Crown 8vo, cloth extra, 3s. 6d. each ; post 8vo, illustrated boards, 2s. each.

The Shadow of the Sword.
A Child of Nature. With Frontispiece.
God and the Man. With 11 Illustrations by Lady Kilpatrick. (FRED. BARNARD).
The Martyrdom of Madeline. With Frontispiece by A. W. COOPER.

Love Me for Ever. With Frontispiece.
Annan Water. | Foxglove Manor.
The New Abelard. | Rachel Dene.
Matt : A Story of a Caravan. With Frontispiece.
The Master of the Mine. With Frontispiece
The Heir of Linne. | Woman and the Man

Red and White Heather. Crown 8vo, cloth extra, 3s. 6d.

The Wandering Jew : a Christmas Carol. Crown 8vo, cloth, 6s.

The Charlatan. By ROBERT BUCHANAN and HENRY MURRAY. Crown 8vo, cloth, with a Frontispiece by T. H. ROBINSON, 3s. 6d. ; post 8vo, picture boards, 2s.

Burton (Robert).—The Anatomy of Melancholy. With Translations of the Quotations. Demy 8vo, cloth extra, 7s. 6d.

Melancholy Anatomised: An Abridgment of BURTON'S ANATOMY. Post 8vo, half-bd., 2s. 6d.

Caine (Hall), Novels by. Crown 8vo, cloth extra, 3s. 6d. each. ; post 8vo, illustrated boards, 2s. each ; cloth limp, 2s. 6d. each.

The Shadow of a Crime. | A Son of Hagar. | The Deemster.

Also LIBRARY EDITIONS of The Deemster and The Shadow of a Crime, set in new type, crown 8vo, and bound uniform with The Christian, 6s. each ; and CHEAP POPULAR EDITIONS of The Deemster and The Shadow of a Crime, medium 8vo, portrait-cover, 6d. each ; cloth, 1s. each.

Cameron (Commander V. Lovett).—The Cruise of the 'Black Prince' Privateer. Post 8vo, picture boards, 2s.

Captain Coignet, Soldier of the Empire: An Autobiography. Edited by LOREDAN LARCHEY. Translated by Mrs. CAREY. With 100 Illustrations. Crown 8vo. cloth, 3s. 6d.

Carlyle (Jane Welsh), Life of. By Mrs. ALEXANDER IRELAND. With Portrait and Facsimile Letter. Small demy 8vo, cloth extra, 7s. 6d.

Carlyle (Thomas).—On the Choice of Books. Post 8vo, cl., 1s. 6d.

Correspondence of Thomas Carlyle and R. W. Emerson, 1834-1872. Edited by C. E. NORTON. With Portraits. Two Vols., crown 8vo, cloth, 24s.

Carruth (Hayden).—The Adventures of Jones. With 17 Illustrations. Fcap. 8vo, cloth, 2s.

Chambers (Robert W.), Stories of Paris Life by.

The King in Yellow. Crown 8vo, cloth, 3s. 6d. ; fcap. 8vo, cloth limp, 2s. 6d.
In the Quarter. Fcap. 8vo, cloth, 2s. 6d.

Chapman's (George), Works. Vol. I., Plays Complete, including the Doubtful Ones.—Vol. II., Poems and Minor Translations, with Essay by A. C. SWINBURNE.—Vol. III., Translations of the Iliad and Odyssey. Three Vols., crown 8vo, cloth, 3s. 6d. each.

Chapple (J. Mitchell).—The Minor Chord: The Story of a Prima Donna. Crown 8vo, cloth, 3s. 6d.

Chaucer for Children: A Golden Key. By Mrs. H. R. HAWEIS. With 8 Coloured Plates and 30 Woodcuts. Crown 4to, cloth extra, 3s. 6d.

Chaucer for Schools. With the Story of his Times and his Work. By Mrs. H. R. HAWEIS. A New Edition, revised. With a Frontispiece. Demy 8vo, cloth, 2s. 6d.

Chess, The Laws and Practice of. With an Analysis of the Openings. By HOWARD STAUNTON. Edited by R. B. WORMALD. Crown 8vo, cloth, 5s.

The Minor Tactics of Chess : A Treatise on the Deployment of the Forces in obedience to Strategic Principle. By F. K. YOUNG and E. C. HOWELL. Long fcap. 8vo, cloth, 2s. 6d.

The Hastings Chess Tournament. Containing the Authorised Account of the 230 Games played Aug.-Sept., 1895. With Annotations by PILLSBURY, LASKER, TARRASCH, STEINITZ, SCHIFFERS, TEICHMANN, BARDELEBEN, BLACKBURNE, GUNSBERG, TINSLEY, MASON, and ALBIN ; Biographical Sketches of the Chess Masters, and 22 Portraits. Edited by H. F. CHESHIRE. Cheaper Edition. Crown 8vo, cloth, 5s.

Clare (Austin), Stories by.

For the Love of a Lass. Post 8vo, illustrated boards, 2s. ; cloth, 2s. 6d.
By the Rise of the River : Tales and Sketches in South Tynedale. Crown 8vo, cloth, 3s. 6d.

Clive (Mrs. Archer), Novels by. Post 8vo, illust. boards, 2s. each.
Paul Ferroll. | Why Paul Ferroll Killed his Wife.

Clodd (Edward, F.R.A.S.).—Myths and Dreams. Cr. 8vo, 3s. 6d.

Coates (Anne).—Rie's Diary. Crown 8vo, cloth, 3s. 6d.

Cobban (J. Maclaren), Novels by.
The Cure of Souls. Post 8vo, Illustrated boards, 2s.
The Red Sultan. Crown 8vo, cloth extra, 3s. 6d. ; post 8vo, illustrated boards, 2s.
The Burden of Isabel. Crown 8vo, cloth extra, 3s. 6d.

Coleman (John).—Curly: An Actor's Story. With 21 Illustrations
by J. C. DOLLMAN. Crown 8vo, picture cover, 1s.

Coleridge (M. E.).—The Seven Sleepers of Ephesus. Fcap. 8vo,
cloth, 1s. 6d.; leatherette, 1s.

Collins (C. Allston).—The Bar Sinister. Post 8vo, boards, 2s.

Collins (John Churton, M.A.), Books by.
Illustrations of Tennyson. Crown 8vo, cloth extra, 6s.
Jonathan Swift. A Biographical and Critical Study. Crown 8vo, cloth extra, 8s.

Collins (Mortimer and Frances), Novels by.
Crown 8vo, cloth extra, 3s. 6d. each ; post 8vo, illustrated boards, 2s. each.
From Midnight to Midnight. | Blacksmith and Scholar.
Transmigration. | You Play me False. | The Village Comedy.
Post 8vo, illustrated boards, 2s. each.
Sweet Anne Page. | A Fight with Fortune. | Sweet and Twenty. | Frances.

Collins (Wilkie), Novels by.
Crown 8vo, cloth extra, many Illustrated, 3s. 6d. each ; post 8vo, picture boards, 2s. each ;
cloth limp, 2s. 6d. each.

Antonina.	My Miscellanies.	Jezebel's Daughter.
Basil.	Armadale.	The Black Robe.
Hide and Seek.	Poor Miss Finch.	Heart and Science.
The Woman in White.	Miss or Mrs.?	'I Say No.'
The Moonstone.	The New Magdalen.	A Rogue's Life.
Man and Wife.	The Frozen Deep.	The Evil Genius.
After Dark.	The Law and the Lady.	Little Novels.
The Dead Secret.	The Two Destinies.	The Legacy of Cain.
The Queen of Hearts.	The Haunted Hotel.	Blind Love.
No Name.	The Fallen Leaves.	

POPULAR EDITIONS. Medium 8vo, 6d. each; cloth, 1s. each.
The Woman in White. | The Moonstone. | Antonina. | The Dead Secret.

Colman's (George) Humorous Works: 'Broad Grins,' 'My Night-
gown and Slippers,' &c. With Life and Frontispiece. Crown 8vo, cloth extra, 3s. 6d.

Colquhoun (M. J.).—Every Inch a Soldier. Crown 8vo, cloth,
3s. 6d.; post 8vo, illustrated boards, 2s.

Colt-breaking, Hints on. By W. M. HUTCHISON. Cr. 8vo, cl., 3s. 6d.

Convalescent Cookery. By CATHERINE RYAN. Cr. 8vo, 1s. ; cl., 1s. 6d.

Conway (Moncure D.).—George Washington's Rules of Civility
Traced to their Sources and Restored. Fcap. 8vo, Japanese vellum, 2s. 6d.

Cooper (Edward H.).—Geoffory Hamilton. Cr. 8vo, cloth, 3s. 6d.

Cornwall.—Popular Romances of the West of England; or, The
Drolls, Traditions, and Superstitions of Old Cornwall. Collected by ROBERT HUNT, F.R.S. With
two Steel Plates by GEORGE CRUIKSHANK. Crown 8vo, cloth, 7s. 6d.

Cotes (V. Cecil).—Two Girls on a Barge. With 44 Illustrations by
F. H. TOWNSEND. Crown 8vo, cloth extra, 3s. 6d.; post 8vo, cloth, 2s. 6d.

Craddock (C. Egbert), Stories by.
The Prophet of the Great Smoky Mountains. Post 8vo, illustrated boards, 2s.
His Vanished Star. Crown 8vo, cloth extra, 3s. 6d.

Cram (Ralph Adams).—Black Spirits and White. Fcap. 8vo,
cloth, 1s. 6d.

Crellin (H. N.), Books by.
Romances of the Old Seraglio. With 28 Illustrations by S. L. WOOD. Crown 8vo, cloth, 3s. 6d.
Tales of the Caliph. Crown 8vo, cloth, 2s.
The Nazarenes: A Drama. Crown 8vo, 1s.

Crim (Matt.).—Adventures of a Fair Rebel. Crown 8vo, cloth
extra, with a Frontispiece by DAN. BEARD, 3s. 6d.; post 8vo, illustrated boards, 2s.

Crockett (S. R.) and others. —Tales of Our Coast. By S. R.
CROCKETT, GILBERT PARKER, HAROLD FREDERIC, 'Q.,' and W. CLARK RUSSELL. With 2
Illustrations by FRANK BRANGWYN. Crown 8vo, cloth, 3s. 6d.

Croker (Mrs. B. M.), Novels by. Crown 8vo, cloth extra, 3s. 6d.
each; post 8vo, illustrated boards, 2s. each; cloth limp, 2s. 6d. each.

Pretty Miss Neville.	Interference.	Village Tales & Jungle
Proper Pride.	A Family Likeness.	Tragedies.
A Bird of Passage.	'To Let.'	The Real Lady Hilda.
Diana Barrington.	A Third Person.	Married or Single?
Two Masters.	Mr. Jervis.	

Crown 8vo, cloth extra, 3s. 6d. each.
In the Kingdom of Kerry. | Beyond the Pale. | Jason, &c. | Some One Else.

Crown 8vo, cloth, gilt top, 6s. each.
Miss Balmaine's Past. | Infatuation. | Terence.

Cruikshank's Comic Almanack. Complete in TWO SERIES. The
FIRST, from 1835 to 1843; the SECOND, from 1844 to 1853. A Gathering of the Best Humour of
THACKERAY, HOOD, MAYHEW, ALBERT SMITH, A'BECKETT, ROBERT BROUGH, &c. With
numerous Steel Engravings and Woodcuts by GEORGE CRUIKSHANK, HINE, LANDELLS, &c.
Two Vols., crown 8vo, cloth gilt, 7s. 6d. each.
The Life of George Cruikshank. By BLANCHARD JERROLD. With 84 Illustrations and a
Bibliography. Crown 8vo, cloth extra, 3s. 6d.

Cumming (C. F. Gordon), Works by. Demy 8vo, cl. ex., 8s. 6d. ea.
In the Hebrides. With an Autotype Frontispiece and 23 Illustrations.
In the Himalayas and on the Indian Plains. With 42 Illustrations.
Two Happy Years in Ceylon. With 28 Illustrations.

Via Cornwall to Egypt. With a Photogravure Frontispiece. Demy 8vo, cloth, 7s. 6d.

Cussans (John E.).—A Handbook of Heraldry; with Instructions
for Tracing Pedigrees and Deciphering Ancient MSS., &c. Fourth Edition, revised, with 408 Woodcuts
and 2 Coloured Plates. Crown 8vo, cloth extra, 6s.

Cyples (W.).—Hearts of Gold. Cr. 8vo, cl., 3s. 6d.; post 8vo, bds., 2s.

Daudet (Alphonse).—The Evangelist; or, Port Salvation. Crown
8vo, cloth extra, 3s. 6d.; post 8vo, illustrated boards, 2s.

Davenant (Francis, M.A.).—Hints for Parents on the Choice of
a Profession for their Sons when Starting in Life. Crown 8vo, cloth, 1s. 6d.

Davidson (Hugh Coleman).—Mr. Sadler's Daughters. With a
Frontispiece by STANLEY WOOD. Crown 8vo, cloth extra, 3s. 6d.

Davies (Dr. N. E. Yorke-), Works by. Cr. 8vo, 1s. ea.; cl., 1s. 6d. ea.
One Thousand Medical Maxims and Surgical Hints.
Nursery Hints: A Mother's Guide in Health and Disease.
Foods for the Fat: The Dietetic Cure of Corpulency and of Gout.

Aids to Long Life. Crown 8vo, 2s.; cloth limp, 2s. 6d.

Davies' (Sir John) Complete Poetical Works. Collected and Edited,
with Introduction and Notes, by Rev. A. B. GROSART, D.D. Two Vols., crown 8vo, cloth, 3s. 6d. each.

Dawson (Erasmus, M.B.).—The Fountain of Youth. Crown 8vo,
cloth extra, with Two Illustrations by HUME NISBET, 3s. 6d.; post 8vo, illustrated boards, 2s.

De Guerin (Maurice), The Journal of. Edited by G. S. TREBUTIEN.
With a Memoir by SAINTE-BEUVE. Translated from the 20th French Edition by JESSIE P. FROTH-
INGHAM. Fcap. 8vo, half-bound, 2s. 6d.

De Maistre (Xavier).—A Journey Round my Room. Translated
by HENRY ATTWELL. Post 8vo, cloth limp, 2s. 6d.

De Mille (James).—A Castle in Spain. Crown 8vo, cloth extra, with
a Frontispiece, 3s. 6d.; post 8vo, illustrated boards, 2s.

Derby (The): The Blue Ribbon of the Turf. With Brief Accounts
of THE OAKS. By LOUIS HENRY CURZON. Crown 8vo, cloth limp, 2s. 6d.

Derwent (Leith), Novels by. Cr. 8vo, cl., 3s. 6d. ea.; post 8vo, 2s. ea.
Our Lady of Tears. | Circe's Lovers.

Dewar (T. R.).—A Ramble Round the Globe. With 220 Illustrations. Crown 8vo, cloth extra, 7s. 6d.

De Windt (Harry), Books by.

Through the Gold-Fields of Alaska to Bering Straits. With Map and 33 full-page Illustrations. Cheaper Issue. Demy 8vo, cloth, 6s.
True Tales of Travel and Adventure. Crown 8vo, cloth, 3s. 6d.

Dickens (Charles), About England with. By ALFRED RIMMER.

With 57 Illustrations by C. A. VANDERHOOF and the AUTHOR. Square 8vo, cloth, 3s. 6d.

Dictionaries.

The Reader's Handbook of Famous Names in Fiction, Allusions, References, Proverbs, Plots, Stories, and Poems. Together with an ENGLISH AND AMERICAN BIBLIOGRAPHY, and a LIST OF THE AUTHORS AND DATES OF DRAMAS AND OPERAS. By Rev. E. C. BREWER, LL.D A New Edition, Revised and Enlarged. Crown 8vo, cloth, 7s. 6d.
A Dictionary of Miracles: Imitative, Realistic, and Dogmatic. By the Rev. E. C. BREWER, LL.D. Crown 8vo, cloth, 3s. 6d.
Familiar Short Sayings of Great Men. With Historical and Explanatory Notes by SAMUEL A. BENT, A.M. Crown 8vo, cloth extra, 7s. 6d.
The Slang Dictionary: Etymological, Historical, and Anecdotal. Crown 8vo, cloth, 6s. 6d.
Words, Facts, and Phrases: A Dictionary of Curious, Quaint, and Out-of-the-Way Matters. By ELIEZER EDWARDS. Crown 8vo, cloth extra, 3s. 6d.

Dilke (Rt. Hon. Sir Charles, Bart., M.P.).—The British Empire.

Crown 8vo, buckram, 3s. 6d.

Dobson (Austin), Works by.

Thomas Bewick and his Pupils. With 95 Illustrations. Square 8vo, cloth, 3s. 6d.
Four Frenchwomen. With Four Portraits. Crown 8vo, buckram, gilt top, 6s.
Eighteenth Century Vignettes. IN THREE SERIES. Crown 8vo, buckram, 6s. each.
A Paladin of Philanthropy, and other Papers. With 2 Illustrations. Crown 8vo, buckram, 6s.

Dobson (W. T.).—Poetical Ingenuities and Eccentricities. Post

8vo, cloth limp, 2s. 6d.

Donovan (Dick), Detective Stories by.

Post 8vo, illustrated boards, 2s. each; cloth limp, 2s. 6d. each.

The Man-Hunter. | **Wanted!**	**A Detective's Triumphs.**
Caught at Last.	**In the Grip of the Law.**
Tracked and Taken.	**From Information Received.**
Who Poisoned Hetty Duncan?	**Link by Link.** | **Dark Deeds.**
Suspicion Aroused.	**Riddles Read.**

Crown 8vo, cloth extra, 3s. 6d. each; post 8vo, illustrated boards, 2s. each; cloth, 2s. 6d. each.
The Man from Manchester. With 23 Illustrations.
Tracked to Doom. With Six full-page Illustrations by GORDON BROWNE.
The Mystery of Jamaica Terrace.   \| **The Chronicles of Michael Danevitch.**

Crown 8vo, cloth, 3s. 6d. each.
The Records of Vincent Trill, of the Detective Service.   \| **Tales of Terror.** [Shortly.

Dowling (Richard).—Old Corcoran's Money. Crown 8vo, cl., 3s. 6d.

Doyle (A. Conan).—The Firm of Girdlestone. Cr. 8vo, cl., 3s. 6d.

Dramatists, The Old.   Cr. 8vo, cl. ex., with Portraits, 3s. 6d. per Vol.

Ben Jonson's Works. With Notes, Critical and Explanatory, and a Biographical Memoir by WILLIAM GIFFORD. Edited by Colonel CUNNINGHAM. Three Vols.
Chapman's Works. Three Vols. Vol. I. contains the Plays complete; Vol. II., Poems and Minor Translations, with an Essay by A. C. SWINBURNE; Vol. III., Translations of the Iliad and Odyssey.
Marlowe's Works. Edited, with Notes, by Colonel CUNNINGHAM. One Vol.
Massinger's Plays. From GIFFORD'S Text. Edited by Colonel CUNNINGHAM. One Vol.

Duncan (Sara Jeannette: Mrs. EVERARD COTES), Works by.

Crown 8vo, cloth extra, 7s. 6d. each.
A Social Departure. With 111 Illustrations by F. H. TOWNSEND.
An American Girl in London. With 80 Illustrations by F. H. TOWNSEND.
The Simple Adventures of a Memsahib. With 37 Illustrations by F. H. TOWNSEND.

Crown 8vo, cloth extra, 3s. 6d. each.
A Daughter of To-Day.   \| **Vernon's Aunt.** With 47 Illustrations by HAL HURST.

Dutt (Romesh C.).—England and India: A Record of Progress

during One Hundred Years. Crown 8vo, cloth, 2s.

Early English Poets.   Edited, with Introductions and Annotations

by Rev. A. B. GROSART, D.D. Crown 8vo, cloth boards, 3s. 6d. per Volume.
Fletcher's (Giles) Complete Poems. One Vol.
Davies' (Sir John) Complete Poetical Works. Two Vols.
Herrick's (Robert) Complete Collected Poems. Three Vols.
Sidney's (Sir Philip) Complete Poetical Works. Three Vols.

Edgcumbe (Sir E. R. Pearce).—Zephyrus: A Holiday in Brazil

and on the River Plate. With 41 Illustrations. Crown 8vo, cloth extra, 5s.

Edwardes (Mrs. Annie), Novels by. Post 8vo, illust. bds., 2s. each.

Archie Lovell.   \| **A Point of Honour**
A Plaster Saint. Crown 8vo, cloth, 3s. 6d.

Edwards (Eliezer).—Words, Facts, and Phrases: A Dictionary of Curious, Quaint, and Out-of-the-Way Matters. Cheaper Edition. Crown 8vo, cloth, 3s. 6d.

Edwards (M. Betham=), Novels by.
Kitty. Post 8vo, boards, 2s. ; cloth, 2s. 6d. | **Felicia.** Post 8vo, illustrated boards, 2s.

Egerton (Rev. J. C., M.A.). — Sussex Folk and Sussex Ways. With Introduction by Rev. Dr. H. WACE, and Four Illustrations. Crown 8vo, cloth extra, 5s.

Eggleston (Edward).—Roxy: A Novel. Post 8vo, illust. boards, 2s.

Englishman's House, The: A Practical Guide for Selecting or Building a House. By C. J. RICHARDSON. Coloured Frontispiece and 534 Illusts. Cr. 8vo, cloth, 3s. 6d.

Ewald (Alex. Charles, F.S.A.), Works by.
The Life and Times of Prince Charles Stuart, Count of Albany (THE YOUNG PRETEN-DER). With a Portrait. Crown 8vo, cloth extra, 7s. 6d.
Stories from the State Papers. With Autotype Frontispiece. Crown 8vo, cloth, 6s.

Eyes, Our: How to Preserve Them. By JOHN BROWNING. Cr. 8vo, 1s.

Familiar Short Sayings of Great Men. By SAMUEL ARTHUR BENT, A.M. Fifth Edition, Revised and Enlarged. Crown 8vo, cloth extra, 7s. 6d.

Faraday (Michael), Works by. Post 8vo, cloth extra, 4s. 6d. each.
The Chemical History of a Candle: Lectures delivered before a Juvenile Audience. Edited by WILLIAM CROOKES, F.C.S. With numerous Illustrations.
On the Various Forces of Nature, and their Relations to each other. Edited by WILLIAM CROOKES, F.C.S. With Illustrations.

Farrer (J. Anson).—War: Three Essays. Crown 8vo, 1s. ; cloth, 1s. 6d.

Fenn (G. Manville), Novels by.
Crown 8vo, cloth extra, 3s. 6d. each : post 8vo, illustrated boards, 2s. each.
The New Mistress. | Witness to the Deed.| The Tiger Lily. | The White Virgin.

A Crimson Crime. Crown 8vo, cloth, gilt top, 6s.

NEW EDITIONS. Crown 8vo, cloth, 3s. 6d. each.

A Woman Worth Winning.	The Story of Antony Grace.
Cursed by a Fortune.	Eve at the Wheel; and The Chaplain's Craze.
The Case of Ailsa Gray.	
Commodore Junk.	The Bag of Diamonds; and The Dark House.
Black Blood.	
Double Cunning.	The Man with a Shadow.
A Fluttered Dovecote.	One Maid's Mischief.
King of the Castle.	This Man's Wife.
The Master of the Ceremonies.	In Jeopardy.

Feuerheerd (H.).—The Gentleman's Cellar; or, The Butler and Cellarman's Guide. Fcap. 8vo, cloth, 1s. [Shortly.

Fin=Bec.—The Cupboard Papers: Observations on the Art of Living and Dining. Post 8vo, cloth limp, 2s. 6d.

Firework=Making, The Complete Art of; or, The Pyrotechnist's Treasury. By THOMAS KENTISH. With 267 Illustrations. Crown 8vo, cloth, 3s. 6d.

First Book, My. By WALTER BESANT, JAMES PAYN, W. CLARK RUS-SELL, GRANT ALLEN, HALL CAINE, GEORGE R. SIMS, RUDYARD KIPLING, A. CONAN DOYLE, M. E. BRADDON, F. W. ROBINSON, H. RIDER HAGGARD, R. M. BALLANTYNE, I. ZANGWILL, MORLEY ROBERTS, D. CHRISTIE MURRAY, MARY CORELLI, J. K. JEROME, JOHN STRANGE WINTER, BRET HARTE, ' Q.,' ROBERT BUCHANAN, and R. L. STEVENSON. With a Prefatory Story by JEROME K. JEROME, and 185 Illustrations. A New Edition. Small demy 8vo, art linen, 3s. 6d.

Fitzgerald (Percy), Works by.
Little Essays: Passages from the Letters of CHARLES LAMB. Post 8vo, cloth, 2s. 6d.
Fatal Zero. Crown 8vo, cloth extra, 3s. 6d. ; post 8vo, illustrated boards, 2s.

Post 8vo, illustrated boards, 2s. each.

Bella Donna.	The Lady of Brantome.	The Second Mrs. Tillotson.
Polly.	Never Forgotten.	Seventy-five Brooke Street.

Sir Henry Irving: Twenty Years at the Lyceum. With Portrait. Crown 8vo, 1s.; cloth, 1s. 6d.

Flammarion (Camille), Works by.
Popular Astronomy: A General Description of the Heavens. Translated by J. ELLARD GORE F.R.A.S. With Three Plates and 288 Illustrations. Medium 8vo, cloth, 10s. 6d.
Urania: A Romance. With 87 Illustrations. Crown 8vo, cloth extra, 5s.

Fletcher's (Giles, B.D.) Complete Poems: Christ's Victorie in Heaven, Christ's Victorie on Earth, Christ's Triumph over Death, and Minor Poems. With Notes by Rev. A. B. GROSART, D.D. Crown 8vo, cloth boards, 3s. 6d.

Fonblanque (Albany).—Filthy Lucre. Post 8vo, illust. boards, 2s.

Forbes (Archibald).—The Life of Napoleon III. With Photogravure Frontispiece and Thirty-six full-page Illustrations. Cheaper Issue. Demy 8vo, cloth, 6s.

Fowler (J. Kersley).—Records of Old Times Historical, Social, Political, Sporting, and Agricultural. With Eight full-page Illustrations. Demy 8vo, cloth, 10s. 6d.

Francillon (R. E.), Novels by.
Crown 8vo, cloth extra, 3s. 6d. each; post 8vo, illustrated boards, 2s. each.

One by One.	**A Real Queen.**	**A Dog and his Shadow.**
Ropes of Sand. Illustrated		

Post 8vo, illustrated boards, 2s. each.

Queen Cophetua.	**Olympia.**	**Romances of the Law.**	**King or Knave?**

Jack Doyle's Daughter. Crown 8vo, cloth, 3s. 6d.

Frederic (Harold), Novels by. Post 8vo, cloth extra, 3s. 6d. each; illustrated boards, 2s. each.

Seth's Brother's Wife.	**The Lawton Girl.**

French Literature, A History of. By HENRY VAN LAUN. Three Vols., demy 8vo, cloth boards, 7s. 6d. each.

Fry's (Herbert) Royal Guide to the London Charities. Edited by JOHN LANE. Published Annually. Crown 8vo, cloth, 1s. 6d.

Gardening Books. Post 8vo, 1s. each; cloth limp. 1s. 6d. each.
A Year's Work in Garden and Greenhouse. By GEORGE GLENNY.
Household Horticulture. By TOM and JANE JERROLD. Illustrated.
The Garden that Paid the Rent. By TOM JERROLD.

Gardner (Mrs. Alan).—Rifle and Spear with the Rajpoots: Being the Narrative of a Winter's Travel and Sport in Northern India. With numerous Illustrations by the Author and F. H. TOWNSEND. Demy 4to, half-bound, 21s.

Garrett (Edward).—The Capel Girls: A Novel. Post 8vo, illustrated boards, 2s.

Gaulot (Paul).—The Red Shirts: A Tale of "The Terror." Translated by JOHN DE VILLIERS. With a Frontispiece by STANLEY WOOD. Crown 8vo, cloth, 3s. 6d.

Gentleman's Magazine, The. 1s. Monthly. Contains Stories, Articles upon Literature, Science, Biography, and Art, and 'Table Talk' by SYLVANUS URBAN.
⁎ *Bound Volumes for recent years kept in stock, 8s. 6d. each. Cases for binding, 2s. each.*

Gentleman's Annual, The. Published Annually in November. 1s.

German Popular Stories. Collected by the Brothers GRIMM and Translated by EDGAR TAYLOR. With Introduction by JOHN RUSKIN, and 22 Steel Plates after GEORGE CRUIKSHANK. Square 8vo, cloth, 6s. 6d.; gilt edges, 7s. 6d.

Gibbon (Chas.), Novels by. Cr. 8vo, cl., 3s. 6d. ea.; post 8vo, bds., 2s. ea.

Robin Gray. With Frontispiece.	**Loving a Dream.** | **The Braes of Yarrow.**
The Golden Shaft. With Frontispiece.	**Of High Degree.**

Post 8vo, illustrated boards, 2s. each.

The Flower of the Forest.	**In Love and War.**
The Dead Heart.	**A Heart's Problem.**
For Lack of Gold.	**By Mead and Stream.**
What Will the World Say?	**Fancy Free.**
For the King. | **A Hard Knot.**	**In Honour Bound.**
Queen of the Meadow.	**Heart's Delight.**
In Pastures Green.	**Blood-Money.**

Gibney (Somerville).—Sentenced! Crown 8vo, cloth, 1s. 6d.

Gilbert (W. S.), Original Plays by. In Three Series, 2s. 6d. each.
The FIRST SERIES contains: The Wicked World—Pygmalion and Galatea—Charity—The Princess—The Palace of Truth—Trial by Jury.
The SECOND SERIES: Broken Hearts—Engaged—Sweethearts—Gretchen—Dan'l Druce—Tom Cobb—H.M.S. 'Pinafore'—The Sorcerer—The Pirates of Penzance.
The THIRD SERIES: Comedy and Tragedy—Foggerty's Fairy—Rosencrantz and Guildenstern—Patience—Princess Ida—The Mikado—Ruddigore—The Yeomen of the Guard—The Gondoliers—The Mountebanks—Utopia.

Eight Original Comic Operas written by W. S. GILBERT. In Two Series. Demy 8vo, cloth, 2s. 6d. each. The FIRST containing: The Sorcerer—H.M.S. 'Pinafore'—The Pirates of Penzance—Iolanthe—Patience—Princess Ida—The Mikado—Trial by Jury.
The SECOND SERIES containing: The Gondoliers—The Grand Duke—The Yeomen of the Guard—His Excellency—Utopia, Limited—Ruddigore—The Mountebanks—Haste to the Wedding.
The Gilbert and Sullivan Birthday Book: Quotations for Every Day in the Year, selected from Plays by W. S. GILBERT set to Music by Sir A. SULLIVAN. Compiled by ALEX. WATSON. Royal 16mo, Japanese leather, 2s. 6d.

Gilbert (William), Novels by. Post 8vo, illustrated bds., 2s. each.
Dr. Austin's Guests. | James Duke, Costermonger.
The Wizard of the Mountain.

Glanville (Ernest), Novels by.
Crown 8vo, cloth extra, 3s. 6d. each; post 8vo, illustrated boards, 2s. each.
The Lost Heiress: A Tale of Love, Battle, and Adventure. With Two Illustrations by H. NISBET.
The Fossicker: A Romance of Mashonaland. With Two Illustrations by HUME NISBET.
A Fair Colonist. With a Frontispiece by STANLEY WOOD.

The Golden Rock. With a Frontispiece by STANLEY WOOD. Crown 8vo, cloth extra, 3s. 6d.
Kloof Yarns. Crown 8vo, picture cover, 1s.; cloth, 1s. 6d.
Tales from the Veld. With Twelve Illustrations by M. NISBET. Crown 8vo, cloth, 3s. 6d.

Glenny (George).—A Year's Work in Garden and Greenhouse:
Practical Advice as to the Management of the Flower, Fruit, and Frame Garden. Post 8vo, 1s.; cloth, 1s. 6d.

Godwin (William).—Lives of the Necromancers. Post 8vo, cl., 2s.

Golden Treasury of Thought, The: An Encyclopædia of QUOTA-
TIONS. Edited by THEODORE TAYLOR. Crown 8vo, cloth gilt, 7s. 6d.

Gontaut, Memoirs of the Duchesse de (Gouvernante to the Chil-
dren of France), 1773-1836. With Two Photogravures. Two Vols., demy 8vo, cloth extra, 21s.

Goodman (E. J.).—The Fate of Herbert Wayne. Cr. 8vo, 3s. 6d.

Greeks and Romans, The Life of the, described from Antique
Monuments. By ERNST GUHL and W. KONER. Edited by Dr. F. HUEFFER. With 545 Illustrations. Large crown 8vo, cloth extra, 7s. 6d.

Greville (Henry), Novels by.
Post 8vo, illustrated boards, 2s. each.
Nikanor. Translated by ELIZA E. CHASE.
A Noble Woman. Translated by ALBERT D. VANDAM.

Grey (Sir George).—The Romance of a Proconsul: Being the
Personal Life and Memoirs of Sir GEORGE GREY, K.C.B. By JAMES MILNE. With Portrait. Crown
8vo, buckram, 6s.

Griffith (Cecil).—Corinthia Marazion: A Novel. Crown 8vo, cloth
extra, 3s. 6d.; post 8vo, illustrated boards, 2s.

Grundy (Sydney).—The Days of his Vanity: A Passage in the
Life of a Young Man. Crown 8vo, cloth extra, 3s. 6d.; post 8vo, illustrated boards, 2s.

Habberton (John, Author of 'Helen's Babies'), **Novels by.**
Post 8vo, illustrated boards, 2s. each; cloth limp, 2s. 6d. each.
Brueton's Bayou. | Country Luck.

Hair, The: Its Treatment in Health, Weakness, and Disease. Translated from the German of Dr. J. PINCUS. Crown 8vo, 1s.; cloth, 1s. 6d.

Hake (Dr. Thomas Gordon), Poems by. Cr. 8vo, cl. ex., 6s. each.
New Symbols. | Legends of the Morrow. | The Serpent Play.
Maiden Ecstasy. Small 4to, cloth extra, 8s.

Halifax (C.).—Dr. Rumsey's Patient. By Mrs. L. T. MEADE and
CLIFFORD HALIFAX, M.D. Crown 8vo, cloth, 3s. 6d.

Hall (Mrs. S. C.).—Sketches of Irish Character. With numerous
Illustrations on Steel and Wood by MACLISE, GILBERT, HARVEY, and GEORGE CRUIKSHANK.
Small demy 8vo, cloth extra, 7s. 6d.

Hall (Owen), Novels by.
Crown 8vo, cloth, 3s. 6d. each.
The Track of a Storm. | Jetsam.
Eureka. Crown 8vo, cloth gilt top, 6s.   [Shortly.

Halliday (Andrew).—Every-day Papers. Post 8vo, boards, 2s.

Hamilton (Cosmo).—Stories by. Crown 8vo, cloth gilt, 3s. 6d. each.
The Glamour of the Impossible. | Through a Keyhole.

Handwriting, The Philosophy of. With over 100 Facsimiles and
Explanatory Text. By DON FELIX DE SALAMANCA. Post 8vo, cloth limp, 2s. 6d.

Hanky-Panky: Easy and Difficult Tricks, White Magic, Sleight of
Hand, &c. Edited by W. H. CREMER. With 200 Illustrations. Crown 8vo, cloth extra, 4s. 6d.

Hardy (Thomas).—Under the Greenwood Tree. Post 8vo, cloth
extra, 3s. 6d.; illustrated boards, 2s.; cloth limp, 2s. 6d.

Harte's (Bret) Collected Works. Revised by the Author. LIBRARY EDITION, in Nine Volumes, crown 8vo, cloth extra, 6s. each.
Vol.   I. COMPLETE POETICAL AND DRAMATIC WORKS. With Steel-plate Portrait.
  „   II. THE LUCK OF ROARING CAMP—BOHEMIAN PAPERS—AMERICAN LEGEND.
  „ III. TALES OF THE ARGONAUTS—EASTERN SKETCHES.
  „ IV. GABRIEL CONROY. | Vol. V. STORIES—CONDENSED NOVELS, &c.
  „ VI. TALES OF THE PACIFIC SLOPE.
  „ VII. TALES OF THE PACIFIC SLOPE—II. With Portrait by JOHN PETTIE, R.A.
  „ VIII. TALES OF THE PINE AND THE CYPRESS.
  „ IX. BUCKEYE AND CHAPPAREL.

Bret Harte's Choice Works, in Prose and Verse. With Portrait of the Author and 40 Illustrations. Crown 8vo, cloth, 3s. 6d.
Bret Harte's Poetical Works. Printed on hand-made paper. Crown 8vo, buckram, 4s. 6d.
Some Later Verses. Crown 8vo, linen gilt, 5s.

Crown 8vo, cloth extra, 3s. 6d. each ; post 8vo, picture boards, 2s. each.
Gabriel Conroy.
A Waif of the Plains. With 60 Illustrations by STANLEY L. WOOD.
A Ward of the Golden Gate. With 59 Illustrations by STANLEY L. WOOD.

Crown 8vo, cloth extra, 3s. 6d. each.
A Sappho of Green Springs, &c. With Two Illustrations by HUME NISBET.
Colonel Starbottle's Client, and Some Other People. With a Frontispiece.
Susy: A Novel. With Frontispiece and Vignette by J. A. CHRISTIE.
Sally Dows, &c. With 47 Illustrations by W. D. ALMOND and others.
A Protegee of Jack Hamlin's, &c. With 26 Illustrations by W. SMALL and others.
The Bell-Ringer of Angel's, &c. With 39 Illustrations by DUDLEY HARDY and others.
Clarence: A Story of the American War. With Eight Illustrations by A. JULE GOODMAN.
Barker's Luck, &c. With 39 Illustrations by A. FORESTIER, PAUL HARDY, &c.
Devil's Ford, &c. With a Frontispiece by W. H. OVEREND.
The Crusade of the "Excelsior." With a Frontispiece by J. BERNARD PARTRIDGE.
Three Partners ; or, The Big Strike on Heavy Tree Hill. With 8 Illustrations by J. GULICH.
Tales of Trail and Town. With Frontispiece by G. P. JACOMB-HOOD.

Post 8vo, illustrated boards, 2s. each.
An Heiress of Red Dog, &c. | **The Luck of Roaring Camp,** &c.
Callfornian Stories.

Post 8vo, illustrated boards, 2s. each ; cloth, 2s. 6d. each.
Flip. | **Maruja.** | **A Phyllis of the Sierras.**

Haweis (Mrs. H. R.), Books by.
The Art of Beauty. With Coloured Frontispiece and 91 Illustrations. Square 8vo, cloth bds., 6s
The Art of Decoration. With Coloured Frontispiece and 74 Illustrations. Sq. 8vo, cloth bds., 6s.
The Art of Dress. With 32 Illustrations. Post 8vo, 1s. ; cloth, 1s. 6d.
Chaucer for Schools. With the Story of his Times and his Work. A New Edition, revised. With a Frontispiece. Demy 8vo, cloth, 2s. 6d.
Chaucer for Children. With 38 Illustrations (8 Coloured). Crown 4to, cloth extra, 3s. 6d.

Haweis (Rev. H. R., M.A.).—American Humorists: WASHINGTON IRVING, OLIVER WENDELL HOLMES, JAMES RUSSELL LOWELL, ARTEMUS WARD, MARK TWAIN, and BRET HARTE. Crown 8vo, cloth, 6s.

Hawthorne (Julian), Novels by.
Crown 8vo, cloth extra, 3s. 6d. each ; post 8vo, illustrated boards, 2s. each.
Garth. | **Ellice Quentin.** | **Beatrix Randolph.** With Four Illusts.
Sebastian Strome. | | **David Poindexter's Disappearance.**
Fortune's Fool. | **Dust.** Four Illusts. | **The Spectre of the Camera.**
Post 8vo, illustrated boards, 2s. each.
Miss Cadogna. | **Love—or a Name.**

Heckethorn (C. W.).—London Souvenirs. (Notes of a LONDON ANTIQUARY.) Crown 8vo, cloth, 6s.   [Shortly.

Helps (Sir Arthur), Books by Post 8vo, cloth limp, 2s. 6d. each.
Animals and their Masters. | **Social Pressure.**
Ivan de Biron: A Novel. Crown 8vo, cloth extra, 3s. 6d. ; post 8vo, illustrated boards, 2s.

Henderson (Isaac).—Agatha Page: A Novel. Cr. 8vo, cl., 3s. 6d.

Henty (G. A.), Novels by.
Rujub, the Juggler. With Eight Illustrations by STANLEY L. WOOD. PRESENTATION EDITION, small demy 8vo, cloth, gilt edges, 5s. ; cr. 8vo, cloth, 3s. 6d. ; post 8vo, illust. boards, 2s.
Crown 8vo, cloth, 3s. 6d. each.
The Queen's Cup. | **Dorothy's Double.**
Colonel Thorndyke's Secret. Crown 8vo, cloth, gilt top, 6s. ; PRESENTATION EDITION, with a Frontispiece by STANLEY L. WOOD, small demy 8vo, cloth, gilt edges, 5s.

Herman (Henry).—A Leading Lady. Post 8vo, bds., 2s. ; cl., 2s. 6d.

Herrick's (Robert) Hesperides, Noble Numbers, and Complete Collected Poems. With Memorial-Introduction and Notes by the Rev. A. B. GROSART, D.D., Steel Portrait, &c. Three Vols., crown 8vo, cloth boards, 3s. 6d. each.

Hertzka (Dr. Theodor).—Freeland: A Social Anticipation. Translated by ARTHUR RANSOM. Crown 8vo, cloth extra, 6s.

Hesse-Wartegg (Chevalier Ernst von).— Tunis: The Land and the People. With 22 Illustrations. Crown 8vo, cloth extra, 3s. 6d.

Hill (Headon).—Zambra the Detective. Crown 8vo, cloth, 3s. 6d. ; post 8vo, picture boards, 2s. ; cloth, 2s. 6d.

Hill (John), Works by.
Treason-Felony. Post 8vo, boards, 2s. | The Common Ancestor. Cr. 8vo, cloth, 3s. 6d

Hoey (Mrs. Cashel).--The Lover's Creed. Post 8vo, boards, 2s.

Holiday, Where to go for a. By E. P. SHOLL, Sir H. MAXWELL, Bart., M.P., JOHN WATSON, JANE BARLOW, MARY LOVETT CAMERON, JUSTIN H. McCARTHY, PAUL LANGE, J. W. GRAHAM, J. H. SALTER, PHŒBE ALLEN, S. J. BECKETT, L. RIVERS VINE, and C. F. GORDON CUMMING. Crown 8vo, 1s. : cloth, 1s. 6d.

Hollingshead (John).—Niagara Spray. Crown 8vo. 1s.

Holmes (Gordon, M.D.)—The Science of Voice Production and Voice Preservation. Crown 8vo, 1s. ; cloth, 1s. 6d.

Holmes (Oliver Wendell), Works by.
The Autocrat of the Breakfast-Table. Illustrated by J. GORDON THOMSON. Post 8vo, cloth limp, 2s. 6d.- Another Edition, post 8vo, cloth, 2s.
The Autocrat of the Breakfast-Table and The Professor at the Breakfast-Table. In One Vol. Post 8vo, half-bound, 2s.

Hood's (Thomas) Choice Works in Prose and Verse. With Life of the Author, Portrait, and 200 Illustrations. Crown 8vo, cloth, 3s. 6d.
Hood's Whims and Oddities. With 85 Illustrations. Post 8vo, half-bound, 2s.

Hook's (Theodore) Choice Humorous Works; including his Ludicrous Adventures, Bons Mots, Puns, and Hoaxes. With Life of the Author, Portraits, Facsimiles and Illustrations. Crown 8vo, cloth extra, 7s. 6d.

Hooper (Mrs. Geo.).—The House of Raby. Post 8vo, boards, 2s.

Hopkins (Tighe), Novels by. Crown 8vo, cloth, 6s. each.
Nell Haffenden. With 8 Illustrations by C. GREGORY. | For Freedom.

Crown 8vo, cloth, 3s. 6d. each.
'Twixt Love and Duty. With a Frontispiece. | The Incomplete Adventurer.
The Nugents of Carriconna.

Horne (R. Hengist). — Orion: An Epic Poem. With Photograph Portrait by SUMMERS. Tenth Edition. Crown 8vo, cloth extra, 7s.

Hugo (Victor).—The Outlaw of Iceland (Han d'Islande). Translated by Sir GILBERT CAMPBELL. Crown 8vo, cloth, 3s. 6d.

Hungerford (Mrs., Author of ' Molly Bawn '), Novels by.
Post 8vo, illustrated boards, 2s. each : cloth limp, 2s. 6d. each.
A Maiden All Forlorn. | A Modern Circe. | An Unsatisfactory Lover.
Marvel. | A Mental Struggle. | Lady Patty.
In Durance Vile.

Crown 8vo, cloth extra, 3s. 6d. each ; post 8vo, illustrated boards, 2s. each ; cloth limp, 2s. 6d. each.
April's Lady. | The Three Graces.
Peter's Wife. | The Professor's Experiment.
Lady Verner's Flight. | Nora Creina.
The Red-House Mystery.

Crown 8vo, cloth extra, 3s. 6d. each.
An Anxious Moment. | A Point of Conscience.
The Coming of Chloe. | Lovice.

Hunt's (Leigh) Essays: A Tale for a Chimney Corner, &c. Edited by EDMUND OLLIER. Post 8vo, half-bound, 2s.

Hunt (Mrs. Alfred), Novels by.
Crown 8vo, cloth extra, 3s. 6d. each ; post 8vo, illustrated boards, 2s. each.
The Leaden Casket. | Self-Condemned. | That Other Person.
Thornicroft's Model. Post 8vo, boards, 2s. | Mrs. Juliet. Crown 8vo, cloth extra, 3s. 6d.

Hutchison (W. M.).—Hints on Colt-breaking. With 25 Illustrations. Crown 8vo, cloth extra, 3s. 6d.

Hydrophobia: An Account of M. PASTEUR'S System ; The Technique of his Method, and Statistics. By RENAUD SUZOR, M.B. Crown 8vo, cloth extra, 6s.

Hyne (C. J. Cutcliffe).—Honour of Thieves. Cr. 8vo, cloth, 3s. 6d.

Impressions (The) of Aureole. Cheaper Edition, with a New Preface. Post 8vo, blush-rose paper and cloth, 2s. 6d.

Indoor Paupers. By ONE OF THEM. Crown 8vo, 1s. ; cloth, 1s. 6d.

Innkeeper's Handbook (The) and Licensed Victualler's Manual. By J. TREVOR-DAVIES. A New Edition. Crown 8vo, cloth, 2s.

Irish Wit and Humour, Songs of. Collected and Edited by A. PERCEVAL GRAVES. Post 8vo, cloth limp, 2s. 6d.

Irving (Sir Henry) : A Record of over Twenty Years at the Lyceum. By PERCY FITZGERALD. With Portrait. Crown 8vo, 1s. ; cloth, 1s. 6d.

James (C. T. C.). — A Romance of the Queen's Hounds. Post 8vo, cloth limp, 1s. 6d.

Jameson (William).—My Dead Self. Post 8vo, bds., 2s. ; cl , 2s. 6d.

Japp (Alex. H., LL.D.).—Dramatic Pictures, &c. Cr. 8vo, cloth, 5s.

Jay (Harriett), Novels by. Post 8vo, illustrated boards, 2s. each.
The Dark Colleen. | **The Queen of Connaught.**

Jefferies (Richard), Books by. Post 8vo, cloth limp, 2s. 6d. each.
Nature near London. | **The Life of the Fields.** | **The Open Air.**
₊ Also the HAND-MADE PAPER EDITION, crown 8vo, buckram, gilt top, 6s. each.

   The Eulogy of Richard Jefferies. By Sir WALTER BESANT. With a Photograph Portrait. Crown 8vo, cloth extra, 6s.

Jennings (Henry J.), Works by.
Curiosities of Criticism. Post 8vo, cloth limp, 2s. 6d.
Lord Tennyson : A Biographical Sketch. With Portrait. Post 8vo, 1s. ; cloth, 1s. 6d.

Jerome (Jerome K.), Books by.
Stageland. With 64 Illustrations by J. BERNARD PARTRIDGE. Fcap. 4to, picture cover, 1s.
John Ingerfield, &c. With 9 Illusts. by A. S. BOYD and JOHN GULICH. Fcap. 8vo, pic. cov. 1s. 6d.
The Prude's Progress : A Comedy by J. K. JEROME and EDEN PHILLPOTTS. Cr. 8vo, 1s. 6d.

Jerrold (Douglas).—The Barber's Chair; and The Hedgehog Letters. Post 8vo, printed on laid paper and half-bound, 2s.

Jerrold (Tom), Works by. Post 8vo, 1s. ea. ; cloth limp, 1s. 6d. each.
The Garden that Paid the Rent.
Household Horticulture : A Gossip about Flowers. Illustrated.

Jesse (Edward).—Scenes and Occupations of a Country Life. Post 8vo, cloth limp, 2s.

Jones (William, F.S.A.), Works by. Cr. 8vo, cl. extra, 3s. 6d. each.
Finger-Ring Lore : Historical, Legendary, and Anecdotal. With Hundreds of Illustrations.
Credulities, Past and Present. Including the Sea and Seamen, Miners, Talismans, Word and Letter Divination, Exorcising and Blessing of Animals, Birds, Eggs, Luck, &c. With Frontispiece.
Crowns and Coronations : A History of Regalia. With 91 Illustrations.

Jonson's (Ben) Works. With Notes Critical and Explanatory, and a Biographical Memoir by WILLIAM GIFFORD. Edited by Colonel CUNNINGHAM. Three Vols. crown 8vo, cloth extra, 3s. 6d. each.

Josephus, The Complete Works of. Translated by WHISTON. Containing 'The Antiquities of the Jews' and 'The Wars of the Jews.' With 52 Illustrations and Maps. Two Vols., demy 8vo, half-bound, 12s. 6d.

Kempt (Robert).—Pencil and Palette : Chapters on Art and Artists. Post 8vo, cloth limp, 2s. 6d.

Kershaw (Mark). — Colonial Facts and Fictions : Humorous Sketches. Post 8vo, illustrated boards, 2s. ; cloth, 2s. 6d.

King (R. Ashe), Novels by.
Post 8vo, illustrated boards, 2s. each.
'The Wearing of the Green.' | **Passion's Slave.** | **Bell Barry.**
A Drawn Game. Crown 8vo, cloth, 3s. 6d. ; post 8vo, illustrated boards, 2s.

Knight (William, M.R.C.S., and Edward, L.R.C.P.). — The
Patient's Vade Mecum: How to Get Most Benefit from Medical Advice. Cr. 8vo, 1s.; cl., 1s. 6d.

Knights (The) of the Lion: A Romance of the Thirteenth Century.
Edited, with an Introduction, by the MARQUESS OF LORNE, K.T. Crown 8vo, cloth extra, 6s.

Korolenko. — The Blind Musician. Translated by S. STEPNIAK and
WILLIAM WESTALL. Crown 8vo, cloth, 1s.

Lamb's (Charles) Complete Works in Prose and Verse, including
'Poetry for Children' and 'Prince Dorus.' Edited, with Notes and Introduction, by R. H. SHEP-
HERD. With Two Portraits and Facsimile of the 'Essay on Roast Pig.' Crown 8vo, cloth, 3s. 6d.
The Essays of Elia. Post 8vo, printed on laid paper and half-bound, 2s.
Little Essays: Sketches and Characters by CHARLES LAMB, selected from his Letters by PERCY
FITZGERALD. Post 8vo, cloth limp, 2s. 6d.
The Dramatic Essays of Charles Lamb. With Introduction and Notes by BRANDER MAT-
THEWS, and Steel-plate Portrait. Fcap. 8vo, half-bound, 2s. 6d.

Lambert (George). — The President of Boravia. Crown 8vo, cl., 3s. 6d.

Landor (Walter Savage). — Citation and Examination of William
Shakspeare, &c. before Sir Thomas Lucy, touching Deer-stealing, 19th September, 1582. To which
is added, A Conference of Master Edmund Spenser with the Earl of Essex, touching the
State of Ireland, 1595. Fcap. 8vo, half-Roxburghe, 2s. 6d.

Lane (Edward William). — The Thousand and One Nights, com-
monly called in England The Arabian Nights' Entertainments. Translated from the Arabic,
with Notes. Illustrated with many hundred Engravings from Designs by HARVEY. Edited by EDWARD
STANLEY POOLE. With Preface by STANLEY LANE-POOLE. Three Vols., demy 8vo, cloth, 7s. 6d. ea.

Larwood (Jacob), Works by.
Anecdotes of the Clergy. Post 8vo, laid paper, half-bound, 2s.
Post 8vo, cloth limp, 2s. 6d. each.
Forensic Anecdotes. | Theatrical Anecdotes.

Lehmann (R. C.), Works by. Post 8vo, 1s. each; cloth, 1s. 6d. each.
Harry Fludyer at Cambridge.
Conversational Hints for Young Shooters: A Guide to Polite Talk.

Leigh (Henry S.). — Carols of Cockayne. Printed on hand-made
paper, bound in buckram, 5s.

Leland (C. Godfrey). — A Manual of Mending and Repairing.
With Diagrams. Crown 8vo, cloth, 5s.

Lepelletier (Edmond). — Madame Sans-Gène. Translated from
the French by JOHN DE VILLIERS. Post 8vo, cloth, 3s. 6d.; picture boards, 2s.

Leys (John). — The Lindsays: A Romance. Post 8vo, illust. bds., 2s.

Lilburn (Adam). — A Tragedy in Marble. Crown 8vo, cloth, 3s. 6d.

Lindsay (Harry, Author of 'Methodist Idylls'), Novels by.
Crown 8vo, cloth, 3s. 6d. each.
Rhoda Roberts.
The Jacobite: A Romance of the Conspiracy of 'The Forty.'

Linton (E. Lynn), Works by.
An Octave of Friends. Crown 8vo, cloth, 3s. 6d.
Crown 8vo, cloth extra, 3s. 6d. each; post 8vo, illustrated boards, 2s. each.
Patricia Kemball. | Ione.   Under which Lord? With 12 Illustrations.
The Atonement of Leam Dundas.   'My Love!' | Sowing the Wind.
The World Well Lost. With 12 Illusts. Paston Carew, Millionaire and Miser.
The One Too Many.   Dulcie Everton. | With a Silken Thread.
The Rebel of the Family.
Post 8vo, cloth limp, 2s. 6d. each.
Witch Stories. | Ourselves: Essays on Women.
Freeshooting: Extracts from the Works of Mrs. LYNN LINTON.

Lucy (Henry W.). — Gideon Fleyce: A Novel. Crown 8vo, cloth
extra, 3s. 6d.; post 8vo, illustrated boards, 2s.

Macalpine (Avery), Novels by.
Teresa Itasca. Crown 8vo, cloth extra, 1s.
Broken Wings. With Six Illustrations by W. J. HENNESSY. Crown 8vo, cloth extra, 6s.

MacColl (Hugh), Novels by.
Mr. Stranger's Sealed Packet. Post 8vo, illustrated boards, 2s.
Ednor Whitlock. Crown 8vo, cloth extra, 6s.

Macdonell (Agnes). — Quaker Cousins. Post 8vo, boards, 2s.

MacGregor (Robert). — Pastimes and Players: Notes on Popular
Games. Post 8vo, cloth limp, 2s. 6d.

Mackay (Charles, LL.D.). — Interludes and Undertones; or,
Music at Twilight. Crown 8vo, cloth extra, 6s.

McCarthy (Justin, M.P.), Works by.

A History of Our Own Times, from the Accession of Queen Victoria to the General Election of 1880. LIBRARY EDITION. Four Vols., demy 8vo, cloth extra, 12s. each.—Also a POPULAR EDITION, in Four Vols., crown 8vo, cloth extra, 6s. each.—And the JUBILEE EDITION, with an Appendix of Events to the end of 1886, in Two Vols., large crown 8vo, cloth extra, 7s. 6d. each.

A History of Our Own Times, from 1880 to the Diamond Jubilee. Demy 8vo, cloth extra, 12s. Uniform with the LIBRARY EDITION of the first Four Volumes.

A Short History of Our Own Times. One Vol., crown 8vo, cloth extra, 6s.—Also a CHEAP POPULAR EDITION, post 8vo, cloth limp, 2s. 6d.

A History of the Four Georges. Four Vols., demy 8vo, cl. ex., 12s. each. [Vols. I. & II. ready.

Reminiscences. With a Portrait. Two Vols., demy 8vo, cloth, 24s.

Crown 8vo, cloth extra, 3s. 6d. each; post 8vo, illustrated boards, 2s. each; cloth limp, 2s. 6d. each.

The Waterdale Neighbours.	**Donna Quixote.** With 12 Illustrations.
My Enemy's Daughter.	**The Comet of a Season.**
A Fair Saxon.	**Maid of Athens.** With 12 Illustrations.
Linley Rochford.	**Camiola:** A Girl with a Fortune.
Dear Lady Disdain.	**The Dictator.**
Miss Misanthrope. With 12 Illustrations.	**Red Diamonds.** **The Riddle Ring.**

The Three Disgraces, and other Stories. Crown 8vo, cloth, 3s. 6d.

'The Right Honourable.' By JUSTIN McCARTHY, M.P., and Mrs. CAMPBELL PRAED. Crown 8vo, cloth extra, 6s.

McCarthy (Justin Huntly), Works by.

The French Revolution. (Constituent Assembly, 1789-91). Four Vols., demy 8vo, cloth, 12s. each.

An Outline of the History of Ireland. Crown 8vo, 1s.; cloth, 1s. 6d.

Ireland Since the Union: Sketches of Irish History, 1798-1886. Crown 8vo, cloth, 6s.

Hafiz in London: Poems. Small 8vo, gold cloth, 3s. 6d.

Our Sensation Novel. Crown 8vo, picture cover, 1s., cloth limp, 1s. 6d.

Doom: An Atlantic Episode. Crown 8vo, picture cover, 1s.

Dolly: A Sketch. Crown 8vo, picture cover, 1s.; cloth limp, 1s. 6d.

Lily Lass: A Romance. Crown 8vo, picture cover, 1s.; cloth limp, 1s. 6d.

The Thousand and One Days. With Two Photogravures. Two Vols., crown 8vo, half-bd., 12s.

A London Legend. Crown 8vo, cloth, 3s. 6d.

The Royal Christopher. Crown 8vo, cloth, 3s. 6d.

MacDonald (George, LL.D.), Books by.

Works of Fancy and Imagination. Ten Vols., 16mo, cloth, gilt edges, in cloth case, 21s.; or the Volumes may be had separately, in Grolier cloth, at 2s. 6d. each.

Vol. I. WITHIN AND WITHOUT.—THE HIDDEN LIFE.

" II. THE DISCIPLE.—THE GOSPEL WOMEN.—BOOK OF SONNETS.—ORGAN SONGS.

" III. VIOLIN SONGS.—SONGS OF THE DAYS AND NIGHTS.—A BOOK OF DREAMS.—ROADSIDE POEMS.—POEMS FOR CHILDREN.

" IV. PARABLES.—BALLADS.—SCOTCH SONGS.

" V. & VI. PHANTASTES: A Faerie Romance.   Vol. VII. THE PORTENT.

" VIII. THE LIGHT PRINCESS.—THE GIANT'S HEART.—SHADOWS.

" IX. CROSS PURPOSES.—THE GOLDEN KEY.—THE CARASOYN.—LITTLE DAYLIGHT.

" X. THE CRUEL PAINTER.—THE WOW O' RIVVEN.—THE CASTLE.—THE BROKEN SWORDS. —THE GRAY WOLF.—UNCLE CORNELIUS.

Poetical Works of George MacDonald. Collected and Arranged by the Author. Two Vols. crown 8vo, buckram, 12s.

A Threefold Cord. Edited by GEORGE MACDONALD. Post 8vo, cloth, 5s.

Phantastes: A Faerie Romance. With 25 Illustrations by J. BELL. Crown 8vo, cloth extra, 3s. 6d.

Heather and Snow: A Novel. Crown 8vo, cloth extra, 3s. 6d.; post 8vo, illustrated boards, 2s.

Lilith: A Romance. SECOND EDITION. Crown 8vo, cloth extra, 6s.

Mackenna (Stephen J.) and J. Augustus O'Shea.—Brave Men

in Action: Thrilling Stories of the British Flag. With 8 Illustrations by STANLEY L. WOOD. Small demy 8vo, cloth, gilt edges, 5s.

Maclise Portrait Gallery (The) of Illustrious Literary Charac-

ters: 85 Portraits by DANIEL MACLISE; with Memoirs—Biographical, Critical, Bibliographical, and Anecdotal—illustrative of the Literature of the former half of the Present Century, by WILLIAM BATES, B.A. Crown 8vo, cloth extra, 3s. 6d.

Macquoid (Mrs.), Works by. Square 8vo, cloth extra, 6s each.

In the Ardennes. With 50 Illustrations by THOMAS R. MACQUOID.

Pictures and Legends from Normandy and Brittany. 34 Illusts. by T. R. MACQUOID.

Through Normandy. With 92 Illustrations by T. R. MACQUOID, and a Map.

Through Brittany. With 35 Illustrations by T. R. MACQUOID, and a Map.

About Yorkshire. With 67 Illustrations by T. R. MACQUOID.

Post 8vo, illustrated boards, 2s. each.

The Evil Eye, and other Stories.	**Lost Rose**, and other Stories.

Magician's Own Book, The: Performances with Eggs, Hats, &c.

Edited by W. H. CREMER. With 200 Illustrations. Crown 8vo, cloth extra, 4s. 6d.

Magic Lantern, The, and its Management: Including full Practical

Directions. By T. C. HEPWORTH. With 10 Illustrations. Crown 8vo, 1s.; cloth, 1s. 6d.

Magna Charta: An Exact Facsimile of the Original in the British

Museum, 3 feet by 2 feet, with Arms and Seals emblazoned in Gold and Colours, 5s.

Mallory (Sir Thomas). — Mort d'Arthur: The Stories of King

Arthur and of the Knights of the Round Table. (A Selection.) Edited by B. MONTGOMERIE RANKING. Post 8vo, cloth limp, 2s.

Mallock (W. H.), Works by.
The New Republic. Post 8vo, picture cover. 2s.; cloth limp, 2s. 6d.
The New Paul & Virginia: Positivism on an Island. Post 8vo, cloth, 2s. 6d.
A Romance of the Nineteenth Century. Crown 8vo, cloth 6s.; post 8vo, illust. boards, 2s.
Poems. Small 4to, parchment, 8s.
Is Life Worth Living? Crown 8vo, cloth extra. 6s.

Margueritte (Paul and Victor).—The Disaster. Translated by
FREDERIC LEES. Crown 8vo, cloth, 3s. 6d.

Marlowe's Works. Including his Translations. Edited, with Notes
and Introductions, by Colonel CUNNINGHAM. Crown 8vo, cloth extra, 3s. 6d.

Massinger's Plays. From the Text of WILLIAM GIFFORD. Edited
by Col. CUNNINGHAM. Crown 8vo, cloth extra, 3s. 6d.

Masterman (J.).—Half=a=Dozen Daughters. Post 8vo, boards, 2s.

Mathams (Walter, F.R.G.S.). — Comrades All. Fcp. 8vo, cloth
limp, 1s.; cloth gilt, 2s.

Matthews (Brander).—A Secret of the Sea, &c. Post 8vo, illustrated boards, 2s.; cloth limp, 2s. 6d.

Meade (L. T.), Novels by.
A Soldier of Fortune. Crown 8vo, cloth, 3s. 6d.; post 8vo, illustrated boards, 2s.
Crown 8vo, cloth, 3s. 6d. each.
The Voice of the Charmer. With 8 Illustrations.
In an Iron Grip. | On the Brink of a Chasm.
Dr. Rumsey's Patient. By L. T. MEADE and CLIFFORD HALIFAX, M.D.
An Adventuress. Crown 8vo, cloth, gilt top, 6s. [Shortly.

Merrick (Leonard), Novels by.
The Man who was Good. Post 8vo, picture boards, 2s.
Crown 8vo, cloth, 3s. 6d. each
This Stage of Fools. | Cynthia: A Daughter of the Philistines.

Mexican Mustang (On a), through Texas to the Rio Grande. By
A. E. SWEET and J. ARMOY KNOX. With 265 Illustrations. Crown 8vo, cloth extra, 7s. 6d.

Middlemass (Jean), Novels by. Post 8vo, illust. boards, 2s. each.
Touch and Go. | Mr. Dorillion.

Miller (Mrs. F. Fenwick).—Physiology for the Young; or, The
House of Life. With numerous Illustrations. Post 8vo, cloth limp, 2s. 6d.

Milton (J. L.), Works by. Post 8vo, 1s. each; cloth, 1s. 6d. each.
The Hygiene of the Skin. With Directions for Diet, Soaps, Baths, Wines, &c.
The Bath in Diseases of the Skin.
The Laws of Life, and their Relation to Diseases of the Skin.

Minto (Wm.).—Was She Good or Bad? Cr. 8vo, 1s.; cloth, 1s. 6d.

Mitford (Bertram), Novels by. Crown 8vo, cloth extra, 3s. 6d. each.
The Gun-Runner: A Romance of Zululand. With a Frontispiece by STANLEY L. WOOD.
The Luck of Gerard Ridgeley. With a Frontispiece by STANLEY L. WOOD.
The King's Assegai. With Six full-page Illustrations by STANLEY L. WOOD.
Renshaw Fanning's Quest. With a Frontispiece by STANLEY L. WOOD.

Molesworth (Mrs.).—Hathercourt Rectory. Post 8vo, illustrated
boards, 2s.

Moncrieff (W. D. Scott-).—The Abdication: An Historical Drama.
With Seven Etchings by JOHN PETTIE, W. Q. ORCHARDSON, J. MACWHIRTER, COLIN HUNTER,
R. MACBETH and TOM GRAHAM. Imperial 4to, buckram, 21s.

Montagu (Irving).—Things I Have Seen in War. With numerous Illustrations. Crown 8vo, cloth, 6s. [Shortly.

Moore (Thomas), Works by.
The Epicurean; and Alciphron. Post 8vo, half-bound, 2s.
Prose and Verse; including Suppressed Passages from the MEMOIRS OF LORD BYRON. Edited
by R. H. SHEPHERD. With Portrait. Crown 8vo, cloth extra, 7s. 6d.

Morrow (W. C.).—Bohemian Paris of To=Day. Written by W. C.
MORROW, from Notes by E. CUCUEL. With 125 Illustrations by EDOUARD CUCUEL. Square 8vo,
cloth, gilt top, 6s. [Shortly.

Muddock (J. E.) Stories by.
Crown 8vo, cloth extra, 3s. 6d. each.
The Golden Idol. [Shortly.
Maid Marian and Robin Hood. With 12 Illustrations by STANLEY WOOD.
Basile the Jester. With Frontispiece by STANLEY WOOD.
Young Lochinvar.
Post 8vo, illustrated boards, 2s. each.
The Dead Man's Secret. | From the Bosom of the Deep.
Stories Weird and Wonderful. Post 8vo, illustrated boards, 2s.; cloth, 2s. 6d.

Murray (D. Christie), Novels by.
Crown 8vo, cloth extra, 3s. 6d. each ; post 8vo, illustrated boards, 2s. each.

A Life's Atonement.
Joseph's Coat. 12 Illusts.
Coals of Fire. 3 Illusts.
Val Strange.
Hearts.
The Way of the World.

A Model Father.
Old Blazer's Hero.
Cynic Fortune. Frontisp.
By the Gate of the Sea.
A Bit of Human Nature.
First Person Singular.

Bob Martin's Little Girl.
Time's Revenges.
A Wasted Crime.
In Direst Peril.
Mount Despair.
A Capful o' Nails.

The Making of a Novelist : An Experiment in Autobiography. With a Collotype Portrait. Cr. 8vo, buckram, 3s. 6d.
My Contemporaries in Fiction. Crown 8vo, buckram, 3s. 6d.

Crown 8vo, cloth, 3s. 6d. each.

This Little World.
Tales in Prose and Verse. With Frontispiece by ARTHUR HOPKINS.
A Race for Millions.

Murray (D. Christie) and Henry Herman, Novels by.
Crown 8vo, cloth extra, 3s. 6d. each ; post 8vo, illustrated boards, 2s. each.
One Traveller Returns. | The Bishops' Bible.
Paul Jones's Alias, &c. With Illustrations by A. FORESTIER and G. NICOLET.

Murray (Henry), Novels by.
Post 8vo, illustrated boards, 2s. each ; cloth, 2s. 6d. each.
A Game of Bluff. | A Song of Sixpence.

Newbolt (Henry).—Taken from the Enemy. Fcp. 8vo, cloth, 1s. 6d. ; leatherette, 1s.

Nisbet (Hume), Books by.
'Bail Up.' Crown 8vo, cloth extra, 3s. 6d. ; post 8vo, illustrated boards, 2s.
Dr. Bernard St. Vincent. Post 8vo, illustrated boards, 2s.
Lessons in Art. With 21 Illustrations. Crown 8vo, cloth extra, 2s. 6d.

Norris (W. E.), Novels by. Crown 8vo, cloth, 3s. 6d. each ; post 8vo, picture boards, 2s. each.
Saint Ann's.
Billy Bellew. With a Frontispiece by F. H. TOWNSEND.
Miss Wentworth's Idea. Crown 8vo, cloth, 3s. 6d.

O'Hanlon (Alice), Novels by. Post 8vo, illustrated boards, 2s. each.
The Unforeseen. | Chance ? or Fate ?

Ohnet (Georges), Novels by. Post 8vo, illustrated boards, 2s. each.
Doctor Rameau. | A Last Love.
A Weird Gift. Crown 8vo, cloth, 3s. 6d. ; post 8vo, picture boards, 2s.
Love's Depths. Translated by F. ROTHWELL. Crown 8vo, cloth, 3s. 6d.

Oliphant (Mrs.), Novels by. Post 8vo, illustrated boards, 2s. each.
The Primrose Path. | Whiteladies.
The Greatest Heiress in England.
The Sorceress. Crown 8vo, cloth, 3s. 6d. ; post 8vo, picture boards, 2s.

O'Reilly (Mrs.).—Phœbe's Fortunes. Post 8vo, illust. boards, 2s.

O'Shaughnessy (Arthur), Poems by :
Fcap. 8vo, cloth extra, 7s. 6d. each.
Music and Moonlight. | Songs of a Worker.
Lays of France. Crown 8vo, cloth extra, 10s. 6d.

Ouida, Novels by. Cr. 8vo, cl., 3s. 6d. ea.; post 8vo, illust. bds., 2s. ea.

Held in Bondage.
Tricotrin.
Strathmore. | Chandos.
Cecil Castlemaine's Gage
Under Two Flags.
Puck. | Idalia.
Folle-Farine.

A Dog of Flanders.
Pascarel. | Signa.
Two Wooden Shoes.
In a Winter City.
Ariadne. | Friendship.
A Village Commune.
Moths. | Pipistrello.

In Maremma. | Wanda.
Bimbi. | Syrlin.
Frescoes. | Othmar.
Princess Napraxine.
Guilderoy. | Ruffino.
Two Offenders.
Santa Barbara.

POPULAR EDITIONS. Medium 8vo, 6d. each ; cloth, 1s. each.
Under Two Flags. | Moths.

Wisdom, Wit, and Pathos, selected from the Works of OUIDA by F. SYDNEY MORRIS. Post 8vo, cloth extra, 5s.—CHEAP EDITION, illustrated boards, 2s.

Page (H. A.).—Thoreau: His Life and Aims. With Portrait. Post 8vo, cloth, 2s. 6d.

Pandurang Hari; or, Memoirs of a Hindoo. With Preface by Sir BARTLE FRERE. Post 8vo, illustrated boards, 2s.

Pascal's Provincial Letters. A New Translation, with Historical Introduction and Notes by T. M'CRIE, D.D. Post 8vo, half-cloth, 2s.

Paul (Margaret A.).—Gentle and Simple. Crown 8vo, cloth, with Frontispiece by HELEN PATERSON, 3s. 6d.; post 8vo, illustrated boards, 2s.

Payn (James), Novels by.
Crown 8vo, cloth extra, 3s. 6d. each ; post 8vo, illustrated boards, 2s. each.

Lost Sir Massingberd.
Walter's Word. | A County Family.
Less Black than We're Painted.
By Proxy. | For Cash Only.
High Spirits.
Under One Roof.
A Confidential Agent. With 12 Illusts.
A Grape from a Thorn. With 12 Illusts.

Holiday Tasks.
The Canon's Ward. With Portrait.
The Talk of the Town. With 12 Illusts.
Glow-Worm Tales.
The Mystery of Mirbridge.
The Word and the Will.
The Burnt Million.
Sunny Stories. | A Trying Patient.

Post 8vo illustrated boards, 2s. each.

Humorous Stories. | From Exile.
The Foster Brothers.
The Family Scapegrace.
Married Beneath Him.
Bentinck's Tutor.
A Perfect Treasure.
Like Father, Like Son.
A Woman's Vengeance.
Carlyon's Year. | Cecil's Tryst.
Murphy's Master. | At Her Mercy.

The Clyffards of Clyffe.
Found Dead. | Gwendoline's Harvest.
Mirk Abbey. | A Marine Residence.
Some Private Views.
Not Wooed, But Won.
Two Hundred Pounds Reward.
The Best of Husbands.
Halves. | What He Cost Her.
Fallen Fortunes. | Kit: A Memory.
A Prince of the Blood.

A Modern Dick Whittington ; or, A Patron of Letters. With a Portrait of the Author. Crown 8vo, cloth, 3s. 6d.
In Peril and Privation. With 17 Illustrations. Crown 8vo, cloth, 3s. 6d.
Notes from the 'News.' Crown 8vo, portrait cover, 1s.; cloth, 1s. 6d.
By Proxy. POPULAR EDITION, medium 8vo, 6d.; cloth, 1s.

Payne (Will).—Jerry the Dreamer. Crown 8vo, cloth, 3s. 6d.

Pennell (H. Cholmondeley), Works by. Post 8vo, cloth, 2s. 6d. ea.
Puck on Pegasus. With Illustrations.
Pegasus Re-Saddled. With Ten full-page Illustrations by G. DU MAURIER.
The Muses of Mayfair : Vers de Société. Selected by H. C. PENNELL.

Phelps (E. Stuart), Works by. Post 8vo, 1s. ea. ; cloth, 1s. 6d. ea.
Beyond the Gates. | An Old Maid's Paradise. | Burglars in Paradise.
Jack the Fisherman. Illustrated by C. W. REED. Crown 8vo, cloth, 1s. 6d.

Phil May's Sketch-Book. Containing 54 Humorous Cartoons. Crown folio, cloth, 2s. 6d.

Phipson (Dr. T. L.), Books by. Crown 8vo, art canvas, gilt top, 5s. ea.
Famous Violinists and Fine Violins.
Voice and Violin : Sketches, Anecdotes, and Reminiscences.

Planche (J. R.), Works by.
The Pursuivant of Arms. With Six Plates and 209 Illustrations. Crown 8vo, cloth, 7s. 6d.
Songs and Poems, 1819-1879. With Introduction by Mrs. MACKARNESS. Crown 8vo, cloth, 6s.

Plutarch's Lives of Illustrious Men. With Notes and a Life of Plutarch by JOHN and WM. LANGHORNE, and Portraits. Two Vols., demy 8vo, half-bound 10s. 6d.

Poe's (Edgar Allan) Choice Works : Poems, Stories, Essays.
With an Introduction by CHARLES BAUDELAIRE. Crown 8vo, cloth, 3s. 6d.
The Mystery of Marie Roget, &c. By EDGAR A. POE. Post 8vo, illustrated boards, 2s.

Pollock (W. H.).—The Charm, and other Drawing-room Plays. By Sir WALTER BESANT and WALTER H. POLLOCK. With 50 Illustrations. Crown 8vo, cloth gilt, 6s.

Pollock (Wilfred).—War and a Wheel : The Græco-Turkish War as Seen from a Bicycle. With a Map. Crown 8vo, picture cover, 1s.

Pope's Poetical Works. Post 8vo, cloth limp, 2s.

Porter (John).—Kingsclere. Edited by BYRON WEBBER. With 19 full-page and many smaller Illustrations. Cheaper Edition. Demy 8vo, cloth, 7s. 6d.

Praed (Mrs. Campbell), Novels by. Post 8vo, illust. bds., 2s. each.
The Romance of a Station. | The Soul of Countess Adrian.

Crown 8vo, cloth, 3s. 6d. each : post 8vo, boards, 2s. each.
Outlaw and Lawmaker. | Christina Chard. With Frontispiece by W. PAGET.
Mrs. Tregaskiss. With 8 Illustrations by ROBERT SAUBER.
Nulma. Crown 8vo, cloth, 3s. 6d.
Madame Izan : A Tourist Story. Crown 8vo, cloth, gilt top, 6s.

Price (E. C.), Novels by.
Crown 8vo, cloth extra, 3s. 6d. each ; post 8vo, illustrated boards, 2s. each.
Valentina. | The Foreigners. | Mrs. Lancaster's Rival.
Gerald. Post 8vo, illustrated boards, 2s.

Princess Olga.—Radna : A Novel. Crown 8vo, cloth extra, 6s.

Proctor (Richard A.), Works by.

Flowers of the Sky. With 55 Illustrations. Small crown 8vo, cloth extra, 3s. 6d.
Easy Star Lessons. With Star Maps for every Night in the Year. Crown 8vo, cloth, 6s.
Familiar Science Studies. Crown 8vo, cloth extra, 6s.
Saturn and its System. With 13 Steel Plates. Demy 8vo, cloth extra, 10s. 6d.
Mysteries of Time and Space. With numerous Illustrations. Crown 8vo, cloth extra, 6s.
The Universe of Suns, &c. With numerous Illustrations. Crown 8vo, cloth extra, 6s.
Wages and Wants of Science Workers. Crown 8vo, 1s. 6d.

Pryce (Richard).—Miss Maxwell's Affections. Crown 8vo, cloth,

with Frontispiece by HAL LUDLOW, 3s. 6d.; post 8vo, illustrated boards, 2s.

Rambosson (J.).—Popular Astronomy. Translated by C. B. PIT-

MAN. With 10 Coloured Plates and 63 Woodcut Illustrations. Crown 8vo, cloth, 3s. 6d.

Randolph (Col. G.).—Aunt Abigail Dykes. Crown 8vo, cloth, 7s. 6d.

Read (General Meredith).—Historic Studies in Vaud, Berne,

and Savoy. With 31 full-page Illustrations. Two Vols., demy 8vo, cloth, 28s.

Reade's (Charles) Novels.

The New Collected LIBRARY EDITION, complete in Seventeen Volumes, set in new long primer type, printed on laid paper, and elegantly bound in cloth, price 3s. 6d. each.

1. **Peg Woffington;** and **Christie John-stone.**
2. **Hard Cash.**
3. **The Cloister and the Hearth.** With a Preface by Sir WALTER BESANT.
4. **'It is Never Too Late to Mend.'**
5. **The Course of True Love Never Did Run Smooth;** and **Singleheart and Doubleface.**
6. **The Autobiography of a Thief; Jack of all Trades: A Hero and a Martyr; and The Wandering Heir.**
7. **Love Me Little, Love me Long.**
8. **The Double Marriage.**
9. **Griffith Gaunt.**
10. **Foul Play.**
11. **Put Yourself in His Place.**
12. **A Terrible Temptation.**
13. **A Simpleton.**
14. **A Woman-Hater.**
15. **The Jilt, and other Stories; and Good Stories of Man and other Animals.**
16. **A Perilous Secret.**
17. **Readiana; and Bible Characters.**

In Twenty-one Volumes, post 8vo, illustrated boards, 2s. each.

Peg Woffington. | **Christie Johnstone.**
'It is Never Too Late to Mend.'
The Course of True Love Never Did Run Smooth.
The Autobiography of a Thief; Jack of all Trades; and James Lambert.
Love Me Little, Love Me Long.
The Double Marriage.
The Cloister and the Hearth.

Hard Cash. | **Griffith Gaunt.**
Foul Play. | **Put Yourself in His Place.**
A Terrible Temptation
A Simpleton. | **The Wandering Heir.**
A Woman-Hater.
Singleheart and Doubleface.
Good Stories of Man and other Animals.
The Jilt, and other Stories.
A Perilous Secret. | **Readiana.**

POPULAR EDITIONS, medium 8vo, 6d. each; cloth, 1s. each.
'It is Never Too Late to Mend.' | **The Cloister and the Hearth.**
Peg Woffington; and **Christie Johnstone.** | **Hard Cash.**

Christie Johnstone. With Frontispiece. Choicely printed in Elzevir style. Fcap. 8vo, half-Roxb. 2s. 6d.
Peg Woffington. Choicely printed in Elzevir style. Fcap. 8vo, half-Roxburghe, 2s. 6d.
The Cloister and the Hearth. In Four Vols., post 8vo, with an Introduction by Sir WALTER BE-SANT, and a Frontispiece to each Vol., buckram, gilt top, 6s. the set.
Bible Characters. Fcap. 8vo, leatherette, 1s.

Selections from the Works of Charles Reade. With an Introduction by Mrs. ALEX. IRE-LAND. Crown 8vo, buckram, with Portrait, 6s.; CHEAP EDITION, post 8vo, cloth limp, 2s. 6d.

Riddell (Mrs. J. H.), Novels by.

Weird Stories. Crown 8vo, cloth extra, 3s. 6d.; post 8vo, illustrated boards, 2s.
Post 8vo, illustrated boards, 2s. each.

The Uninhabited House.
The Prince of Wales's Garden Party.
The Mystery in Palace Gardens.

Fairy Water.
Her Mother's Darling.
The Nun's Curse. | **Idle Tales.**

Rimmer (Alfred), Works by. Large crown 8vo, cloth, 3s. 6d. each.

Our Old Country Towns. With 54 Illustrations by the Author.
Rambles Round Eton and Harrow. With 52 Illustrations by the Author.
About England with Dickens. With 58 Illustrations by C. A. VANDERHOOF and A. RIMMER.

Rives (Amelie, Author of 'The Quick or the Dead?'), Works by.

Barbara Dering. Crown 8vo, cloth, 3s. 6d.; post 8vo, picture boards, 2s.
Meriel: A Love Story. Crown 8vo, cloth, 3s. 6d.

Robinson Crusoe. By DANIEL DEFOE. With 37 Illustrations by

GEORGE CRUIKSHANK. Post 8vo, half-cloth, 2s.

Robinson (F. W.), Novels by.

Women are Strange. Post 8vo, illustrated boards, 2s.
The Hands of Justice. Crown 8vo, cloth extra, 3s. 6d.; post 8vo, illustrated boards, 2s.
The Woman in the Dark. Crown 8vo, cloth, 3s. 6d.; post 8vo, illustrated boards, 2s.

Robinson (Phil), Works by. Crown 8vo, cloth extra, 6s. each.
The Poets' Birds. | The Poets' Beasts.
The Poets and Nature: Reptiles, Fishes, and Insects.

Rochefoucauld's Maxims and Moral Reflections. With Notes
and an Introductory Essay by SAINTE-BEUVE. Post 8vo, cloth limp, 2s.

Roll of Battle Abbey, The: A List of the Principal Warriors who
came from Normandy with William the Conqueror, 1066. Printed in Gold and Colours, 5s.

Rosengarten (A.).—A Handbook of Architectural Styles. Trans-
lated by W. COLLETT-SANDARS. With 630 Illustrations. Crown 8vo, cloth extra, 7s. 6d.

Rowley (Hon. Hugh), Works by. Post 8vo, cloth, 2s. 6d. each.
Puniana: Riddles and Jokes. With numerous Illustrations.
More Puniana. Profusely Illustrated.

Runciman (James), Stories by. Post 8vo, bds., 2s. ea.; cl., 2s. 6d. ea.
Skippers & Shellbacks. | Grace Balmaign's Sweetheart. | Schools & Scholars.

Russell (Dora), Novels by.
A Country Sweetheart. Crown 8vo, cloth, 3s. 6d.; post 8vo, picture boards, 2s.
The Drift of Fate. Crown 8vo, cloth, 3s. 6d.

Russell (Herbert).—True Blue; or, 'The Lass that Loved a Sailor.'
Crown 8vo, cloth, 3s. 6d.

Russell (W. Clark), Novels, &c., by.
Crown 8vo, cloth extra, 3s. 6d. each; post 8vo, illustrated boards, 2s. each; cloth limp, 2s. 6d. each.

Round the Galley-Fire.	An Ocean Tragedy.
In the Middle Watch.	My Shipmate Louise.
On the Fo'k'sle Head.	Alone on a Wide Wide Sea.
A Voyage to the Cape.	The Good Ship 'Mohock.'
A Book for the Hammock.	The Phantom Death.
The Mystery of the 'Ocean Star.'	Is He the Man?	The Convict Ship.
The Romance of Jenny Harlowe.	Heart of Oak.	The Last Entry.

The Tale of the Ten.

A Tale of Two Tunnels. Crown 8vo, cloth, 3s. 6d.

The Ship: Her Story. With 50 Illustrations by H. C. SEPPINGS WRIGHT. Small 4to, cloth, 6s.

Saint Aubyn (Alan), Novels by.
Crown 8vo, cloth extra, 3s. 6d. each; post 8vo, illustrated boards, 2s. each.
A Fellow of Trinity. With a Note by OLIVER WENDELL HOLMES and a Frontispiece.

The Junior Dean.	The Master of St. Benedict's.	To His Own Master.
Orchard Damerel.	In the Face of the World.	The Tremlett Diamonds.

Fcap. 8vo, cloth boards, 1s. 6d. each.
The Old Maid's Sweetheart. | Modest Little Sara.

Crown 8vo, cloth, 3s. 6d. each.
Fortune's Gate. | Gallantry Bower: A Story of a Fair Impostor.

Mary Unwin. With 8 Illustrations by PERCY TARRANT. Crown 8vo, cloth, 6s.

Saint John (Bayle).—A Levantine Family. A New Edition.
Crown 8vo, cloth, 3s. 6d.

Sala (George A.).—Gaslight and Daylight. Post 8vo, boards, 2s.

Scotland Yard, Past and Present: Experiences of Thirty-seven Years.
By Ex-Chief-Inspector CAVANAGH. Post 8vo, illustrated boards, 2s.; cloth, 2s. 6d.

Secret Out, The: One Thousand Tricks with Cards; with Entertain-
ing Experiments in Drawing-room or 'White' Magic. By W. H. CREMER. With 300 Illustrations. Crown
8vo, cloth extra, 4s. 6d.

Seguin (L. G.), Works by.
The Country of the Passion Play (Oberammergau) and the Highlands of Bavaria. With
Map and 37 Illustrations. Crown 8vo, cloth extra, 3s. 6d.
Walks in Algiers. With Two Maps and 16 Illustrations. Crown 8vo, cloth extra, 6s.

Senior (Wm.).—By Stream and Sea. Post 8vo, cloth, 2s. 6d.

Sergeant (Adeline), Novels by.
Under False Pretences. Crown 8vo, cloth, gilt top, 6s.
Dr. Endicott's Experiment. Crown 8vo, cloth, 3s. 6d.

Shakespeare for Children: Lamb's Tales from Shakespeare.
With Illustrations, coloured and plain, by J. MOYR SMITH. Crown 4to, cloth gilt, 3s. 6d.

Shakespeare the Boy. With Sketches of the Home and School Life,
the Games and Sports, the Manners, Customs, and Folk-lore of the Time. By WILLIAM J. ROLFE
Litt.D. With 42 Illustrations. Crown 8vo, cloth gilt, 3s. 6d.

Sharp (William).—Children of To-morrow. Crown 8vo, cloth, 6s.

Shelley's (Percy Bysshe) Complete Works in Verse and Prose.
Edited, Prefaced, and Annotated by R. HERNE SHEPHERD. Five Vols., crown 8vo, cloth, 3s. 6d. each.

Poetical Works, in Three Vols.:
Vol. I. Introduction by the Editor; Posthumous Fragments of Margaret Nicholson; Shelley's Corre-
spondence with Stockdale; The Wandering Jew; Queen Mab, with the Notes; Alastor,
and other Poems; Rosalind and Helen; Prometheus Unbound; Adonais, &c.
,, II. Laon and Cythna: The Cenci; Julian and Maddalo; Swellfoot the Tyrant: The Witch of
Atlas; Epipsychidion; Hellas.
,, III. Posthumous Poems; The Masque of Anarchy; and other Pieces.

Prose Works, in Two Vols.:
Vol. I. The Two Romances of Zastrozzi and St. Irvyne: the Dublin and Marlow Pamphlets; A Refu-
tation of Deism; Letters to Leigh Hunt, and some Minor Writings and Fragments.
II. The Essays; Letters from Abroad; Translations and Fragments, edited by Mrs. SHELLEY.
With a Biography of Shelley, and an Index of the Prose Works.

Sherard (R. H.).—Rogues: A Novel. Crown 8vo, cloth, 1s. 6d.

Sheridan's (Richard Brinsley) Complete Works, with Life and
Anecdotes. Including his Dramatic Writings, his Works in Prose and Poetry, Translations, Speeches,
and Jokes. Crown 8vo, cloth, 3s. 6d.
The Rivals, The School for Scandal, and other Plays. Post 8vo, half-bound, 2s.
Sheridan's Comedies: The Rivals and **The School for Scandal.** Edited, with an Intro-
duction and Notes to each Play, and a Biographical Sketch, by BRANDER MATTHEWS. With
Illustrations. Demy 8vo, half-parchment, 12s. 6d.

Sidney's (Sir Philip) Complete Poetical Works, including all
those in 'Arcadia.' With Portrait, Memorial-Introduction, Notes, &c., by the Rev. A. B. GROSART,
D.D. Three Vols., crown 8vo, cloth boards, 3s. 6d. each.

Signboards: Their History, including Anecdotes of Famous Taverns and
Remarkable Characters. By JACOB LARWOOD and JOHN CAMDEN HOTTEN. With Coloured Frontis
piece and 94 Illustrations. Crown 8vo, cloth extra, 3s. 6d.

Sims (George R.), Works by.
Post 8vo, illustrated boards, 2s. each; cloth limp, 2s. 6d. each.

The Ring o' Bells.	**Dramas of Life.** With 60 Illustrations.
Mary Jane's Memoirs.	**Memoirs of a Landlady.**
Mary Jane Married.	**My Two Wives.**
Tinkletop's Crime.	**Scenes from the Show.**
Zeph: A Circus Story, &c.	**The Ten Commandments:** Stories.
Tales of To-day.	

Crown 8vo, picture cover, 1s. each; cloth, 1s. 6d. each.

The Dagonet Reciter and Reader: Being Readings and Recitations in Prose and Verse
selected from his own Works by GEORGE R. SIMS.
The Case of George Candlemas. | **Dagonet Ditties.** (From *The Referee.*)

Rogues and Vagabonds. Crown 8vo, cloth, 3s. 6d.; post 8vo, picture boards, 2s.; cloth limp, 2s. 6d.
How the Poor Live; and **Horrible London.** With a Frontispiece by F. BARNARD.
Crown 8vo, leatherette, 1s.
Dagonet Abroad. Crown 8vo, cloth, 3s. 6d.; post 8vo, picture boards, 2s.; cloth limp, 2s. 6d.
Dagonet Dramas of the Day. Crown 8vo, 1s.
Once upon a Christmas Time. With 8 Illustrations by CHARLES GREEN, R.I. Crown 8vo,
cloth gilt, 3s. 6d.

Sister Dora: A Biography. By MARGARET LONSDALE. With Four
Illustrations. Demy 8vo, picture cover, 4d.; cloth, 6d.

Sketchley (Arthur).—A Match in the Dark. Post 8vo, boards, 2s.

Slang Dictionary (The): Etymological, Historical, and Anecdotal.
Crown 8vo, cloth extra, 6s. 6d.

Smart (Hawley), Novels by.
Crown 8vo, cloth 3s. 6d. each; post 8vo, picture boards, 2s. each.

Beatrice and Benedick.	**Long Odds.**
Without Love or Licence.	**The Master of Rathkelly.**

Crown 8vo, cloth, 3s. 6d. each.

The Outsider.	**A Racing Rubber.**

The Plunger. Post 8vo, picture boards, 2s.

Smith (J. Moyr), Works by.
The Prince of Argolis. With 130 Illustrations. Post 8vo, cloth extra, 3s. 6d.
The Wooing of the Water Witch. With numerous Illustrations. Post 8vo, cloth, 6s.

Snazelleparilla. Decanted by G. S. EDWARDS. With Portrait of
G. H. SNAZELLE, and 65 Illustrations by C. LYALL. Crown 8vo, cloth, 3s. 6d.

Society in London. Crown 8vo, 1s.; cloth, 1s. 6d.

Somerset (Lord Henry).—Songs of Adieu. Small 4to, Jap. vel., 6s.

Spalding (T. A., LL.B.).—Elizabethan Demonology: An Essay on the Belief in the Existence of Devils. Crown 8vo, cloth extra, 5s.

Speight (T. W.), Novels by.

Post 8vo, illustrated boards, 2s. each.

The Mysteries of Heron Dyke.
By Devious Ways, &c.
Hoodwinked; & Sandycroft Mystery.
The Golden Hoop,
Back to Life.

The Loudwater Tragedy,
Burgo's Romance.
Quittance in Full.
A Husband from the Sea.

Post 8vo, cloth limp, 1s. 6d. each,

A Barren Title.　|　Wife or No Wife?

Crown 8vo, cloth extra, 3s. 6d. each.

A Secret of the Sea. | The Grey Monk. | The Master of Trenance.
A Minion of the Moon: A Romance of the King's Highway.
The Secret of Wyvern Towers.
The Doom of Siva.
The Web of Fate. (This Story forms the GENTLEMAN'S ANNUAL for 1890). Demy 8vo, 1s.

Spenser for Children. By M. H. TOWRY. With Coloured Illustrations by WALTER J. MORGAN. Crown 4to, cloth extra, 3s. 6d.

Spettigue (H. H.).—The Heritage of Eve. Crown 8vo, cloth, 6s.

Stafford (John), Novels by.
Doris and I. Crown 8vo, cloth, 3s. 6d.
Carlton Priors. Crown 8vo, cloth, gilt top, 6s.

Starry Heavens (The): A POETICAL BIRTHDAY BOOK. Royal 16mo, cloth extra, 2s. 6d.

Stedman (E. C.), Works by. Crown 8vo, cloth extra, 9s. each.
Victorian Poets.　|　The Poets of America.

Stephens (Riccardo, M.B.).—The Cruciform Mark: The Strange Story of RICHARD TREGENNA, Bachelor of Medicine (Univ. Edinb.) Crown 8vo, cloth, 3s. 6d.

Sterndale (R. Armitage).—The Afghan Knife: A Novel. Post 8vo, cloth, 3s. 6d.; illustrated boards, 2s.

Stevenson (R. Louis), Works by.
Crown 8vo, buckram, gilt top, 6s. each ; post 8vo, cloth limp, 2s. 6d. each.
Travels with a Donkey. With a Frontispiece by WALTER CRANE.
An Inland Voyage. With a Frontispiece by WALTER CRANE.

Crown 8vo, buckram, gilt top, 6s. each.
Familiar Studies of Men and Books.
The Silverado Squatters. With Frontispiece by J. D. STRONG.
The Merry Men.　|　Underwoods: Poems.
Memories and Portraits.
Virginibus Puerisque, and other Papers. | Ballads.　　| Prince Otto.
Across the Plains, with other Memories and Essays.
Weir of Hermiston.

A Lowden Sabbath Morn. With 27 Illustrations by A. S. BOYD. Fcap. 8vo, cloth, 6s.
Songs of Travel. Crown 8vo, buckram, 5s.
New Arabian Nights. Crown 8vo, buckram, gilt top, 6s.: post 8vo, illustrated boards, 2s.
The Suicide Club; and The Rajah's Diamond. (From NEW ARABIAN NIGHTS.) With Eight Illustrations by W. J. HENNESSY. Crown 8vo, cloth, 3s. 6d.
The Stevenson Reader: Selections from the Writings of ROBERT LOUIS STEVENSON. Edited by LLOYD OSBOURNE. Post 8vo, cloth, 2s. 6d.; buckram, gilt top, 3s. 6d.

Stockton (Frank R.).—The Young Master of Hyson Hall. Illustrated by VIRGINIA H. DAVISSON. Crown 8vo, cloth, gilt top, 6s.　　　　　　　*[Shortly.*

Storey (G. A., A.R.A.).—Sketches from Memory. With 93 Illustrations by the Author. Demy 8vo, cloth, gilt top, 12s. 6d.

Stories from Foreign Novelists. With Notices by HELEN and ALICE ZIMMERN. Crown 8vo, cloth extra, 3s. 6d.; post 8vo, illustrated boards, 2s.

Strange Manuscript (A) Found in a Copper Cylinder. Crown 8vo, cloth extra, with 19 Illustrations by GILBERT GAUL, 5s.; post 8vo, illustrated boards, 2s.

Strange Secrets. Told by PERCY FITZGERALD, CONAN DOYLE, FLORENCE MARRYAT, &c. Post 8vo, illustrated boards, 2s.

Strutt (Joseph). — The Sports and Pastimes of the People of England; including the Rural and Domestic Recreations, May Games, Mummeries, Shows, &c., from the Earliest Period to the Present Time. Edited by WILLIAM HONE. With 140 Illustrations, Crown 8vo, cloth extra, 3s. 6d

Swift's (Dean) Choice Works, in Prose and Verse.   With Memoir,
Portrait, and Facsimiles of the Maps in 'Gulliver's Travels.' Crown 8vo, cloth, 3s. 6d.
Gulliver's Travels, and **A Tale of a Tub.** Post 8vo, half-bound, 2s.
Jonathan Swift: A Study. By J. CHURTON COLLINS. Crown 8vo, cloth extra, 8s.

Swinburne (Algernon C.), Works by.

Selections from the Poetical Works of
A. C. Swinburne. Fcap. 8vo 6s.
Atalanta in Calydon. Crown 8vo, 6s.
Chastelard: A Tragedy. Crown 8vo, 7s.
Poems and Ballads. FIRST SERIES. Crown 8vo, or fcap. 8vo, 9s.
Poems and Ballads. SECOND SERIES. Crown 8vo, 9s.
Poems & Ballads. THIRD SERIES. Cr. 8vo, 7s.
Songs before Sunrise. Crown 8vo, 10s. 6d.
Bothwell: A Tragedy. Crown 8vo, 12s. 6d.
Songs of Two Nations. Crown 8vo, 6s.
George Chapman. (See Vol. II. of G. CHAPMAN'S Works.) Crown 8vo, 3s. 6d.
Essays and Studies. Crown 8vo, 12s.
Erechtheus: A Tragedy. Crown 8vo, 6s.
A Note on Charlotte Bronte. Cr. 8vo, 6s.

A Study of Shakespeare. Crown 8vo, 8s.
Songs of the Springtides. Crown 8vo, 6s.
Studies in Song. Crown 8vo, 7s.
Mary Stuart: A Tragedy. Crown 8vo, 8s.
Tristram of Lyonesse. Crown 8vo, 9s.
A Century of Roundels. Small 4to, 8s.
A Midsummer Holiday. Crown 8vo, 7s.
Marino Faliero: A Tragedy. Crown 8vo, 6s.
A Study of Victor Hugo. Crown 8vo, 6s.
Miscellanies. Crown 8vo, 12s.
Locrine: A Tragedy. Crown 8vo, 6s.
A Study of Ben Jonson. Crown 8vo, 7s.
The Sisters: A Tragedy. Crown 8vo, 6s.
Astrophel, &c. Crown 8vo, 7s.
Studies in Prose and Poetry. Cr. 8vo, 9s.
The Tale of Balen. Crown 8vo, 7s.
Rosamund: A Play. Crown 8vo, 6s.

Syntax's (Dr.) Three Tours: In Search of the Picturesque, in Search
of Consolation, and In Search of a Wife. With ROWLANDSON's Coloured Illustrations, and Life of the
Author by J. C. HOTTEN. Crown 8vo, cloth extra, 7s. 6d.

Taine's History of English Literature. Translated by HENRY VAN
LAUN. Four Vols., small demy 8vo, cloth boards, 30s.—POPULAR EDITION, Two Vols., large crown
8vo, cloth extra, 15s.

Taylor (Bayard). — Diversions of the Echo Club: Burlesques of
Modern Writers. Post 8vo, cloth limp, 2s.

Taylor (Tom).—Historical Dramas: 'JEANNE DARC,' ''TWIXT AXE
AND CROWN,' 'THE FOOL'S REVENGE,' 'ARKWRIGHT'S WIFE,' 'ANNE BOLEYNE,' 'PLOT AND
PASSION.' Crown 8vo, 1s. each.

Temple (Sir Richard, G.C.S.I.).—A Bird's-eye View of Pictur-
esque India. With 32 Illustrations by the Author. Crown 8vo, cloth, gilt top, 6s.

Tennyson (Lord): A Biographical Sketch. By H. J. JENNINGS. Post
8vo, portrait cover, 1s.; cloth, 1s. 6d.

Thackerayana: Notes and Anecdotes. With Coloured Frontispiece and
Hundreds of Sketches by WILLIAM MAKEPEACE THACKERAY. Crown 8vo, cloth extra, 3s. 6d.

Thames, A New Pictorial History of the. By A. S. KRAUSSE.
With 340 Illustrations. Post 8vo, cloth, 1s. 6d.

Thomas (Annie).—The Siren's Web: A Romance of London
Society. Crown 8vo, cloth, 3s. 6d.   [Shortly.

Thomas (Bertha), Novels by.
Proud Maisie. Crown 8vo, cloth, 3s. 6d.
The Violin-Player. Crown 8vo, cloth, 3s. 6d.; post 8vo, picture boards, 2s.
Cressida. Post 8vo, illustrated boards, 2s.

Thomson's Seasons, and The Castle of Indolence. With Introduction by ALLAN CUNNINGHAM, and 48 Illustrations. Post 8vo, half-bound, 2s.

Thornbury (Walter), Books by.
The Life and Correspondence of J. M. W. Turner. With Eight Illustrations in Colours and
Two Woodcuts. New and Revised Edition. Crown 8vo, cloth, 3s. 6d.

Post 8vo, illustrated boards, 2s. each.
Old Stories Re-told. | **Tales for the Marines.**

Timbs (John), Works by. Crown 8vo, cloth, 3s. 6d. each.
Clubs and Club Life in London: Anecdotes of its Famous Coffee-houses, Hostelries, and
Taverns. With 41 Illustrations.
English Eccentrics and Eccentricities: Stories of Delusions, Impostures, Sporting Scenes,
Eccentric Artists, Theatrical Folk, &c. With 48 Illustrations.

Transvaal (The). By JOHN DE VILLIERS. With Map. Crown 8vo, 1s.

Trollope (Anthony), Novels by.
Crown 8vo, cloth extra, 3s. 6d. each; post 8vo, illustrated boards, 2s. each.
The Way We Live Now. | **Mr. Scarborough's Family.**
Frau Frohmann. | **Marion Fay.** | **The Land-Leaguers.**
Post 8vo, illustrated boards, 2s. each.
Kept in the Dark. | **The American Senator.**
The Golden Lion of Granpere. | **John Caldigate.**

Trollope (Frances E.), Novels by.
Crown 8vo, cloth extra, 3s. 6d. each ; post 8vo, illustrated boards, 2s. each.
Like Ships upon the Sea. | Mabel's Progress. | Anne Furness.

Trollope (T. A.).—Diamond Cut Diamond. Post 8vo, illust. bds., 2s.

Trowbridge (J. T.).—Farnell's Folly. Post 8vo, illust. boards, 2s.

Twain's (Mark) Books.
Crown 8vo, cloth extra, 3s. 6d. each.
The Choice Works of Mark Twain. Revised and Corrected throughout by the Author. With Life, Portrait, and numerous Illustrations.
Roughing It; and The Innocents at Home. With 200 Illustrations by F. A. FRASER.
The American Claimant. With 81 Illustrations by HAL HURST and others.
Tom Sawyer Abroad. With 26 Illustrations by DAN BEARD.
Tom Sawyer, Detective, &c. With Photogravure Portrait.
Pudd'nhead Wilson. With Portrait and Six Illustrations by LOUIS LOEB.
Mark Twain's Library of Humour. With 197 Illustrations by E. W. KEMBLE.

Crown 8vo, cloth extra, 3s. 6d. each ; post 8vo, picture boards, 2s. each.
A Tramp Abroad. With 314 Illustrations.
The Innocents Abroad; or, The New Pilgrim's Progress. With 234 Illustrations. (The Two Shilling Edition is entitled Mark Twain's Pleasure Trip.)
The Gilded Age. By MARK TWAIN and C. D. WARNER. With 212 Illustrations.
The Adventures of Tom Sawyer. With 111 Illustrations.
The Prince and the Pauper. With 190 Illustrations.
Life on the Mississippi. With 300 Illustrations.
The Adventures of Huckleberry Finn. With 174 Illustrations by E. W. KEMBLE.
A Yankee at the Court of King Arthur. With 220 Illustrations by DAN BEARD.
The Stolen White Elephant.
The £1,000,000 Bank-Note.
Mark Twain's Sketches. Post 8vo, illustrated boards, 2s.
Personal Recollections of Joan of Arc. With Twelve Illustrations by F. V. DU MOND. Crown 8vo, cloth, 6s.
More Tramps Abroad. Crown 8vo, cloth, gilt top, 6s.
An Author's Edition de Luxe of the Works of Mark Twain, in 22 Volumes (limited to 600 numbered copies, of which 600 are for sale in Great Britain), is in preparation, and a Prospectus will shortly be ready.

Tytler (C. C. Fraser-).—Mistress Judith: A Novel. Crown 8vo, cloth extra, 3s. 6d. ; post 8vo, illustrated boards, 2s.

Tytler (Sarah), Novels by.
Crown 8vo, cloth extra, 3s. 6d. each ; post 8vo, illustrated boards, 2s. each.
Lady Bell. | Buried Diamonds. | The Blackhall Ghosts.
Post 8vo, illustrated boards, 2s. each.
What She Came Through. | The Huguenot Family.
Citoyenne Jacqueline. | Noblesse Oblige. | Disappeared.
The Bride's Pass. | Saint Mungo's City. | Beauty and the Beast.
Crown 8vo, cloth, 3s. 6d. each.
The Macdonald Lass. With Frontispiece. | Mrs. Carmichael's Goddesses.
The Witch-Wife. | Rachel Langton. | Sapphira.
A Honeymoon's Eclipse. [Shortly.

Upward (Allen), Novels by.
A Crown of Straw. Crown 8vo, cloth, 6s.
Crown 8vo, cloth, 3s. 6d. each ; post 8vo, picture boards, 2s. each.
The Queen Against Owen. | The Prince of Balkistan.
'God Save the Queen!' a Tale of '37. Crown 8vo, decorated cover, 1s ; cloth, 2s.

Vashti and Esther. By 'Belle' of The World. Cr. 8vo, cloth, 3s. 6d.

Vizetelly (Ernest A.), Books by. Crown 8vo, cloth, 3s. 6d. each.
The Scorpion: A Romance of Spain. With a Frontispiece.
With Zola in England: A Story of Exile. With 4 Portraits.

Wagner (Leopold).—How to Get on the Stage, and how to Succeed there. Crown 8vo, cloth, 2s. 6d.

Walford's (Edward, M.A.) County Families of the United Kingdom (1900). Containing the Descent, Birth, Marriage, Education, &c., of 12,000 Heads of Families, their Heirs, Offices, Addresses, Clubs, &c. Royal 8vo, cloth gilt, 50s. [Preparing.

Waller (S. E.).—Sebastiani's Secret. With 9 Illusts. Cr. 8vo, cl.,6s.

Walton and Cotton's Complete Angler; or, The Contemplative Man's Recreation, by IZAAK WALTON; and Instructions How to Angle, for a Trout or Grayling in a clear Stream, by CHARLES COTTON. With Memoirs and Notes by Sir HARRIS NICOLAS, and 61 Illustrations. Crown 8vo, cloth antique, 7s. 6d.

Walt Whitman, Poems by. Edited, with Introduction, by WILLIAM M. ROSSETTI. With Portrait. Crown 8vo, hand-made paper and buckram, 6s.

Warden (Florence).—Joan, the Curate. Crown 8vo, cloth, 3s. 6d.

Warman (Cy).—The Express Messenger, and other Tales of the Rail. Crown 8vo, cloth, 3s. 6d.

Warner (Charles Dudley).—A Roundabout Journey. Crown 8vo, cloth extra, 6s.

Warrant to Execute Charles I. A Facsimile, with the 59 Signatures and Seals. Printed on paper 22 in. by 14 in. 2s.
Warrant to Execute Mary Queen of Scots. A Facsimile, including Queen Elizabeth's Signature and the Great Seal. 2s.

Washington's (George) Rules of Civility Traced to their Sources and Restored by MONCURE D. CONWAY. Fcap. 8vo, Japanese vellum, 2s. 6d.

Wassermann (Lillias) and Aaron Watson.—The Marquis of Carabas. Post 8vo, illustrated boards, 2s.

Weather, How to Foretell the, with the Pocket Spectroscope. By F. W. CORY. With Ten Illustrations. Crown 8vo, 1s.; cloth, 1s. 6d.

Westall (William), Novels by.
Trust Money. Crown 8vo, cloth, 3s. 6d.; post 8vo, illustrated boards, 2s.

Crown 8vo, cloth, 6s. each.
As a Man Sows. | **A Red Bridal.**
With the Red Eagle.

NEW EDITIONS. Crown 8vo, cloth, 3s. 6d. each.
A Woman Tempted Him. | **Nigel Fortescue.** | **Ralph Norbreck's Trust.**
For Honour and Life. | **Ben Clough. | Birch Dene.** | **A Queer Race.**
Her Two Millions. | **The Old Factory.** | **Red Ryvington.**
Two Pinches of Snuff. | **Sons of Belial.** |
Roy of Roy's Court. | **The Phantom City.** | **Strange Crimes.**

Westbury (Atha).—The Shadow of Hilton Fernbrook: A Romance of Maoriland. Crown 8vo, cloth, 3s. 6d.

White (Gilbert).—The Natural History of Selborne. Post 8vo, printed on laid paper and half-bound, 2s.

Wilde (Lady). — The Ancient Legends, Mystic Charms, and Superstitions of Ireland; with Sketches of the Irish Past Crown 8vo, cloth, 3s. 6d.

Williams (W. Mattieu, F.R.A.S.), Works by.
Science in Short Chapters. Crown 8vo, cloth extra, 7s. 6d.
A Simple Treatise on Heat. With Illustrations. Crown 8vo, cloth, 2s. 6d.
The Chemistry of Cookery. Crown 8vo, cloth extra, 6s.
The Chemistry of Iron and Steel Making. Crown 8vo, cloth extra, 9s.
A Vindication of Phrenology. With Portrait and 43 Illusts. Demy 8vo, cloth extra, 12s. 6d.

Williamson (Mrs. F. H.).—A Child Widow. Post 8vo, bds., 2s.

Wills (C. J.), Novels by.
An Easy-going Fellow. Crown 8vo, cloth, 3s. 6d. | **His Dead Past.** Crown 8vo, cloth, 6s.

Wilson (Dr. Andrew, F.R.S.E.), Works by.
Chapters on Evolution. With 259 Illustrations. Crown 8vo, cloth extra, 7s. 6d.
Leaves from a Naturalist's Note-Book. Post 8vo, cloth limp, 2s. 6d.
Leisure-Time Studies. With Illustrations. Crown 8vo, cloth extra, 6s.
Studies in Life and Sense. With 36 Illustrations. Crown 8vo, cloth, 3s. 6d.
Common Accidents: How to Treat Them. With Illustrations. Crown 8vo, 1s.; cloth, 1s. 6d.
Glimpses of Nature. With 35 Illustrations. Crown 8vo, cloth extra, 3s. 6d.

Winter (John Strange), Stories by. Post 8vo, illustrated boards, 2s. each; cloth limp, 2s. 6d. each.
Cavalry Life. | **Regimental Legends.**
Cavalry Life and Regimental Legends. LIBRARY EDITION, set in new type and handsomely bound. Crown 8vo, cloth, 3s. 6d.
A Soldier's Children. With 34 Illustrations by E. G. THOMSON and E. STUART HARDY. Crown 8vo, cloth extra, 3s. 6d.

Wissmann (Hermann von). — My Second Journey through Equatorial Africa. With 92 Illustrations. Demy 8vo, cloth, 16s.

Wood (H. F.), Detective Stories by. Post 8vo, boards, 2s. each.
The Passenger from Scotland Yard. | **The Englishman of the Rue Cain.**

Woolley (Celia Parker).—Rachel Armstrong; or, Love and Theology. Post 8vo, illustrated boards, 2s.; cloth, 2s. 6d.

Wright (Thomas, F.S.A.), Works by.
Caricature History of the Georges; or, Annals of the House of Hanover. Compiled from Squibs, Broadsides, Window Pictures, Lampoons, and Pictorial Caricatures of the Time. With over 300 Illustrations. Crown 8vo, cloth, 3s. 6d.
History of Caricature and of the Grotesque in Art, Literature, Sculpture, and Painting. Illustrated by F. W. FAIRHOLT, F.S.A. Crown 8vo, cloth, 7s. 6d.

Wynman (Margaret).—My Flirtations. With 13 Illustrations by J. BERNARD PARTRIDGE. Post 8vo, cloth limp, 2s.

Yates (Edmund), Novels by. Post 8vo, illustrated boards, 2s. each.
The Forlorn Hope. | Castaway.

Zangwill (I.). — Ghetto Tragedies. With Three Illustrations by A. S. BOYD. Fcap. 8vo, cloth, 2s. net.

'ZZ' (L. Zangwill).—A Nineteenth Century Miracle. Cr. 8vo, 3s. 6d.

Zola (Emile), Novels by. Crown 8vo, cloth extra, 3s. 6d. each.
The Fortune of the Rougons. Edited by ERNEST A. VIZETELLY.
The Abbe Mouret's Transgression. Edited by ERNEST A. VIZETELLY. [Shortly.
His Excellency (Eugene Rougon). With an Introduction by ERNEST A. VIZETELLY.
The Dram-Shop (L'Assommoir). With Introduction by E. A. VIZETELLY.
The Fat and the Thin. Translated by ERNEST A. VIZETELLY.
Money. Translated by ERNEST A. VIZETELLY.
The Downfall. Translated by E. A. VIZETELLY.
The Dream. Translated by ELIZA CHASE. With Eight Illustrations by JEANNIOT.
Doctor Pascal. Translated by E. A. VIZETELLY. With Portrait of the Author.
Lourdes. Translated by ERNEST A. VIZETELLY.
Rome. Translated by ERNEST A. VIZETELLY.
Paris. Translated by ERNEST A. VIZETELLY.
Fruitfulness (Fécondité). Translated by E. A. VIZETELLY. [Shortly.

With Zola in England. By ERNEST A. VIZETELLY. With Four Portraits. Crown 8vo, cloth, 3s. 6d.

SOME BOOKS CLASSIFIED IN SERIES.
*** For fuller cataloguing, see alphabetical arrangement, pp. 1-26.*

The Mayfair Library. Post 8vo, cloth limp, 2s. 6d. per Volume.

Quips and Quiddities. By W. D. ADAMS.
The Agony Column of 'The Times.'
Melancholy Anatomised: Abridgment of BURTON.
A Journey Round My Room. By X. DE MAISTRE. Translated by HENRY ATTWELL
Poetical Ingenuities. By W. T. DOBSON.
The Cupboard Papers. By FIN-BEC.
W. S. Gilbert's Plays. Three Series.
Songs of Irish Wit and Humour.
Animals and their Masters. By Sir A HELPS.
Social Pressure. By Sir A. HELPS.
Autocrat of Breakfast-Table. By O. W. HOLMES.
Curiosities of Criticism. By H. J. JENNINGS.
Pencil and Palette. By R. KEMPT.
Little Essays: from LAMB'S LETTERS.
Forensic Anecdotes. By JACOB LARWOOD.

Theatrical Anecdotes. By JACOB LARWOOD.
Ourselves. By E. LYNN LINTON.
Witch Stories. By E. LYNN LINTON.
Pastimes and Players. By R. MACGREGOR.
New Paul and Virginia. By W. H. MALLOCK.
The New Republic. By W. H. MALLOCK.
Muses of Mayfair. Edited by H. C. PENNELL.
Thoreau: His Life and Aims. By H. A. PAGE.
Puck on Pegasus. By H. C. PENNELL.
Pegasus Re-saddled. By H. C. PENNELL.
Puniana. By Hon. HUGH ROWLEY.
More Puniana. By Hon. HUGH ROWLEY.
The Philosophy of Handwriting.
By Stream and Sea. By WILLIAM SENIOR.
Leaves from a Naturalist's Note-Book. By Dr ANDREW WILSON.

The Golden Library. Post 8vo, cloth limp, 2s. per Volume.

Songs for Sailors. By W. C. BENNETT.
Lives of the Necromancers. By W. GODWIN.
The Autocrat of the Breakfast Table. By OLIVER WENDELL HOLMES.
Tale for a Chimney Corner. By LEIGH HUNT.

Scenes of Country Life. By EDWARD JESSE.
La Mort d'Arthur: Selections from MALLORY.
The Poetical Works of Alexander Pope.
Maxims and Reflections of Rochefoucauld.
Diversions of the Echo Club. BAYARD TAYLOR.

Handy Novels. Fcap. 8vo, cloth boards, 1s. 6d. each.

A Lost Soul. By W. L. ALDEN.
Dr. Palliser's Patient. By GRANT ALLEN
Monte Carlo Stories. By JOAN BARRETT.
Black Spirits and White. By R. A. CRAM.

Seven Sleepers of Ephesus. M. E. COLERIDGE
Taken from the Enemy. By H. NEWBOLT.
The Old Maid's Sweetheart. By A. ST. AUBYN.
Modest Little Sara. By ALAN ST. AUBYN.

My Library. Printed on laid paper, post 8vo, half-Roxburghe, 2s. 6d. each.

The Journal of Maurice de Guerin.
The Dramatic Essays of Charles Lamb.
Citation and Examination of William Shakspeare. By W. S. LANDOR.

Christie Johnstone. By CHARLES READE.
Peg Woffington. By CHARLES READE.

The Pocket Library. Post 8vo, printed on laid paper and hf.-bd., 2s. each.

Gastronomy. By BRILLAT-SAVARIN.
Robinson Crusoe. Illustrated by G. CRUIKSHANK
Autocrat of the Breakfast-Table and The Professor at the Breakfast-Table. By O. W. HOLMES.
Provincial Letters of Blaise Pascal.
Whims and Oddities. By THOMAS HOOD.
Leigh Hunt's Essays. Edited by E. OLLIER.
The Barber's Chair. By DOUGLAS JERROLD.

The Essays of Elia. By CHARLES LAMB.
Anecdotes of the Clergy. By JACOB LARWOOD.
The Epicurean, &c. By THOMAS MOORE.
Plays by RICHARD BRINSLEY SHERIDAN.
Gulliver's Travels, &c. By Dean SWIFT.
Thomson's Seasons. Illustrated.
White's Natural History of Selborne.

Popular Sixpenny Novels. Medium 8vo, 6d. each ; cloth, 1s. each.

All Sorts and Conditions of Men. By WALTER BESANT
The Golden Butterfly. By WALTER BESANT and JAMES RICE.
The Deemster. By HALL CAINE.
The Shadow of a Crime. By HALL CAINE.
Antonina. By WILKIE COLLINS.
The Moonstone. By WILKIE COLLINS.
The Woman in White. By WILKIE COLLINS.
The Dead Secret. By WILKIE COLLINS.

Moths. By OUIDA.
Under Two Flags. By OUIDA.
By Proxy. By JAMES PAYN.
Peg Woffington; and Christie Johnstone. By CHARLES READE.
The Cloister and the Hearth. By CHARLES READE.
It is Never Too Late to Mend. By CHARLES READE.
Hard Cash. By CHARLES READE.

THE PICCADILLY NOVELS.

LIBRARY EDITIONS OF NOVELS, many Illustrated, crown 8vo, cloth extra, 3s. 6d. each.

By Mrs. ALEXANDER.

Valerie's Fate.
A Life Interest.
Mona's Choice.
By Woman's Wit.

By F. M. ALLEN.—Green as Grass.

By GRANT ALLEN.

Philistia. | Babylon.
Strange Stories.
For Maimie's Sake,
In all Shades.
The Beckoning Hand.
The Devil's Die.
This Mortal Coil.
The Tents of Shem.
The Great Taboo.
Dumaresq's Daughter.
Duchess of Powysland.
Blood Royal.
I. Greet's Masterpiece.
The Scallywag.
At Market Value.
Under Sealed Orders.

By M. ANDERSON.—Othello's Occupation.

By EDWIN L. ARNOLD.

Phra the Phœnician. | Constable of St. Nicholas.

By ROBERT BARR.

In a Steamer Chair.
From Whose Bourne.
A Woman Intervenes.
Revenge!

By FRANK BARRETT.

The Woman of the Iron Bracelets.
The Harding Scandal.
Under a Strange Mask.
A Missing Witness.
Was She Justified?

By 'BELLE.'—Vashti and Esther.

By Sir W. BESANT and J. RICE.

Ready-Money Mortiboy.
My Little Girl.
With Harp and Crown.
This Son of Vulcan.
The Golden Butterfly.
The Monks of Thelema.
By Celia's Arbour.
Chaplain of the Fleet.
The Seamy Side.
The Case of Mr. Lucraft.
In Trafalgar's Bay.
The Ten Years' Tenant.

By Sir WALTER BESANT.

All Sorts & Conditions.
The Captains' Room.
All in a Garden Fair.
Dorothy Forster.
Uncle Jack.
World Went Well Then.
Children of Gibeon.
Herr Paulus.
For Faith and Freedom.
To Call Her Mine.
The Revolt of Man.
The Bell of St. Paul's.
The Holy Rose.
Armorel of Lyonesse.
S. Katherine's by Tower
Verbena Camellia, &c.
The Ivory Gate.
The Rebel Queen.
Beyond the Dreams of Avarice.
The Master Craftsman.
The City of Refuge.
A Fountain Sealed.
The Changeling.
The Charm.

By AMBROSE BIERCE—In Midst of Life.

By PAUL BOURGET.—A Living Lie.

By J. D. BRAYSHAW.—Slum Silhouettes.

By ROBERT BUCHANAN.

Shadow of the Sword.
A Child of Nature.
God and the Man.
Martyrdom of Madeline
Love Me for Ever.
Annan Water.
Foxglove Manor.
The New Abelard.
Matt. | Rachel Dene
Master of the Mine.
The Heir of Linne.
Woman and the Man.
Red and White Heather.
Lady Kilpatrick.

ROB. BUCHANAN & HY. MURRAY.

The Charlatan.

By ROBERT W. CHAMBERS.

The King in Yellow.

By J. M. CHAPPLE.—The Minor Chord.

By HALL CAINE.

Shadow of a Crime. | Deemster. | Son of Hagar.

By AUSTIN CLARE.—By Rise of River.

By ANNE COATES.—Rie's Diary.

By MACLAREN COBBAN.

The Red Sultan. | The Burden of Isabel.

By MORT. & FRANCES COLLINS.

Transmigration.
Blacksmith & Scholar.
The Village Comedy.
From Midnight to Midnight.
You Play me False.

By WILKIE COLLINS.

Armadale. | After Dark.
No Name. | Antonina
Basil. | Hide and Seek.
The Dead Secret.
Queen of Hearts.
My Miscellanies.
The Woman in White.
The Law and the Lady.
The Haunted Hotel.
The Moonstone.
Man and Wife.
Poor Miss Finch.
Miss or Mrs.?
The New Magdalen.
The Frozen Deep.
The Two Destinies.

By WILKIE COLLINS—continued.

'I Say No.'
Little Novels.
The Fallen Leaves.
Jezebel's Daughter.
The Black Robe.
Heart and Science.
The Evil Genius.
The Legacy of Cain.
A Rogue's Life.
Blind Love.

By M. J. COLQUHOUN.

Every Inch a Soldier.

By E. H. COOPER.—Geoffory Hamilton

By V. C. COTES.—Two Girls on a Barge

By C. EGBERT CRADDOCK.

His Vanished Star.

By H. N. CRELLIN.

Romances of the Old Seraglio.

By MATT CRIM.

The Adventures of a Fair Rebel.

By S. R. CROCKETT and others.

Tales of Our Coast.

By B. M. CROKER.

Diana Barrington.
Proper Pride.
A Family Likeness.
Pretty Miss Neville.
A Bird of Passage.
'To Let.' | Mr. Jervis.
Village Tales.
Some One Else.
The Real Lady Hilda.
Married or Single?
Two Masters.
In the Kingdom of Kerry
Interference.
A Third Person.
Beyond the Pale.
Jason.

By W. CYPLES.—Hearts of Gold.

By ALPHONSE DAUDET.

The Evangelist; or, Port Salvation.

By H. COLEMAN DAVIDSON.

Mr. Sadler's Daughters.

By ERASMUS DAWSON.

The Fountain of Youth.

By J. DE MILLE.—A Castle in Spain.

By J. LEITH DERWENT.

Our Lady of Tears. | Circe's Lovers.

By HARRY DE WINDT.

True Tales of Travel and Adventure.

By DICK DONOVAN.

Tracked to Doom.
Man from Manchester.
The Chronicles of Michael Danevitch.
Vincent Trill.
The Mystery of Jamaica.
Terrace.
Tales of Terror.

By RICHARD DOWLING.

Old Corcoran's Money.

By A. CONAN DOYLE

The Firm of Girdlestone.

By S. JEANNETTE DUNCAN.

A Daughter of To-day. | Vernon's Aunt.

By A. EDWARDES.—A Plaster Saint.

By G. S. EDWARDS.—Snazelleparilla.

By G. MANVILLE FENN

Cursed by a Fortune.
The Case of Ailsa Gray.
Commodore Junk.
The New Mistress.
Witness to the Deed.
The Tiger Lily.
The White Virgin.
Black Blood.
Double Cunning.
Bag of Diamonds, &c.
A Fluttered Dovecote.
King of the Castle
Master of Ceremonies.
Eve at the Wheel. &c.
The Man with a Shadow
One Maid's Mischief.
Story of Antony Grace.
This Man's Wife.
In Jeopardy.   [ning.
A Woman Worth Win-

By PERCY FITZGERALD.—Fatal Zero.

By R. E. FRANCILLON.

One by One.
A Dog and his Shadow.
A Real Queen.
Ropes of Sand.
Jack Doyle's Daughter.

By HAROLD FREDERIC.

Seth's Brother's Wife. | The Lawton Girl.

By PAUL GAULOT.—The Red Shirts.

By CHARLES GIBBON.

Robin Gray.
Loving a Dream.
Of High Degree
The Golden Shaft.
The Braes of Yarrow.

By E. GLANVILLE.

The Lost Heiress.
A Fair Colonist.
The Fossicker.
The Golden Rock.
Tales from the Veld.

THE PICCADILLY (3/6) NOVELS—*continued.*

By E. J. GOODMAN.
The Fate of Herbert Wayne.

By Rev. S. BARING GOULD.
Red Spider. | Eve.

By CECIL GRIFFITH.
Corinthia Marazion.

By SYDNEY GRUNDY.
The Days of his Vanity.

By OWEN HALL.
The Track of a Storm. | Jetsam.

By COSMO HAMILTON.
The Glamour of the Impossible.
Through a Keyhole.

By THOMAS HARDY.
Under the Greenwood Tree.

By BRET HARTE.
A Waif of the Plains. | A Protégée of Jack
A Ward of the Golden | Hamlin's.
Gate. (Springs. | Clarence.
A Sappho of Green | Barker's Luck.
Col. Starbottle's Client. | Devil's Ford. (celsior.'
Susy. | Sally Dows. | The Crusade of the ' Ex-
Bell-Ringer of Angel's. | Three Partners.
Tales of Trail and Town | Gabriel Conroy.

By JULIAN HAWTHORNE.
Garth. | Dust. | Beatrix Randolph.
Ellice Quentin. | David Poindexter's Dis-
Sebastian Strome. | appearance.
Fortune's Fool. | Spectre of Camera.

By Sir A. HELPS.—Ivan de Biron.

By I. HENDERSON.—Agatha Page.

By G. A. HENTY.
Rojub the Juggler. | The Queen's Cup.
Dorothy's Double.

By JOHN HILL. | The Common Ancestor.

By TIGHE HOPKINS.
'Twixt Love and Duty. | Nugents of Carriconna.
The Incomplete Adventurer.

By VICTOR HUGO.
The Outlaw of Iceland.

By Mrs. HUNGERFORD.
Lady Verner's Flight. | The Coming of Chloe.
The Red-House Mystery | Nora Creina.
The Three Graces. | An Anxious Moment.
Professor's Experiment. | April's Lady.
A Point of Conscience. | Peter's Wife. | Lovice.

By Mrs. ALFRED HUNT.
The Leaden Casket. | Self-Condemned.
That Other Person. | Mrs. Juliet.

By C. J. CUTCLIFFE HYNE.
Honour of Thieves.

By R. ASHE KING.
A Drawn Game.

By GEORGE LAMBERT.
The President of Boravia.

By EDMOND LEPELLETIER.
Madame Sans-Gêne.

By ADAM LILBURN.
A Tragedy in Marble.

By HARRY LINDSAY.
Rhoda Roberts. | The Jacobite.

By HENRY W. LUCY.—Gideon Fleyce.

By E. LYNN LINTON.
Patricia Kemball. | The Atonement of Leam
Under which Lord? | Dundas.
'My Love!' | Ione. | The One Too Many.
Paston Carew. | Dulcie Everton.
Sowing the Wind. | Rebel of the Family.
With a Silken Thread. | An Octave of Friends.
The World Well Lost.

By JUSTIN McCARTHY.
A Fair Saxon. | Donna Quixote.
Linley Rochford. | Maid of Athens.
Dear Lady Disdain. | The Comet of a Season.
Camiola. | The Dictator.
Waterdale Neighbours. | Red Diamonds.
My Enemy's Daughter. | The Riddle Ring.
Miss Misanthrope. | The Three Disgraces.

By JUSTIN H. McCARTHY.
A London Legend. | The Royal Christopher.

By GEORGE MACDONALD.
Heather and Snow. | Phantastes.

By PAUL & VICTOR MARGUERITTE
The Disaster

By L. T. MEADE.
A Soldier of Fortune. | The Voice of the Charmer
In an Iron Grip. | On the Brink of a
Dr. Rumsey's Patient. | Chasm.

By LEONARD MERRICK.
This Stage of Fools. | Cynthia.

By BERTRAM MITFORD.
The Gun-Runner. | The King's Assegai.
Luck of Gerard Ridgeley. | Rensh. Fanning's Quest.

By J. E. MUDDOCK.
Maid Marian and Robin Hood. | Golden Idol.
Basile the Jester. | Young Lochinvar.

By D. CHRISTIE MURRAY.
A Life's Atonement. | The Way of the World.
Joseph's Coat. | Bob Martin's Little Girl
Coals of Fire. | Time's Revenges.
Old Blazer's Hero. | A Wasted Crime.
Val Strange. | Hearts. | In Direst Peril.
A Model Father. | Mount Despair.
By the Gate of the Sea. | A Capful o' Nails.
A Bit of Human Nature. | Tales in Prose & Verse.
First Person Singular. | A Race for Millions.
Cynic Fortune. | This Little World.

By MURRAY and HERMAN.
The Bishops' Bible. | Paul Jones's Alias.
One Traveller Returns. |

By HUME NISBET.
'Bail Up!'

By W. E. NORRIS.
Saint Ann's. | Billy Bellew.
Miss Wentworth's Idea.

By G. OHNET.
A Weird Gift. | Love's Depths.

By Mrs. OLIPHANT.
The Sorceress.

By OUIDA.
Held in Bondage. | In a Winter City.
Strathmore. | Chandos. | Friendship.
Under Two Flags. | Moths. | Roffino.
Idalia. (Gage. | Pipistrello. | Ariadne.
Cecil Castlemaine's | A Village Commune.
Tricotrin. | Puck. | Bimbi. | Wanda.
Folle Farine. | Frescoes. | Othmar.
A Dog of Flanders. | In Maremma.
Pascarel. | Signa. | Syrlin. | Guilderoy.
Princess Napraxine. | Santa Barbara.
Two Wooden Shoes. | Two Offenders.

By MARGARET A. PAUL.
Gentle and Simple.

By JAMES PAYN.
Lost Sir Massingberd. | Under One Roof.
Less Black than We're | Glow-worm Tales
Painted. | The Talk of the Town.
A Confidential Agent. | Holiday Tasks.
A Grape from a Thorn. | For Cash Only.
In Peril and Privation. | The Burnt Million.
The Mystery of Mir- | The Word and the Will.
By Proxy. (bridge. | Sunny Stories.
The Canon's Ward. | A Trying Patient.
Walter's Word. | A Modern Dick Whit-
High Spirits. | tington.

By WILL PAYNE.
Jerry the Dreamer.

By Mrs. CAMPBELL PRAED.
Outlaw and Lawmaker. | Mrs. Tregaskiss.
Christina Chard. | Nulma.

By E. C. PRICE.
Valentina. | Foreigners. | Mrs. Lancaster's Rival.

By RICHARD PRYCE.
Miss Maxwell's Affections.

By Mrs. J. H. RIDDELL.
Weird Stories.

By AMELIE RIVES.
Barbara Dering. | Meriel.

By F. W. ROBINSON.
The Hands of Justice. | Woman in the Dark.

By HERBERT RUSSELL.
True Blue.

THE PICCADILLY (3/6) NOVELS—*continued.*

By CHARLES READE.

Peg Woffington; and Christie Johnstone.
Hard Cash.
Cloister & the Hearth.
Never Too Late to Mend
The Course of True Love Never Did Run Smooth; and Single-heart and Doubleface.
Autobiography of a Thief; Jack of all Trades; A Hero and a Martyr; and The Wandering Heir.

Griffith Gaunt.
Love Little, Love Long.
The Double Marriage.
Foul Play.
Put Y'rself in His Place
A Terrible Temptation.
A Simpleton.
A Woman-Hater.
The Jilt, & other Stories; & Good Stories of Man and other Animals.
A Perilous Secret.
Readiana; and Bible Characters.

By W. CLARK RUSSELL.

Round the Galley-Fire.
In the Middle Watch.
On the Fo'k'sle Head
A Voyage to the Cape.
Book for the Hammock
Mystery of 'Ocean Star'
Jenny Harlowe.
An Ocean Tragedy.
A Tale of Two Tunnels.

My Shipmate Louise.
Alone on Wide Wide Sea.
The Phantom Death.
Is He the Man?
Good Ship 'Mohock.'
The Convict Ship.
Heart of Oak.
The Tale of the Ten.
The Last Entry.

By DORA RUSSELL.

A Country Sweetheart. | The Drift of Fate.

By BAYLE ST. JOHN.

A Levantine Family.

By ADELINE SERGEANT.

Dr. Endicott's Experiment.

By GEORGE R. SIMS.

Once Upon a Christmas Time.

By HAWLEY SMART.

Without Love or Licence.
The Master of Rathkelly.
Long Odds.

The Outsider.
Beatrice & Benedick.
A Racing Rubber.

By T. W. SPEIGHT.

A Secret of the Sea.
The Grey Monk.
The Master of Trenance
The Doom of Siva.

A Minion of the Moon.
The Secret of Wyvern Towers.

By ALAN ST. AUBYN.

A Fellow of Trinity.
The Junior Dean.
Master of St. Benedict's.
To his Own Master.
Gallantry Bower.

In Face of the World.
Orchard Damerel.
The Tremlett Diamonds.
Fortune's Gate.

By JOHN STAFFORD.—Doris and I.
By R. STEPHENS.—The Cruciform Mark.
By R. A. STERNDALE.

The Afghan Knife.

By R. LOUIS STEVENSON.

The Suicide Club.

By ANNIE THOMAS.—The Siren's Web.
By BERTHA THOMAS.

Proud Maisie. | The Violin-Player

By FRANCES E. TROLLOPE.

Like Ships upon Sea.
Anne Furness.

Mabel's Progress.

By ANTHONY TROLLOPE.

The Way we Live Now.
Frau Frohmann.
Marion Fay.

Scarborough's Family.
The Land Leaguers

By IVAN TURGENIEFF, &c.

Stories from Foreign Novelists.

By MARK TWAIN.

Mark Twain's Choice Works.
Mark Twain's Library of Humour.
The Innocents Abroad.
Roughing It; and The Innocents at Home.
A Tramp Abroad.
The American Claimant.
Adventures Tom Sawyer
Tom Sawyer Abroad.

Tom Sawyer, Detective.
Pudd'nhead Wilson.
The Gilded Age.
Prince and the Pauper.
Life on the Mississippi.
The Adventures of Huckleberry Finn.
A Yankee at the Court of King Arthur.
Stolen White Elephant.
£1,000,000 Bank-note.

By C. C. FRASER-TYTLER.

Mistress Judith.

By SARAH TYTLER.

Buried Diamonds.
The Blackhall Ghosts.
The Macdonald Lass.
The Witch-Wife.

Mrs Carmichael's Goddesses. | Lady Bell.
Rachel Langton.
Sapphira

A Honeymoon's Eclipse.

By ALLEN UPWARD.

The Queen against Owen | The Prince of Balkistan.

By E. A. VIZETELLY.

The Scorpion: A Romance of Spain.

By F. WARDEN.—Joan, the Curate.
By CY WARMAN.

The Express Messenger.

By WILLIAM WESTALL.

For Honour and Life.
A Woman Tempted Him
Her Two Millions.
Two Pinches of Snuff.
Roy of Roy's Court.
Nigel Fortescue.
Birch Dene.
The Phantom City.

A Queer Race.
Ben Clough.
The Old Factory.
Red Ryvington.
Ralph Norbreck's Trust.
Trust-money
Sons of Belial.
Strange Crimes.

By ATHA WESTBURY.

The Shadow of Hilton Fernbrook.

By C. J. WILLS.—An Easy-going Fellow.
By JOHN STRANGE WINTER.

Cavalry Life and Regimental Legends.
A Soldier's Children.

By MARGARET WYNMAN.

My Flirtations.

By E. ZOLA.

The Fortune of the Rougons.
The Abbe Mouret's Transgression.
The Downfall.
The Dream. | Money.
Dr. Pascal. | Lourdes.
The Fat and the Thin

His Excellency.
The Dram-Shop.
Rome. | Paris.
Fruitfulness.

By 'Z Z.'

A Nineteenth Century Miracle.

CHEAP EDITIONS OF POPULAR NOVELS.

Post 8vo, illustrated boards, 2s. each.

By ARTEMUS WARD.

Artemus Ward Complete.

By EDMOND ABOUT.

The Fellah.

By HAMILTON AÏDÉ.

Carr of Carrlyon. | Confidences.

By Mrs. ALEXANDER.

Maid, Wife, or Widow?
Blind Fate.
Valerie's Fate.

A Life Interest.
Mona's Choice.
By Woman's Wit.

By GRANT ALLEN.

Philistia. | Babylon.
Strange Stories.
For Maimie's Sake.
In all Shades.
The Beckoning Hand.
The Devil's Die.
The Tents of Shem.
The Great Taboo

Dumaresq's Daughter.
Duchess of Powysland.
Blood Royal. | [piece.
Ivan Greet's Master.
The Scallywag.
This Mortal Coil.
At Market Value.
Under Sealed Orders.

By E. LESTER ARNOLD.

Phra the Phœnician.

BY FRANK BARRETT.

Fettered for Life.
Little Lady Linton.
Between Life & Death.
Sin of Olga Zassoulich.
Folly Morrison.
Lieut. Barnabas.
Honest Davie.
A Prodigal's Progress.

Found Guilty.
A Recoiling Vengeance.
For Love and Honour.
John Ford, &c.
Woman of Iron Bracelets
The Harding Scandal.
A Missing Witness.

By SHELSLEY BEAUCHAMP.

Grantley Grange.

By FREDERICK BOYLE.

Camp Notes.
Savage Life.

Chronicles of No man's Land.

TWO-SHILLING NOVELS—*continued.*

By Sir W. BESANT and J. RICE.

Ready-Money Mortiboy
My Little Girl.
With Harp and Crown.
This Son of Vulcan.
The Golden Butterfly.
The Monks of Thelema.

By Celia's Arbour.
Chaplain of the Fleet.
The Seamy Side.
The Case of Mr. Lucraft.
In Trafalgar's Bay.
The Ten Years' Tenant.

By Sir WALTER BESANT.

All Sorts and Conditions of Men.
The Captains' Room.
All in a Garden Fair.
Dorothy Forster.
Uncle Jack.
The World Went Very Well Then.
Children of Gibeon.
Herr Paulus.
For Faith and Freedom.
To Call Her Mine.
The Master Craftsman.

The Bell of St. Paul's.
The Holy Rose.
Armorel of Lyonesse.
S.Katherine s by Tower
Verbena Camellia Stephanotis.
The Ivory Gate.
The Rebel Queen.
Beyond the Dreams of Avarice.
The Revolt of Man.
In Deacon's Orders.
The City of Refuge.

By AMBROSE BIERCE.

In the Midst of Life.

BY BRET HARTE.

Californian Stories.
Gabriel Conroy.
Luck of Roaring Camp.
An Heiress of Red Dog.

Flip. | Maruja.
A Phyllis of the Sierras.
A Waif of the Plains.
Ward of Golden Gate.

By ROBERT BUCHANAN.

Shadow of the Sword.
A Child of Nature.
God and the Man.
Love Me for Ever.
Foxglove Manor.
The Master of the Mine.
Annan Water.

The Martyrdom of Madeline.
The New Abelard.
The Heir of Linne.
Woman and the Man.
Rachel Dene. | Matt.
Lady Kilpatrick.

By BUCHANAN and MURRAY.

The Charlatan.

By HALL CAINE.

The Shadow of a Crime. | The Deemster.
A Son of Hagar.

By Commander CAMERON.

The Cruise of the 'Black Prince.'

By HAYDEN CARRUTH

The Adventures of Jones.

By AUSTIN CLARE.

For the Love of a Lass.

By Mrs. ARCHER CLIVE.

Paul Ferroll.
Why Paul Ferroll Killed his Wife.

By MACLAREN COBBAN.

The Cure of Souls. | The Red Sultan.

By C. ALLSTON COLLINS.

The Bar Sinister.

By MORT. & FRANCES COLLINS.

Sweet Anne Page.
Transmigration.
From Midnight to Midnight.
A Fight with Fortune.

Sweet and Twenty.
The Village Comedy.
You Play me False.
Blacksmith and Scholar
Frances.

By WILKIE COLLINS.

Armadale. | After Dark.
No Name.
Antonina.
Basil.
Hide and Seek.
The Dead Secret.
Queen of Hearts.
Miss or Mrs.?
The New Magdalen.
The Frozen Deep.
The Law and the Lady
The Two Destinies.
The Haunted Hotel.
A Rogue's Life.

My Miscellanies.
The Woman in White.
The Moonstone.
Man and Wife.
Poor Miss Finch.
The Fallen Leaves.
Jezebel's Daughter.
The Black Robe.
Heart and Science.
'I Say No!'
The Evil Genius.
Little Novels.
Legacy of Cain.
Blind Love.

By M. J. COLQUHOUN.

Every Inch a Soldier.

By C. EGBERT CRADDOCK.

The Prophet of the Great Smoky Mountains.

By MATT CRIM.

The Adventures of a Fair Rebel.

By B. M. CROKER.

Pretty Miss Neville.
Diana Barrington.
'To Let.'
A Bird of Passage.
Proper Pride.
A Family Likeness.
A Third Person.

Village Tales and Jungle Tragedies.
Two Masters.
Mr. Jervis.
The Real Lady Hilda.
Married or Single?
Interference.

By W. CYPLES.

Hearts of Gold.

By ALPHONSE DAUDET.

The Evangelist; or, Port Salvation.

By ERASMUS DAWSON.

The Fountain of Youth.

By JAMES DE MILLE.

A Castle in Spain.

By J. LEITH DERWENT.

Our Lady of Tears. | Circe's Lovers.

By DICK DONOVAN.

The Man-Hunter.
Tracked and Taken.
Caught at Last!
Wanted!
Who Poisoned Hetty Duncan?
Man from Manchester.
A Detective's Triumphs
The Mystery of Jamaica Terrace.
The Chronicles of Michael Danevitch.

In the Grip of the Law.
From Information Received.
Tracked to Doom.
Link by Link
Suspicion Aroused.
Dark Deeds.
Riddles Read.

By Mrs. ANNIE EDWARDES.

A Point of Honour. | Archie Lovell.

By M. BETHAM-EDWARDS.

Felicia. | Kitty.

By EDWARD EGGLESTON.

Roxy.

By G. MANVILLE FENN.

The New Mistress.
Witness to the Deed.

The Tiger Lily.
The White Virgin.

By PERCY FITZGERALD.

Bella Donna.
Never Forgotten.
Polly.
Fatal Zero.

Second Mrs. Tillotson.
Seventy-five Brooke Street.
The Lady of Brantome.

By P. FITZGERALD and others.

Strange Secrets.

By ALBANY DE FONBLANQUE.

Filthy Lucre.

By R. E. FRANCILLON.

Olympia.
One by One.
A Real Queen.
Queen Cophetua.

King or Knave?
Romances of the Law.
Ropes of Sand.
A Dog and his Shadow.

By HAROLD FREDERIC.

Seth's Brother's Wife. | The Lawton Girl.

Prefaced by Sir BARTLE FRERE.

Pandurang Hari.

By EDWARD GARRETT.

The Capel Girls.

By GILBERT GAUL.

A Strange Manuscript.

By CHARLES GIBBON.

Robin Gray.
Fancy Free.
For Lack of Gold.
What will World Say?
In Love and War.
For the King.
In Pastures Green.
Queen of the Meadow.
A Heart's Problem.
The Dead Heart.

In Honour Bound.
Flower of the Forest.
The Braes of Yarrow.
The Golden Shaft.
Of High Degree.
By Mead and Stream.
Loving a Dream.
A Hard Knot.
Heart's Delight.
Blood-Money.

By WILLIAM GILBERT.

Dr. Austin's Guests.
James Duke.

The Wizard of the Mountain

By ERNEST GLANVILLE.

The Lost Heiress.
A Fair Colonist.

The Fossicker.

TWO-SHILLING NOVELS—*continued*.

By E. C. PRICE.
Valentina. | Mrs. Lancaster's Rival.
The Foreigners. | Gerald.

By RICHARD PRYCE.
Miss Maxwell's Affections.

By JAMES PAYN.
Bentinck's Tutor. | The Talk of the Town.
Murphy's Master. | Holiday Tasks.
A County Family. | A Perfect Treasure.
At Her Mercy. | What He Cost Her.
Cecil's Tryst. | A Confidential Agent.
The Clyffards of Clyffe. | Glow-worm Tales.
The Foster Brothers. | The Burnt Million.
Found Dead. | Sunny Stories.
The Best of Husbands. | Lost Sir Massingberd.
Walter's Word. | A Woman's Vengeance.
Halves. | The Family Scapegrace.
Fallen Fortunes. | Gwendoline's Harvest.
Humorous Stories. | Like Father, Like Son.
£200 Reward. | Married Beneath Him.
A Marine Residence. | Not Wooed, but Won.
Mirk Abbey | Less Black than We're
By Proxy. | Painted.
Under One Roof. | Some Private Views.
High Spirits. | A Grape from a Thorn.
Carlyon's Year. | The Mystery of Mir-
From Exile. | bridge.
For Cash Only. | The Word and the Will.
Kit. | A Prince of the Blood.
The Canon's Ward. | A Trying Patient.

By CHARLES READE.
It is Never Too Late to | A Terrible Temptation.
Mend. | Foul Play.
Christie Johnstone. | The Wandering Heir.
The Double Marriage. | Hard Cash.
Put Yourself in His | Singleheart and Double-
Place | face.
Love Me Little, Love | Good Stories of Man and
Me Long. | other Animals.
The Cloister and the | Peg Woffington.
Hearth. | Griffith Gaunt.
The Course of True | A Perilous Secret.
Love. | A Simpleton.
The Jilt. | Readiana.
The Autobiography of | A Woman-Hater.
a Thief. |

By Mrs. J. H. RIDDELL.
Weird Stories. | The Uninhabited House.
Fairy Water. | The Mystery in Palace
Her Mother's Darling. | Gardens.
The Prince of Wales's | The Nun's Curse.
Garden Party. | Idle Tales.

By AMELIE RIVES.
Barbara Dering.

By F. W. ROBINSON.
Women are Strange. | The Woman in the Dark
The Hands of Justice. |

By JAMES RUNCIMAN.
Skippers and Shellbacks. | Schools and Scholars.
Grace Balmaign's Sweetheart.

By W. CLARK RUSSELL.
Round the Galley Fire. | An Ocean Tragedy.
On the Fo'k'sle Head. | My Shipmate Louise.
In the Middle Watch. | Alone on Wide Wide Sea.
A Voyage to the Cape. | Good Ship 'Mohock.'
A Book for the Ham- | The Phantom Death.
mock. | Is He the Man?
The Mystery of the | Heart of Oak.
'Ocean Star.' | The Convict Ship.
The Romance of Jenny | The Tale of the Ten.
Harlowe. | The Last Entry.

By DORA RUSSELL.
A Country Sweetheart.

By GEORGE AUGUSTUS SALA.
Gaslight and Daylight.

By GEORGE R. SIMS.
The Ring o' Bells. | Zeph.
Mary Jane's Memoirs. | Memoirs of a Landlady.
Mary Jane Married. | Scenes from the Show.
Tales of To-day. | The 10 Commandments.
Dramas of Life. | Dagonet Abroad.
Tinkletop's Crime. | Rogues and Vagabonds.
My Two Wives. |

By ARTHUR SKETCHLEY.
A Match in the Dark.

By HAWLEY SMART.
Without Love or Licence. | The Plunger.
Beatrice and Benedick. | Long Odds.
The Master of Rathkelly. |

By T. W. SPEIGHT.
The Mysteries of Heron | Back to Life.
Dyke. | The Loudwater Tragedy.
The Golden Hoop. | Burgo's Romance.
Hoodwinked. | Quittance in Full.
By Devious Ways. | A Husband from the Sea

By ALAN ST. AUBYN.
A Fellow of Trinity. | Orchard Damerel.
The Junior Dean. | In the Face of the World.
Master of St. Benedict's | The Tremlett Diamonds.
To His Own Master. |

By R. A. STERNDALE.
The Afghan Knife.

By R. LOUIS STEVENSON.
New Arabian Nights.

By BERTHA THOMAS.
Cressida. | The Violin-Player.

By WALTER THORNBURY.
Tales for the Marines. | Old Stories Retold.

By T. ADOLPHUS TROLLOPE.
Diamond Cut Diamond.

By F. ELEANOR TROLLOPE.
Like Ships upon the | Anne Furness.
Sea. | Mabel's Progress.

By ANTHONY TROLLOPE.
Frau Frohmann. | The Land-Leaguers.
Marion Fay. | The American Senator.
Kept in the Dark. | Mr. Scarborough's
John Caldigate. | Family.
The Way We Live Now. | Golden Lion of Granpere

By J. T. TROWBRIDGE.
Farnell's Folly.

By IVAN TURGENIEFF, &c.
Stories from Foreign Novelists.

By MARK TWAIN.
A Pleasure Trip on the | Life on the Mississippi.
Continent. | The Prince and the
The Gilded Age. | Pauper.
Huckleberry Finn. | A Yankee at the Court
Mark Twain's Sketches. | of King Arthur.
Tom Sawyer. | The £1,000,000 Bank-
A Tramp Abroad. | Note.
Stolen White Elephant. |

By C. C. FRASER-TYTLER.
Mistress Judith.

By SARAH TYTLER.
The Bride's Pass. | The Huguenot Family
Buried Diamonds. | The Blackhall Ghosts.
St. Mungo's City. | What She Came Through
Lady Bell. | Beauty and the Beast.
Noblesse Oblige. | Citoyenne Jaqueline.
Disappeared. |

By ALLEN UPWARD.
The Queen against Owen. | Prince of Balkistan.
'God Save the Queen!'

By AARON WATSON and LILLIAS WASSERMANN.
The Marquis of Carabas.

By WILLIAM WESTALL.
Trust-Money.

By Mrs. F. H. WILLIAMSON.
A Child Widow.

By J. S. WINTER.
Cavalry Life. | Regimental Legends.

By H. F. WOOD.
The Passenger from Scotland Yard.
The Englishman of the Rue Cain.

By CELIA PARKER WOOLLEY.
Rachel Armstrong; or, Love and Theology.

By EDMUND YATES.
The Forlorn Hope. | Castaway.

By I. ZANGWILL.
Ghetto Tragedies.